CHRIS BERRY
TOUGH
WORLD

GREAT N ORTHERN

TOUGH WORLD by Chris Berry

First published in Great Britain in 2021 by Great Northern Books

ISBN: 978-1-914227-16-5

Cover design by Caroline Berry

Great Northern Books
PO Box 1380, Bradford,
West Yorkshire, BD5 5FB

www.greatnorthernbooks.co.uk

Chris Berry is from the north of England and lives near Leeds. He has written for the *Yorkshire Post* for over 20 years. He is the author of crime thriller novels and several autobiographies. He's a keen sportsman and runs several distances up to half marathons. Born in Kingston upon Hull, he is a staunch Yorkshireman. His hometown rugby league club is Hull Kingston Rovers. *Tough World* is his third novel.

Also by Chris Berry

FICTION

TOUGH SEASON
TOUGH SEASON IN THE SUN
TOUGH WORLD

NON FICTION

BOXY & ME A Love That Never Died

THE MAKING OF FARMER CHRIS

TONY CHRISTIE The Song Interpreter

JOE LONGTHORNE The Official Autobiography

SUGAR IN THE MORNING Joe Longthorne

LES BATTERSBY & ME Bruce Jones

BOXSTER'S STORY The Truth Behind The Bull

THE J.D. IRELAND STORY

www.chrisberry.tv

PRAISE FOR TOUGH SEASON IN THE SUN

Tough Season in the Sun is a great read and just as enthralling as its predecessor *Tough Season*. What you've written is a perfect TV mini-series waiting to happen and in Greg you've created a superhero. **Gary Walker**

What a gripping, compelling read. I found the story fast moving with plenty of action and intrigue from start to finish. It had many twists and turns and sex and scandals. I cannot wait for the next one.
Alisdair Mackie

What a great read it has been! Really enjoyed the thrill of it all and the setting of Lanzarote. Highly recommended! Can't wait for the next one.
Janet Hague

My favourite books are by Conn Iggulden, John Grisham, Lee Child, George RR Martin and Simon Scarrow. The biggest compliment I could give Chris is that I would rate his writing to be of an equal standard to these authors.
   Tough Season in the Sun is a fantastic follow-up novel to the first and the story is equally as gripping.
Steven Rostron

Tough Season in the Sun is a great read for all that like thrillers not just rugby league fans. Well written to keep you wanting to get to the next chapter, and then the next book. Keep them coming!
Walter Armitage

Having read *Tough Season*, the first in the series, this second book does not disappoint. Even up to the last few pages it kept you on your toes.
Ken Knott

If you enjoy a crime thriller this book will tick the box. Following on from his first book featuring Greg, a rugby league player, this one is set in sunny Lanzarote. A well written thriller will always keep your attention and *Tough Season in the Sun* does just that.
Sarah Pulleyn

I loved the first book and was looking forward to reading about what Greg would get up to. I wasn't disappointed! I highly recommend it!
David Pickup

Thoroughly enjoyed this second outing of Greg Duggan's new beginning, or so he thought. Delightful characters thrown into the mix all leading to a dramatic conclusion. Well done Chris Berry for using the greatest toughest team sport on Earth, Rugby League on which you started the shenanigans.
Kindle Customer

Thoroughly enjoyed the first in the series *Tough Season*, and *Tough Season in the Sun* did not disappoint at all. The sport and crime are still great elements and Greg has some up close and personal times – no extra training needed!
Frank Healy

Hurry up with number three, not to spoil things for others but you haven't half left us with a cliffhanger at the end. Great read!
Janet Booth

Finished! Wow, wow, wow! Think it was even better than the first! It's a cracking good crime thriller and a real page turner. As much as I enjoyed *Tough Season*, this second in the series was even more enjoyable.
Amanda Clarke

Brilliant stuff! This time our all-conquering hero Greg Duggan blazes a brand-new trail of destruction in the steaming heat of Lanzarote. Greg takes it all in his stride as the plots thicken, the bullets fly and the bodies are left scattered both on and off the rugby field. It all boils down to the pulsating Judgment Day winner-takes-all final in front of a vociferous, packed stadium. Fantastico!
Darryl Wills – Yorkshire Evening Post

Love this book. Couldn't put it down. Would highly recommend it.
Kristy Wolfenden

A fabulous read which captured rugby league at its best. The characters are believable and fun. An extremely entertaining read!
Helen G.

I thought *Tough Season* was good! This one is even better! What a fantastic read. Every chapter keeps you gripped to the end. You will love the cliffhanger!
Grahame Frodsham

Get the publisher to get a wriggle on. Fantastic writing!
Vivienne Litherland, Wire Fan

Just read both your books. They are great. Can't wait for No.3.
Dot Pursell, St Helens Fan

My daughter bought me both *Tough Season* and *Tough Season in the Sun* and can honestly say I really enjoyed them both. As rugby league is central to the story lines they grabbed me from the start and were hard to put down. I'm waiting for the third book in the series and I have never said that before!
Tony Southerington, Hull KR Fan

You won't be disappointed. Real treat having rugby league intertwined.
Si Jones, Batley Fan

AUTHOR'S NOTE

Tough World is the third crime thriller novel in the Greg Duggan series. In the first two *Tough Season* and *Tough Season in the Sun* I took Greg from his perennially struggling lower division, hometown rugby league club to the sunshine of Lanzarote, playing for a club that made it to Super League. This time we follow Greg's on- and off-field trials, tribulations and triumphs in Australia and the South Pacific islands nation of Vanuatu, amidst the Rugby League World Cup.

As with *Tough Season in the Sun* I have personal experience of each location in *Tough World*. Efate is a beautiful island of the Republic of Vanuatu and is where most of the action takes place. Its murder rate is nowhere near the rate at which it appears in *Tough World* and I have no reason to believe there is corruption to the extent I have imagined here, nor are any of the characters either political, police or rugby league officialdom anything other than in my imagination.

What is very real is that I have stayed at Breakas Beach Resort, which I use as the England team's Vanuatu headquarters, and it is as beautiful as I have attempted to portray, with wonderful staff who will do anything for you. There really is a Hideaway Island that certainly does have the world's only underwater post office and the snorkelling among crystal blue waters and coral with beautifully coloured fishes is very real too.

While all of the characterisations in my books are largely fictitious I have as usual had great fun putting in the names of friends, family members and now friends through those of you who read my books. I hope those that find themselves in *Tough World* can have a smile about this.

One person who is certainly not fictitious is the wonderful Vanuatu singer songwriter Vanessa Quai and I do hope that if you enjoy this book that you look up Vanessa's music on YouTube. 'Life is Good' the song I use to turn into 'Greg is Good' is a really fantastic sunshine/reggae song and I love 'Light It Up'. I played these so much during the writing of *Tough World*.

I specifically used Byron Bay as it is where my eldest son Russ lives with his partner Alex and he really does run a wine shop in the town and has, speaking as a proud dad, won several awards in the wine trade. It is a fabulous seaside resort well-respected for its surfing. Byron Bay Bluesfest is also a very real live music festival that I've attended both times that my wife Pauline and I have visited Australia. It is a stunning 5-day international event and I've been very fortunate to see the Doobie Brothers, Larry Graham of Graham Central Station, Joss Stone, Buddy Guy and even Tom Jones.

Once again I am extremely grateful to my publishers Great Northern Books – particularly David Burrill for all his constant support, owner Peter Crangle, and to Ross and Roger. It is a team effort getting a book published and everyone plays their part, including my lovely wife Pauline who keeps topping up the malt whisky and my lovely daughter Caroline who has once again excelled herself in producing this amazing front cover.

· Enjoy! And let's all get together again in *Tough Season – The French Connection*, the fourth in the Greg Duggan series!

Chris

TOUGH WORLD

CHAPTER 1

The kick to his stomach that took away his breath didn't kill him, but the kick that lashed out at his temple, followed by another for good measure and a final stamp on the back of his head most certainly did. Brutal. No gun.

His ring finger and small finger of his left hand had been chopped off by an axe as he'd attempted to flee. His assailant had only had one objective and had achieved it with minimum effort and fuss. Job done. Money in the bank.

The Dressing Room
He was nervous. He'd taken an age to get ready. Couldn't even lace up his boots, his hands were shaking so much. He wanted to do well, make a good impression.

The Dressing Down
'Beyond belief!'
Greg Duggan's best mate, Aussie Kenny Lomax had been used to being astounded by Greg's remarkable on-field brilliance and yet confounded by his off-field antics. He'd stood shoulder-to-shoulder alongside him on rugby league grounds through all of their highs in the past two years in Super League playing for Lanzarote Eruption.

Those highs had included Greg's dramatic, last-gasp try in the play-off final that had brought about Eruption's promotion to the elite league two years previously.

Greg had followed that up by helping Eruption to a Challenge Cup semi-final and being just one step away from the Super League Grand Final in the Canary Island club's first campaign.

Kenny had also been there each time Greg had hit rock bottom in his personal life, which was becoming a regular occurrence. What had just happened was yet another calamity in his recent roll call of disaster that had appeared to have hit the accelerator pedal in the past season and had seen Eruption struggle to match their first season in Super League. Kenny's words were delivered in friendship but also in exasperation.

'*You're your own worst enemy, mate.*'

Kenny and Greg were on video call on WhatsApp.

Greg could only give his smile-cum-grimace and familiar slight shrug. He didn't disagree with his best mate's sentiments.

The Earlier Dressing Down

'*Vamos! Y no vuelvas!*'

She had rasped out the words like a viper delivering venom.

'Go and don't come back' had been the translation. Greg had had no defence. It had been another chapter drawing to its close. He knew only too well he'd been heading for this moment.

His world had not been right for months. He'd not been thinking straight. Too much going on inside his head. Too many thoughts, demons, taking control. He hadn't been in a good place for a while.

'*Estas despedido!*'

It was more than all over. She'd sacked off their relationship and she'd sacked him from the club too. He would never play for Eruption again. He'd not built that into any equation and had been shocked, but now that it had happened, he wasn't unduly concerned.

What the hell was going on with his life? He should surely have been concerned about it? Distraught? But he felt nothing except, he had to admit now, relief. He couldn't explain it.

As he always seemed to, he'd gone from hero to zero. And just at the moment he had no appetite to get back to being a hero.

Kenny was trying his best to help him through, but Greg had felt alone for a long time before this. He shouldn't be feeling this way. He'd had everything going his way the previous season when Eruption had established themselves with the big boys.

He'd had rave reviews about his performances that first season. He'd won the hearts of the islanders.

He'd enjoyed a fantastically physical relationship with Maria Cavaleros who had taken overall control of the club, but he'd blown it. Enjoying similarly passionate liaisons with the island's leading political figure Yurena Aguilar hadn't been his sharpest move.

Greg now afforded himself an ironic smile, a raising of his eyebrows and a shake of his head, thinking about it. Not his best move. He smiled, ironically, at himself again.

He'd had a great two years in Playa Blanca and had built fantastic memories. It was time to build some more, once he'd got his head straight, got back home, seen his son. A few months going back to normal life in England.

Dressed to kill

'I don't bloody well care! Just get off your fat arse and do something about it!'

Her heels clacked as she made her way purposefully and stridently from the building wearing a striking ruby red dress that stopped just before her knees, matching stilettos.

Businesslike, pretty and sexy all in one.

This was fast becoming a living nightmare rather than the grand celebration she had planned and overseen throughout. Firing her fingers at her phone's buttons, she moved straight to the following call, propelling similar vitriol at her next victim.

She was very much a woman in a man's world, well aware of being so and as such she was taking no prisoners. She wanted action. Call number three maintained the momentum of fury as she approached her car.

'It's me. Just what the hell do you think you're doing! … That's utter crap and you know it! …'

She stopped just at the door of her Joss JPI coupe that matched her dress, while she listened. The other voice took immediate control.

'Hold your nerve. We are only days away … okay? … right,

gotta go.'

She shook her head. There were other works at play of which the bearer of these words didn't have a bloody clue.

Balance redressed

When the charred remains of a body were found on the island of Efate in the south Pacific archipelago nation of Vanuatu, little did the island's authorities suspect this was to be something of more global consequence. It was simply a body, an unexplained death.

That's how it was until investigations began into the disappearance of one of the three major representatives of the Rugby League World Cup Organising Committee, days prior to the start of the Rugby League World Cup to be held in Australia and the South Pacific.

Debutant Dressed and Ready for Action

When blond-haired, 6-year-old Kyle Duggan appeared from the dressing room with the rest of his team there were cheers and applause from parents, grandparents, aunts, uncles and family friends.

The red and white Hopton Under 7s were about to play their first game of the season against Ludding Vale. Greg was there, back home to watch his son's first game.

His world might have been falling apart, but this was one bright spot as he stood on the touchline alongside his ex-wife Diane and her new husband Paul with their 18-month-old daughter Lily beside them in a buggy.

Greg was a proud dad. He had been sad that he'd not been around much in the past two years and had been missing his son growing up. Never before had he realised just how important this all was, to be there for his son, not only now but whenever possible.

Maybe that's why things had worked out the way they had, bringing him back home after nearly two and a half years in the Canary Islands. He didn't believe in fate, but he could see how it could be seen that way.

Thirty minutes later he was extremely angry, but also even more proud if that could have been possible as little blond Kyle showed his dad that he'd already learned a thing or two about the game.

Dressed to thrill

'Don't say a word,' she had whispered, wearing a smile that had meant everything to him and a white figure-hugging thin strapped dress that showed off her stunning lithe body, beautiful breasts and perfect pins. She let the flimsy material slip softly to the floor revealing her nakedness except for delicate panties of silk and white lace, organza ribbon with a diamante in the centre and crystal side straps. She was enjoying the moment just as much as he.

'We have all night to talk ... but right now ...' She let the words slip away as their lips met, danced and their tongues made their first play.

Immediately they were back in time. Their kiss the most beautiful, sensual moment either had experienced since ... well, since their last time.

Greg had been thinking again of last night, his first back in England in a non-playing capacity, and of them together like this. Susie had been one of the pieces of his jigsaw that had been missing from his life. This had been the other, his son.

Last night had put things back right in many ways and now here, stood on the touchline watching Kyle, he had been able to smile again.

Greg's world was to be rocked just minutes later as his Samsung sprang to life. His mum's voice.

'Greg, it's your dad. I think he's going to ...'

His mum's emotion took control at the other end of the call. Her voice cracking.

'How soon can you get here?'

CHAPTER 2

'... *What a turn of pace! It's Venus! He's just come on for his international debut and he's in acres of space, they won't catch him. Oh, what another excellent try from the speedster who has really come of age this season in Super League ... but I'm afraid this isn't going to be enough to save England!*'

Greg had just turned up the DAB radio in the Range Rover Evoque Sport he'd hired the day previously on landing back in England. It was a million miles different to the beat-up bangers he'd driven when playing for Hopton Town and working as a garage mechanic.

Those days had been less than three years ago. How his life had changed. This was a brand-new motor, not some ancient Alfa Romeo. He shook his head as he realised he'd probably be returning it tomorrow.

He had turned up the volume because he'd heard the radio commentary on the latest England game before the Rugby League World Cup was to get under way, he'd heard Vinny's name – Vincent Venus – the young player he'd played alongside for the past few seasons for Lanzarote Eruption and Hopton Town.

Greg was only half listening.

His mind was suddenly full of bad news. He knew he had to leave England again, leave Kyle, leave Susie who he had just seen for the first time in two years. So much for settling to a normal life.

It had been a long time since he'd seen his mum and dad, but it didn't matter how long it had been. He knew he had to go. He looked across and smiled at Kyle sat in the passenger seat.

It all seemed so daft. Stupid really. Just as he'd got back for his son and Susie it was his dad that needed him, or in reality his mum.

Kyle had pulled on his shirt for the team Greg had started with over 20 years ago. Not only that, but he had scored a superb try.

That had been Greg's prouder-than-proud bit, but there had also been a dark side that he hadn't remembered happening when he'd been a kid playing. The vitriol, the obscene, awful language of some of the parents who should have known better. And it was towards the young referee. Greg could not believe how grown men and women could act in such a way to someone else's child.

He now looked across again at Kyle. His son was now sat munching a well-earned bag of crisps with a can of Coca Cola in the Range Rover's cup holder and a Mars bar ready to follow. He quickly switched back to being the proud dad. He beamed at his son, taking his hand briefly off the steering wheel to ruffle Kyle's shock of thick blond hair.

'And there's young half-back Stu Wainwright coming on for his first game in an England shirt … this lad's had an amazing last two years. He hasn't got long to make an impression here …'

Stu was another of Greg's playing colleagues. Both Stu and Vinny had made it to the England team. Greg was proud of them too, but right now he was even more proud of his son.

'Dad!'

Kyle whipped his father back into the real world and touched his heart.

'Can you stay with us, please? Forever.'

CHAPTER 3

Greg was frustrated. He had so wanted to spend more time with Kyle and Susie. He'd quite fancied chatting with Diane too, catching up. They'd retained a decent relationship, talking mainly about their son, since their break-up.

They'd been teenage sweethearts since high school and had married when they were both just turned 20.

Diane still thought fondly of him, he knew that much, and the feeling was mutual. They also both wanted the best for their son. But Diane was now married to Paul, and they had Lily.

Maybe he was just a rolling stone, then thought how much of an idiot he sounded, thinking that way. It was almost as though he had a clue about what he was trying to justify. He'd enjoyed the company of other women, end of story.

He was now 30. The only real constant in his life for years had been Susie and he'd just been back with her again for the first time in two years the night previously.

He smiled as he thought of her again. She made him feel good just thinking about her. He tried to equate everything, why he'd been with some of the other girls, but swiftly moved on.

Maybe he really didn't have a clue about life, love, girls, people. Maybe he was fairly useless at all that. Maybe he was just a rugby league player. Maybe.

What was with all of these maybes entering his head. Get a grip, man.

He'd taken Kyle back to Diane and Paul. He'd had a cuppa with them but had felt he was intruding at their home on a new-build estate on the edge of Hopton.

Diane hadn't said anything. It had been just a feeling. Paul wasn't unwelcoming but had been busying himself elsewhere in the house. It wasn't ideal. Greg decided to go.

'You know you're welcome any time ...'

Diane had said the words affectionately, smiling at him as he'd given his son another ruffle of his hair before leaving. They, Greg and Diane, had held each other very briefly. There was no great feeling in the tiny embrace. Life had moved on.

'My Mr Cool, mmm ...'

She was straddling him now, enjoying being back in her favourite position, riding him. Younger women and even girls in their twenties, thirties or even forties would have been proud. She had been ready for him in heels, black lacy suspender belt and stockings. She knew what he liked.

This gorgeous, sensual older woman who enjoyed fondling her own breasts in the height of passion as she rose and fell in tandem with their combined movement, had always excited him.

'You saved my life ...'

They'd enjoyed what they both never seemed to tire of and were now relaxing from another fulfilling evening.

She was looking into his eyes and he back into hers. He loved the way she did that. She was propping her head up with her hand, her elbow on the bed, smiling the way she did, the way her eyes danced and her blonde hair caressed her shoulders. They kissed again, this time softly, their tongues lingering.

Greg never boasted about his great performances on the field or helping friends, colleagues, his ex-wife and son, and Susie.

He didn't argue that he hadn't saved her. He knew he had. He just let it ride, much as Susie had just done in her own way.

He also knew Susie was just being gentle and playful. He loved that about her. Yes, he'd saved her when she'd been caught up in the crossfire of the mess he'd had to sort out in Lanzarote. And he had possibly saved her life.

But he'd also felt that to a large degree her plight at the time had been down to what had been going on in his life. He'd felt responsible. He put his hand to her cheek now, softly holding it in his big hand.

'You save my life every time we are together.'

He said it with more romance, more feeling, than he had anticipated. Christ, he was starting to say things that seemed out of a script, what was all that about?

For all that he'd more recently been with Maria Cavaleros, owner of the Lanzarote Eruption Super League team, it was always Susie who pushed his buttons, it was Susie who he fancied like crazy, it was Susie he wanted to be with when it all came down to it.

'*Shhhh …*'

Susie was looking into his eyes. She put her fingers to her own lips and then onto his.

'*Hold me Greg …*'

This embrace meant something more. Greg felt it.

Susie knew Greg had to go, almost as quickly as he'd returned. He'd told her about his dad.

In some ways it was perhaps the best thing. It saved any words from her.

Life had changed for her in the past twelve months. She hadn't discussed it.

It was best left. He was going half the way around the world and this time she knew it might be the last time for them. She probably wouldn't see him again.

There was a tear in her eye as she held him, her head next to his shoulder as they embraced tightly. Susie didn't want him to see.

A few years ago Greg possibly wouldn't have noticed, but right now he felt it. There was something in Susie's embrace that said this might be a final goodbye. He couldn't put his finger on it as to why.

This was so different, the way she held him, the way it seemed she really didn't want to let him go. He felt he shouldn't ask. He knew he wasn't imagining it.

Greg had never questioned Susie seriously about what else was ever going on in her life. Over the years she had talked about her family, her grown-up children and their families. She had talked of her friends.

Greg realised he'd let things go unsaid, unquestioned, and right now he wished he hadn't, he wished they had talked more.

They had shared laughter, fun, intimacy.

She'd cried on his shoulder when they had seen an older couple dancing, proper ballroom dancing, clearly loving being together and moving as one. She had said it had reminded her of her mum and dad doing the same at a dance hall or even just at home as she had been growing up.

Greg had been privileged to be there for her then, seen her emotions. It had been a moment that had meant more to him than any other. When they had talked more deeply there had been similar moments, yet there had also been an unseen dividing line. Things that had been left unsaid. From both sides.

He hadn't felt all of this as strongly as he did now, sat on the plane up high over the United Kingdom and bound for Australia.

What hadn't she said last night?

Susie had never held him that way before. He knew that it meant there was something unsaid. He felt he should have asked.

But then maybe it was best that he hadn't. Maybe she'd wanted to say something but couldn't.

All these bloody maybes!

'Mr Duggan?'

Greg had fallen asleep not long into the first part of the long haul, the seven-hour flight to Abu Dhabi.

He'd intended to take in *No Time To Die*, the last James Bond film to feature Daniel Craig in the title role that had been delayed due to the worldwide epidemic the year previously, and *The Hitman's Wife's Daughter's Uncle's Dogs' Bodyguard* or something like that, with Freddie Reynolds and Samuel L. Jackson reprising their roles of earlier films, on the in-flight movies, but he'd dropped off instead. Plenty of time. He had another sixteen hours in the sky to come after Abu Dhabi.

'Excuse me, sir. Could you come with me please?'

Strange request. He cocked his head slightly with no idea why he was being asked to follow. The maroon and pink bedecked and not unpretty flight attendant escorted him through Economy class to Business and First class to a class he'd never heard of before, on a deck above.

He'd never even known that planes had other levels.

This was a mini version of a luxurious hotel suite, a mini-apartment in the sky with a living room, en suite facilities and bedroom.

Really? What the hell was this all about? Why was he here?

'Mr Duggan, good of you to join us.'

There were two of them in the room.

He knew he wasn't dreaming, that this was for real, but it was also truly out of this world, one hell of an upgrade.

Greg's expression said it all. His eyes, one second wide, next second trying to work out what was happening.

'Sit down, Greg, make yourself comfortable.'

Two well-dressed, highly attractive women.

The one who had introduced him was probably in her late-40s to mid-50s, perhaps even into her 60s at a touch. Blonde-to-fair hair, shoulder length, attractive figure, beautiful face. She was now seated.

The other was also slim, also shapely, possibly a little older but no less pretty, platinum blonde, marginally smaller than the other. Greg sat.

They were in a leather upholstered room with sofa and armchair, coffee table, laptops and large widescreen TV. Greg sat to the left of the sofa, platinum blonde across from him in the armchair.

'Drink?'

Having just woken and having been seemingly transported to some kind of parallel universe this all seemed surreal.

The 'mile high club' popped into his mind, he shook away the thought with a little pressing together of his lips, slight exhalation through his nose, raising of his eyebrows and shrug of his shoulders.

'Tea.'

The platinum blonde whom he'd taken as slightly older fed him information.

'This is an Airbus A380. This is what's called The Residence. It's a three-roomed apartment. There's this room, a bathroom ... and a bedroom.'

She paused momentarily in her delivery. She had crossed her legs. Was that a hint of a stocking top as her skirt rode up a little?

'As you might imagine, this doesn't come cheap, and neither do we.'

Greg resisted temptation in asking anything, no matter what she had been implying.

Was she flirting? He shook himself out of the thought almost instantly. Why was his brain hard-wired this way? He laughed inwardly at himself without giving away any other outer show of his thoughts, or so he hoped. He knew there had to be an ulterior motive at play.

Not that Greg was complaining. This was far more comfortable and better company than being lumped in with 500-600 others down in Economy where a six-foot-three guy like him would struggle for leg room at the best of times.

He'd stick this out for as long as he could. No innuendo intended.

Two attractive women, luxury accommodation, bedroom – there he went again, couldn't stop himself, could he?

Experience told him to be wary, especially during his time on Lanzarote. He'd encountered a new level of female power out there.

Reality was starting to kick in. Why, really, was he here? One, he wouldn't get invited somewhere like this, that obviously cost a bomb, for no reason. Two, what were they after?

As if on cue the platinum blonde who had a cultured, or in Greg's vocabulary posh, accent got to the point.

'Have you ever heard of The International Centre for Integrity in Sport?'

It wasn't as though Greg needed any time for his answer, he hadn't a clue. He gave a simple slight shake of his head, bottom lip just over his top lip. The woman asked another.

'Why are you going to Australia?'

Greg's next thought was already in his brain before he could do anything about it. If these women had the dosh to afford this kind of thing, they would surely already know why he was there? They'd have their sources. There was something too assured about them.

He'd never rated himself as the sharpest knife in the drawer when working people out, but Integrity in Sport? What was that all about?

He also knew he had every right not to tell them why he was heading Down Under, but what was the point? Why keep quiet? He had nothing to hide. He wasn't going Down Under for anything other than his parents. He slanted his eyes, pursed his lips.

He wasn't about to get over friendly with them. He was relaxed. Just give it to them straight.

'My dad's ill. He might be dying.'

He looked directly at the blonde. He didn't smile and neither did she. For the next ten seconds it was a stare-off. It seemed much longer. It all seemed so unnecessary.

If she wanted to play games, fair enough. He'd given her his answer. She had known it anyway, Greg was sure of that much.

There was a knock at the door. The stewardess arrived with silver salver service adorned by china tea pot, cups and saucers and a coffee pot. This was beyond bizarre, like stepping back in time to *Downton Abbey*. When was the butler due?

Platinum blonde's face relaxed, she allowed herself a forced smile.

'He said you were good.'

Greg slanted his eyes at her once again, cocked his head slightly, asking the question without using words. It was Greg's way. Keep words to a minimum. She smiled. Their sparring was clearly entertaining her. He spoke.

'Your job gets you this?'

Greg nodded in the direction of what he saw in front of him and raised his eyebrows. Platinum blonde smiled again.

'It's a very serious business. In our line of work it's important to stay well out of the way.'

Greg raised his eyebrows, this time almost mockingly. He watched her reaction to his. Her reaction was a shrug that she maintained for perhaps a second longer than was really necessary. He added another question.

'Who?'

Greg left it there, one syllable this time, one word. No explanation. He'd heard what she'd said previously. The recommendation. He'd said he was good. Who was this who had said this?

'How would you describe your relationship with Maria Cavaleros?'

Platinum blonde had sidestepped responding to him with another question. Where was this going?

Why were they mentioning Maria?

Greg chose to sidestep her question in return for her swerve of his.

'Why are you going to Australia?'

It was his turn to ask the same question. He kept his poker face as she held hers. This wasn't exactly getting either of them anywhere, but Greg had time to kill. It wasn't as though he had anywhere to be but back downstairs in Economy, watching a Bond movie.

But what the fuck was all this about?

The widescreen TV burst into life. Maria was there on screen, pictured with somebody else whose face was blurred out.

If Greg's current hosts had been anticipating he would turn into some green-eyed monster at the sight of this and subsequent frames that took the couple from arm-in-arm, clearly enjoying a night out, to intimacy on Papagayos beach in Playa Blanca they hadn't done their homework properly.

If they had been expecting more from Greg by way of reaction they were going to be mightily disappointed.

The next frame made all the difference in the world.

CHAPTER 4

'Aww mate, the Pommies are really under the pump. They'll get through their group, but they've sure got their work cut out if they want to make it past the quarters ...'

Former Kangaroos international Ricky Johnson was talking on Queensland Sports Radio as Greg made his way down the coast in a Mitsubishi Pajero Sport hire car picked up from Brisbane airport.

They were talking about the game he'd been half-listening to in the Range Rover Evoque when Greg had Kyle with him. It had been a disaster for the England team in a pre-tournament warm-up game.

Greg had harboured hopes of being named in the World Cup squad until injury had intervened during the season. He'd recovered match fitness and had been playing well again towards the end of the season, but by then others had gone in front of him in the squad.

The show's presenter was another former player too, Clint Newsome, who had played out the end of his career in Super League in England after ten seasons in Australia's NRL.

'And it all gets under way in just two days when the Roos play the opening game against Wales at Stadium Australia.'

Johnson and Newsome rated England's chances of winning the competition at less than zero following two catastrophic defeats Down Under – at Anzac Oval in Alice Springs and against the small island nation of Niue at the Alofi Stadium in the South Pacific.

England fans were mystified. Whoever had come up with the idea of taking the team to the baking-hot centre of Australia the day following their arrival in the country, after a 22-hour flight covering 11,500 miles, followed up with two flights taking in a further 3600 miles to play a second game on one of the South Pacific's most isolated islands two days later needed, exceedingly politely of course, their heads examining!

Greg shook his head in disbelief.

Three of his Eruption teammates had made the England squad – Vinny Venus, Stu Wainwright and John Cloudsdale. They all deserved to be selected for the World Cup, but they hadn't deserved this kind of preparation.

'For any Pommies tuning in right now, you boys took one hell of a beating …'

Clint was enjoying the moment, playing to the Aussie listeners and flagrantly plagiarising a commentary from one of the England international football team's worst defeats decades ago. He went on.

'To some of you Pommies listening in, g'day to you, and in the words of one of your favourite songs, you might have been asking "where the … (the presenter added his own bleep at this point) … is Alice?" but not any more …

'Just in case you don't know, Alice is a little town in the middle of our great island with a population of just over 30,000 … Alice is home to just four rugby league teams that play in the Central Australia Conference. And if you didn't hear the result it was Alice 12 England 4.'

He'd been building up to his pay-off line.

Ricky Johnson was no less damning, initially sounding as though he may have been about to offer some kind of reasoning.

'Aww mate, come on, be fair …'

Greg couldn't help but smile. He could feel them egging each other on in the studio or on Zoom or any streaming service. Wherever they were speaking they could see each other and were controlling their hysterics while sending their Aussie listeners into a state of delirium. Ricky added,

'… Alice is a big place …'

He let it hang in the air a second longer before blitzing.

'… compared to Nieu … do you know the island has a population of just 1,600? … Most schools in Oz have a bigger number … and again – to be fair – they have won internationals before, against Malta and the Cook Islands, but Nieu 24 England 22 … really?'

Greg had heard enough.

'The competition starts in less than 48 hours and you're telling me this now! Do you need me to come down there and wipe your backsides for you! Get it fixed!'

She was getting mightily sick of people passing the buck to her with their problems instead of finding solutions. Her stress level was at an all-time high, looking down from her office at the 83,500-seater Stadium Australia in Sydney where final rehearsals were taking place for the Grand Opening, a spectacular affair in keeping with the country's previous achievements.

This was all set to be the most inclusive Rugby League World Cup tournament with men's, women's, wheelchair, physical disability (PDRL) competitions and first ever LGBT international game called 'The Pink' all to be held in Australia and various islands in Oceania.

It was to be Australia's biggest single-sport international competition and for one woman the years of planning were about to come to fruition, but as she looked out on the mass of colour presently bathing the ground she received a call that was to stop her in her tracks.

'Yes!'

She had been abrupt, anticipating the call to be another line manager not prepared to make their own decision.

'Who the hell are you?!'

The voice made it clear. Zoe Miller felt her world stop revolving.

'What?!'

The Rugby League World Cup Organising Committee chief executive's anger and frustration of seconds before had been replaced by a numbness.

She held on to the balcony railing from where, seconds previously she had considered herself the proudest person in Australia. This couldn't be happening now, could it?

'No. I'm still here. What do you want me to do?'

CHAPTER 5

Byron Bay, one of Australia's favourite seaside towns, was where Greg's folks had set up home after leaving the UK.

Greg's head was mashed. He'd flown from Lanzarote to England to Australia in the past three days. What the hell had that thing been all about up in the sky with the two women. And that picture they had shown at the end? That couldn't have been true could it? He wasn't so daft that he didn't realise how everything could be doctored to look not what it was.

Susie. That embrace. He knew it meant something that hadn't been said.

Kyle. He wanted to be with his son. He wanted to be with Susie.

His dad was struggling to take top spot in his brain. It didn't mean he wasn't thinking about him or his mum, and how she was feeling. He'd come 11,000 miles for Christ's sake, he told himself, as he was driving. At least he was here. It was just that life appeared to be getting more complicated, even though he liked to keep it simple.

Yes, he usually brought things on himself, but just at the moment he had a fair old mix of stuff to deal with, including finding a new club, new employment. Maybe now was the time to get an agent. Maybe he'd go back to being a mechanic.

He smirked at himself over that thought.

Nah, he couldn't see himself having to resort back to his initial trade, but then he wasn't getting carried away with any high ideas about himself either. Maybe an agent might be worth a go.

Greg was now within half an hour of Byron Bay and could see the banners proclaiming the latest international BluesFest festival.

As he drove closer his mindset flicked between several people.

Kyle – he knew he didn't want to miss his son growing up, that he wanted to be a part of his son's life. He wanted to be around when Kyle wanted his breakfast in a morning, to go out and have a kick-about with a football or to pass a rugby ball.

Susie – he loved with all his heart, he was at his happiest when he was with her, okay Kyle too, but that was a different ballpark. He raised his eyebrows and smiled as he realised he was talking balls.

Maria – the women on the plane? The questions? The pictures? Just what had been going on there? Maybe there had been more to his sacking than met the eye.

Now, around ten miles from Byron Bay, thoughts finally began flooding his head about his mum and dad.

Tina and Trev Duggan had both been active, sports oriented, always in trim and in tune with nature and the outdoor life. Consequently, their sons, Greg and Colin had grown up enjoying adventurous and rigorous holidays that regularly included long-distance walking, running, mountain climbing, wild water swimming, cycling and just about anything that involved hard toil, spirit and determination.

Their weekends had included taxiing the boys to their respective matches, competitions or outdoor pursuits – whether rugby league, cross country, cyclo-cross and swimming in Greg's case, or mountain climbing, hiking and tennis in Colin's – but Tina and Trev had also followed their own passions, feeling just as strongly about leading their own lives.

Greg had never been surprised about much they did and when his parents had announced they were quitting their jobs and about to travel the world he had already added 'and not coming back' in his head. Greg had been 19 and Colin 21 when their parents had started their big adventure.

Tina and Trev had made their way across Europe and Asia, had fallen in love with the Far East including India, Hong Kong and China and had enjoyed Japan before heading for the South Pacific taking in Fiji and New Zealand.

Australia turned out to be their final destination. They had alluded to living there in the past, even with the boys when they were younger, and they had found their own paradise in Byron Bay just two hours south of Brisbane, its people, way of life, surfing, food, the music. They had invested everything they had in staying there.

That had been a decade ago and Greg had only seen them in the flesh twice since, once when he and Diane had married and six years ago when his grandfather had died. They'd come back for both, but Greg had never visited them until now. Was it going to be too late for his father?

Greg lived his life, they lived theirs and they talked every so often on Messenger or WhatsApp, sometimes by video link.

They'd had slightly more contact during the recent pandemic, which had abated almost completely around eight months ago, but their calls had still only been numbered on the fingers of one hand over the past eighteen months and if they lasted longer than twenty minutes it was a miracle. Greg wasn't big on conversation.

Tina and Trev were both in their early fifties and from the video calls they'd shared, until the call that had brought about Greg's journey, they had both looked in good shape, cracking shape actually. Tina was definitely very much still a looker with her bleached blonde tousled hair and svelte figure.

Greg could tell his dad had put on a few pounds but was still well appointed. They both looked younger than their actual age.

Losing his dad crossed Greg's mind as he drove closer.

What would it mean to him? They were still a close family unit even if they were thousands of miles apart. They didn't stay in touch often enough, or at least Greg wasn't generally the one to make the first move, but that didn't mean they didn't love each other.

His dad not being around? He honestly had no real idea what it would mean.

'*Gregory!*'

His mum beamed at him from just outside the doors of the

hospital reception area where she stood looking splendidly young, wearing shorts and t-shirt. She smiled the way she always had, the way he always remembered, so full of warmth.

Thousands of miles might have separated them, but nothing could stop him seeing that smile whenever he thought of her.

Tina knew her son wasn't one to immediately embrace, even though she also knew he wanted to. She made the decision for him as he approached. She wasn't in floods of tears, she didn't break down when she saw him, she was similar to her son. Didn't need many words.

'*It's great to see you.*'

She expressed it just the way his mum always did. Total sincerity, not a flash of any underlying feelings over how long it had taken and that it had taken something like this to get him out there. Just love.

'*Come on, let's see your dad.*'

She'd not prepared him for anything, other than in the call she'd made initially. The subsequent calls they'd shared over arrangements and arrival times had never included Dad appearing on-screen. Greg hadn't asked why. It was either bad or they both had their reasons why he wasn't shown.

It was bad.

Greg's world was shattered in the instant he saw him. There was nothing that could have prepared him for this moment. He knew instantly why his mum hadn't shown him on-screen, hadn't mentioned anything about his condition and why she had made the call.

Whatever had been Greg's worst case scenario beforehand couldn't have been worse than what he saw in front of him.

He pictured his dad as he was when he was growing up. It was a kneejerk reaction on seeing him. His mum had been so right to call.

Greg's first thought was not how he was, but how long he had left.

Tina saw Greg sway. She knew her sons and she knew that Greg, for all his front with people he didn't really know, was a straightforward lad, someone who never saw far into the future because he was too much in the day.

Not a criticism, just how he lived his life.

Tina knew this would hit him like a sledgehammer as it had her, but she also knew he wouldn't have coped with it very well any other way. At least this way she could do something first-hand about the bits he would be blown into.

Greg was her little lad who had held her hand so tightly that first day he went to school and hadn't wanted her to leave. She knew this was another time he'd wobble.

His dad was dying. Of that there was little doubt.

Greg struggled to find words at the best of times. He was bereft here. Whatever thoughts had gone through his mind in those final miles toward the hospital were gone.

Tina knew instinctively what was coming next. She answered while Greg was nowhere even near formulating a question.

'*Not long.*'

She held his hand. Her voice breaking.

He clutched her hand tightly, more so than he'd ever held it before. He knew it was too much, relaxed his grip a little. She'd had time work out how she was going to deal with Greg.

Colin who was on his way too.

Tina turned her attention back to Trev, but spoke again to Greg.

'*I'm so pleased you're here.*'

She turned back towards her son, her eyes glazed with tears, not yet running down her face, but welling up. She put her free hand near to her mouth.

'*It has all happened so quickly. We didn't know what to do for the best, but then ...*' her voice was breaking, just like her heart.

CHAPTER 6

'... get him on a flight ... really? ... well track him down!'

It was the first good news Shane Chislett, the England coach, had heard for weeks. His team's first game in the competition was to be the day following the official opening of the tournament in Sydney. His plans were in tatters. He was desperately short of fit players.

England's disastrous warm-up games had not been his idea, and had robbed him of half of his preferred starting 13.

He knew that his remaining charges possessed more than enough power, finesse and creativity to win their opening game with ease against one of the game's emerging nations, Vanuatu. But beating the Pacific islanders was not really the issue.

England had been installed as second favourites to win the World Cup, after Australia. They were clinging to that status but no-one now saw them as likely to overthrow the men in green and gold if they reached the final.

Others such as the New Zealand and Papua New Guinea teams were already licking their lips at the prospect of playing them in the quarters or semis.

'Where have we reached in the investigation into the body?'

He was trying to appear calm. This was one of several items on the agenda in today's briefing of his team. But solving what had occurred was a problem. Danford was well aware that their investigative resources would struggle to deal with anything out of the ordinary.

Danford Napakauranga police commissioner for Vanuatu had held the office for the past twenty years and in that time had been more used to dealing with the impact of natural disasters, domestic violence and occasional robberies rather than unexplained murders. His was a land where cyclones and earthquakes were more frequent than murder.

His police presence on Efate, the Republic of Vanuatu's

third largest island, that only hosts a population of 68,000 was stretched to its limit. They already had enough on their plate with the impending arrival of the England international rugby league team and their supporters.

Hosting World Cup games was great news for the island, for its tourism, but for Danford this was a serious headache.

An unexplained murder. A body in the manner it had been destroyed, was something else.

Add a huge influx of nearly 5000 people due in the next two days, to an airport that was barely able to cope with its visitor traffic at the best of times, and there was very real stress already.

The whole nation was preparing for a bounce in trade, as well as the most momentous sporting event in its history.

This body, what remained of it, was the last thing Danford needed right now. The spotlight would be projected on he and his team.

There had been rumours that his deputy Elenola Taneo was impressing the local politicians and that Danford was feeling the heat.

'*We are waiting for SOCO to finish. And we are still working on Erakor, but it is becoming more difficult. There are so many people coming on to the island that we may lose evidence.*'

Alex Lui was in charge of the investigation and giving his report. He was in his late 20s, good-looking with jet black hair and recently promoted to Vanuatu CID. This was his first murder case. Danford had been his mentor.

Erakor Island is one of the many small islands littered off Efate and is only a two-minute water bus hop from the mainland. It is home to one of the island's most prestigious hotel and spa complexes and is one of the main island's most popular resorts with beautiful sandy beaches and excellent snorkelling among the coral and crystal blue waters.

'*There must be witnesses and evidence, SOCO are doing what they can but we could do with more of our team to ask around.*'

'*Thank you Alex. Let's increase our presence there today.*'

Danford was addressing the meeting in the police

headquarters in Port Vila. The room included his would-be challenger Elenola, Alex Lui and a dozen others in the operations room.

'*Now let's turn our attention to the Municipal Stadium and security all over town ...*'

Zoe Miller knew she had to do this. There was no other way. She had been successful in sport and then in business.

She had become the country's greatest heptathlete twenty years ago, earning a gold medal at the Olympics and had gone on to start her first fitness centre, which had grown into over 100 centres throughout Australia and New Zealand before she had sold her controlling stake in the company.

Zoe had since taken on roles with Sport Australia, Aussie Rules and latterly the NRL, that had led to her appointment as chief executive for the Rugby League World Cup.

She was presently 'seven miles from Sydney, and a thousand miles from care', a phrase well-known to those who visited Manly, the seaside resort that was also beginning to burst at its seams with rugby league fans.

She had taken the Fast Ferry service from Sydney as instructed, a 20-minute journey to Manly Wharf and was now heading for The Corso, a plaza of cafés, bars and shops.

'*You got me?*'

Zoe whispered as she made her way along the Corso toward the beach.

'*Uh-huh,*' was the reply.

This had been all too swift in setting up, this was not something where she was in control.

There had been no time to plan, but she'd tried as best she could. She hadn't got to this point in her career without help and she sure as hell needed it now, but as fast as she was trying to figure out what was going on, time was being eaten up. The call she'd taken had been an hour ago.

In that time, she'd made calls using a new pay-as-you-go 'burner' phone. She kept several but none were close when she'd received the call. She hadn't come this far in her career without knowing her way around the block and devices that could be used and ditched without trace had proved useful.

She had sent a text on the one number she needed and prayed there would be an immediate reply. She had also managed a change of clothing, as she had felt this whole escapade or whatever was to follow would be better suited to a jeans and t-shirt op, or even her running gear.

She had learned to keep various alternatives of clothing either in her office or car at all times. She chose joggers, top and a baseball cap. Better for running if she had to. She didn't know what to expect.

To fail to prepare was to prepare to fail she'd once been told – and she did not fail, ever.

'I don't know what the hell's going on here …'

Zoe's breathing was steady while she walked and talked through her phone while listening on ear bud headphones. She was trying to keep a calmness. Inside she was worried as hell.

'We'll soon find out …'

At least the voice was reassuring, a voice she trusted. It spoke again.

'Just do what you always do … keep calm …'

'Easier said than done …'

Zoe was quick with her riposte, but it hadn't been one of venom, merely stating fact. She couldn't have felt any more impotent than right now.

The voice was as patient and observant as it could be. Didn't try to contradict. Left a space, time for consideration. It was only seconds, but it proved sufficient.

'Clear head … Understand? … Zoe? …'

The voice was holding firm. Trying hard to keep her on course yet understanding.

Zoe had abandoned any final arrangements that were to be made for the start of the competition. She'd had no choice.

The voice tried again, this time with greater concern, wanting to hear at least something.

'Zoe?'

CHAPTER 7

'Get it out … spread it!'

It wasn't a game. The voice from the sidelines was trying his best not to be exasperated, he was known for his ability to maintain a straight face when the television cameras were on him during a game, not to let his emotions surface, but his patience had been wearing thin.

Shane Chislett had enjoyed a fabulous playing career in England and Australia and had become one of Super League's and the NRL's most respected coaches in the past decade since he'd finished on the park.

He'd completed a remarkable double-double in winning Grand Finals in both countries as player and coach and had played international rugby league over a period of thirteen seasons.

He had taken on the role as head coach of England six months prior to the World Cup competition.

Never before had he been involved in such a shambles. Who, in God's name, had sent he and his charges out to Alice Springs! Why the hell? Centre of Australia, baking hot conditions. Just what had this all been about? – Nieu, for Christ's sake! Where the hell was that? He'd had to Google it and then still couldn't believe where his players were going when they should have been preparing and taking everything in their stride professionally.

He blamed himself. The itinerary had been decided long before he'd taken over as coach, but he should have looked more closely and he should have pulled them out of both games.

The games had done nothing for his players. England were the big guns, the superstars, the pitches were light years behind what they were used to, but for the opposition these were their very own cup finals. These had been intended as warm-up games, of little consequence apart from a run-out for the whole squad. They had been anything but!

Perhaps this was all just down to some well-meaning idiot somewhere who was trying what the sport was forever keen on, in taking the game to far-flung corners, giving others those amazing experiences, once in a lifetime games.

Nah! He might have accepted that at first, but he wasn't that naïve! There was so much happening around him that wasn't right. He didn't know why, but whoever it was that was behind it needed sorting – and quickly. Chislett would deal with it.

It was he who had expressed the need for more players. Having flown out with the requisite 31-player squad he was currently down to just 16 fully fit players after the two warm-up games in Alice and Nieu.

Chislett shook himself back to the guys in front of him, now finally in a practice session at the kind of ground they should have been using all along.

'Come on boys ... re-set ... and go again ...'

Chislett clapped his hands to urge the players on in their workout at Dolphin Stadium, home of Redcliffe Dolphins in Brisbane, the Queensland Cup competition's most successful team and with ambitions of joining the NRL.

He'd organised this himself, through his Queensland connections having played for Brisbane for three seasons, and had relocated the squad to somewhere much more in keeping with what everyone would have expected.

For the first time in a week everyone was happier with accommodation, their hotel, facilities and the feel-good was coming back to where it had been when they had set off from England.

His problem was that he now needed a full deck of fit players. Reinforcements were being contacted or were on their way, but whether they would all arrive before their opening match in Vanuatu was in the lap of the Gods.

His first new charge was heading straight for him. Shaun Chislett had never played or coached against him as his last two seasons had been spent coaching in Australia, but he knew all about him.

There was a nod of acceptance and a clasp of hands greeting from both Chislett and Greg as they came face to face.

'*I hear your dad's not good.*'

Greg gave the briefest of nods and the briefest of replies.

'*Yeah.*'

Chislett wasn't in the mood for messing about with pleasantries.

'*You in the right frame of mind?*'

Greg looked Chislett in the eye. He hadn't driven up for the past two hours from Byron Bay just to say Hi.

Greg had known he couldn't do much at the hospital, apart from comfort his mum. He'd told her about the call. She knew he'd want to go. Col had turned up.

Tina knew Greg had done the right thing in coming. Greg had said he would stay, but both Tina and Col had known there was little point. There was no malice from either of them.

Greg nodded again at Chislett. This time firmer.

'*I'll get changed.*'

Greg made straight for the dressing room. He turned from Chislett to go, but then swiftly turned back.

'*My dad's dying ... That's why I'm here ... in Australia ...*'

Minimalistic speech was Greg's stock in trade. Action rather than words was always his thing. He raised his eyebrows while taking a deep breath, lips firm, then twitched ever so slightly. Another little inhale through his nose. A little shake of the head.

'*My brother just arrived ... he's better at all that than me ... I got your call ... I'm here to play Mr Chislett ...*'

Greg's eye narrowed as he sought to rid his coach of any doubt.

'*... and I'm here to win, whatever it takes ...*'

CHAPTER 8

Zoe's self-preservation kicked in. This was wrong. She needed more time. Thinking time. This smelled bad. Everything. She needed to win back control. She ditched the mic and the earbuds, dived into a nearby café bar. She mumbled something to the barista about needing the toilet. He pointed.

She made for the rear of the building, passing the single toilet and heading for a fire door. Pressing the release bar, she made her way out and into a yard and refuse area that led to an alleyway.

She had calculated this was a set-up.

She didn't know quite how, but even the voice she thought she could trust. There had been something about that too. The voice had been too calm for someone who allegedly hadn't known anything until she had called. The voice knew something. She was sure of it, or if she wasn't 100 per cent sure, she wasn't prepared to gamble.

Zoe hadn't had time to disseminate any details while she'd been in the stadium but there had been something that had clicked in her brain as she had been making her way on the Corso.

As she made her way down the alley, she heard raised voices coming from where she had just left. She had been right. This was no time for standing still. It was time to disappear.

'That's better boys!'

Shane Chislett was back with his players and coaching staff on the Redcliffe Dolphins ground, and their latest recruits.

He'd been buoyed by two other new charges in addition to Greg – prop Billy Ecktenstall and stand-off Owen Fenchurch who had both been over in Sydney as they had come over as possible signings for NRL clubs for next season. All three would be straight into the opening group game against Vanuatu.

'Greg, we got this … you, me, Vinny … let's go!'

Stu Wainwright was calling the shots at scrum-half in the practice game, which had been arranged behind closed doors with Redcliffe's second string.

Greg was full of pride. Four years earlier, Stu and Vincent Venus had been teenage lads cutting their teeth with his hometown club Hopton Town. All three had then played together at the newly formed Lanzarote Eruption and had all become stars of Super League.

Now they were all here, along with Eruption teammate of the past two seasons, John Cloudsdale.

Greg couldn't care less about the roundabout way in which he'd made it back to England duty from having played a couple of games at the end of the previous season. He was here and up for it all.

'*Great play guys …*'

Chislett voiced it out loud as he saw the three weave their magic. OK, it was a practice match rather than the real thing but it had been a beautiful sight. Stu had received at the play-the-ball, had stepped off his right, shimmying left and deftly creating the space for Greg to charge on to. Greg had dummied one player, gone through the gap and produced a fantastic reverse pass for Vinny to gallop in under the posts. It was exquisite and not the first time they had performed it either.

'*Just like the Challenge Cup semi-final!*'

Vinny was ebullient. Stu grinned as the trio embraced in celebration.

'*Bring on Vanuatu!*'

While Greg shared the sentiment he wasn't about to get carried away. Exuberance was one thing, cockiness another and he sensed that part of the England players' undoing in Nieu and Alice might have been that they had expected to win by just turning up.

Vanuatu would have players who would rise to an occasion and as underdogs anyone could win if the opposition didn't concentrate.

In the stands there were reporters from the English and

Australian press, broadcast media and social media bloggers who had been allowed into the sessions. It was another part of the World Cup organisers' plans to make this the most open competition in the world.

At least a dozen had been watching and taking photographs. They were tapping reports into their respective tablets and laptops, updating websites, blogs, Facebook pages, WhatsApps, Instagram, Twitter, TikTok and every other feed possible with the latest news from the England camp. Greg's name brought a mix of headlines.

Duggan leaves dying dad's bedside for England call ... Former Eruption star gives up woman troubles for World Cup ... Forgotten Hero reignites campaign ...

The headlines were already alive throughout the world by the time the session was completed. There were more, plus photographs and videos of the move made by the three players. So much for this being a behind-doors session.

Greg knew everyone in the squad except for prop Freddie South. The rest he'd either played against with Lanzarote Eruption or he'd met in the course of his two international appearances to date, both against France, home and away fixtures.

Freddie had been playing for the Roosters in Sydney for the past three seasons having won everything he could in Super League. He'd not done so badly in the NRL either, making it to the Grand Final twice and picking up quite a following for his no-nonsense straight-ahead style of play. He was a tackle machine.

Greg and Freddie had an immediate mutual respect.

They'd been on opposite sides in the earlier session that day, a 20-minute 7-a-side runout, and Greg had never been hit so hard in a clean tackle, but he wasn't going to show that to Freddie on his first day with the squad. Freddie had nodded briefly after it, lips pressed hard together but in full appreciation of Greg's response.

Greg called Col when he reached his room in the salubrious

Brisbane Riverside Emporium Hotel.

Dad was comfortable. He was fine or as fine as he could be. Mum was okay. Bearing up. Greg didn't feel as bad about having gone with Col around.

Greg flung off his clothing, checked the mini fridge for water, sure enough there was a bottle as well as a bar of chocolate. Downed half the bottle, opened the bar while turning on the shower. Took a bite and stepped in.

The power shower relaxed him. He'd had a shower at the ground but this was more relaxing. The warmth felt good on his body, his muscles. He'd not trained properly since the end of the season and now he had two days to get match fit.

He knew the timescale was ridiculous, but he felt good about the day, being back out on the park, and he'd been surprised that he hadn't been totally out of condition. It had only been three weeks since the season had ended but he had maintained his fitness through running daily.

He felt that although he probably wasn't totally match fit that he should be okay for the Vanuatu game. He wasn't feeling glib about England's opponents, he just didn't have anything like the time to devote to getting himself back to 100 per cent.

He would run in the morning. Early rise, through the streets of Brisbane. Get back for breakfast having completed his first session for the day and still complete any other session Shane had planned for them. The flight out to Vanuatu was in the early afternoon.

Greg was determined to make the most of a chance he'd thought had come and then gone through injury earlier in the season.

Realistically at 30 years of age he was unlikely to play in another World Cup when it came around in five years' time. This was his time to perform on the biggest stage and maybe, just maybe reach the final and beat Australia, the odds-on favourites.

Shower time was when Greg often contemplated, when he considered everything calmly. Things came to him. It was stimulating.

Susie. Find out what was wrong with her, or what was wrong with them as a couple. There was definitely something she wasn't telling him. Was she ill? Was she seeing someone else?

He wouldn't like it if she said that she'd moved on, but he'd totally get it. He'd not been around much, but he would still find it hard to take.

Greg knew deep down that he loved her, always had right from the first time their eyes had danced at each other. He had wanted her ever since, and still now. Christ, if she'd said she could come out he'd gladly pay the flight then and there.

Kyle popped into his head.

'Kinell!!'

He said it aloud, but to himself.

Greg couldn't believe it. He gave himself a hard time.

'For God's sake!'

He said it to no-one in his room. He hadn't rung his son since getting off the plane, even though he had sent a text. What the hell time was it now in the UK? Was he nine hours ahead or ten hours behind? Would Kyle be at school?

Two calls had to be made. Kyle and Susie. He'd get on with both of them when he'd finished. Now enjoy. Stop thinking. Let the water beat against his body. Breathe.

His phone sprang to life as he stepped out of the bathroom.

By the time he reached it the caller had gone. He took a quick look at his 'recents' in his call list. Fate could do amazing things and his first thought or hope was that maybe it was Diane with Kyle, or maybe it was Susie.

It was nobody he knew, or at least it didn't come up with any name he had stored, probably just some sales call. He flung it back on the bed. A minute later it pinged with a message that was to change everything.

'Get out of your room NOW! Just go. NOW!'

If this had hit Greg four years ago when he had been working full-time as a garage mechanic and part-time as a rugby league player for perennial strugglers Hopton Town he'd have thought twice about this kind of message.

He'd have immediately questioned it, dismissed it, thought it ridiculous, but after what he'd been through in recent times, and the positions he'd been put into, his brain switched to overdrive.

Someone here was desperately serious. He had to move fast.

Greg made for the door of the room he'd inhabited for less than half an hour, his hand reaching out before thinking that caution may be better.

He computed what had been said once again. The messenger had tried to ring him. Greg hadn't got to it in time. A message had come, which also required greater time, which probably meant there was either little or no time.

He didn't try the door to the corridor.

CHAPTER 9

Disappearing was all very well, but when you've been an icon, shown on 30-foot-high posters and on television, it's not so easy.

Zoe Miller had been the All-Australian equivalent of the illustrious All-American grid iron, basketball and athletics stars.

Her face had appeared on billboards throughout Australia in the buildup to the Sydney Olympics where she had won her gold medal two decades ago. She'd become the sport's pin-up girl.

After her athletics career she had launched her gym business and then taken high-profile managerial roles. She was widely held in high esteem for being able to get the job done whatever it took – and her usual starting point had been to trust nobody and then work out who earned it. She was very much in that mode right now. One of her colleagues on the Rugby League World Cup Organising Committee had gone missing. Now she needed to do the same. Run.

She needed her wits about her. She needed to know who she could trust, and fast.

The voice at the end of the line, as she had made her way to Manly Beach, was not one of those she could trust any longer, of that she was certain. As certain as she could be. She had trusted the voice before. Her instinct had now told her different.

Zoe Miller would find the answers. She would not give in.

The management of rugby league's greatest ever showpiece occasion had taken up nearly every waking hour of her existence in the past six months, but all of that was in the past right now, even though the opening ceremony was less than 48 hours away.

'You ready?'

Zoe had been looking out across Sydney harbour, the other

side of the spit of land that sees Manly bordered by water on both east and west sides. She'd alerted her brother Jordan, when the original meeting that she'd now swerved had been arranged. She'd said that she might need his boat, and fast. Escape strategy. Always have two or three alternatives.

It was Jordan asking the question. She nodded. It was time to go. She didn't yet know what she was running from, but she was most certainly getting away.

Greg was on his way too. All he knew about his room so far, having only stepped in a short while ago, was that other than the door on to the hotel corridor, there were also doors out to what he now hoped would prove to be a balcony. That was exactly what he found, but not exactly as he might have hoped.

Greg had no idea whose voice it had been on his phone, but for the moment that didn't matter. Just get out. Just do as the caller had said.

Greg's room was on the 5th floor. He looked down on a bustling Brisbane below and the river traffic on the Brisbane River. He didn't have time. Decide and go. His and the other rooms right along the side of the hotel all had balconies. The balconies to each room were all of the similar style, size and opulence. Quality but small spaces.

Each balcony had a gap of what seemed four to five feet between each and the only means of getting across was to stand on the three-foot-high wall to jump across to the other. Whoever had been the designer had clearly not taken in the need for escape routes for people fleeing their rooms.

Greg had little chance of a run-up to land safely on the next balcony. His mind flittered briefly. Stay and tackle whoever was due at his door head on? But if they were armed, what then? Knives, guns? Why was he in danger, for God's sake? What had he done?

All thoughts were quickly rendered useless a split second later when there was a knock at his door and a voice calling his name. Without another thought he was standing on the wall, flinging his arms in order to gain the momentum and flight needed. He jumped.

'Boss?'

Alex Lui was at the commissioner's door. It wasn't so much a question as gaining his attention.

'Looks like we may have something … on the body on Erakor … oh, and … Sablan is on his way … just seen him making his way across …'

'Sablan?'

Commissioner Danford Napakauranga and Winston Sablan, Prime Minister of Vanuatu, had been at South Pacific University together. He knew Winston would not venture over to the police department without good reason, even though their respective offices were no more than a few hundred yards apart.

Danford was immediately on high alert. But first he wanted to know what Alex had found out and whether that was the reason for Winston's interest.

'What do we know?'

Greg landed firmly on the neighbouring hotel room balcony wall, hopped on to the floor, tried the doors. Locked! Fuck!

He made an instant decision to move on. He hopped onto the wall again giving himself a run-up to leap for the next balcony along.

Greg's legs were now pumping in the air like a long jumper aiming for a new personal best. He landed well once again with the sole of one foot on the wall and combining a quick next move with a two-footed jump down into the balcony area.

Again, it looked locked. The sound of any breakage might increase the chance of his being found. He didn't bother to check, thinking more about creating any distance he could between himself and any would-be pursuers. Another run-up, another balcony, again clearing it with ease.

This time the balcony doors were open. He felt he could hear voices coming from where he'd started his leaps, but this was no time for looking back and, just as he'd watched Daniel Craig playing Bond on the plane for his last time, he mused, this was no time to die. Idiot. Think of how to get out of this, not films.

He went through the open balcony doors, finding it marginally odd that the curtains were shielding the sunlight. It was still a bright sun-kissed early evening.

Greg began pulling the black cloth aside with just one thing on his mind, to get back out onto the hotel corridor and get to a teammate, someone from the England party or a hotel official. At least that would give himself time to try and work out what was going on. His entry was not exactly the easiest, despite the doors not being closed.

As he shifted the curtain he heard the sound of crashing at the other side. It sounded like metal. Several people were swiftly cursing but this was no time for considering anything further other than his own plans. Greg pulled back the curtain further and made his way into the room.

Suddenly he couldn't see a thing.

There was brightness thrown into his face and now those voices he'd just heard were louder. These weren't voices of those who might be pursuing him, but voices that seemed to be cursing each other as well as him.

The light was too strong. Blinding. Greg put his right hand over his eyes to shield them and attempt to refocus. Within seconds everything was all too clear. What was before him was a picture that set him back apace. What the holy fuck was this?

There must have been at least a dozen people in the room. They were filming, or at least they had been until Greg's untimely arrival.

The contraption he'd heard falling must have been a mic boom that one member of the room's populous had been holding so that it was out of the camera's view.

There were bright white lights to the other side of the room. It had been those that had temporarily blinded him. There were screens and three people holding different size video cameras capturing the action from every conceivable angle.

Two of the cameras were being held by women, one by a

man. There was a warmth in the room, not of conviviality but more an animal warmth, perhaps unsurprising given the number of people, and no doubt the reason for the balcony doors being open.

On the bed was a woman.

No, strike that, Greg quickly established, not a woman, but it appeared a man dressed as one.

He/she was wearing black stockings with a black satin basque and suspenders, plus bright red stiletto shoes and was tied by the wrists to the headboard and by the ankles to God knows where! For fuck's sake, what had he stumbled into now?

He/she was wearing a long blonde-haired wig and far from being annoyed by Greg's presence had clearly been taken with him. He/she turned his head by way of affection and with a huge smile.

'Now this is more like it boys and girls ...'

Others in the room may have been angry with Greg over his entrance, causing havoc with the camera and lighting crew, but the blonde-haired masculine voice that came from the bed-bound body was clearly excited by Greg. It certainly seemed that way, so far as gravity was concerned, not that Greg had been about to leer.

'I certainly didn't see you coming darling. I don't know who ordered you, but thank God they did ...'

Having fled his room so abruptly Greg hadn't had time for clothing, apart from his boxers and it appeared he had arrived on the set of some weird porn movie dressed like Brad out of *The Rocky Horror Picture Show*. He kind of fitted in with the scene, which was worrying.

Greg was soon put into little doubt that his presence was not required, by a woman who was similarly attired to the bed-bound guy/girl but holding a hand-held digicam.

'Piss off, you fucking interloping weirdo!'

Him, the weirdo? Dear God! Get out of there!

Greg took in another male, somewhat similarly attired to the one with the currently 12 o'clock appendage.

Greg had no words! He didn't have many in his locker at the best of times, but this was a real head-shaker. What the hell really goes on in hotel rooms?

He needed to keep moving and made for the door that he'd calculated should bring him back into the corridor to make his escape from whoever was chasing him.

He turned the handle.

He opened the door gingerly. He wanted to hear, or rather he did not want to hear, sounds coming from the corridor, so that he could get to where he could be safe.

Greg now thought again about the voice. Was that because he'd heard it before? No real time just yet to consider properly. Think. Get to safety.

He opened the door enough to take a look – to the right, the direction in which he had come from; and left, checking all activity.

There were people in the corridor. He could see what appeared to be two men at the door of the first room he'd reached on his initial leap but hadn't entered.

The men looked as though they were on a mission, and it didn't look like they were on a charitable one at that. This wasn't a social call, he could tell that much. He couldn't see them clearly, but for a second thought he'd seen one of them before. He had no idea where.

Greg could perhaps make his move from this room if these two went into the other room where they were currently at the door. He chose that he'd be better going left down the corridor.

He was about to commit himself when he heard activity coming from the other end of the corridor. Couldn't see anyone. He shut the door.

'*What the hell …!!!*'

It was the voice of the woman who'd just given him an earful.

The bedroom had exploded with action once again. Equipment that the sound and light crew had just put back into place after Greg's entrance was crashing down once again.

This time it was accompanied by the bustling in of a man who it seemed hadn't been as adept at leaping across balconies as Greg, judging by the way he was holding his ankle.

The star of the movie wasn't nearly as inviting as he/she had been over Greg's arrival on the set. Expletives were firing off in all directions, but the much-tethered cross-dresser managed as good-natured a response to the latest intrusion as was possible given the circumstances.

'My dear man. Can you not see I am working ...'

The 'dear man' referred to was currently as blinded by the remaining lighting that had stayed upright as Greg had been.

Quickly realising the man who'd made his entry probably couldn't make out immediately where he was, or who was who, and that his eyes would take valuable seconds to become accustomed, Greg slipped around the other end of the curtains shielding the balcony doors as the sound and lighting crew scrabbled around getting their equipment back together.

He was back outside on the balcony in seconds.

Where to go now? What had happened here in the past few minutes?

He'd only been in Australia less than 24 hours, but after travelling 11,000 miles the previous day, having received a call-up for England, having seen his dad, having comforted his mum and having taken part in two training sessions having not played at all for weeks, it looked like he had now appeared on the set of a weird porno while fleeing someone or some people who were after him for God knows what. Jeez!

Forget that. One thing at a time. Get to safety. Get away. He heard a sound. The doors on to the balcony of the first room he'd tried were opening. He crouched low and moved back closer to the doors where he was now, two balconies on from them.

He could hear shouting inside the room he'd just left. He raised up, only slightly, to see whether the balcony two rooms away was now occupied. It wasn't. Greg made his move.

Greg was determined to put as much space between him and

those who were on his tail. Forget why they were on it, just go.

Three more balconies had now been added to his run, his adrenaline now flowing. Stupid thoughts came in to his mind. Balcony running? New sport? Like free running?

More like an easy way to provide himself with a permanent long-term injury if he got it wrong.

It was as he took in the latest balcony he'd landed on and was catching his breath from a third consecutive leap that he took a glance back for the first time since leaving his porn movie session.

Encouragingly he hadn't heard anyone behind him. He'd also been pleasantly surprised that his bare feet hadn't taken a battering at every landing and that he'd not landed awkwardly. Every cloud, he thought briefly.

He was starting to think more clearly now. Had he put enough distance, room-wise between himself and anyone following him? There was only one way to find out.

He decided to try the doors leading to the balcony of the third room he'd reached, the sixth in total. Struck lucky. Slightly open.

'Greg?'

Greg was dumbfounded.

'Greg, *what are you doing here? And why are you in my bedroom? ... with just your boxers on?*'

Speechless didn't even begin to describe it. This was a larger suite than his, in fact a very large suite looking at it now. Greg had noticed the balconies had become longer on the last two he'd arrived at, but he hadn't twigged that meant the rooms or suites were similarly larger.

The questions were being asked by someone he knew. It was a kind of surreal feeling, but a positive vibe at last nonetheless.

She didn't need any sixth sense to work out something was very wrong.

CHAPTER 10

'Just what is going on?'

Zoe had made it to Newcastle Harbour, New South Wales. Jordan had pushed his new Eastport 32 cruiser all the way. It was designed more for bay and coastal cruises than an ocean-going dash, but he had responded to his sister's need for speed.

He had set off again immediately Zoe had disembarked, heading straight back for Sydney Harbour.

Zoe had purchased three new burner phones at the first Coles store she had laid eyes on and had immediately opened one while checking out the number she had needed on one of her two regular mobile phones.

This had all been about safety first, giving herself space, time to think. Forget the World Cup. But that was what this was all about, wasn't it?

Her first call on the burner had been to a number that she had stored on her regular World Cup phone simply as 'Him'.

The recipient of her question was frustrated.

'You tell me ... where the hell did you get to? ... and where are you?'

That was all Zoe needed. She hung up.

There, in the third line was the real question that was on the lips of her colleague. That was all they, whoever they were, wanted to know.

She flung the first new burner phone straight into the Hunter River. One phone down, two to go. Don't trust anybody. Don't stay anywhere too long. Don't keep hold of suspect phones that could be triangulated to find out where a call had been made.

This was a time to make sure she had a future.

It was already a testing day for Danford Napakauranga and his force. The impending arrival of Prime Minister Winston Sablan, as Alex Lui had mentioned was another cause for concern for Danford.

Efate was now less than 48 hours from hosting its biggest ever sporting event. Vanuatu versus England in the World Cup.

Camera crews and tourists were everywhere, the Vanuatu national rugby league team were enjoying their training at the stadium that had increased its seating capacity due to temporary stands having been added on three sides of the ground.

On the face of it this should have been a cause for celebration. A huge payday for the island nation archipelago, which would go a long way towards improving facilities and infrastructure, particularly in Port Vila.

Efate was to play host to three games in all. It was to be a massive shot in the arm for Vanuatu. First up was their own massive fixture against England.

The locals who knew their sport were excited because they had heard that Nieu had beaten England and they, Vanuatu had beaten Nieu twice. Maybe, just maybe, this island nation that had only won a handful of games against other emerging nations might find England on a wobble.

The island press, the *Vanuatu Daily Post*, which had gone more online than print in the recent past, had printed thousands of additional copies each day in the week leading up to the game, buoyed by greater advertising spends including a huge daily property section as the locals realised this was their opportunity to attract foreign investment. The same was true for Radio V, the radio station that broadcast throughout the islands.

Typically, the business and financial end of the spectrum weren't so much concerned about the sport itself, more what it would do for the island's tourism – and more adroitly what it could do for them.

There had been a report of a body found on Erakor Island, which had headlined in the early part of the week, but largely the *Post* and Radio V were concentrated on the game.

Prime Minister Winston Sablan dressed smart but casual, and looking good for his early-60s was determined that the island nation was not going to waste this opportunity to be portrayed as sunny, friendly and smiling – and for that reason he wanted Erakor Island, one of Efate's prime destinations, unfettered by police tape and back open once again, as though nothing had happened.

'Just two days is all I'm asking, Danford. Tomorrow and the day of the game. Then you can go back to your duties.'

Danford was acutely aware that this was not so much a request as an edict. Back to his duties? Winston had been a long-time acquaintance but Danford found him very flaky and even more so since he had become prime minister.

Despite being close the two had fallen out many times and ever since Winston had made his way into politics Danford had seen him become what he saw as a political stereotype, more interested in his own well-being than that of the people he was serving.

Winston had made the finding of a dead body sound like it was a petty crime that could be held over.

Danford was also aware that Winston had a personal interest in Erakor Island – he owned it!

'There has been a development …'

Danford wanted Winston to know that delaying an investigation was not an option. He looked daggers at Winston, who had felt he had made his point already and was preparing to leave. Winston wasn't for turning.

Winston looked Danford straight in the eye, leaning in towards him from where he was satnding opposite Danford's desk. Danford remained seated, unintimidated.

'Danford. Two days … two days and you can do whatever you like … just get rid of anything that looks like a crime scene until then …'

Winston turned to leave. He was frustrated and concerned that his friend might not be agreeing to play ball. Danford wasn't happy.

'Tell me again, Winston. Where did you have your operation?'

Winston turned back towards Danford. Curious, but already anticipating the kind of reply he was used to in their disagreements from the past.

'*The one where you lost your fucking balls!*'

Danford had lost any patience he had with Winston and clearly the feeling was mutual. Friendship could only stretch so far.

Winston smiled back at Danford, but it was a hollow smile, one full of anger. Danford knew this wasn't playing well and he hadn't intended it to. He also knew Elenola Taneo, his deputy commissioner, stood to gain from any fallout, but he was damned if he was going to let Winston run roughshod over any inquiry he was undertaking.

Winston wasn't for rising any more to Danford's baiting.

'*Two days. That's all Danford. Two days ...*'

He turned, again. He made to leave. On reaching Danford's office door he turned once more.

'*Just do it, Danford ... you cannot afford the consequences ...*'

Danford had hardly ever been taken aback by anything Winston had said, but Winston's last retort prompted his near-jerk reaction. He didn't slam a fist against his desk or hurl anything at a wall, he just stated where the case had reached.

'*Winston ... we are waiting for SOCO ...*'

Danford paused.

Winston was waiting now. He wanted more. He motioned for Danford to carry on, but Danford had his own reasons why he only wanted to give so much.

'*Winston, you know I cannot disclose anything to you. It is an on-going investigation, and one that we need to keep on-going.*'

Petulance was all Danford could discern instantly from Winston's reaction. He'd been hoping for more, something that would tell him his instinct was right and that his call to the station had been instigated by some higher authority.

Danford knew only too well that Winston had a lot of baggage. Any number of Achilles heels. He'd keep him in check. He felt a manipulation going on.

What concerned him was why.

In some ways Winston's role as Prime Minister sounded very

grand, and it kind of was, but with an overall population across over 65 inhabited islands of less than 300,000 there were limits to power. It might be a grand title if you were in Australia or the UK, but here? It didn't exactly bring you huge advantages. Or did it?

That's what Danford was beginning to wonder. Maybe, just maybe, it was time to look a little further into Winston's world? Why would Winston be threatening him now?

Winston Sablan had left about an hour ago. Danford had made calls, sent emails. He had then taken a walk over to Port Vila Municipal Stadium to check on the progress of security for the game.

Ringing out into the night air was the sound of Vanuatu's favourite songstress Vanessa Quai rehearsing her set for half-time in the game versus England. Vanessa's 'Life Is Good' made him feel good.

It was Alex Lui who broke his boss's feel-good mood. Developments had just taken another massive turn.

CHAPTER 11

'Boss, you need to look at something ...'

Alex Lui was a well-mannered young man who was ambitious to go far in either the police force on Vanuatu or in Australia.

'... according to this report from SOCO it looks likely our body is a man called Bob Rudd ... we're just waiting on forensics, but we know he arrived on the island five days ago and that he hasn't been seen for the past three days ... the last confirmed sighting we have of him was making his way east of Port Vila towards Erakor village. Bob Rudd is ... was ... the finance director for the Rugby League World Cup ...'

Danford closed his eyes, put his right palm to his face and massaged his temple as he thought. He'd been considering whether he should accede to Winston's demands and lay-off the crime scene at Erakor Island.

This news told him there was no way he could do that. The Australian police would now be involved, and would no doubt be arriving once this information reached them.

An island nation of sunshine and smiles was what the tourists and rugby league followers would see across most of Efate, but those visiting Erakor Island would see police tape and sealed-off areas near to the hotel, restaurant and where scuba diving took place.

Alex hadn't finished though.

'And that's not all ... take a look at this ...'

Alex moved from his chair so that Danford could sit down and take a close look at the video that had already made it to YouTube and was now going viral on social media.

Danford closed his eyes once again having watched it. Inhaled deeply, then exhaled just as much while pinching the bridge of his nose with the thumb and forefinger of his left hand.

What he had just seen was a new nightmare – and even closer to home.

CHAPTER 12

The surprises just kept on coming in Greg's most recent room arrival. No sooner had he been amazed to see the naked woman, who he hadn't seen for over a year, than within seconds he was also in the company of a similarly naked six-foot-six young man he knew only too well.

Suddenly, Greg's boxers leant him an overdressed feeling.

'Greg, dude, what are you doin' in here man? ... and like that? ...'

Vinny Venus spread his palms in front of him, his words at first purely asking a question and then slightly raising his voice in incredulity.

Greg offered up the words that many have uttered since time immemorial in such circumstances.

'It's not what it looks like.'

CHAPTER 13

She heard the knock on the door. She had opened her eyes, closed them again. The sun streamed in and she recalled that fabulous warm feeling of her eyelids not being enough to keep out the sunlight, as though they were translucent. It was a beautiful moment sending her back to her teenage years.

Broke.

She wasn't anywhere near that position financially, but it's exactly where she had come to now. The village of Broke was home to no more than 300. Home. This is where she'd grown up. The Hunter Region in Singleton Shire, part of the Broke-Fordwich wine region of the Hunter Valley. A land of trees, countryside and where she had run and run and run to become one of the fittest women on Earth.

Rock shelters close by had once been a favourite haunt of her growing up, exploring where her indigenous ancestors' paintings were now a significant draw, some depicting Baiame, the Sky Father, who had created the world through dreaming.

This area where she had spent so much time was now a tourism honey pot for those exploring their heritage and for the wine tasting.

Zoe had used her second burner phone to contact her dad, Coen who had driven out to the outskirts of Newcastle to collect her, no questions asked. Her mum Marli had been overjoyed to see her, but had immediately recognised her daughter was troubled. All Zoe had wanted right then had been somewhere to hide away, take her time, somewhere she could think and plan. No better place than home.

It was only now that she was here and had enjoyed resting up overnight that it dawned on Zoe how she could have, in doing so, unwittingly put her parents in danger.

What if she had been followed? But then why would she have been followed? The meeting in Manly? What had that all been intended to be about?

Zoe began to relax. She'd not had anybody on her tail since abandoning her headphone and mic wires and fleeing from the back of the coffee bar.

She couldn't be sure of that of course, but there had been no-one following her on the ocean between Sydney and Newcastle, nobody had been waiting at Newcastle Harbour. And there had been nothing she'd noticed following her and her dad back home.

She thought now of what could have brought about the call she'd received and the meeting she had avoided. She knew there were those who held grudges against her leadership, her colour of skin, her sexual preference and just plainly and simply did not like her.

It had been Zoe who had pushed so hard for the now imminent Rugby League World Cup to be even more inclusive of all society.

She was overseeing the Women's World Cup running alongside the tournament. Nobody held a grudge that way. The Physical Disability RL World Cup, the Wheelchair Rugby League World Cup, but the inaugural LGBT World Cup demonstration game labelled 'The Pink' between teams representing the Southern and Northern Hemisphere had been a different matter.

There were those who had vehemently disagreed with the inclusion of 'The Pink' and Zoe had been accused, in some quarters, of pandering to her own whims, her own kind. Those who disagreed said they were not homophobic, but at a time when politicians were being extra careful, especially with a federal election imminent in Australia, the words politically correct kept coming forward and Zoe's best laid plans had been kept in order.

Talk was, amongst those who did not share her volition, that the brash, attractive former Olympic pin-up had abused her privileged position.

Zoe couldn't see how the LGBT Pink could have caused the

call she had received.

She'd had flak for it, but it had passed. It had now become an accepted part of the whole Rugby League World Cup extravaganza – and for her part, yes, Zoe felt good about having inspired it. She had felt it would help put the sport ahead of the rest. Her own legacy to the game that her father had once played.

Now at her window looking out on the gorgeous Hunter Valley there was a part of her that had wished she'd gone along to the meeting. At least she'd not be going through this right now, turning things over and over in her head.

But she had felt that she may have been walking into a trap, and she hadn't trusted the voice of the person on her wire. Someone whom she had thought she could trust implicitly.

She had stepped away, out of it all. She was still close enough to reappear in time for the opening ceremony and the opening game that was to follow between Australia and Wales in Stadium Australia.

Everything was in place, the work had all been done. She'd be better off here for now, at home, out of the way – or then again, maybe not, if it brought unwanted attention.

She wanted to go back. For goodness' sake, she had been living and breathing this whole extravaganza for long enough. She deserved to be there.

What to do? The knock came on her door once again. For a second Zoe panicked. Letting her vivid imagination run wild. She thought about who may be knocking without saying anything and why she hadn't heard either of her parents moving around this morning. And then.

'*Honey, are you okay?*'

The world hadn't completely changed. It was her mum's voice. She beckoned Zoe to the kitchen where she was as bright and busy as ever making breakfast when Zoe put in her appearance.

It was as Zoe sat at the kitchen table that her worst fears were to resurface. It was her mum who delivered the innocuous line that exploded in Zoe's brain like the salvo of a cannon.

'*Your dad's gone to collect your friend …*'

Marli's words had spilled out so easily, no trace of concern, so innocent. Zoe was facing away from her mother at the time. She was grateful for it being that way as her mum couldn't see her initial reaction. Friend? What the hell? Zoe braced herself and answered her mother hopefully just as innocently.

'*Oh great … I wasn't expecting anyone …*'

Why was dad picking up whoever it was? That didn't make any sense. If someone was trailing her, surely they'd have their own transport? Zoe felt an impending doom. What might have already happened to her father? What had she done by coming back home?

CHAPTER 14

Greg was taking in breakfast with the rest of the England team in the hotel. Spirits were running high. They were heading out to Vanuatu for their first game in the tournament in three hours and everyone was up for getting under way.

The first two friendly games had been just that so far as the team was concerned, even though nobody had enjoyed losing in Nieu or Alice Springs.

Now was when the real deal started.

Another two players drafted into the squad had touched down at Brisbane airport overnight – Troy Whittingham and Mason Bell, centre and second row respectively.

The new recruits would be back on a plane out of the same airport heading for Efate.

Greg was sitting with Vinny, Stu, John Cloudsdale and Freddie South.

Vinny had been holding court around the table telling of the previous evening's odd visitation to his suite, by a boxers-only-clad Greg.

'I just came out of the bathroom and there he was, with my girl!'

Vinny's voice and manner were incredulous, yet jovial. He was keeping it cool as Greg had asked. Whatever had gone on last night Greg would find out his own way and in his own time. He'd informed the hotel management about someone having been in his room and had asked to be moved immediately to a suite next to Vinny and Gina.

It was Gina Irvine he had seen naked after his balcony running exercise.

Gina Irvine, the late Bob Irvine's daughter who had gifted his daughter ownership of Lanzarote Eruption. Gina Irvine aka Jenny Juniper, recording artist and singer-songwriter performer who had met and fallen in love with Vinny two years ago and they had managed to remain as a couple in all that time.

The suite had been hers, not Vinny's. She'd surprised him, dropping by as she was due to appear in a headline slot at the world-famous Byron Bay BluesFest in a couple of weeks' time. Her career having taken a massive upsurge in the past year with an award-winning album. Vinny's suite had been next door, the one Greg had ended up occupying.

They'd been enjoying a last night before the England team headed out for Vanuatu.

'*Greg. You okay? Just heard about last night.*'

Shane Chislett was similar to Greg in respect of few words. Greg's nod was enough for him. No fuss.

Freddie South had played under Chislett in England and Australia. He made a nod to his former club and now international boss, then turned to Greg as Chislett had moved on.

'*Christ mate, what have you done?*'

Greg looked at his new teammate quizzically.

'*I have never, and I mean never, known him to talk with players about anything other than the game. He just doesn't. It's not his style.*'

Greg, Vinny and Stu looked at each other not knowing what to make of Freddie's comment. It was left to Vinny to bring it all back to something humorous.

'*Maybe he just fancies you, boss!*'

He and Stu had always carried on calling Greg boss, as he had been their player-coach at Hopton. The three had come through a lot together and both Vinny and Stu held their 'boss' in high esteem, aside from when he turned up in their bedroom in his boxers!

'*Surprise!*'

Zoe hadn't needed to worry. Her worst fears had soon been allayed on his return.

Marli had simply smiled when Jess had come in. Jessica was Zoe's closest friend when she had been growing up in Broke. They had laughed, cried and played together. Jess had also been an accomplished athlete and they had trained alongside each other for many years, running for New South Wales.

They'd not seen each other for years but uncannily Marli had been talking with Jess's mum around the time Zoe had rung to ask her dad for a ride back home. It turned out Jess was going to be coming home to visit at the same time and the mums had cooked up the idea of a reunion.

'Mum! How did you manage to keep a straight face? I'd wondered who it could be ...'

Zoe was so relieved and ran down to Jess who she had seen emerging from her dad's car. This was a good thing. Zoe had waved her finger naughtily at her mum as she had spoken to her, but with the biggest smile she had managed for days.

Jess was all smiles too. While Zoe had a lot to think about, this was a welcome diversion. What would an hour or two matter?

'It's great to see you, Zoe. It's been too long ... now, where's that wine?'

The old friends hugged each other close, walked back to the Miller's house arm-in-arm and began catching up, while way off in the distance, avoiding being noticed, which was difficult in Broke, a pickup parked up and its driver watched.

CHAPTER 15

'It's as bad as it gets ...'

Alex Lui was summing up what he had just shown Danford.

Danford Napakauranga had thought he'd seen it all on Efate and the other islands that made up the Republic of Vanuatu. He'd been commissioner for the past twenty years but had served in the Vanuatu Police Force (VPF) and the paramilitary Vanuatu Mobile Force (VMF) for over forty years.

He'd seen the island's development in the past decade and how agriculture and fishing, for so long the island's major industries, were fast becoming overtaken by tourism.

Vanuatu's tax haven status had also attracted big names in industry from around the world and a smattering of film idols, performers and sports moguls.

Offshore banking now held an important position in the economy and the growth was increasing. He'd seen how greed made people. Winston Sablan now fitted that category.

Danford knew just how important many on the island felt the next two days were to Efate's and Vanuatu's future.

Despite the unwanted title of Most Disaster Prone Country in the World through earthquakes, cyclones, volcanoes, hurricanes and tsunamis, tourists had found Efate and were arriving in increasing numbers every year.

He also knew that what he had seen on screen hours ago was not what Winston Sablan would have wanted to become public.

'Boss, it just got worse ...'

Alex Lui was watching as Winston marched across to the police headquarters.

Winston was not a happy man. If he'd been frustrated the day previously, he was verging an apoplectic now, almost purple with rage.

He wasted no time on entering Danford's office, but whatever Winston was planning on saying was fast obliterated by the commissioner.

'*Don't even think about it, Winston. Before you say a word let me tell you one thing. This ...*'

He pointed to the hard copy of an image that had appeared on screen

'*... this is an absolute disgrace. It disgusts me. I uphold law and order here. And I know that you know what is going on and that you have not done a damned thing about it. If you have come over here in your high and mighty manner once again, ready to stop my work, think again. I will not let you dictate to me how this police force goes about its business. The tape stays up on Erakor, the police presence will be strengthened there and everywhere we can, and you will not do a damned thing about it. Do I make myself clear?*'

Winston Sablan was even further enraged, but he also knew that what he had also seen on the video that was now trending on social media had handed Danford Napakauranga all of the cards. This was not a battle he could win right now, but he would win later and Danford wouldn't be able to do, as he put it himself, a damned thing about that either.

Alex Lui raised his eyebrows as he saw Sablan leave.

Danford held his face firm, as though chewing slightly on the inside of his mouth. He was ready now for what he knew would no longer just be about upholding law and order but his own personal war with officialdom.

Danford spoke calmly to Alex.

'*I want everyone here in an hour. Get me every officer on the island. We are going to ensure that this island is as safe as it can be – and we're going to find out just why we have the dead body of an international organisation here and who is promoting this filth and degradation.*'

It was as Danford was finishing his instructions to Alex Lui that rapid shotgun fire was heard, followed by shrieks and wailing as the drama unfolded just yards from the police headquarters.

CHAPTER 16

'We're here to win a game, nothing more ...'

Shane Chislett was being questioned by the world's press at the Port Vila Municipal Stadium. Asked what he'd been expecting on arriving at the stadium, no larger than a small rugby league club's facility back in England, he remained resolute.

'It really doesn't matter what venue we have to play at, we just need to win games. Sure, this might be a bit small but I'm absolutely certain there will be a fantastic atmosphere and we're taking nothing for granted ...'

Chislett nodded in the direction of the journalist who had asked the question.

He'd fielded everything professionally without giving away what he really felt, that the ground was a shit-hole, the surface was unplayable and his team had been brought here because of some kind of pandering to the Emerging Nations Rugby League Organisation that was apparently starting to carry some weight in the increase of the sport.

Chislett had got off lightly until an Aussie journalist intervened.

'Shane, Grace Elliott, Australia Today. How hurt are you by the accusation that has been made about you. Over personally managing your team to throw games?'

Chislett was knocked way off beam. He'd never been called a cheat in all his time as a player or coach – and he'd never thrown games. He'd never heard the accusation. Was she making this up? He would normally have answered on the spot to any question but he had been so taken aback.

Where the fuck had it come from?

Annie Laing was the England team's Media & Communications Manager and as such responsible for the smooth running of the press briefings.

She had been about to thank everyone when Grace Elliott had piped up. She was now, having seen Shane Chislett's reaction, swiftly on the case to wrap up the proceedings.

'Thank you everyone ... as I'm sure you know we've just arrived and Shane needs to ensure the team is properly prepared. The players will be available for a photocall in around half an hour. There will be another press briefing in the morning.'

Grace Elliott wasn't a woman to be ignored, nor was she about to step back from the damage she had just inflicted. Like a boxer seeing an open cut above the eye, she jabbed again.

'I'm sorry, but can we take it from Shane's non-comment that there is some truth in the allegation?'

There was a hush around the room as every reporter worth his or her salt gathered themselves for what heir new headline might be.

Shane Chislett, in his broad northern twang and bluff style, had rallied. He had put his hand up towards Annie Laing to let her know he had this. He would deal with it. He had prided himself, up until now, on his handling of the media ever since his playing days.

'I can tell you this. I have never thrown a game of anything in my life ...'

Chislett was keeping his blood from boiling at this point. Holding back the emotion as best he could. He continued.

'I always play to win. And you can tell your newspaper I will be suing for defamation of character for any broadcast or print of purely scurrilous rumour ...'

'... And one more thing ...'

Grace Elliott had held this next nugget back rather like a southpaw-style boxer jabbing away at first and then cutting loose.

Shane Chislett had been relatively proud of his rallying effort. The defamation of character line had come to him spontaneously.

Grace had measured him up for her next blast, which was to be wholly unexpected.

'The Pink? Are you in favour, or not?'

Shane wasn't, but not because of any homophobic tendency. He felt that, personally, the sport he loved and had played since he was a kid was being used here just to tick boxes, but as the England coach he could not afford to say any of it. This time he reacted quickly.

'I just want our great game to be played, watched and loved by as many people as possible all around the world, that's why we're here, to promote this fantastic sport. This has always been a sport that is more about family than race, creed, skin or gender.'

Grace wasn't about to give up her thread.

'I'm sorry Shane but did you not say in an interview that 'these people' should not be playing rugby league? How inclusive is that?'

Shane Chislett once again had the wind knocked temporarily out of his sails. When had he ever said that?

'I think that is quite enough for today Ms Elliott.'

Annie Laing now took over. This had gone far too far. Once again, she thanked everyone for attending and the two dozen or so journalists and photographers made their way out onto the park where Greg and his teammates were becoming accustomed to their new surroundings.

Greg and the rest of the squad were looking at the Port Vila ground shaking their heads in dismay. This was an accident waiting to happen. But there was no time to complain about it. The game was tomorrow.

That night they would watch the tournament opener on the television at the beautiful Breakas Beach Resort Hotel just 6 kilometres from Port Vila.

Grace Elliott watched on as the England team shook their heads – and smiled.

CHAPTER 17

'What is happening on this island?'

Danford looked up from where he had been cradling the man shot outside the police headquarters. He was looking up into Alex Lui's eyes.

Winston had been taken to Port Vila Central Hospital, hanging by a thread to his life, having been hit by at least two of the bullets everyone had heard being fired.

Danford had stayed where Winston had fallen.

His question had been part rhetorical and more of despair. Occasionally altercations in village communities had escalated beyond domestic feuds into murder, but this was something new. Assassination of the country's premier.

Social media and Radio V had leapt on the incident and the headline was already that Winston had died, before explaining later in the type that this was still speculation and the country's prime minister and surgeons were fighting for his life.

Annie Laing had picked up the news about the island's prime minister before the England party had been informed through the authorities. Annie had also come across the dead body story on Erakor Island, which hadn't as yet come out as public knowledge that it may involve some high-ranking person in the Rugby League World Cup management. She would ensure nothing was planned out that way for the England team.

'Who in their right minds mentioned a bloody … run …'

Freddie South was a prop who enjoyed the car crash of a tackle, the close combat and to offload a pass when he could. He was a modern-day prop forward, lean yet at the same time immensely strong, fit and powerful. He did not attribute any of this to running, even though he did his fair share and his stats confirmed it. But running? Running the streets? He didn't see the sense in it.

Greg, who was running alongside his new buddy, loved

running. He always had, but even he hadn't suggested that the whole squad should run back from Port Vila to the Breakas Beach Resort.

Vinny was totally enjoying it, not even breaking sweat. He went past them having sauntered for a while near the back. He'd heard Freddie's comment and ran backwards for a short while talking to Freddie and Greg.

'*It could have been me guys … all I said was it's about the length of a parkrun to get back to where we're staying … keep smiling boys!*'

With that, Vinny Venus had turned and was away. The squad and coaching staff, plus a few of the Team England officials who also ran, were strung out a good half a mile from front to back by the time the leaders of the pack Vinny, another winger Jericho Pallagi and one of the centres Sam Rivers were within half a mile of returning to Breakas.

It was a good-natured run, more to give some form of exercise after having been on the plane for three hours. There was no hollering at anyone to put a shift in. It would do for the late afternoon, with a training session in the morning to work on moves and plays particularly with those who had just joined the squad.

Greg and Freddie were in the middle of the pack, neither sauntering nor flat out, just doing enough to stretch and flex and keep everything ticking over in their respective engines.

There was someone else beyond the back markers, a mix of a couple of the bigger lads, some of the coaching staff and one of the more casual runners from the staff.

He wasn't running. He'd hired a car. He was gradually making his way past the runners, his eyes seeking out someone who had already caused him pain. Greg Duggan.

CHAPTER 18

'It's the 16th staging of the tournament that began in 1954 and has seen Australia win the title far more than any other nation. Only England and New Zealand have been the other winners and in truth it is hard to look beyond those three for this tournament's winners, but it's here and 16 nations will start their campaigns over the next few days seeking to become champions of the world! Welcome to the Rugby League World Cup Finals direct from Stadium Australia!'

It was the build-up Zoe had been hoping for including a magnificent spectacle of Australian culture with a cast of thousands on the pitch and the surrounding track producing an opening event that included rock perennials Midnight Oil with Jessica Mauboy and rapper Tasman Keith performing a powerful and emotional rendition of 'First Nation'. Midnight Oil would headline on the Legends stage at BluesFest in Byron Bay in a couple of weeks.

Zoe sat back, relaxed that it had all gone well, no hiccups. It had been fun watching it on the television. She hadn't felt any tension at all. It hadn't been important that she was missing. This was all about the competition from now on, in all of its separate spheres. Jess was stopping over. It had been like old times. They'd swapped stories over their respective careers.

'Do you think you'll go back?'

Zoe hadn't confided the real reason she had found herself back home, it was too soon to give that kind of detail. She smiled a thoughtful smile at her friend.

'If you'd asked me that before I landed here yesterday, I'd probably have answered it unequivocally yes, but you know ...'

Zoe looked around her and out into the darkness that was now drawing in and shrugged her shoulders. She gave more of a sigh to go with it all than she had anticipated.

'Maybe I'm done with the city life, Sydney, Melbourne ... maybe it's time to come home ...'

She smiled again at Jess. They let a moment linger. It was Zoe who broke it.

'*More wine, I believe your glass is somewhat empty once again young lady!*'

All the pomp and ceremony was over. The England team was gathered at Breakas where a cinema size screen had been brought in under the canopy at the bar to show the first game – Australia vs Wales.

TV show host Bethany Best had hyped the game as much as she could, but the celebrity guests – film hero Russell Crowe and TV presenter Adam Hills, who was due to play in the Physically Disabled Rugby League World Cup team for England despite being an All-Australian boy – held out little hope for the Wales team.

It was the same story in the commentary area with commentator Bruce Anderson and summariser Aussie legend Wayne Ferryman offering only pleasantries towards the boys from the valleys while concentrating on their green and gold superstars of the sport.

At half-time they were eating their words.

Wales had come out passing the ball around the park and fleet of foot – and when they didn't have possession they were working hard in defence. The underdogs went in leading at the break by 6 points to nil. They had shut out the World Cup holders who looked shell-shocked as they left the paddock.

'*Over-confidence from the Roos, play after play out of their skin from the Welsh Dragons who are breathing fire here at Stadium Australia ...*'

Bruce Anderson's final comments before the ad break were what every Aussie fan had on their mind.

'*What has happened to our boys? Come back and join us after these words from our sponsors.*'

'*Yes, still here ... she is and so am I ... she's not going anywhere ...*'

The pickup driver had been around all day. He'd managed a bit of kip, he'd acted as though he were a tourist and had taken himself off out of the way as best he could but he was still conspicuous in a town of no more than 250 people. He'd been in Broke since the morning, had seen Jess come and not go. He was settling in for the night in the cab listening to the footy.

'Yeah, I know mate, not a great start …'

It had been his only conversation of the day, apart from when he'd gone for supplies earlier. Every other message had been a text. He was talking about the game.

'Get Out Of The Vehicle!'

The firmness of the knock on his pickup window had made him jump almost out of his skin. The figure he saw was clad in a black mask with black balaclava and pretty much head to toe in black. It could only mean one thing. He was in big trouble.

'Get Out! Now!'

He now saw the gun, with a silencer, which meant to him it was intended to be used.

'Get out or I shoot!'

Now he was even more alarmed. This wasn't meant to be a dangerous op. He'd taken it because he needed the money.

He thought about starting the engine and getting the hell out of this little town, already fearing the consequences if he were to do exactly as the figure in black had said or if he didn't. This hadn't been in his script.

He opened the door to the pickup.

CHAPTER 19

Every bar or restaurant on Efate was now full to the rafters with supporters of either England or Vanuatu. Huge numbers of islanders having come over by boat. In every bar or restaurant there was a screen showing the tournament opener.

The England fans were in full voice singing their hearts out, and they had been enjoying Australia's embarrassing first half. The Wales team included players of Super League and NRL experience, but no way were they in the same league as the Roos.

Greg felt the same as many, as he watched the game at Breakas. This had to be a temporary blip. Their coach would have them in the hutch at half-time, settle their nerves and they would come out what they were – world-beaters – he was sure of it.

Danford had been staring at his glass for some time. He and Alex Lui were back at the police headquarters. Earlier, in the late afternoon, they had received the news that Danford had been anticipating.

Winston had been pronounced dead, never having regained consciousness, at around 5pm. Vanuatu's prime minister had been assassinated.

Danford now cradled his glass of kava, Vanuatu's most popular and celebrated brew. Alex listened to his boss. He had learned a great deal about upholding standards and unwavering spirit and determination from him. Danford's voice crackled with emotion now.

'... *he was a good man* ...'

He nodded as if to affirm the fact. Inhaled deeply, exhaled just as deeply.

'... *I love this island. It is my soul. My heart beats for it. Everything I do, everything I am is right here ... but right at this very moment* ...'

He gave a casual cocking of his head, lips tightly pursed.

'Right at this very moment I hate what this island is becoming … for the whole of my life this has been a safe place … largely safe from what is happening now … but it is changing … and these deaths, these murders …'

Danford let the sentence go. It was what he was leading to next that would reinvigorate his protégé Alex Lui.

'But I'll tell you this …'

Danford had taken a slug of the kava and now placed his glass firmly back on his desk.

'I will do everything in my power to bring about justice for these crimes, these murders. We will find the perpetrator or perpetrators and we will do our damnedest to make this island safe once more.'

He picked up his glass again, Alex did the same, they clinked glasses and Danford ended his police sermon with a toast.

'To Winston …'

As they finished up and headed out of the headquarters Danford put his arm on Alex's shoulder. He had a big beaming smile on his face now.

'Tomorrow is not just another day, it is a day when we show the world what Vanuatu is really like …'

Alex smiled a firm-lipped smile at his boss, looking him in the eyes, nodded and went on his way.

Radio V, the *Vanuatu Daily Post* and every media outlet was all over the assassination, as was social media on the internet.

The murder of the prime minister had eclipsed the viral video that had been the talk earlier and Vanuatu vs England, headline news for the previous few days had been demoted in the running order.

There was speculation that the game might not go ahead, but this was quickly rebuffed by the island's deputy prime minister Ben Santo.

The second-half of Australia versus Wales had started the same way as the first-half had ended, with a second try out wide to Wales to flying winger Ewan Jones, who had been scoring for fun in Super League all season. The conversion had been missed, but the Welsh were 10-0 up and daring to dream, while the Roos looked totally out of sorts.

'Well, mate, I've never seen an Aussie footy side play like this. I cannot see coach Jaime Pagano allow it to go on like this too much longer. He's gotta make changes in personnel, not just to spell players but get them going.'

Bruce Anderson had a knack for voicing as a commentator what the rest of the Aussie supporters were thinking. This was a disaster. If they didn't do something soon they could really be under the pump for the rest of the tournament.

'It doesn't bear thinking about – and I'm usually the most optimistic guy around ...'

Anderson knew this would bring about guffaws at homes and bars all around the country who had heard his rather less optimistic but perfectly fair opinions in the past. He savoured the moment and anyone who knew him well would have seen his smile in the commentary position as he continued.

'... but, if our beloved Roos lose here, which is unthinkable I know, but you're seeing what I'm seeing and it isn't clever, then their next hit up is against Fiji, and those boys are big units and always up for a battle ... Wayne, this could be all over for the Roos before the final cushy one against Lebanon!'

Wayne Ferryman wasn't quick off the mark either. Anderson jumped in at the hesitation.

'... there you have it ... even the great Wayne Ferryman is worried, as well we all might be ... this is a horror show and no mistake ...'

The play of the ball had been stopped for a short while as one of the Aussies received treatment, hence Anderson's opportunity to milk the Roos' imminent demise.

'This World Cup could bring about more shocks than we've seen in my lifetime. Look at England. Defeats in Nieu and in Alice Springs. I'm not saying we should expect Wales vs Vanuatu in the final, but maybe it's not going to be as cut and dried a tournament as many were predicting.'

Greg's day had been far less stressful than his previous day of hopping balconies. He had relaxed and had spoken to Kyle not once but twice during the day, firstly when he'd woken that morning at 5am Australia time and he'd just caught Kyle at 8pm UK time. He'd called his son again at 6pm Port Vila time after returning from the run and at 8am UK time.

'My next game is tomorrow, Dad ...'

Greg felt saddened that he wouldn't be there.

'You just keep playing like I saw you last weekend. You were great ...'

Greg closed his eyes, picturing again his son not just playing but loving playing. It was as he had been.

'Wish you were here, Dad. Do you think you could get back in time?'

It had made Greg smile and at the same time had brought tears to his eyes. They talked about school, Kyle was really enthusiastic. He was more upbeat about it than Greg could ever remember he had been.

When they signed off Greg felt good, but with an emptiness too.

Making contact with Susie was another matter completely. He'd tried. But nothing. This had happened at times before. When it had, Greg had always told himself that she had found somebody else.

He'd never liked it, always hoped it had never happened, but he was a realist. He loved being with her, the passion they had for each other, their whole being. He also loved her nipples now he started letting himself go, her bum, her breasts, her ... enough already he told himself with an inner smile.

He left a couple of voice messages, a couple of texts, WhatsApp, but still nothing. That last embrace they'd shared still rankled. It felt like an end, but he didn't know why. Was it just that she couldn't fully end it? Was it something completely different? Was she ill? He'd keep trying.

'Bloody Amazing!!!'

Freddie South was up on his feet applauding. The Wales hooker Dai Hughes had just gone over for their third try of the game.

Stadium Australia was in uproar with the Welsh ex-pats and those fans who had made the journey. Delirium was perhaps a better description. Painted faces of the national colours of red, white and green; flags and banners being waved furiously and what sounded like thousands of Welsh men and women belting out songs.

'And Australia seem to have no answer to the Welsh Dragons tonight.'

Bruce Anderson had been happy to hype the situation at half-time, believing that the Aussies' class would tell, but now fifteen minutes into the second stanza there was little life to be seen in Jaime Pagano's charges.

'Aww mate, I think the time has come to ring those changes for Jaime. He's persisted with these boys on the park for long enough. I'm not sure why he hasn't used his interchanges at all as yet ...'

Wayne Ferryman's patience had worn thin. He knew the Roos were totally under the pump now, as the conversion sailed through the posts.

'One more score by Wales and this game could be over, I can't believe I'm saying it.

'We've got to say that, as much as Australia haven't played well, this team from Wales really has played above and beyond their expected level, but look here, look what's happening now ...'

As Anderson continued with his commentary Greg was looking at the screen and gave the broadest of smiles.

'And on comes Kenny Lomax ...'

Anderson had already mentioned the other three, but it was Kenny who had brought the smile to Greg's face.

Kenny had won everything in the game and three years ago had turned up at Hopton Town as they were languishing at the foot of the professional ladder in England. He and Greg had done everything they could to keep Hopton from going under, but their combined efforts had come too late.

They had played together again for Eruption where they had brought the island of Lanzarote immediate success in reaching Super League and had now spent two highly satisfactory seasons there, culminating in Greg's sacking, but not for playing reasons!

Kenny had last played for his country three and a half years ago. Injury had brought about the end of his glittering run in the green and gold and by the time he was fit again his international career had been consigned to the bin, but his form had been such that he'd forced his way back to selection. Now 37, he was by far the oldest member of the team. Bruce Anderson was a fan.

'… *can one of the greatest players ever to pull on the green and gold jumper roll back the years here? We certainly need something …*'

Wayne Ferryman had played alongside Kenny in four previous World Cups, Australia had won three of them. He had nothing but good vibes for his compatriot.

'*Aww, Bruce, if there's one player you need at a time like this, it is this man. These guys out on the park don't seem to know what day it is. Kenny will spark something that's for sure. He's been pulling up trees in the Super League for the last couple of seasons and from what I've seen he's been playing the best footy of his career.*'

The England team was transfixed at Breakas. Their own start since arriving in the southern hemisphere hadn't exactly been auspicious but their games so far had been meaningless, a run out for tired limbs from a Super League season, more about regaining match fitness.

This, on the other hand, was a catastrophe in the making for the Aussies. Not one of the England party could have considered in their wildest dreams that Wales would be leading 16-0 going into the last quarter of the game.

Greg had enjoyed the best times of his own career playing alongside Kenny. As much as he wanted the Aussie team to fail here, he also wanted his good mate to do well.

Greg had been so wrapped up in watching the game that he hadn't noticed until now the beautiful woman who walked past him where he was standing at the bar area looking back at the huge screen showing the game.

Greg's eyes wandered, as they were somewhat inclined. Blonde, slim, at first glance late 20s, early 30s? Radiant smile, not that she had been smiling at him, had she?

Danford wasn't watching the game. He'd stayed a while at police headquarters.

'*Chief. You got a minute?*'

Danford had been so caught up in his thoughts that he hadn't been aware of her. He'd had no idea how long Elenola Taneo had been watching him. They'd rarely seen eye to eye in the past.

Elenola had been born on the Vanuatu island of Espiritu Santo, the nation's largest island and where Spanish explorer Fernandez de Queiros had first claimed the island archipelago for his country in 1606. Elenola normally worked out of Luganville on Santo, the island's largest town. She was attractive, raven-haired and in her early 40s.

'*Winston Sablan was a good man …*'

Elenola was straight to the point, she never arrived anywhere without trying to tackle things the moment she had landed.

They would need to work even more closely together in the coming days as they oversaw two murder inquiries and coped with keeping everyone safe as Efate's population was about to increase to an all-time high, albeit for a few days.

She normally commuted by air the 168 miles between Espiritu Santo and Efate a couple of times each week, but she was now to be on Efate for the duration of the Rugby League World Cup games and the murder investigations. She had flown into the airport in Port Vila having taken the Luganville flight.

Danford had sensed a 'but' coming to her assertion of Winston's qualities and he wasn't wrong. Elenola was also not without compassion or empathy.

'*… look chief, I know you and Prime Minister Sablan went back a long way …*'

Elenola was watching Danford's eyes, expression and any manner he was now about to adopt. He stretched out his arms and his hands on his desk in front of him, took a deep breath, then clasped his hands in thoughtful mode, almost prayer-like, under his nose.

'Winston and I did go back, yes ...'

He paused, looked into Elenola's eyes, serious.

'... so, whatever your 'but' is about him, you needn't worry on my account. I am a policeman first and foremost deputy commissioner. And what is more important right now is to protect others on the island. We are going to need to work together, all of us, particularly you, Alex and myself ...'

Elenola was already ahead of her chief.

'That's why I'm here tonight, direct from my flight, because there are some things you need to know about Winston Sablan ...'

The beautiful woman came back past Greg once more, on her way to where she had been sitting previously. Was she a member of the England party at Breakas?

He'd heard that England had booked the whole place. His eyes followed her once again. Greg gave the slightest of smiles, in case her eyes caught his as she went past.

She looked great and smelled great. Her perfume was intoxicating. He then thought again more of Susie before his eyes returned to the game as the commentator's decibels reached a personal high for the night.

'You little ripper!'

Bruce Anderson once again summed up the nation's feelings in one short line. Three words that didn't fully explain what had just happened.

'Finally! We've got a game here! And it's Special K who has put Australia on the board for the first time in this World Cup. Wayne, that was pure magic, the little runaround off a pass from Vellidale.'

Wayne Ferryman was suddenly energised, as were most of the rest of the stadium.

'Aww mate, that's such a relief. The boys needed to get over the whitewash and that's something Kenny has been a wizard at for nearly twenty years now. Still a long way to go.'

'But now all around Australia, wherever you're watching this game you can all have hope. Who would have thought we'd need

that in our opening game of the tournament? I've said it before and I'll say it again, none of these teams are to be taken for granted. You do that and you're on the road to failure. Right, settle in, settle down everybody. If this kick goes over the Roos need two more converted scores. Fifteen minutes to go.'

The atmosphere around the pool and on the sofas under the covered area near the bar at Breakas where everyone was watching the game had been slightly dampened. The Aussies struggling for what seemed the first time in years had given hope to everyone, but probably more significantly those who were more likely to win the trophy if they didn't, notably New Zealand and England – with Papua New Guinea and France slightly further back.

'Oh! Here we go!'

Australia had secured the conversion to take the game to 16-6 in Wales' favour. Wales had kicked the ball back to the men in green and gold – and now they were running with purpose for what seemed the first time in the game.

'You can feel the electricity so much now it is crackling all around the ground! … And there he goes again! … Kenny Lomax, we bow down to you sir! He's hauled down on the Wales 20-metre line.'

Bruce Anderson was enjoying whipping up the fervour in homes throughout the country and now, almost when it looked as though the unspeakable may have been on the cards, an Australia defeat in the opening game, he had something to hold on to.

'Lomax plays the ball and Elton Richards collects. Ohhh! He's thrown out the most outrageous dummy and he's gone through the gap. He's sprinting towards the line. Glyn Thomas, the Welsh full-back is covering – and that's an amazing … oh, would you believe it … Thomas rags Richards just short of the line but Lomaxxxxxx!!!!!! Yessss!'

Australia's World Cup had well and truly begun! Just shy of seventy minutes into the competition and with the conversion they had narrowed the gap to 16-12. The Aussie supporters were in raptures, the Welsh fans sang as though their very being now depended on it. The stadium was alight.

'*And this is what the Rugby League World Cup is all about!*'

It was the cry of a now wholly enthusiastic Bruce Anderson.

'*We, I'm sorry, let's not be too partisan here … hey forget that, we, all Australians want to win this World Cup like no other before it because of this standard of competition. Wherever you are watching all over the world, this is what makes our sport the best in the world!*'

It was a hyperbole frenzy from Bruce. He hadn't truly believed the standard of the game had increased, but he was prepared to use it, especially now that the Aussies were still at this present moment in a hole.

It was coming up to ten minutes left in the game.

In Broke, Zoe gave a smile as she watched her parents who were glued to the screen.

Greg had already seen the writing on the wall. Only four points from drawing level against a team that had given everything in the first sixty but looked out on their feet.

He'd turned his attention more and more towards the blonde girl. She had looked him in the eye, briefly, as she'd passed, he was sure of it.

'*Wow, what a hit up! … and that puts a different complexion on the next nine minutes … Kenny Lomax is spark out!*'

A hush came over the stadium as the player who had dragged the Green & Gold Machine back from oblivion lay prostrate while medics rushed to his aide. The referee Pierre Marseilles had no hesitation in sending the perpetrator of Lomax's head shaker, prop Berwyn Evans, to the bin.

'*And Wales are reduced to twelve for the remainder of this game, but how much damage has been done here? Or has Kenny Lomax done enough for the rest of the boys to pull this through? I can't see him getting up from this … hold on though … just a second everybody …*'

Kenny Lomax was rising, slowly, back on his haunches. The medics were looking closely. The crowd at the ground saw him moving on the big screen. The swell of noise grew and carried on into a tidal wave of noise as Kenny Lomax moved from his haunches to his feet. Capping it all was his famed gap-toothed grin that shone out of the screen as he returned to action.

Australia took the option of a penalty kick for two points, slotting it over and bringing them within two points of Wales with eight minutes left on the clock and Wales down one player.

Greg watched his former teammate of the past three seasons and was in awe of his ability and tenacity. He already knew Kenny would be getting back up and into the game. He'd seen it happen many times previously. This man was not just a magician on the park, he was also a miracle man of remarkable comebacks.

Wales held on.

There was no way they should have been able to on form, class and with one man down, but hold on they did for the next six minutes. The clock on the big screen was ticking down and Aussie eyes were glancing at it every other second.

Greg's eyes were glancing elsewhere, while also becoming more wrapped up in the game. The blonde girl. He couldn't help it. She was stunning.

Don't be a fool, he told himself, you've too much at stake here. The game coming up. In the team for tomorrow. Forget it. Think Kyle. Think Susie. Think England.

'Two minutes on the clock! Two points in the ball game! What a way to start this World Cup! And Wales have the ball on the Australia 20-metre line. All they have to do is hold on to the ball. It's stick it up the jumper time!'

Bruce Anderson was giving it large on the commentary. Inside, his Aussie heart was pounding, but in his profession this was why he did this job.

'Aww, you know what, if these boys in red take this game it will be the biggest wake-up call the Roos have ever had – and maybe they've needed it, because without Kenny Lomax they would have been dead in the water by now.'

Wayne Ferryman was taking the pragmatic view.

Greg's mobile phone reverberated on the bar. He never saw the end of the game.

CHAPTER 20

'You came … I wasn't sure you would …'

She looked even more amazing than he'd thought at first glance. She'd sent the number of her bungalow. Breakas included hotel accommodation and bungalows on the beach. Had she really noticed him just by walking to the bar? Her voice sounded sultry, beckoning.

Greg was curious, as well as excited by her. Something had gone wrong between him and Susie, he could feel it. Maybe they were over at last, maybe she had found someone who was more, available. Maybe he should just get on with, life.

'I nearly didn't …'

She had been sitting on the veranda area, probably so that he knew he was at the right bungalow. He had stopped himself from walking in.

Less incriminating to his teammates or England officials if any were in close vicinity. This was not the night for any other kind of activity before their first big game in the tournament, but he was taken with her.

Greg also wanted to make sure that this wasn't a set-up. There was something about the way in which she had appeared, going past, making eye contact, that he would have just liked and accepted a few years ago, but why was she there now? He'd been under the impression that the England squad and staff had booked out the whole of Breakas.

'What's your name?'

Greg had become a little more social media savvy in recent years. If she lied now it would prove she was a non-starter for him despite how she looked. He'd find out confirmation of who she was by asking around at Breakas.

She smiled easily.

'Karla …'

Karla smiled a little more. Her long blonde hair framed her

gorgeous face. She was wearing a beautiful strappy white lace cocktail dress. She'd dispensed with her sandals having walked across the beach from the bar at the hotel to her bungalow.

'*Drink? … I have wine, beer, kava …*'

Karla had taken the initiative.

Nothing wrong with a drink. That wasn't committing himself to a night of unbridled passion. Well, not just yet anyway. Stop it, he told himself. There was nothing to be gained from this, apart from the obvious. Think straight. Go back to his suite.

Greg decided on the sociable route.

'*Beer, thanks …*'

It was just a drink, nothing more. Karla handed him a bottle from the refrigerator.

'*What made you come?*'

She put her head to one side slightly, looked into his eyes, her tongue played on her lips.

'*Your text was … how did you get my mobile number?*'

Greg had hesitated. It had dawned on him. How had she got it? This woman was beautiful, alluring, sexy, but there were too many questions that needed asking and he needed to rest up for the game tomorrow.

What was her last name? She hadn't given that, although maybe she'd just given her first name because this was exploratory on both sides? But she hadn't answered how she had got his number.

Karla was watching him, she was easy, relaxed. She sipped at the cocktail she had brought over from the bar area.

'*What are you thinking?*'

Karla tipped her head to one side as she spoke. He liked the way she did that. There was a certain degree of playfulness in them both. He rested his head back on the right side of his shoulder, looked somewhere in the distance in the sky, but nowhere in particular, to his left.

'*What I'm thinking …*'

he said, as he brought his eyes to meet hers, watching for reaction to what he was about to say.

'... is why? ... why me? ... why tonight? ... why no last name? and the number? ...'

He looked her straight in the eye now for any sign of weakness, any look that told him this should stop right now.

Yesterday he had been tipped off seconds before someone came into his hotel room in Brisbane. Today he had been pretty much propositioned by a beautiful, glamorous woman, tomorrow he had a World Cup game. Was it all linked?

Karla took a deep breath.

'My name is Karla Karelia. I am from Poland, but my family moved to Australia when I was 6 years old. I am not married. I am here on my own because I prefer it that way. I liked the way we looked at each other. I believe in love at first sight, or something like that. Maybe attraction at first sight would be better. Would you like me to go on ... oh, yes, your number ... we share a mutual friend ... will that do?'

She took up her glass but before savouring her cocktail, to go with her cocktail dress, she covered off that answer too.

'Jen ... Jen Juniper? ... I appeared in a video to one of her songs ... oh, and all this is okay, really it is ... I can understand why you would need to know all this ...'

He would check with Gina aka Jen. This was too much to take in right now. His first thought? It was too contrived. Why here? Now? It was time to call it quits, no matter how enticing.

'Thanks for the beer, I'm turning in. Big day tomorrow ...'

Greg began to make his way back to his room, away from the bungalows and in the main building of the hotel. He'd chosen not to look back after a slight smile. She hadn't looked disappointed.

He'd moved on in his thoughts by the time he'd reached his room. Tomorrow's game was what counted now, that's why he was there. He called Col to check on how Mum was coping and how Dad was doing. No change. He called Susie again. No answer. It was too late now for another call to Kyle, but his game was in the morning, so he sent him a text.

Final text was to Gina.

CHAPTER 21

Hideaway Island was one of Efate's most popular tourist destinations. It had achieved worldwide fame for its underwater post office, where visitors would send their postcards back home via the only underwater post mistress Lena Kalotiti, who would scuba dive each day to serve customers and post mail.

The small island just a couple of hundred metres off Efate and noted for coral, scuba diving, crystal clear waters and all colours of fish was reached every hour by waterbus.

This was now the latest part of Efate to receive police incident taping sealing off a section of its beach. It was another murder scene set to test the investigative personnel of the Vanuatu Police Force.

Danford had struggled to believe what he was hearing when the call had come in. He was shaking his head at the scene now. He and Elenola had gone straight out, it was no more than five minutes from their headquarters in Port Vila.

'How long?'

Danford asked of the forensic team busily surveying its third body in a matter of days and second within hours. It was going to be a long night and an even longer day as everything else on the island ramped up towards the kick-off at Port Vila Municipal Stadium.

'Chief …'

Elenola had thought she would be prepared for anything.

'It's Lena.'

CHAPTER 22

Zoe touched down at Port Vila International Airport early the next morning. She and Jess had been watching the 4x4 parked up in Broke most of the previous day. Despite looking in keeping with the area, being a pickup, everyone would know it wasn't local, not least because of its plates, but also because Broke was such a small community that everybody knew everyone – and everybody knew everyone's business, including their vehicles.

The local Neighbourhood Watch Alliance had been a regular feature of Broke even before such schemes and organisations were adopted in every community. They looked after their own and this vehicle, unbeknown to the driver, had become its principal news and focus for the day.

It had been a full-on tour-de-force from Zoe's old friends and family that had located where the black Ford Ranger had last been sold and the owner's name, although they suspected it was stolen.

Another neighbour big into photography had managed to take enough clear stills of the driver and through the driver's purchase of fuel and a coffee at a truck stop on the main highway fingerprints had been taken from the discarded cup. An ex-police chief had retired to Broke and had called in a favour.

Their man in the vehicle had been Grady Sorenson, twice convicted of armed robbery and with a string of other crimes. Twice jailed. Known to have worked in organised crime. Always armed.

The good people of Broke had jumped him before he had time to equip himself with his firearm. One of the figures clad all in black toting the gun with the silencer, backed up by two others similarly clothed, led Grady from his vehicle, taking his keys and phone from him, hog-tied him and bundled the career villain into the back of his own pickup.

The last Zoe had seen of him was his vehicle going past the family residence that she left minutes later. She was alongside her father in his car. He drove her to Newcastle Interchange where she boarded the fast train to Sydney airport.

She now had Grady's mobile phone and was sending texts on his behalf to whoever was his paymaster. She would find out who this was later.

Jess and Zoe hadn't just reminisced during their day together. Zoe had confided in her old friend what had gone on in Sydney. They had set their minds to why Zoe had received the message she had. Zoe had filled several gaps for Jess in terms of the World Cup Organising Committee and the Rugby League International Authority.

Jess had said that it all stank and that it all seemed to her, from what Zoe had said, that she, Zoe, was best out of it all.

Zoe's nature was not to quit – and then the news had appeared during the previous day that Bob Rudd's body had been found on Efate.

Bob Rudd, former financial whizz-kid in his heyday and finance director of the Rugby League World Cup. He'd said he'd needed a few days to get his head straight over something about a week ago and there were some last-minute problems in Efate that needed solving.

Now he was dead and Zoe had been summoned to some clandestine meeting that she'd bottled because she'd smelled something really bad. She'd had an armed man near to her doorstep. Could she be next?

Why had Bob Rudd ended up the way he had in Vanuatu? And why hadn't she felt able to trust an ally when the going had got tough?

Zoe's fellow passengers to Port Vila had included the last of those heading out to watch the game, but there was also a group of probably twenty or so who didn't look as though they had boarded for fun, they looked to Zoe like a delegation of some sort; and although she hadn't been aware, there were two more on the flight who had their own reasons for being there.

'*Zoe Miller?*'

Zoe knew she didn't exactly look the way she had twenty years ago at the Olympics, but she had made a point of keeping up her hoodie to her top and a buff to cover her mouth and chin while on board.

She'd only moved her buff from her face to take a drink on the flight when she had been recognised by a woman next to her who professed to being a fan.

She'd gone on to ask for Zoe's autograph. Zoe obliged. Other conversation from Zoe was not forthcoming, but she needn't have worried. This woman could talk for Australia.

Det Supt Erin Jackson had clocked Zoe as she had been boarding the flight but hadn't been able to place her. One of those moments where someone is seen out of context. Erin hadn't thought any more about it. She had plenty on her mind.

This case had come up at either just the right or just the wrong time for her. Had she been sent here to get her out of the way while some promotion was decided? Or was this a test case to once again check her tenacity or suitability for the next bigger role?

Greg was in game-day mode and had woken early, around 6.30am to get out for a run before anyone else was up and about. He also wanted to ensure he was giving his body enough time to restore its energy in the afternoon ready for the evening kick-off.

Shane Chislett had scheduled a light session after breakfast followed by a squad meeting.

But Greg wasn't alone in the early hours of the day. As he left the Breakas complex, heading out on to Pango Road and passing the mobile kava bar, there were others.

Jericho Palaggi, Sam Rivers and Aaron Fielding all looked as fresh as they had on the run back from the stadium the previous evening, less than twelve hours ago. They hurtled past Greg, who was running at a decent lick but nowhere near their pace, with a cheery cry of 'good morning'.

The trio played for Super League champions, the Ravens,

and there were four more of their teammates in the England squad. They made up an impressive and lethal backs division back home. They were heading off way into the distance within the next thirty seconds.

'*Listen up everybody! We will be working with the Vanuatu Police Force through Commissioner Napakauranga. When we were deployed yesterday it was in response to the murder of Bob Rudd, finance director with the Rugby League World Cup Organising Committee, however since then two more murders have taken place, both citizens of Vanuatu.*

'*The other two murders are not our primary concern, although local information suggests they may have a connection with the murder of Rudd.*

'*I would like our investigations to centre wholly on his murder – and if in doing so we overlap with information on the murders of prime minister Winston Sablan and Lena Kalotiti we should share information with the Commissioner and his team.*'

Detective Superintendent Erin Jackson of the Australian Federal Police Authority was briefing her team at the Vanuatu Police Headquarters with Danford, Elenola and Alex Lui all present. It was 8am. There had been no time for signing in to hotels, all baggage had been brought with the team of twenty-five that had flown.

'*There is also Vanuatu's first match in the World Cup tournament tonight, against England, and this town is going to be crawling with people inside the next few hours as the excitement builds.*

'*I want us out of here, to have cleaned up this case, as soon as possible, but I'm not looking at cutting corners to do so.*'

The Detective Superintendent turned to the Commissioner.

'*Commissioner Napakauranga can tell you what they have so far.*'

She knew already that the Vanuatu Police Force had nothing, or at best very little. It established her team's position.

Once Danford had relayed the evidence so far Erin Jackson took over once again.

'*I want to know everything about this man from birth to death,*

I want his history, his career, what he ate, drank, his vices. Family, friends, what people thought of him, how he gained the positions he had attained, his bank accounts, personal details, sexual preferences, why he was here? And why he is now dead? And I want it all on my desk in the next hour! Go!'

Elenola Taneo and Alex Lui were in awe.

Danford Napakauranga had seen grandstanding from big fish before, and wished he had half the resources that Erin Jackson had at her disposal.

Erin Jackson's team quickly fired up their laptops and mobile phones and began gathering information. It was an impressive set-up. Within minutes, members of the team were leaving the building bound for Erakor Island.

CHAPTER 23

'Axe to be yielded as Roos fail in World Cup opener'.

The NRL website made much kinder reading than either *The Sydney Morning Herald* or *The Australian* that morning and the broadcast news was having a field day too.

'Where did it all go wrong?'; *'Nightmare start'*; *'Embarrassment!'*; and *'Killer Wales leave Roos blubbering'* were just a smattering of the headlines and social media was much, much worse. All except Kenny Lomax were in the firing line. Wales had hung on to take the opening tie 16-14.

England head coach Shane Chislett was playing it all down in his first press conference of the day, held next to the infinity pool at Breakas.

'Obviously it's not what the Aussies would have wanted, but I'm sure they will bounce back. It's only one game. There's a long way to go in this competition and our campaign gets under way tonight, but it won't be easy. Every team deserves to be here.'

Chislett wouldn't be drawn on further questions over whether the Aussies had been over-confident, which they had; and ill-prepared, which it seemed they had been also, all apart from Kenny.

The heavy-set, hard-as-nails coach was concentrated on just one task. England's first game in the competition.

'Look, we know our results haven't been clever leading up to this game but this is now the main stage. Vanuatu have pulled off some good wins and they will be looking forward to cutting us down as their first big scalp. It's our job to make sure that doesn't happen.'

Chislett was grateful there had been no repetition of the female journalist who had tried to make him look homophobic in the previous press briefing. Media and Relations Manager Annie Laing had restricted numbers into the briefing and Grace Elliott hadn't been granted a press pass.

'How are you this morning?'

She cocked her head to one side as he looked round to her. He couldn't help but smile back.

Sod it, Greg now thought. He'd not looked into what she had told him last night as yet. He really had been in game mode since getting up and would probably remain that way until the eighty minutes were up.

Karla had arrived at breakfast in Breakas just as Greg was heading for fruit, cereal and juice, perhaps to be rounded off with a coffee. She sounded as provocatively sexy as she had the night before, and for someone who had just surfaced she looked as cute as the day.

Her smile reminded Greg of Susie, the same cheeky look, the same suggestive eyes. And her beach minidress of blue and primrose worked well with her beautiful blonde hair.

'*Perhaps when you have returned triumphant this evening we might …*'

She purposely wavered a little, to watch how the line was going.

'*… meet again?*'

Greg was caught in one of those moments where he wanted to say why not, but then he had not checked her out, as he'd intended to. His answer was a non-committal 'maybe'.

She hmphed. It was a kind of semi-exasperated sound. She turned and walked away over to a section of the breakfast area not inhabited by the England party.

Chislett announced that the light session he had planned was on the beach in front of the Breakas Resort. All basic stuff as he now believed that getting the basics right, completing their possession stats, fast ball handling when in possession and a hard running defensive line would provide the platform.

'*Look at Australia last night. That's what can happen without the basics. We've had two tough warm-up games, but none of that matters now. Tonight's starting thirteen is: Aaron Fielding, Jericho Pallagi, Sam Rivers, Troy Whittingham, Vincent Venus, Owen Fairclough, Stu Wainwright, Freddie South, Ash Tyson, Billy Ecktenstall, Mason Bell, Mick Green and Greg Duggan.*'

Interchanges: Gary Walker, Phil Parkin, Richard Dee and Charlie Cole.'

There were a few gasps or at very least sounds of shock around the room. Regulars for the past half-dozen England games Regan Phillips, Jason Neve, Tyler Rodgers and Kane Heath had all been dumped from the seventeen. Chislett felt the aura and responded. Nipping it in the bud as best he could.

'We are gonna need every one of you at some point in this campaign. We've already lost six players to injury. If you're in, good luck to you and try to keep hold of your spot; if you're out, be supportive. This has got to be Team England from now on – and these Vanuatu players aren't going to give a shit how good you think you are!'

It took more than an hour for Erin Jackson's team to have her dossier fully in place on the life and times of Bob Rudd, but one person who had been on the same plane had a head start and knew exactly where she was headed.

'We need to talk …'

CHAPTER 24

It was all she had said, no introduction was necessary on the heavily camera-fed intercom she was facing after hiring a Suzuki Jimny from Vila Rentacar.

She had seen at least three cameras trained on the device and all around, and they were on swivel too, moving to get the best angles.

There was no verbal reply. The electronic gates opened. The intercom had been placed in such a way that she'd had to get out of the vehicle. Back inside, she made her way down the immaculate white stone driveway.

Greg was back in his room. He'd run seven miles before breakfast. He and the rest of the seventeen selected for the game had spent an hour on the beach with the coaching staff, largely working on drumming the basics back into their heads. Completing their sets of six tackles with the ball. Going back the requisite ten metres quickly when on defence for each play of the ball.

Tactical coaches on plays and moves took over for another half hour after that, purely to work on a few moves between pairings.

Fielding, Pallagi and Rivers were already a strong working unit with their club side, so too were Wainwright and Venus, Greg also; and there were others that had worked well together in the past.

It was now around 1pm. The squad had had lunch together, all prepared to a strict diet laid down by the England party's dietician. They'd taken their own chefs who had taken over the hotel kitchen.

Greg was settling in for an afternoon of nothingness, relax, call everyone – Col, talk with Mum, try Susie, again, he still hadn't given up hope with her. She'd had a habit of going to ground like this at times over their several years of seeing each other. But, that way she had been before he'd left, it gnawed at his brain. There was something.

He couldn't contact Kyle just yet, as it would be the early hours of the morning back in England, but he wanted to talk with his son, tell him how proud he was of him and give him some nice words before his game.

The thing was, Greg's kick-off was at 7pm and he was 10 hours ahead of Kyle. It would be 9am in England. Kyle's game was at 11am. He'd ring him an hour before kick-off.

'He's been restless, but he seems okay, well, as okay as he's ever going to be … yeah, Mum's doing well … she's just gone for a break … there's nothing any of us can do …'

Col was steady as a rock. Always had been.

'You're starting the game? That's great! Hey, all the news is about Vanuatu over here. And last night's game, wow! The Aussies are getting a real panning by everyone over here, but that's some serious shit going down where you are. Their prime minister has been assassinated, did you know? … and they've found the body of one of the World Cup organisers there too. Go steady bud! … and don't do your usual thing and find yourself in the middle of it … that's all I'm saying.'

Greg had heard the talk around the breakfast area about the trouble on the island but there hadn't been much more than that, just talk and it had moved on.

Greg had been more concerned furthering his partnership with Freddie South and Freddie's fellow prop Billy Ecktenstall. It was always good to have the big guys on-side.

'I thought I might find you here …'

For fuck's sake! How the hell had she got past security, which was meant to be all over their section of the complex.

'… I also thought that maybe I could help you … relax?'

Karla's eyes sparkled. The hotel was all on one level, sprawling over several acres, and each room or suite had a generous veranda looking out onto the ocean where she was standing provocatively. It was a gorgeous view, complete with palm trees, beach and sea – and now Karla. The scene looked immaculate.

Greg knew that now was about getting set for tonight's game, not taking on what would probably amount to extra curricula activity. But he looked at her and Christ, the way she looked was sensational. Susie? Were they still …? What were they? Greg closed his eyes for a second, bit the inner underside of his lip slightly. He opened them again. Resist?

She looked amazing and she was there. She was wearing, hardly wearing, a white bikini that covered very little, more a collection of string.

Lust was rearing its head, so to speak, once again.

Here she was, at his door, smiling, enticing. There wasn't much he had to do but say yes.

CHAPTER 25

'I thought we had agreed this was a bad idea.'

Zoe hadn't been expecting an entirely open-armed greeting and she'd not been disappointed. She was passed a drink. She had no intention of drinking it. She knew this was dangerous territory. She looked her host directly in the eye.

'We had ...' she said with emphasis on the past tense. *'But then you murdered Bob Rudd ... or should I say, Bob Rudd was murdered ... here ... on your island, or again ... the island where you choose to live ...'*

'Your point is what exactly?'

The host, owner of the private beachfront estate at Paradise Beach, the millionaire's playground on Efate, was talking, in between lengths of the pool.

She stopped. Jumped out, lithe, effortless and was handed a towel by one of her well-torsoed young gentlemen who adorned the place, as well as beautiful girls. She could see Zoe's eye had strayed ever so slightly, towards one of the girls. It was enough to spot a weakness, and she was good at spotting those – she'd spotted that with poor old Bob Rudd too.

'More champagne? Something on the rocks? Or something to really help you loosen up?'

Temptation was dripping from Zoe's host's mouth and eyes. She wanted Zoe to be sucked into her world, and she'd made a pretty good fist of it so far.

She was now drying herself by patting down her glistening naked body in front of her. Whether she was purposely trying to entice her or not, Zoe found that she couldn't have cared less. All she could see was a woman with a lovely figure. Her breasts were perky, irresistibly so and, well, the rest of her was similarly perfectly proportioned.

'Why?'

She had to cut through all this. But everything was heading

in one very certain direction and the flower of her own personal southern hemisphere was responding.

The temptress now wore nothing but her smile in front of Zoe. She padded over to where Zoe was watching her, her satin auburn hair caressing her shoulders, her makeup looking as good as when she had gone into the pool. Her nipples erect and clearly excited and anticipatory.

She held out her hand delicately to Zoe, beckoning her to take it, willing her to hold hands. It was enticement, erotica, engagement and empowerment all bound into one small gesture.

'Come … let's get in the pool together … I want you …'

She mouthed the last three words, rather than saying them even in a whisper.

There were worse places she could have been. She could have been caught up in city life, running meetings, being a highly paid executive or instead she could be being wined and propositioned on a gorgeous island in the South Pacific by a beautiful woman who had many faults, but who wanted her badly. And Zoe found she now wanted her too.

When they slipped into the water, hardly making a ripple, holding each other close, it was as close to heaven as Zoe had come in her life.

CHAPTER 26

'*Mmmm* ...' Karla's face showed an ecstasy borne out of fulfilment as she turned her head to where Greg was behind her on the bed, thrusting with a momentum that she was reciprocating with her bum, holding her cheeks softly but firm.

'*Ohhh baabyyy ...*'

Det Supt Erin Jackson's reputation for wanting everything done in the minimum amount of time and yet complaining that her team hadn't given her what she had wanted was legendary.

They hadn't rolled their eyes in her direct line of vision when she had given the hour ultimatum, but they had met the deadline with the customary reaction.

Four hours later they had achieved a background on the 'charcoal man' they had so nicknamed after seeing the photographs taken on Erakor Island and at the morgue.

Their findings had provided varied conjecture over why he might have been on the island of Efate and finally Erakor Island but no real clues.

In his position of finance director of the Rugby League World Cup and with four games set to be played in Port Vila he had every reason to be there, to check on costings, ensure that everything was ticking along nicely and with a week to go perhaps he had been on the island to sign off on final deals and other work that may have still been required.

'*He was bent, had to be ...*'

This was Erin Jackson's standpoint. She saw so many gaps, quirks, anomalies, call them whatever, there were just too many oddities, stuff that didn't fit right. She had Bob Rudd down as a man who had abused his position, payments for services that only he would know what these services were.

'*... could he have been blackmailed?*'

Erin was pacing, as though in a trance, trying to make some sense of what she was reading. Her second-in-command Marlon

Razni was maintaining a silence. He'd worked with Erin for the past three years and knew how she led a case. This was classic. Come in all guns blazing, the big I am, create a culture of pace and pressure. Then begin disseminating. He couldn't knock it. It generally worked for her authority.

She turned to him.

'Your thoughts?'

He'd known it was coming. He always went along with her initial assumptions to placate but then added his humble thoughts. She held a respect for him. No other colleague had lasted longer than six months with her.

'Bent. Yeah, I go with that.'

He nodded, while rubbing his chin with his right hand.

'Definitely something like blackmailed, something that someone had over him – yeah, blackmailed … but I'm reading there's more about this guy …'

Erin motioned for him to carry on.

'He didn't need to be here … like NEED to be here … on Efate …'

'So why was he?'

Erin had felt the same, she paced again.

'A woman? … a man? … money? … bank accounts don't give any impression anything was wrong, he didn't look in trouble …'

'No problems at home either, or at least nothing on here.'

Marlon pushed his hands forward towards the information on the screen.

'Doesn't mean all is right, but worth checking …'

'Looks like whatever he was into he was like soap …'

Marlon looked quizzical. Erin explained.

'… slippery?'

'Obviously not slippery enough.'

'Someone caught up with him, caught on to whatever wheeze he'd thought up … he's a finance man for God's sake, an accountant … surely it's got to be about money?'

CHAPTER 27

'Lena wasn't exactly an angel,'

Alex Lui began his opening assessment of the world's only underwater post mistress.

This was not news to Danford but he refrained from comment. Her role had been eye-catching and had been enhanced by her body, which she had kept in shape. Lena had been regularly called upon for photographs with the island's visitors and was seen as a celebrity, playing up to her fame.

'She enjoyed the publicity her role brought her – and she played on it. She received a good deal of attention.'

Elenola wanted to get to the facts.

'But what does that tell us, Alex? She was a good-time girl who became caught up with someone who took advantage of her? Maybe she was just in the wrong place at the wrong time?'

Danford interjected before Alex had time to move on to his notes, the nitty-gritty detail that Elenola had meant.

'I can tell you that Lena came from a family of modest means. I remember that much. When the underwater post office was started she had been working on Hideaway Island as a scuba diving instructor to the hotel guests. She was the obvious choice – young, pretty, photographable ...'

Alex now wondered why Danford had given him the task of looking into Lena's life when he already had prior knowledge of her. Danford was quick to put Alex right.

'... but beyond that I know very little about her ... what do you have Alex? ...'

'Lena was 32 years of age, unmarried. She had a child, a boy, Santos, at 17 who is now 15 and a good kid, no trouble. She is from Pango. Her father is a farmer growing kava, keeping a few cattle for beef. She achieved decent results at school and swam for Vanuatu in the Oceania Junior Swimming Championships. She's worked on Hideaway for 16 years, having started there while at school. I'm

visiting Hideaway this afternoon.'

Elenola had wanted to uncover information Danford hadn't known about his old pal Winston Sablan, not for any other reason than to make it all worthwhile. She had known that Danford had given her a poisoned chalice in trying to find anything after perhaps 40 years of friendship.

'Winston Sablan. Port Vila-born. Youngest of twelve children. Married four times. Seven children. Prime Minister for the past four years. A member of our island nations' government for over thirty. Worked his way up through village chiefdom. Prior to government he was a used car salesman and ventilation specialist. Known as a man who always got what he wanted, one or two 'casualties' in terms of friendships gone sour over the years ...'

Danford raised his arm.

'Like who? Recent?'

Elenola had led up to this moment where she felt Danford would interject. She'd hit pay dirt. Something her chief didn't know?

Five minutes later all three were on their way. Danford and Elenola on the trail of stray friendships – and Alex to Hideaway Island.

CHAPTER 28

The England tour bus arrived at Port Vila Municipal Stadium at 4pm. Three hours prior to kick-off. Shane Chislett wanted his team totally prepared in as relaxed a manner as possible.

Since lunch every member of the starting thirteen and those on the bench had been in their rooms sleeping or resting up.

Greg's afternoon had been somewhat more energetic than Chislett might have planned. He knew professionally before a big game that rest was important but, well, this woman. This game was against a team that rated lower than the lowest rank he'd been playing with Hopton Town.

Now that he was at the ground he felt it maybe hadn't been such a good idea. He was knackered, or at the very least not where he should have been at this time before a game.

The Vanuatu national side had already arrived. They had also been together overnight and during the day leading up to the game at the home of prominent Vanuatu businessman and former prime minister Sela Natavanu.

They had enjoyed his Paradise Beach Estate where they had swum, run and worked out in his own grounds that included an Olympic-size pool, running track, rugby league ground that was probably better than the one at Port Vila.

Vanuatu's head coach was Dane Mitchell. He'd been in the job for ten years and had taken the nation from unknowns to one of the leading Emerging Nations. While they were 100,000-1 outsiders to win the tournament and 100-1 to beat England and Papua New Guinea in the group games they were favourites to beat Greece. They had come a long way. They'd gone from 32nd nation in the world to 16th in just four years.

Ben Mara was Vanuatu's hero. Ben had established himself firstly in the Queensland Cup competition where Dane Mitchell had been his mentor before going on to the Sydney League and then signing for the Sea Eagles where he had enjoyed three successful years working his way into the NRL side before moving north to the Cowboys, where he had found his home.

Ben was the national side's talisman, a stand-off who could also play hooker, full-back or centre. He was working alongside players with limited experience for his home nation, but he loved wearing the badge and the shirt. And he was there to meet the England team off the coach.

'Shane! Good to see you mate! Been a while …'

Ben was one of the nicest guys in the NRL, a player who respected his good fortune in having had someone like Dane Mitchell help him along the way. He had already vowed that when his playing days were over he would commit himself to building on what Aussie-born Dane had achieved.

There was talk of a Vanuatu side based in Port Vila taking part in the Queensland Cup competition a few years ahead.

Other than Ben Mara the rest of the Vanuatu side was made up largely of unknowns. Two others had Queensland Cup credentials, having played for clubs in the tournament, but having not made it as regulars – Zac Santo and Antony Marango.

'Should be a great atmosphere in Vila tonight. It's been rockin' all day … hey Freddie, good to see you too man …'

There was a solid embrace between the two players.

Port Vila Stadium was buzzing. The islanders were knowledgeable about the game and although they knew more about the NRL in Australia, as games were shown in the bars, they also saw Super League games from the UK and knew many of the players.

'Catch up with you guys later!'

Ben disappeared into the stadium.

'Gina, yeah …'

Greg had been next to Freddie when his phone had exploded into life with the lead break of White Stripes' 'Seven Nation Army'. Freddie had very nearly jumped out of his skin!

'Yeah, said she knows you …'

Gina had apologised for not having rung back sooner. Yes, she knew Karla. Nice girl, Polish she remembered and yes, they may have talked about what had happened with Lanzarote Eruption as that would have been a topic at the time and there may have been mention of Greg along the way, but beyond that there wasn't much else she could add. Not the best of pals, not the worst, more acquaintance.

Had Greg imagined that Karla had made Gina's friendship bigger than it appeared? Whichever way, it hadn't really provided Greg with any truly negative answers he'd been looking for. Gina knew her. Karla hadn't lied.

Two minutes later, after coming off the call with Gina, Greg's phone began the White Stripes' anthem once again. This time Freddie had moved on within the ground. It was worse news, from Col.

'... he's struggling Greg ...'

Col was keeping a lid on it. Dad was slipping away. The doctors didn't know how long, but his breathing had become more laboured and he wasn't able to communicate very well. Greg asked after mum.

'She's coping ...'

There was no attempt at asking Greg to come back, no pressure.

'Crap timing this, just before your game ...'

Greg suddenly felt drained from his afternoon delight, from his incoming calls and was emotionally spent.

'... there's no way you could get back now if he goes in the next hours. There's nothing you can do anyway ... I just wanted to let you know ... you know ...'

Greg had felt stressed about leaving them in Byron Bay, not over-stressed, but enough for it to be another thing in his life that wasn't right. Not sufficient to drop it all and get back with Col and his parents. But it didn't help. He had started thinking again about Karla, the women on the plane, the warning to get out of his room. He'd had a cracking afternoon with Karla and Gina's comments about her hadn't been negative. Let it go. He had a game to play.

CHAPTER 29

Zoe had enjoyed the most sensual, entertaining and at times energetic afternoon with her host, which had started in the pool and had transferred to the bedroom where both had enjoyed exploring each other in tenderness and mutual affection.

They now laid together, sated.

Zoe and her host had flirted over social media, phone and by text but this had been their first time together. She had harboured hopes it would be this good.

For Zoe this was now time to find out more about this woman. She felt as though she had already known her through their WhatsApp video chats and Zoom calls but had felt that something this intimate might have created more of a bond.

'Why did you do it?'

Zoe was propped up by one elbow with her left hand cradling the left-hand side of her chin and her hand supporting her left cheek.

This suddenly didn't seem right. Why was she asking? But then a lot of people in Zoe's world in organising the World Cup hadn't seemed totally right all the time either. Bob Rudd being one of those.

She'd been used to the machinations of business, being reliant upon deals being made and ideals having to be diluted in order that other parties got what they wanted.

Zoe had wanted this to be the biggest, most inclusive sport event in the world. She had her high ideals, but in order to meet them she had had to enlist others, others who could cut through all of the problems, find her solutions.

Ultimately, these people had not become involved for altruistic reasons but to line their own pockets.

Zoe wasn't unaware this would be the case. She wasn't naïve. She had seen things happen in business before, but the past three months, as the tournament had been getting closer, had seen everything escalate beyond her wishes.

This woman had been in her camp over 'The Pink' and had made things happen.

At first Zoe had been so taken with the support she had been receiving, which hadn't been forthcoming in other quarters, that she had been blind to someone using her hopes and dreams, in her name, and creating something she would never have intended. Is that what this beautiful, alluring woman had done?

Zoe wanted things so badly, for the tournament, but not that much that she would have gone to the extreme lengths that it now seemed her host had gone to, in her name.

Her host looked her straight in the eye, winked at her, smiled and then slid out of the bed and picked up her drink. She walked over to the window, looking out towards the ocean from Paradise Beach.

'*Did I say I'd done anything?*'

She smiled again at Zoe. She took a long slow drag on her cocktail. She turned again to the ocean.

'*Bob Rudd was a chancer. He thought he had it all worked out. He thought he had you in his pocket …*'

She turned again to Zoe, who had purposely stayed where she was in bed.

Zoe didn't want to give her host any impression that she was particularly uneasy about anything. In her heart, Zoe wanted that with this woman again and again, regardless of anything.

'*I'm not a murderer, Zoe …*'

Zoe's host came back towards the bed, seductively sliding her body in alongside the former Olympic athlete. She whispered into Zoe's ear as she nuzzled into her.

'*… but I know how to look after those I care about …*'

Zoe closed her eyes as her host began taking her to another world once more. This was what she had craved for, someone to fulfil her desires.

She knew, in the small recesses of her mind, that she might be being taken in by this woman but by the next few seconds Zoe was past caring. This would do for now.

CHAPTER 30

Sela Natavanu was a man on the march back to power. He had been prime minister before Winston Sablan and had been swept out of government on the back of a political crisis that had seen several in his government accused of having embezzled funds that should have gone to getting the country back on its feet after major cyclone damage.

He'd since managed to amass a huge fortune that nobody really knew how.

There were plenty of theories. The common ones had included sex and drugs.

Sela's return to the political landscape was to be achieved through his daughter Nene Natavanu. Nene was bright, ambitious and her father's daughter in all respects.

They were Ni-Vanuatuans, part of the island nation's indigenous population, and wanted the best for their Melanesian ethnic groups. Getting a woman elected was no easy task.

'Mr Natavanu. Detective Superintendent Erin Jackson of the Australian Federal Police Authority. My colleague Detective Razni. We are conducting inquiries into the murder of Bob Rudd. The body that was found on Erakor Island?'

Erin had made the decision to go straight to Natavanu's palatial residence of Paradise Beach Estate. Marlon had been establishing links that Rudd had had on the island and Rudd had met with Natavanu on several occasions.

Marlon had found the connection with Sela Natavanu via accessing Rudd's office in Australia. They'd found his flight arrival time into Port Vila. Marlon had checked with Bauerfield, Port Vila's airport. Rudd had landed ten days ago.

Security cameras had captured the moment when he had left the airport where he had been picked up by the driver of a silver-grey Mercedes. Natavanu's driver.

'Tragic news, inspector.'

Sela Natavanu didn't exactly look beset with heartache.

He had anticipated a call at some stage but had expected it to be Danford. The Australian Federal Police Authority involvement was another level, but he wasn't fazed.

'You knew Mr Rudd?'

Sela answered without hesitation. He appeared relaxed, happy to give an explanation of his relationship with Rudd.

'We were businessmen conducting business interests. I was instrumental in bringing the World Cup games here through providing the necessary funding Bob required. A great coup for our nation, an opportunity for us to show the world our beautiful country.'

They were sitting on luxurious garden sofas that looked out to the ocean. Detective Razni, Marlon, was next up to the plate with a question.

'How hard?'

Natavanu acted as though he either hadn't heard properly or hadn't understood.

'How hard did you have to 'work' ...'

Marlon didn't buy this businessman routine.

'How much did it cost you Mr Natavanu? How much was Mr Rudd holding you to ransom? And why? Why was he able to?'

Sela Natavanu was calm, assured.

'Detective, I would like to say I have no idea where you're heading with these questions, but I believe you may be under some misapprehension over who I am and what I can influence ...'

Marlon was about to wade in once again, but Erin raised her arm slightly towards Natavanu while rising from the sofa.

'Mr Natavanu. Thank you. You have been most generous with your time.'

Sela nodded. Erin motioned for Marlon to leave too. They reached the side of the house where they would make their way around to their vehicle. Erin turned back to Natavanu.

'Enjoy the game ...'

Erin had chosen to leave without giving any greater hassle. Marlon had played his role well in the good-cop, bad-cop routine they had adopted.

CHAPTER 31

'Good evening Australia, New Zealand, Papua New Guinea and the rest of the world from Port Vila Municipal Stadium on Efate, one of Vanuatu's island archipelago on an historic night for their people and their national rugby league team.'

Channel 17's anchor for the evening was Sydney-born Brandi Hurrell and she was bigging up the game which for her had special significance.

'I have special memories of Efate and Espiritu Santo, the two most populated islands, as my mum's family came from Vanuatu. The people here are so friendly and we have been warmly welcomed by everyone.'

Brandi then changed from bright and upbeat to sincere and sobering to acknowledge the previous day's events on the island.

'But firstly, we must not forget that the past 24 hours has seen tragedy in the murders of prime minister Winston Sablan and well-respected local woman Lena Kalotiti, in addition to the news that Rugby League World Cup finance director Bob Rudd's body has also been identified on Erakor Island. There will be a minute's silence before the game tonight in their memory.'

'This is it boys.'

The team had been out on the park running their drills with the coaching staff, practising the high-bomb, kicks, grubbers, checking out the playing surface. The crowd had responded. And for a small ground, even an hour before kick-off, it was packed to the limit and beyond.

Greg had been looking all around the ground and there wasn't a gap anywhere in the stands. They'd been told that the capacity had been raised to 10,000 for the game from a previous best of around 5,000 when Vanuatu had welcomed Fiji as a warm-up game. Spectators were still arriving. A big screen had been installed just outside the ground and another in Port

Vila near the market place. Thousands who couldn't get tickets would watch there.

Shane Chislett continued his preparatory words for his opening game in charge of a World Cup team as coach. He'd played in two World Cups previously.

'*Complete your sets. Make good field position. Tackle hard. I know this all sounds basic, but it is exactly what is needed. You are all playing at a higher level week-in, week-out than any of this team BUT you should know never to underestimate ANY team …*'

Chislett looked around at his players.

'*This is their World Cup Final. Dane (Mitchell) will be firing them up for it and with that crowd, their players will be elevated two or three levels above their usual standard.*'

Chislett now turned directly to Greg. He let fly!

'*And I will not fucking tolerate ANY ignorance of my orders!*'

Sod the mild-mannered approach, Chislett had been simmering over this, and he was now ready to fire off both barrels.

'*Duggan, you fucking idiot! What the hell were you doing screwing around this afternoon?*'

Chislett was in Greg's face now, Chislett's face now red with rage. Greg gave no answer apart from the look of astonishment written all over his face.

'*You're dropped. To the bench. Give you time to reflect on how important this game is to you. And think yourself bloody lucky you're not out of this tournament completely already.*'

Chislett turned back to the rest of his charges. He let his rage dissipate slightly.

'*You see, it's all about control … self control …*'

He gave another sideways glance at Greg.

'*Now let's get out on that paddock and control this game.*'

Brandi Hurrell made the announcement as she received the news through her earpiece.

'*… and there has been a last-minute change to the England team … Greg Duggan, who only joined the England squad earlier a couple of days ago and was all set to start will be on the bench …*

there was no indication of any pulled muscle or complication when he was on the field warming up earlier, so we can only assume it is a tactical switch ...'

As Brandi asked her panel of rugby league experts to give their thoughts Greg was caught up in his own.

How had Chislett found out? How had he known? So far as Greg was aware Chislett and the other coaches were in another part of the hotel.

Who had shopped him? Did he have anyone in the squad who'd felt they'd had their noses pushed out in some way because he was there?

Shit! He remembered now that he'd been so consumed with the phone calls he'd received from Col and Gina and how they had scrambled his brain that he hadn't called Kyle.

It was only minutes before going out on to the park, or in Greg's case on to the bench. Kick-off time in Port Vila was 7pm, which meant it would be close to 9am back home. He still had time. In fact, the timing might be spot on. Kyle might just be having his breakfast before heading off for his game with Diane.

'The sound in this little ground is deafening!'

Commentator Brad Kearns was struggling to make himself heard over the hubbub that had greeted the Vanuatu players as they had appeared on the pitch. He continued with his own decibel level increased.

'We are 2000 kilometres north-west of Brisbane in the South Pacific and I cannot hear myself speak, so I hope you can hear me back home or wherever you are watching ... last night the competition began with a phenomenal win for Wales against the Green & Golds ... it's not what any Aussie would have wanted, but it was fantastic for the tournament ... I'm not suggesting lightning will strike twice in this opening Group B game but you just don't know ...'

The England team also came out to a big reception. Thousands of England supporters had made the journey, first from the UK to Australia and then the additional three-and-a-half-hour flight to Port Vila.

'*Laurie, what can we expect in these opening minutes? Will Vanuatu be able to draw on this crowd and go hard for the opening twenty minutes? Or will England aim to steamroller over them in the same time? Have you ever heard a noise like this before?*'

Laurie Northey had played NRL, Super League and international rugby league. He was Brad Kearns' summariser for the evening and chuckled along with Brad's final comment.

'*Aww mate, probably not as loud as this in such a small ground but it reminds me of the PNG Stadium in Port Moresby. The people there just love their national sport and here, well it is something really special to be here tonight … how I think it will start? I don't know, but this crowd has got to be worth something to their team.*'

From cacophonous sound to silence was achieved in the matter of a split second. The minute's silence was impeccably observed by the whole crowd. There were tears for Winston Sablan but far more were shed for Lena Kalotiti and pretty much none for Bob Rudd.

The respective national anthems were played as the Vanuatu side, bedecked in their colours of lime green, gumdrop green, black and red, with a daub of yellow, stood to one side of the match officials and the England players in white shirts with the red St George's cross emblazoned across their chests to the other.

Brad Kearns was still smarting, as every Aussie was, from the previous evening's result. He couldn't help but mention it again in his run-up to the kick-off.

'*On paper everything points to this being a walk in the park for the England team but we all know what happened last night. Australia bombed against Wales. Who would have seen that one coming? And England lost to Nieu in their last international before this comp. This crowd would just go wild if their heroes were to score early.*'

Greg's mental state could not have been much worse at the moment.

As he sat with the other interchange players he knew his focus should have been on the game, watching, so that when he came on he could have an influence, but he wasn't finding it easy. Kyle, his dad, Susie, plus what had been happening over the last couple of days. The women on the plane, the call in his room in Brisbane, Karla. He wasn't over-bothered about the dressing down from Shane. He'd made a swift apology as the team had left the dressing room. Shane was right, he knew.

Brad Kearns was enjoying being at the helm on commentary duty at Port Vila.

'Listen to that roar! I'm coming here again! Book me in for the next match here already, I love these people in their greens and blacks and reds … and we're under way!!'

Vanuatu's full-back Zac Santo kicked off high into the early evening sky and the roar reached yet new levels of intensity.

The ball hung in the air for what seemed like at least a second longer than normal and the extra 'hang time' allowed the galloping, enthusiastic Vanuatu speedsters to put immediate pressure on the England team.

Winger Potefa Tanna and centre Tony Soromon were arriving on the scene just inside the England 20-metre line as England full-back Aaron Fielding launched himself in the air, but beating them both was 16 stones of muscle in the form of second row forward Sitivani Kato who had flown into the sky marginally before Fielding.

It was a flight path destined to end with devastating impact but somehow the airborne missile that was Kato contorted, so that his back was now to the England line, stretched out an elongated arm and palmed the ball back towards the nation's most gifted player Ben Mara.

Ben Mara ran straight on to the ball without losing step, sidestepped the England defence, went straight through the gap and touched down under the posts.

The crowd, already super-hyped, were delirious – Brad Kearns was in commentary dreamland!

'Kato was Superman. Eight point nine seconds! We are not even ten seconds into the game and Emerging Nation status Vanuatu playing their first ever World Cup Finals group game and against one of the favourites for this comp are ahead!

'I cannot hear myself think let alone speak here at Port Vila! That was absolutely off the chart!'

Zac Santo slotted over the conversion and it was Vanuatu 6 England 0.

'Australia last night, maybe England tonight, what price a New Zealand failure tomorrow. I'm telling you – this tournament looks like being thrill a minute – or second!'

While Brad Kearns was losing himself in an orgy of rugby league frenzy Greg was already lost in his own world of loss – losing his dad was becoming even more real, losing his son was getting closer if he didn't do something about it, losing Susie looked nailed on and if it wasn't why the hell had he just slept with Karla?

His head was spinning as the crowd erupted once again.

'Vanuatu to receive the ball from an England kick-off to resume this game. Aaron Fielding kicks the ball nearly as high as his counterpart Santo, but it's a longer kick and there's not the same time for the onrushing England players to replicate Vanuatu's move.'

This time it was ex-Queensland Cup player Antony Marango who was underneath the ball as it fell. Keen to make an impact Vinny Venus and Troy Whittingham were on him before he could make yardage, but Marango was no slouch and had a real ball-handling brain.

As he attempted to break free he saw his brother Peter in space and tucked it away to him out of the back of his hand. Peter had never made it across the ocean to try his hand in higher grade but he'd been Vanuatu's hooker for the past seven years and could spot a gap.

Peter Marango went through a flat-footed England line, in between a despairing Billy Ecktenstall and Owen Fenchurch, and the crowd went wild again.

'The Marango brothers have carved something out of nothing here and Vanuatu are already on the halfway line where Peter Marango is hauled to the ground by a brilliant tackle from Freddie South.'

Urged on by a now baying crowd who were enjoying every moment the Vanuatu players found extra energies, greater speed of thought and turn of pace than some had ever imagined. Straight in behind Peter Marango at the play-the-ball was scrum-half Dom Spokeyjack, another ever present in the side over the past seven years.

Dom feigned to go right, took the ball past second row forward Big Mick Green and passed the ball out of the palm of his hand to Port Vila-born Jayson Kaloros. The centre showed the quickest of hands to feed the ball straight on to his wing partner, 18-year-old Samuel Timatua who moved electrifyingly quickly next to the touchline.

Vinny Venus was on his way, covering from the other side of the field to assist Jericho Pallagi. It was as though Timatua had wings as he leapt with ball in one hand over Pallagi and with an outstretched arm landed it safely and fairly inside the try line.

'This is astounding! If you're watching at home or wherever you are and if you haven't watched our amazing sport before, this is just something amazing! ... young Samuel Timatua has just rewritten the international history books. He's just gone over for the fastest second try ever recorded in international rugby league history!'

Clocked at one minute and twenty-five seconds Samuel Timatua's try took the Vanuatu lead out to 10-0, but with a tricky conversion attempt from way out on the touchline this time Zac Santo missed.

England hadn't had the ball in their hands, apart from placing it on a kicking tee to kick off which they were now undertaking again. It was a nightmare start.

Shane Chislett was unflappable. There were no histrionics from him. He hadn't anticipated being two tries down after two minutes, but he knew there were another seventy-eight to go and that the game would yet change.

'And this crowd is going totally bananas! I hope they've enough supplies of their local liquor kava because if it carries on like this Port Vila is going to be rocking well into the night!'

Laurie Northey hadn't been able to get in too much in the opening minutes as Brad Kearns had sent his commentary, a little like the Vanuatu performance, into a new stratosphere.

He took his turn now.

'Look, we know England are a good team and they're going to come back in this game when they get the ball in hand, but for these countrymen and women who have come from all the islands to be here, what a special night. Even if they stopped the game now this will be something to tell their children and grandchildren in years to come.'

Brad was having none of the years to come bit.

'Come on Laurie! This is the here and now. This game is about belief, it's about heart, it's about shocks and twists and turns. It was Australia's nightmare last night, tonight it's England under the pump. Wowee! I love this game of ours!'

Sela Natavanu was as enthused as the rest of the Vanuatu supporters.

Natavanu had hired the portable grandstand seating that now ran the full length of the 100 metres opposite the grandstand side. He'd also hired further portable grandstand seating to both ends of the ground; and had filled in the gaps at both ends of where the permanent grandstand finished. Taking up one corner of the ground there was now an immaculate looking three-storey building that would become a gymnasium after the World Cup but presently gave a magnificent view of the ground from its third tier with hospitality facilities.

It looked tremendous in its regalia of green, black and red – Vanuatu's national flag colours. Sela Natavanu had ambitions for his island nation's progress in years to come and this, plus the portable grandstand seating, which he had already decided would not find its way back to the Australian hirer, were all within his plans to put Vanuatu even more on the sporting map. Nena could take the credit. He would simply enjoy.

Sela's guests included those who had supported him when he had been prime minister and business colleagues from the islands. They also included a neighbour who had been hosting the Rugby League World Cup chief executive.

Zoe had chosen to come out of hiding. She couldn't stay out of sight forever. She had been kept under wraps by her sensual host at Paradise Beach and had been ghosted into Sela's game-day hospitality building courtesy of her host's blacked-out Porsche windows.

Greg's head was truly a shed. He was watching the game, but not watching. One of those stares that made it look as though he was intent on the game but in reality he was as far away from it as he could be.

He was passed a water bottle. He took it without thinking. There was a whisper.

'Don't look back. Look underneath.'

What? What the hell? He took a drink first, it was welcome. He put his hand to the underside of the container which felt as though there was something taped to it. He loosened the tape and put what was taped into the side pocket of his England zip jacket.

Seconds later, without turning his head to check looking at anyone, he took it out of his pocket with his hand faced down but his thumb holding what had been taped. He turned it over. It was a very short note. He put it back in his pocket.

'Ohh, that's another superb sidestep by Ben Mara! He's gone clean through the would-be tacklers and he's offloaded a fabulous pass to Benaminio Finau who is tackled well by England's Big Mick Green. Vanuatu are back in possession after a period where England have been working their way back into this game Laurie.'

'That's right Brad. Vanuatu couldn't keep up the pace of that frenetic start. England are coming back into it now. You can sense they're rediscovering their mojo with some terrific ball handling and completing their sets. You can see they are not panicking, just trying to get in the groove.'

Dane Mitchell had worked hard with his team, getting them into shape. He knew all about the intensity of big games with big crowds and this really was a big crowd for his players. The official capacity with all of the new, hired-in seating was around 6,500 but everywhere there were spectators shoehorned into the ground and it wouldn't at all have been a surprise if it was over double that figure.

Hardly a big crowd in relative terms to Stadium Australia

but for Port Vila, Efate and Vanuatu a tremendous crowd. Mitchell knew that would work in his favour while they were leading and help if they went behind, but he had also known that it would generate a nervous excitement among his players that weren't used to it, and that it would be energy-sapping later on – regardless of the adrenaline.

That was why at 20 minutes into the game he began his interchanges. Spelling the big guys was his first move. Bong Spokeyjack, Dom's much larger brother, came on in place of Alfia Taiwia; and Azariah Tangis for Andrew Nickiau.

Shane Chislett didn't follow suit. He wanted his starting 13 to get into the game, take a proper hold. He'd seen enough underdogs start well and then fade as the favourites took control. His feeling was that they had got themselves into this mess and it was their duty to get them back out.

Greg was relieved that Shane hadn't made the same call as Mitchell.

'And there's the first quality move from England … it's Freddie South who has made the bust, between Soromon and Kato. They're two big fellas but Freddie, who's had a good spell with the Roosters in the NRL was too clever for them there. He sold them both the dummy and he's charging into the Vanuatu half.

'Zac Santo and Peter Marango have him, but still he travels. Bong Spokeyjack has joined the party here. He's shrugging them off as though they're nothing, but they are all big men. Ooof! That's got to send him down. It's a juddering tackle from Benaminio Finau. And he's finally going … ohh, but not before he puts out an arm and flips the ball out!'

Brad Kearns was in raptures over what the big England prop forward had just achieved.

Stu Wainwright took the ball and quick of thought and deed he darted off his right foot, round the back of South and his Vanuatu melee, and looked to straighten up. As he looked, jinked and made as though to pass he saw, out of the very corner of his eye, a galloping Vinny Venus itching for the ball to be played.

'And Wainwright has moved so fast there that the Vanuatu

defence is caught for numbers … ohhhh! What a pass!! He's floated it straight into the arms of Vincent Venus and it's perfect timing. Try time, England! The Eruption pair combine yet again, as they have done now for the past three seasons for their club.'

Brad Kearns privately feared the worst for Vanuatu, even though they still held the lead, which was cut to 10-6 when Aaron Fielding slotted over the conversion in front of the posts.

'Vanuatu may have shipped their first points but full credit to this crowd! They are enjoying themselves. It's a carnival atmosphere.'

The next ten minutes followed an increasingly familiar pattern. England making good yardage with the ball in hand and setting up good positions without getting the ball over the line – and Vanuatu sticking to their guns, but not making as much yardage as the England players.

At the half-hour mark, and sticking to his game plan, Dane Mitchell brought on fresh legs in the shape of Daniel Smith and Jason Natou. Daniel was the son of an English businessman who had settled in Vanuatu for tax purposes; Jason came from Vanuatu's furthest-flung, most southerly populated island, Anatom. They replaced Tony Soromon and Jayson Kaloros.

Greg again looked Shane Chislett's way. The England coach was in consultation with his staff. It looked like they were discussing a change.

'Cloudsdale, Parkin – you're on!'

The announcement had come from Chislett.

'And it's a first interchange from England with two big fellas John Cloudsdale and Philip 'The Butcher' Parkin coming on to relieve Mason Bell and Big Mick Green. Still no sign of playmaker Duggan, Laurie?'

While Laurie Northey responded to Brad Kearns, Greg breathed a huge sigh of relief and rested back. Barring an injury in the ten minutes before half-time he wouldn't be used.

Another five minutes passed with both sides running up the ball hard and England still edging the field position. It had been a hard-fought first half.

Everything changed with four minutes to go before the break.

CHAPTER 32

The ball had been spiralled high into the now early evening sky by the boot of Zac Santo off the last tackle in Vanuatu's latest set. It hung for even longer than his first kick in the game. Underneath it was the capable Aaron Fielding for England.

Zac Santo, having executed the kick, was taken out late, just a split second late with the perpetrator being an eager-to-impress free-running Lanzarote player John Cloudsdale. He'd just come on, was fired up and had gone in hard.

After what had been a great first half for him, Zac was now presently on another planet.

But that was only part of the tale.

Aaron Fielding, who had been underneath the ball as it hurtled back downwards had been similarly taken out. It was another interchange player also looking to make his mark who had inflicted the damage – Bong Spokeyjack.

Bong had leapt marginally later than Aaron, but the crunch that was heard as head met chin was shattering. Blood appeared instantly on Bong, but was largely from Aaron.

All four players were down.

The next moments were chaos.

The ball hadn't been spilled from Aaron Fielding's grasp. He and Bong Spokeyjack had had their eyes firmly fixed on its descent and as their heads smashed together the ball had hit Fielding and Spokeyjack in turn as it had come down on the England 20-metre line.

The medics from both nations were off like sprinters from the sidelines fearing the worst. Both players had been at least two feet in the air when it had happened and had little control over where they landed – and in Aaron Fielding's case the second impact was when his head crashed to the ground, jarring his neck and sending another splintering sound through his body.

The crowd, so wrapped up in the game, saw the players go

down, but also saw the ball tumbling away.

It was Ben Mara who reacted quickest of them all and he hacked the ball on towards the England try line. The Vanuatu supporters were urging Mara on, Sam Rivers and Stu Wainwright were covering as fast as they could.

In a matter of seconds the pitch had become part battleground with wounded men; part euphoria with Ben Mara going over and landing downward pressure on the ball to score; and part apoplectic with England players who felt the referee Cory Jones of New Zealand should have immediately called a halt to play.

Greg was more immediately concerned that he would be called upon to come on for Fielding who, along with Santo, was out cold. He would normally have been just waiting for his chance to explode on to a game, but not right now.

It was pandemonium on the pitch. Verbals were flying, the medics were doing their best to attend to all four players who were all currently prostrate.

'And New Zealand referee Cory Jones has awarded the try! … or has he? … Is he going to the screen for confirmation? … First concern must surely go to the health of Aaron Fielding and Bong Spokeyjack. They both look spark out.'

Brad Kearns was attempting to keep up with everything.

'Yeah Brad, just looking at the other two – Zac Santo and John Cloudsdale – who also went down. Santo is back sitting up now, but Cloudsdale, who was the villain in their clash by being just too late arriving, seems to have copped it far worse …'

Laurie Northey was doing his level best at assisting Kearns with handling the drama that was unfolding from the two collisions.

'You're right mate, looks like Cloudsdale hasn't come out of it too clever, he looks in immense pain. Ohh, just look at his face! Santo, meanwhile, looks a bit groggy and wondering what day it is … but the other two guys is where there is real concern …'

'Oh no. I don't like this …'

Laurie Northey had seen the face of one of the medics.

'I've never seen a medic in as much shock on the footy field as

I've just seen there. This looks really bad ...'

'Yeah. Let's hope it all looks far worse than it actually is. Here's the playback now, ohh ...'

Brad Kearns refrained from sensationalising any further. He continued relaying the information as best he could.

'Bong Spokeyjack is also in a bad way, but it seems nowhere near as bad as Aaron Fielding.'

On field, referee Corey Jones had rightly become more concerned with the players' welfare than the scoreline.

The initial hubbub over whether the try was to stand had been quelled as players and officials from both teams calmed themselves. Drinks were liberally distributed. For once the crowd had hushed, understanding the seriousness of the situation.

Greg looked at what had been passed to him once again.

'Fielding's moving. They're going very carefully with him and rightly so ... there's still a great deal of concern out there, lot of arms flailing about ... Spokeyjack's up on his haunches ... that's a better sign ...'

While Brad Kearns had been concentrating on the battered and broken, Laurie Northey had spotted the next action.

'There's movement in the crowd down by the far corner, Brad, between the temporary grandstands where there have been so many standing ...'

'Yeah, it looks like they're trying to bring an ambulance through and on to the pitch.'

In the ensuing minutes Vanuatu's Zac Santo and Bong Spokeyjack left the field of play, assisted by medics, to applause from the crowd; with John Cloudsdale stretchered off and Aaron Fielding taken straight to Port Vila Hospital. The crowd reaction also being one of huge applause.

Finau and Nickiau came back on for Vanuatu. Charlie Cole made his first appearance and Mason Bell reappeared, leaving Greg as the only player not to have played a part in the first half, unless he was suddenly called upon in the next three minutes.

Greg couldn't believe that he'd been left sidelined. He'd expected Chislett to use him after the injuries to Fielding and

Cloudsdale, but he hadn't. Why? Surely Chislett couldn't have been that pissed with him? But maybe so.

Brad Kearns couldn't believe the try had been given!

'*And after all that, the referee has gone back to the try line and has quite simply awarded Ben Mara and Vanuatu the try!*'

'*He's not even gone to the screen. There were no red cards, yellow cards or putting players on report. We all know that Mr Jones likes to keep the game flowing and is extremely lenient, but really? No cards? Giving the try without going upstairs to the big screen?*'

The decision reignited the spectators.

Vanuatu were now 14-6 up and it was Antony Marango who slotted over the conversion, taking over kicking duties from Zac Santo. The game restarted at 16-6 to Vanuatu after a ten-minute break.

Three minutes later it was half-time. It had been straightforward play since the resumption with both sides easing their way back into the game.

The half-time interval set the whole crowd bouncing along to the sunshine sound of Ni-Vanuatu songstress Vanessa Quai and her band playing her reggae infused YouTube hit 'Life Is Good' which the Vanuatu supporters sang along to as though it was their team's anthem.

The England fans and those of other nations who had come over for the game caught the mood. 'Beautiful Day' was next up, before her last number that had the crowd smiling and singing along once again.

Vanessa had rapper Hip Tuta join her on stage for 'Light It Up' at which point from nowhere thousands of glow-sticks appeared. They'd all been taped on the underside of the seats and Vanessa engaged the crowd by telling them they all had a special gift to light up their lives, the game and to hold them up for the swift return of England player Aaron Fielding.

Vanuatu's princess of pop had proved the perfect half-time for the crowd at the game and judging by the immediate response at the ground and online there would be many more views of her YouTube channel.

Greg had been relieved he'd not been called upon earlier in the first half, but why hadn't Shane Chislett put him on at the end of the half? But the note he'd read? Maybe that was the reason? Did Chislett know?

'DO NOT come on until after the 50th minute,' had been the instruction on the bottle.

What the hell was this all about?

'If this is what it's like all the time in Vanuatu book me in!'

These were the words of Brad Kearns as the World Cup on Channel 17 came back after an ad break.

'Wonderful songs from Vanessa Quai, amazing support from the islanders and a team that is performing way above expectation. Laurie, it's all looking good, good, good ...'

Laurie Northey acknowledged Greg's nod to Vanessa's lyric from 'Life is Good' and also praised the people of Vanuatu before Brad passed over the baton to pitchside reporter Karen Stonehouse who had news from both teams.

'Brad, let's start first with Aaron Fielding. We are told he's now in a bed in the hospital in Port Vila awaiting news on an X-ray to his jaw and a brain scan. He's concussed, but the good news is he is now talking and sitting up ... Vanuatu's Bong Spokeyjack is not concussed but his head injury means he will also play no further part in this game ... better news for Vanuatu's Zac Santo ... he will be back on-field at some point in this second half, but bad news for John Cloudsdale for England who will go in to hospital for tests on his back and left hip after this game ... that means England are down two players from their available seventeen ...'

It all pointed to Greg coming on, certainly sooner rather than later. Could he delay his entrance if he was called before the clock went to 50 minutes? What would happen if he didn't? Was he back in the middle of something once again? What the hell was going on?

Vanuatu came out for the second half to a magnificent reception from their supporters all crammed into the stands. It looked as though there were at least two people to every seat.

'This crowd seems to be growing every time you look across the

ground ...'

Brad Kearns' assessment wasn't wrong. The first-half performance and the mini-Vanessa Quai concert at half-time had brought even more. Everyone wanted to be in and no matter how. Brad returned to the game itself.

'Can they do it? Can they beat England, Laurie?'

'Aww mate, who can say? This next 40 will give us the answer, but I'll tell you this. If their noses are ahead with a minute to go or if they need a score by then, this crowd will do all it can.'

It was England to kick off the second half. They had only two interchange players left on their bench – Billy Ecktenstall, who'd played the first half hour; and Greg, as yet unused.

Zoe Miller was enjoying herself. She still had questions that needed answering, but being here in the South Pacific, watching a game that she had played a part in bringing to the islands was vindication of her efforts these past months.

The opening to the second 40 minutes was just as loud as the first half, but without the amazing on-field scenes. Dane Mitchell had been a wily campaigner in his playing days and had known when to press the accelerator pedal and when to watch the opposition do it. He'd told his charges to be prepared for an upping of the tempo from England in the second half.

Dane's one concern had been when his team reached the hour mark. That last twenty minutes of the game was when fit, professional teams usually imposed themselves more greatly.

Dane and his coaching team had done all they could with the players that included farmers, fishermen, tradesmen and salesmen, but he knew a time might come when they would have to dig deeper than they'd perhaps ever done before.

The break had recharged both sides and the first eight minutes of the second half saw them cancel each other out, but on the ninth minute, the 49th of the game, Gary Walker, who had replaced Greg in the starting lineup, made his first real break of the night.

He eluded two tacklers and had just Azariah Tangis in front of him. Gary, often the joker in the pack in the dressing room, was not laughing as he turned his ankle over while trying to come off his right foot to go left.

Azariah crashed him to the ground, turning the already sore ankle over again. Walker was in agony. The medics rushed on. This time referee Cory Jones stopped the game as Walker had gone down with the ball in hand. The clock was stopped at 49 minutes 55 seconds.

Greg looked up at the big screen showing the time. How could this be?

If he went on now, would that be okay with whoever had sent him the note? Who had sent it? What would five seconds do? Surely the clock would start even before he came on? How would that make a difference to anything?

Shane Chislett motioned for both Billy Ecktenstall and Greg to warm up while he awaited a signal from the medics on the field. There was a shake of the head and a tumbling roll of hands signalling a change was necessary.

While warming up, Greg looked across to Chislett and saw him look to the screen. He was looking at the clock! No! Chislett couldn't have been involved in the note, could he?

Chislett lifted his chin in Greg's direction and nodded for him to go on.

Greg was stripping off his jacket and making his way towards the official on the line.

What was five seconds to anyone anyway?

The England supporters applauded Gary Walker as he was helped from the field.

Greg was like a singer going on to the stage. When he hit it, it was like a light-bulb moment. He hadn't been properly focused on the game when he'd been on the sidelines but now, stepping on to the park in front of this audience, tightly packed into this little ground thousands of miles into the ocean, Greg was suddenly primed and ready to rock!

CHAPTER 33

He had his mouthguard slightly out of his mouth as he made his way towards Stu Wainwright who was ready to receive the ball at acting half-back, behind the play-the-ball player Owen Fenchurch, who had taken hold of the ball from Gary Walker.

'Just give me that ball Stu!'

Stu didn't need any second bidding. Fenchurch played the ball back to him, the clock began moving from 49 minutes 55 seconds, Wainwright passed the ball straight to a rampaging six-foot-three Duggan who looked his first tackler Alfie Taiwai straight in the eye, stepped slightly and palmed him away as though swatting a fly, destroying another, Sitivano Kato with a brutal hand-off and he was in daylight.

Thirty metres from the Vanuatu line and the England supporters' voices were finally in the ascendancy as they were buoyed by this supercharged man.

'And Greg Duggan has made his presence felt with his first carry of the game, look at this guy go!'

Brad Kearns had seen Super League games but had rarely seen Eruption. Not until now had he realised the power of Greg Duggan in the flesh.

Greg was amazed how easy he had made the bust with his first play. While ever he had been sitting on the bench he hadn't felt up for the game, he'd been lost in all the other thoughts, but now that he was on the park all that mattered was the ball he was carrying.

Brad Kearns was just as fired up.

'This is just what this game needed – and it is certainly what England needed. Ohhh! That's sublime!'

Greg had only Jayson Kaloros to beat in front of him. The young centre had never played against anyone like him before. Greg sashayed his hips, it was enough for Kaloros to stand flat-footed and Greg changed course to go straight in under the posts. Vanuatu 16 England 10.

Greg took absolute control, demanding the kicking tee and slotting over the conversion before anyone else in the team had realised they needed a new kicker as Fielding was no longer on the park. Vanuatu 16 England 12 – after 50 minutes and 22 seconds!

'Now, Laurie, what kind of impact player is that? Greg Duggan has only been on the paddock for 27 seconds!'

Brad Kearns was as enthusiastic as anyone over genuine rugby league talent. He was delighted that the game had taken another dramatic twist.

There was a noticeable change of atmosphere in one part of the ground.

Sela Natavanu had been suddenly incensed. He left his party.

It was now all about Greg. He took the kick-off. No other player on either side had touched the ball in the game since he'd taken the pass from Stu Wainwright.

Greg was a past-master at the laconic. Few words, big deeds. He didn't even tell Stu Wainwright verbally what was to happen next, just prior to kicking off he spread both his hands behind his back. He then approached the ball as though he was going to wallop it high into the floodlit night sky, but five paces into his ten-pace run-up he changed his body shape and instead of lifting the ball high off the tee he kicked it along the floor, following it immaculately to the 10-metre line.

Ben Mara figuratively kicked himself. It was basic stuff. It was the basic stuff you played against teams that were a little naïve or inexperienced. Vanuatu were both.

Before Brad Kearns could draw breath in wonder and amazement at how one man had come on under two minutes ago and totally transformed the course of the game, Greg had retrieved the ball, dummied Benjaminio Finau and Samuel Timatua and run back into open space again. Again he was facing the hapless Jayson Kaloros for the second time in just over a minute, who was playing out of position having taken over the full-back role from Zac Santo.

'Wow! Wow! Wow!'

It was all commentator Brad Kearns could say. He shook his head momentarily, looked at his summariser and Laurie Northey and said absolutely nothing. He was totally gobsmacked by what he'd just witnessed inside two extraordinary minutes, before regaining his power of speech and eulogising.

'Breathtaking! Honestly, I just didn't know what to say for a second there. Sometimes words really are not enough. Greg Duggan has single-handedly turned this game on its head! Not one England or Vanuatu player has touched this ball since he took hold of it and he's still holding it now. Just watch the possession stats in a minute. It won't read England 100 per cent – it will read Greg Duggan!'

The clock now showed 51 minutes 35 seconds. Incredible. Greg had gone in under the posts, he'd slotted the conversion over and within thirty seconds he was back kicking off again! Vanuatu 16 England 18.

The home side's supporters were in a state of shock.

Greg placed the ball back on the kicking tee and this time put his hands open behind and widespread behind him and then pressed them down low. Stu Wainwright knew this move, so too did Vinny Venus – and earlier that day Freddie South had been brought up to speed with what was to come.

Ben Mara was watching more intently this time. He knew another move was on.

There was no way Vanuatu were going to fall for another of Greg Duggan's party pieces. Ben Mara howled across at his players, gumshield removed. All of their good work was being undone by one man and he was running his own one-man show.

Brad Kearns had taken a deep breath as Greg had positioned the ball and walked back to commence his run up for the kick. He then pitched back in again.

'Well, here we go again with The Magician! He's cast a spell over this game, that is for sure. What can Greg Duggan do next? … Oh … wow!'

Kearns almost choked on the water he'd just downed,

thinking he had enough time.

Greg was now even controlling his commentary, because Kearns' reaction to what he'd just seen had caused him to half-splutter, half-laugh at Greg's latest outrageous play.

Greg had started out on his approach to the kick, coming at the ball in a slight arc from the left with all of the impression being that it would head over to the right side of the field. A normal play.

But in the course of his run-up – and just two metres before launching his boot at the ball – he altered course and, keeping his balance, managed to wing the ball up high to the left, high and hanging and again short enough that his teammates were to now join the Duggan party.

Ben Mara's team had been left flat-footed again. It was a move Greg had only used once before, when playing junior rugby league. He'd remembered about it when he'd watched Kyle play, although he'd used it when he was about 13 and the success of his previous kick-off he'd been inspired to give it a go.

'Duggan's put it up high and look at this charge on the left-hand side of the field. These guys knew this move was on. It's another unique kick-off. Welcome to the Greg Duggan Masterclass everybody!

'... and it's Freddie South, one of the other new recruits, who has claimed the ball just over 10 metres into the Vanuatu half with their players struggling to engage in anything like a tackle since Greg came on. South has taken it up to the Vanuatu 30-metre line before he has a hand laid on him. Antony Marango has made ground, and now he has him, but South has slipped he ball out one-handed and basketball style to Stu Wainwright who scampers past Sitivani Kato and Tony Soromon, angles his run across field and sends an immaculate kick through on the floor for winger Vincent Venus to pick it up just before the line and touch it down behind the posts! Wow! Try!!!!'

Greg slotted over the conversion again, approximately 53 seconds after having done so previously.

'Vanuatu 16 England 24! I don't think I have ever seen a game change so rapidly. Just under four minutes ago this England team

was losing by 10, they're now ahead by 8. And I'll say it again. One man has changed the whole course of the game.'

Once again Greg kicked off, back to the now shell-shocked Vanuatu in their green, black and red.

The Vanuatu crowd was now properly hushed for the first time in the game, but the England supporters were dancing in the stands and making up for the islanders' disappointment.

Greg's kick-off this time was a more regulation affair. There were only so many tricks he could pull out in one game.

Potefa Tanna collected Greg's kick on the Vanuatu 20-metre line, this time there were no rampaging England players only a yard off, steaming in. Tanna had enough time to catch, reset and charge the ball up.

Tanna was Efate born-and-bred and from Port Vila. He was the man who scored all the tries for his home club and was eager to get Vanuatu back in the game. As he upped the gears before reaching the tackle of six-foot-four and mass of ginger-haired Billy Ecktenstall, who had just come on for Mason Bell, Tanna tried his trademark step off his right foot that had served him well for the past four seasons and had seen him score several times for his nation. He felt something crack.

There was no way back, he lost all pace in a split second and a juggernaut in the shape of Ecktenstall was heading his way. The Vanuatu crowd gasped in unison.

Out of nowhere Greg appeared and tackled his own player, taking him out sideways.

In the nano-second from seeing what had happened to Tanna, Greg had recognised the impact Billy's force might have on the Vanuatu player, highly likely making his injury far worse.

'I know I keep saying this … but I cannot believe what we've just seen!'

Brad Kearns was starting to think Greg was rewriting rugby league history.

'Greg Duggan has taken out one of his own players … and he's done it to save Vanuatu's Potefa Tanna …'

But there was something else.

'... *aww now, listen to this ... this is something I have never ever witnessed before ... this man, who has just turned around England's fortunes, the man who has ripped the heart out of the Vanuatu team in little under four minutes since he came on is now being cheered and applauded by the Vanuatu supporters ...*'

On the field Greg had been quick to apologise to Billy, who initially wanted to nail him to the nearest wall for what he'd done.

The supporters of both teams had seen what Greg had done and why. Potefa Tanna had gone down clutching the ball and Greg had not only dealt with a rampaging Billy, he had also shielded him from any other onrushing player.

The Vanuatu supporters were on their feet as one!

They had learned Greg's name in the past four minutes, as the speakers around the ground had kept mentioning who had scored.

They now chanted his name in time to Vanessa Quai's 'Life Is Good' changing the lyric to 'Greg is Good'. It flowed. It had a beat. It had rhythm.

Greg couldn't help but smile. He looked all around the ground and applauded the fans in return.

Vanuatu captain Ben Mara came over to him and shook his hand. Some of the others in the team came too while Potefa Tanna was first assessed before he was helped from the paddock.

'*Mate, that was so sporting of you! I don't know how you made the decision to do that so quickly!*'

Greg acknowledged Ben Mara's words with his customary shrug, at doing what had come to him spontaneously. There were tears in Brad Kearns' eyes and a frog in his throat as he expounded.

'*Ladies and gentlemen, you have not just seen a masterclass in these past five minutes, you have also seen a true gentleman of the sport that we all love. Greg Duggan take a bow!*'

Brad Kearns then joined in with a rendition of 'Greg is Good' before his summariser and pundit Laurie Northey suggested that his career remain in commentary rather than singing.

Greg's sportsmanship had uncannily revitalised the Vanuatu crowd who had been so touched by the England player's effort on their own player's behalf that, having sung to Greg, it was as though they had collectively realised their contribution to this World Cup was to be the sunny, happy friendly islands nation and to enjoy everything about being involved.

While the Vanuatu supporters had refound their voices the fortunes of their team were to continue on a downward spiral as the rest of the England team upped their game. The last 25 minutes saw the boys from the northern hemisphere rattle in five more tries, two more to Greg and every try scored converted by him. Vinny had gone over for his hat-trick try with Big Mick Green and Stu Wainwright also scoring.

Full Time: Vanuatu 16 England 54.

'And now, we have Player of the Match, Greg Duggan …'

Pitchside reporter Karen Stonehouse asked Greg whether he'd ever tackled a teammate in a match before. Greg, by now, was typically deadpan about it. It wasn't that big a deal. He shrugged his shoulders.

'I just did what I did.'

Few words, as usual. Greg was more action man than erudite speaker. Karen Stonehouse was determined to make him smile, at the very least.

'… and now you're the star of a reggae tune! You're a Vanuatu hero!'

Greg couldn't help but allow a smile to appear, although he typically didn't let himself go. This time he gave a slight shrug of the shoulders. He really didn't know what to say.

Karen Stonehouse could see he wasn't too forthcoming with the words. She went for one final attempt, still very enthusiastically, unperturbed by Greg's manner.

'You made such an immediate impact tonight Greg, what were you thinking before you came on when your team was 10 points behind?'

Greg shook his head, as though trying to clear it. He shrugged again, a bigger shrug this time. He looked to one side, gathering his thoughts. He gave a smile as he turned back to the camera.

'*I don't think, Karen. I just do. I'm a rugby league player. I'm playing for England. It's an honour. We won, that's all that matters.*'

Greg smiled back at Karen.

Sela Natavanu hadn't returned to the party. He'd been angered. Although it may not have been discernible to many in his party, it had certainly made an impression on Zoe.

Zoe may have enjoyed her day with her host including watching the game with her, while being well looked after by Sela Natavanu's colleagues, but for all that she had enjoyed herself she hadn't bought either her host's words that she hadn't been involved in Bob Rudd's murder.

What she had done, so well she'd thought to herself, was to have kept her anonymity. She'd arrived at Bauerfield having kept her face well covered, except for passport control, had travelled to her host alone and had put on shades and a floppy sunhat to go to the game in the Porsche. There had only been around 15-20 guests in Natavanu's party, none of whom she believed would have recognised her.

Zoe was wrong.

CHAPTER 34

'*Do you know how much that five seconds cost me?*'

It was rhetorical.

'*This man. He's in the way. It's time we took him out of the way.*'

There was no need for reply. It was an instruction, not a matter to be discussed. Action was the only requirement.

Greg was congratulated by everyone in the England changing room on his return from the post-match interview, and when Shane Chislett returned he was also forthcoming in praise but typically northern in not getting carried away.

'*Good work, Greg.*'

He then turned to the rest.

'*That's one win boys, against a team everybody expected us to beat. They're going to expect the same against Greece in three days' time. And so am I. Take it easy tonight and tomorrow morning, then we'll start with some light training in the afternoon. Enjoy your evening.*'

Greg's mind was already elsewhere again.

Kyle! He'd only been able to send a quick text before.

He was about to make the call to Diane, to speak with his son when he noticed he had two missed calls. Col ... and Susie!

At last, was Greg's initial reaction to Susie finally having tried to contact him. He rang Col. It could be the most imminent.

Greg felt hollow as he hit Col's name on his phone. He kept thinking about the days when he and Col were kids, the holidays, what they did, Dad always having a laugh with them.

He wasn't gone.

Col said he had left him a voicemail, but Greg had rung without listening to it. If he had he'd have known. Dad was no worse, no better. They'd watched the game. Col and Mum. It was a really nice call.

Diane was next up. Greg couldn't believe it had been a week already since he'd seen his son make his debut. So much had happened to him in that time.

'They're just about to kick off. The club put on your game in their clubhouse and we've all been watching. It was dire until you came on. You should have heard Kyle cheering you, saying "That's my dad". Well done you.'

Diane's last three words were delivered in a more affectionate way than he'd heard from her in a long while.

Somehow, in Greg's mind, Kyle had brought him back closer to Diane, a little bit more like when they were first together. But she had married Paul and they now had a daughter.

'I'll ring you if he scores or I'll get Kyle to use my phone to ring you …'

Again, Di's words were delivered with affection. Was he missing something here? Was something else going on that he didn't know about? It made him want to ask about Diane and Paul, how they were getting on, but he refrained. It wasn't his place, and he didn't want to get in the way.

Susie was next. Greg had decided that he would listen to any voicemail messages to check on whether she had left one but she hadn't. There was just the message from Col.

He tried. As he was waiting for an answer he almost knew there wouldn't be one. He comforted himself that at least she had rung.

Somehow this gorgeous woman, quite a bit older than him but a stunning, sensuous, sexy blonde, and so far as he'd always been concerned, beautiful in every way inside and out, was always in his heart no matter what else was happening in his life.

Sure, he'd been with other women, even today, but with Susie it had always seemed right, even when it had been wrong.

She hadn't answered. No different to what he'd anticipated. No worries. Maybe she'd call again, but at least now he'd known she'd tried. It was hope, that was all, but it would do for now.

He left a message on her voicemail. It was more affectionate than he'd ever realised he could be. He knew something was wrong.

'Where are you?'

Greg's phone had sprung to life immediately he'd left his

message. He'd looked at the screen of his Samsung to see whether it was any name he'd stored, someone he knew. No name appeared.

It was Karla. The way she'd said the words was as though they had been together years, rather than minutes.

She was either insatiable, clingy or something didn't add up. He was now going for the latter. But he also wanted to know why? Why was she coming on to him all the time? He smiled inwardly. Maybe it was worth exploring her apparent insatiability?

'I'm in your room …'

Christ! How the hell had she managed that again?

'I'm just …'

Greg could feel her seduction already. Her breath was steamy, enticing, intoxicating.

'… waiting … patiently …'

The two smart women on the Airbus; the warning to get out of his hotel room in Brisbane; now this sexy girl all over him on Efate. He didn't know what it all amounted to but there was something.

He hadn't learned much over his lifetime, he mused, but he had learned particularly in the past four years about people not being as they might seem. Karla Karelia certainly fitted into that category. But why? What was she up to?

'Zoe? … Zoe Miller?'

Zoe hadn't wanted to turn at all, as she had known this would blow what she had intended, to remain unknown. She had realised her poster girl status of two decades ago might still give way to recognition even though her face was older and her hair quite different to those days.

She was still at Sela Natavanu's party at the stadium. Nobody had come up to her and said, 'Aren't you …?'

Her role as chief executive for the Rugby League World Cup wasn't one that had particularly propelled her name back in the public eye.

She had felt relatively safe from recognition at the party as at least half of the people there seemed to have probably not been born when she was at the top of her game.

'Detective Superintendent Erin Jackson, Australian Federal Police Authority. Is there somewhere we can talk? Privately?'

Zoe was trying not to look stunned. She had been totally aware that Bob Rudd having been murdered would have consequences for her, at least in that she would be questioned. She was on Efate. She just hadn't been ready right now.

'I remember watching you when I was a little girl.'

Erin was doing her usual thing. An easy-going introduction. Put the interviewee at ease.

Zoe found them a small room on the next level down from where the party was still in full swing. Her host had conveniently disappeared? She'd been around until just before Erin had arrived. It amplified Zoe's suspicions about her.

'I wanted to be like you. Hell, I think we all did. You made running a sexy sport, with your fantastic braided hair and your colourful fingernails … my only problem was I had all that, but not the ability …'

Zoe smiled at Erin graciously. This woman was soft-soaping her, fawning about her. She'd seen it all before from agents to companies wanting to use her to sell something. This cop was working her way through to asking her the questions she had really come along with.

'Why are you here Ms Miller?'

She knew that this question was the hardest for her to answer truthfully. She was here because of Rudd, because of what had happened in Manly … at Broke … but also because of her host. She was here because of …

Erin Jackson was entertained by watching the cogs turn around in Zoe's head. She knew that Zoe would have been sent on the 'Way to speak with Media' courses designed at firing questions back to questions instead of answering directly or answering with a completely different agenda to the question itself.

It was not lost on Zoe that the detective superintendent

had purely used her last name when she'd broken from the childhood memories to her real reason for being there.

'*I'm here for the World Cup, Detective Superintendent.*'

Erin let Zoe have her first answer without questioning, as though she'd accepted it. She went back to the soft soap routine.

'*These islanders gave England a good game I understand.*'

Zoe nodded. The cop wasn't here for the chit-chat. She was just gearing up for the next hit. It came swiftly.

'*Your financial director, Bob Rudd … we're looking into his murder … anything you can tell us?*'

Zoe cocked her head slightly.

'*I'm not sure what you mean, superintendent.*'

Zoe had told herself to stay tight-lipped, let the cop do the running. Now she'd responded quickly to her, too quickly.

Erin took her time, this time.

She'd had a feeling about this ever since Marlon and the rest of the team, in the course of their contacts, had come up with Zoe Miller having disappeared, just gone off-grid, for the past three days; then, in the course of checking the Bauerfield CCTV footage checking for anyone they could, for whatever tenuous link, they had come up with Zoe Miller.

Erin had thought the same as Zoe's initial answer. She was chief executive of the World Cup after all, she had every reason to be here.

But here, and not at the opening ceremony the previous day? Really? And she had made a beeline for Paradise Beach, near to where they now knew Bob Rudd had been a visitor. What wasn't Zoe Miller telling her – and most importantly of all, why?

'*What are you hiding, Zoe?*'

Not sure what she meant, indeed. She backed up her question with another.

'*What is it you know that we don't and why are you not prepared to tell me right now?*'

CHAPTER 35

The England team emerged from the stadium to board their coach.

A huge crowd of both England and Vanuatu supporters had gathered, the reggae tune went up once more, but this time a few of the Vanuatu supporters had convinced their friend, the half-time concert pop star and islands' favourite Vanessa Quai to sing 'Life Is Good,' but as 'Greg Is Good'.

The Vanuatu team came out too, to head back to their camp and prepare for their next game, and the coming together of the supporters, players and music merged to become a street party with everyone involved.

This truly was a friendly island.

Greg wasn't one for blowing his own trumpet, but he could not help himself but sing and dance along with what was going on. He danced with Vanessa Quai as she sang. The local kava was flowing nicely. The Channel 17 and Cloud TV cameras caught the occasion.

This was what Zoe had hoped the World Cup matches being played in different areas in Australia and Oceania would bring about, but right now she wasn't able to enjoy it herself.

'Greg is so good, good, good, Greg is so wonderful, smiles away our pain today, tomorrow'll be a brighter day …'

The whole assembled crowd were now singing along as Vanessa's band, who'd hastily reassembled some of their kit, added to the atmosphere. The England supporters started a conga-train, which the Vanuatu supporters also joined and some of the members of both teams.

Port Vila Municipal Stadium had never known a party quite like it. If ever there had been an advertisement for playing some of the games in a remote location in the South Pacific this was it.

Vanuatu had been given three games to stage on Efate at

Port Vila. The next was to be England again, playing another Emerging Nation qualifier Greece; and finally Vanuatu versus Greece. Vanuatu, England and Greece would all travel to Papua New Guinea for their games against them.

This game had always been nailed on to have been the biggest of the three hosted in Efate, and it had exceeded all the locals' expectations.

Greg had made himself such a hero with that one move where he'd saved Potefa Tanna from further injury that England were almost guaranteed the Vanuatu fans would be on their side against Greece.

'Greg is so good, good, good – Greg is so good, good, good' the rest of the team mocked him on the way back to Breakas about an hour or so later than planned after all the partying.

It seemed that Billy Ecktenstall, the man he'd creamed out of the way to protect the unfortunate Vanuatu winger, was now leading the chorus.

'Dad! Dad! I scored two tries! ...'

Kyle was being prompted by his mother in the background and he was so excited.

'Yeah Mum ... Yes ... I'll tell him ... and Dad, guess what? We won! Like you! ... got to go. Mum's buying crisps and Coke ... Muuuum!!!! ...'

Kyle's voice trailed off in the distance, then came back.

'Bye Dad!! ... You did amazing in your game! You played amazing!! Dad is so good, good, good – Dad is so wonderful!! Bye! ... love you!'

Greg's face couldn't have shown a wider smile than he was giving right now, listening back to Kyle's message while on the coach going back to Breakas. His boy. He was so proud.

He looked again at his phone. There was nothing more. No message from Susie. Nothing more from Byron Bay.

Greg had covered everything. He'd tried to have contact with his son, who had called him back with a great report of his own game, so enthusiastic. He'd kept in touch with Col, about his dad. Susie had tried to get in touch.

And he'd helped England to their first win and unintentionally made himself a hero on the island through one spontaneous decision. Not a bad day.

And now tonight, if she was still there and for however long it lasted, Greg kind of knew that he was stepping into an unknown.

He wanted Susie, but he had Karla. It wasn't the way he would have wanted it to be, despite how sexy Karla was, he would still prefer to be with Susie. If only she could be there, right now, there would be none of this. What was it that she hadn't said? Maybe it was something he hadn't said?

Forget all that. As Susie would have said, 'But you were not available', so too now Greg thought that Susie wasn't either, and this woman was wanting him – and she was there, and she was available, and he was.

He still wasn't at all certain about her, in fact he knew that there was probably enough about her that was not right, but he loved what she was doing to him, how she was enticing him. He knew he was possibly playing with fire.

It was an unknown he was prepared to play along with for the time being and maybe find out more. Why was she so wanting to be with him?

And Greg wasn't wrong about the unknown, when he opened the door to his suite on his return.

CHAPTER 36

'Ssshhhh!'

It was now near to midnight and the hotel was close to darkness apart from wall lights in the corridor. Greg had felt a calmness sweep over him as he had headed for his suite. When he'd opened the door he'd made for turning on some form of lighting.

Karla, it had to be her, but with such a lack of light he couldn't be one hundred per cent certain until he felt her touch, smelled her perfume, her body shape. She glided towards him, guided his hand into hers.

'Come with me. I am going to give you the most fulfilling night you have ever had ...'

She led Greg to the beautiful double king size bed. In the darkness Greg could just make out that Karla was wearing something that looked as though it must be black.

As they moved as one, he felt his hand brush against her side. Flesh. Thigh, hip, bum – and lace material around the hip, attached by what felt like a thin strap. She was walking slowly, clicking on the flooring. Heels.

They reached the bed and Karla made him sit down. She then produced a blindfold, made for sleeping, and in some cases not for sleeping!

'Put this on darling ...'

She breathed with, it seemed to Greg, as much sexually charged intent as possible.

Greg was obedient. He did as he'd been instructed and, he found, with little trepidation except being already concerned about why she was seducing him.

Hell of a way to go though, was one thought that crashed through his mind making him smile at himself.

Bloody idiot, why was he letting her do this? And then, another voice was telling him, 'Go on, enjoy it while you can'.

He was also absolutely aware that an apparently harmless donning of a blindfold might be used against him in some way if he was not careful. He told himself not to get carried away with Karla's explicit attention, which was starting to accelerate.

'Just relax and let me take over ...'

Karla purred.

'You've already had a fantastic, spectacular night ... now I'm just going to send you to another planet ...'

Greg managed to resist the urge to mention the seventh planet from the sun at this point as he didn't want her to think of him as an arsehole.

Yes, he wanted to know what this sexy lady was all about and this way, playing along with whatever her game was, might be his best move. He might have been knackered from his earlier exploits, but this was still welcome.

In nothing more than seconds Greg found himself naked and totally aroused. He was now holding Karla's luscious bum cheeks with his hands just inside her suspender straps as she hovered her southern comfort just above his face before lowering for him to engage. Karla's face, had he been able to see it, would have given Greg cause to smile.

Her eyes were closed. She was in her own Karlaland, cupping her breasts and playing with her erect, upturned nipples as she rode his tongue and lips. It was all proving highly intoxicating for them both, certainly by the murmurs of deep satisfaction coming in waves.

So far as Greg was concerned this was an infinitely better way to find out information than he'd been used to when he'd been caught up in previous problems at Hopton Town and with Lanzarote Eruption – even though he'd actually found out precious little so far.

Karla had been right. Greg was feeling good. It seemed as though she was enjoying the night just as much as he.

So, why? What was it? What was it that he kept coming back to? Part of him was saying don't spoil what was happening, and another was saying 'hold on' this can't be real.

She had to be after something, didn't she? Appearing when she had, with no real explanation. She'd said about love at first sight, which now seemed more like lust at first sight.

'*Yeah, lover … Mmm, yeah … that's … ohh, that's … it … there … mmm … keep going … oh … yeah … ummm …*'

Karla was riding Greg now and he was responding to her rhythm with an occasional playful spank of her bum as encouragement without being over-zealous. She had taken off his blindfold. His big hands were now caressing her. It was with a gentleness that seemed incongruous for such a big man. Their rhythm increased as they reached peak, their bodies and voices in harmony, combining in the perfect dual climax.

Whatever Greg had steeled himself over, that something might happen while he was making love with Karla, that she might in some way have been able to conjure up danger for him elsewhere, hadn't taken place. Maybe he'd been too cynical about her, maybe he'd been coloured by all of the bad side of what he'd seen in the past few years and now couldn't tell bad from good?

'*Well?*'

She smiled sweetly as she rested her face against the palm of her hand, her elbow propping her as she lay next to him. Her question had been delivered cheekily rather than enquiring.

There had been no disguising their mutual satisfaction and Greg knew it had been a special time. This woman was something else, as she had said she was. He couldn't knock her passion and intimacy in the bedroom, nor her beauty. She had raised her eyebrows as she'd asked the question. One arched a little higher than the other.

Greg was loosening up towards her. Not just in bed, but also as a relationship. He could feel it. He was relaxed as he asked her,

'*Why do you prefer to be on your own?*'

He asked it delicately, softly. It was the only thing Greg could think of that Karla had said previously that he could put his finger on that was not quite right.

Maybe there was something in her past? He was already starting to think more affectionately about her, more on her side than being cynical.

Karla closed her eyes, just for a second or two. Was she calculating what to tell him? Was her next line going to be a lie?

She breathed out deeply. She slumped back on the bed as though her elbow that had been supporting her had given way with the strain of what she was thinking. She exhaled deeply once again. Greg watched. Eventually, she smiled, but not the cheeky or confident smile of previously. Her eyes were moist.

'It's not something I can talk about …'

She dabbed at the corners of her eyes. Licked her lips lightly, that had become dry. Put her left hand to her face with her middle finger touching slightly on the underside of her nose and her index finger feeling her breath from her left nostril. It was a calming influence.

'… not at the moment … I just can't …'

Greg was part wanting to be understanding but was also part not wanting to be caught out. This was either acting or real. Maybe she was a good actress? Able to put on the waterworks in an instant? She had certainly just made a dramatic change from temptress to tainted in seconds.

Greg still didn't know what he was letting himself in for with Karla. He couldn't be sure that he hadn't missed something that was important and would have shown her to be suspect.

So maybe she was this beautiful girl on her own, a couple of thousand miles from home. He wanted so much to buy it, but he still couldn't be sure.

CHAPTER 37

'*Now, Ms Miller.*'

Det Superintendent Erin Jackson was settling herself in for what she sensed was likely to be a protracted evening. Det Marlon Ranzi was alongside her. They had taken Zoe to the police headquarters. It was Erin's way of trying to crank up the pressure.

'*We can take these all individually, and we will, but what I really want to know is why you are here in Vanuatu, why you disguised yourself on the flight over here, why you disappeared from Sydney two days ago, why you were not present at the opening ceremony of a World Cup when you are chief executive of its organisation, why your financial director was over here and why you are staying with the person you are in Paradise Beach.*'

Erin stopped at this point. Breathed deeply. Bowed her head, cocked it slightly as she raised it again, and smiled the kind of smile that told of her frustration already with Zoe, lips firmly together.

Erin shrugged her shoulders at Zoe. Held out her hands. Gave her an exasperated expression.

Zoe was not forthcoming. It looked all set to be the long night Erin had anticipated.

In seconds it was all set to be much longer and much more dramatic than she had ever imagined.

'*Get down on the floor right now! ... Right NOW!!! ... Do IT!!! ... Don't think! Just do it!*'

Det Superintendent Erin Jackson had a gun at her throat. Det Marlon Razni too. Zoe had a hood put over her head and was bundled away from the police headquarters.

'*Don't move!! ... Stay down!! ... If you want to stay alive, just DO IT!*'

CHAPTER 38

Sela Natavanu was a powerful man on the island. He had invested heavily in recent ventures. Right now, he was an extremely unhappy man – and when Sela was unhappy the whole of Efate knew about it. He was pacing his villa. His phone on loudspeaker.

'Listen to me! I will not, I repeat, will not be made a fool of! Last night was a shambles! I was told this was a slick operation, show me that it is, or I am out!'

Greg awoke to the sunshine bursting through into his suite. He felt the warmth on his face. He opened his eyes, then closed them feeling the sun warm his eyelids. No early morning run today after last night's exertions on the pitch – and in the bed.

The bed. Karla. He turned over and let the day go on without him.

'What in hell's name ...?'

It was all Danford could muster as he surveyed the detritus from what had obviously been some kind of raid of the police headquarters. He had been made aware of a problem when the cleaner orderly had alerted him something was very wrong as he had approached the headquarters finding the doors wide open.

The three of them currently on site – Theo, the orderly, Alex Lui and Danford Napakauranga, stood in bewilderment. Desks and chairs upturned and broken, paper and files littered all around and, it appeared, every laptop or computer had been thrown to the floor, broken or both.

Danford's office had been ransacked. The glass between his room and the rest of the office was shattered.

Karla was there. Something had connected for him with her last night. Maybe it had been her vulnerability, that moment when he had seen her emotions take over. She may not have confided in him whatever was wrong, but she had at least opened up to him. He felt a bond.

Even though he wanted to keep on his guard, he couldn't

help but feel an attachment to her.

'Hi.'

She smiled. Even that one word made Greg melt further towards her. He smiled too. She appeared softer. Maybe it was just the morning time, that moment when a guard is down before full awakening brings back reality, but she looked younger, someone who needed him. They kissed, just delicately, prettily. A kiss that suddenly meant so much more.

'*Boss, check this out …*'

Alex had been going through the CCTV footage from cameras positioned all around the headquarters. Two had been taken out but that still left half a dozen.

By now the place was alive with other staff and members of Det Supt Jackson's team who were all busily putting the offices back into shape. Desks and chairs were largely okay, as were the laptops and computers. Whoever had done this had not aimed at destroying anything, it seemed, apart from Danford's office glass.

'*10.35 last night … Det Supt Jackson and Det Razni … and a woman …*'

Alex Lui skipped on to 10.45.

'*… and this …*'

Six masked intruders, all dressed head to toe in black, appeared on screen – two with machetes, two holding rifles, the other two with shotguns. Their entry was from various parts of the building into the main area and then a single shot blew Danford's glass apart. There appeared to be a lot of shouting although there was no sound on the video.

Jackson, Razni and – although Napakauranga and Lui didn't know who she was at the time – Zoe, all hit the deck as guns were placed against the cops' heads. First, Zoe was hooded and bundled away; then Jackson and Razni were hooded and bound up before they too were escorted out of the building.

Elenola had now appeared and was watching the action behind Alex who was seated and Danford stood. Elenola offered her first contribution.

'*Why is the woman not bound? What's so special about her?*'

Alex gave his assessment.

'*She's the reason they came?*'

Danford looked to Alex.

'*We have any more? Anything that shows us a vehicle? Direction they were going?*'

Alex shook his head.

'*The cameras that record the exterior of the building were taken out beforehand. These guys knew what they were doing.*'

'*Yeah. Ruger rifles and Glock guns. These guys are not just tooled up for something like this. This was a professional job, made to look like it was amateur by the mess.*'

'*Jackson was evidently on the right track, in some way, judging by the actions here. Do we know the woman?*'

He saw blankness from both Elenola and Alex.

'*First base, run her picture through the system, see what falls out; and let's get weaving around the town and the rest of the island as to where our colleagues from Australia have been taken ...*'

Danford paused.

'*And while we are all at it, we still have three murders to solve ...*'

The England squad was in good form at breakfast. It had been good news about Aaron Fielding. He had arrived back from hospital having recovered from his concussion sustained in the game and even better news was that his jaw had not been broken as first feared.

He was out for at least the next game, against Greece, but Chislett now had numbers back and new players were arriving to be able to cope.

Full-back Steve 'Rocking' Docking who had made a name for himself with Super League's Grand Final serial winners Jagston Jaguars had flown in that morning with his teammate of many years, centre or back row forward Neil 'Brickie' Duncan who had earned his nickname on account of his early career when he'd been unsure that rugby league was for him or to become a bricklayer. The name, like his bricks, had stuck.

Gary Walker (ankle) and John Cloudsdale (back and hip)

were also ruled out and Jericho Pallagi, Troy Whittingham and 'Big' Mick Green were all carrying knocks, but there was now a growing spirit in the camp with a victory under their belt.

Greg arrived at breakfast with Karla. None of the rest of the squad had their wives or partners with them, but Greg had felt it was natural to turn up together. They'd spent the night in the same bed. What was the problem?

It appeared there was none. There was no mention of them turning up as a couple. There was no awkward moment.

'Focus boys. That's what we need ...'

Breakfast had finished and the whole squad was in the outside bar area. Chislett was holding court.

'Easier day today boys. We will take a look at this Greece team, watch their game against Papua New Guinea from last night. Greece gave them a bit of a game, a bit like Vanuatu did with us. Okay PNG ran out easy winners in the end but until about 65 minutes there was only six points in it.'

The training sessions were to be held in the afternoon and early evening, followed by morning and afternoon the next day. The day following was the next game. Greek fans were already arriving on the island.

'If we tell ourselves any of this is going to be easy, that's when we will be found out. We have, on paper, the easiest route to the quarters. Australia thought they had an easy group, now look what could happen if they lose to Fiji! They could be out.'

Zoe was back with her host. She had been returned to her by the hooded gang following the raid on the police headquarters, where her would-be assailants had hooded her, as Elenola Taneo had commented, but not bound her.

She had spent the night back in the arms and the bed of her host. It had been a relief after being taken in for further questioning.

'Who were those men? Were they yours?'

Zoe and her host had just returned from a run. Her host had the same slim running figure as Zoe. They had run seven and a half miles at a decent but not stressful pace. It felt good to be out running, doing what she had always enjoyed.

They had showered together. Zoe hadn't mentioned her rescuers until now. She had been gauging the best time to bring it out.

'What has happened to the police investigators? The man and woman?'

Zoe stopped towelling her host down and asked her the question she had been meaning to ask since she had arrived.

'Who are you? ... I mean, who are you really? ...'

Zoe was still asking her questions lightly, with care. She was entranced by this beautiful, gorgeous and sexy woman. Things hadn't changed in that way, nor did she want them to.

Their run had only increased Zoe's desire for her. Her body was one thing, wonderfully lithe, perfect perky breasts, cute booty, slender legs – but it was the way she smiled at her while they were running, the way her eyes also seemed to smile, and then the way they touched, the way they held hands – their fingers entwined as though they had been born for each other, but there was so much now that she needed to know about her.

There had been no way Zoe could ever see that this woman wouldn't be in her life, but all of this, whatever this was that had happened last night? It all put a new complexion on their relationship.

Zoe's lover had stopped drying her and was looking into Zoe's eyes, smiling once again the smile that released Zoe's endorphins. She couldn't help but reciprocate. Their lips met, their towels slipped to the floor, they embraced and then their passion took hold once more.

'I am yours ...'

Zoe's lover whispered the words so seductively into Zoe's ear. It took just those three to send her heart racing and to forget everything else.

It turned into a morning that Zoe had never experienced before, sending her into ecstasy as her lover explored her time and again with every sensual touch and kiss.

CHAPTER 39

'Boss, they've been spotted. Detective Superintendent Jackson and Detective Razni ... on Kakula Island!'

Kakula Island was to the north-west of Efate and had been a private island that had harboured big dreams of turning into an exclusive resort. The hotel had been built, but its timing had not been great. It had suffered from the ravages of Cyclone Pamela, Cyclone Jean and Cyclone Christine and its investor had gone bust.

Jackson and Razni had been dumped overboard from a powerboat just 50 metres from the shore, cut loose from their ropes that had bound them just prior to being heaved into the sea. Fishermen setting off from Paonangisu on the mainland had noticed people on the island during the afternoon. The local policeman in the area was dispatched across the strait to bring them back.

Danford was relieved. The possible scenario of having two detectives' deaths on his islands would have brought about even greater presence from his Australian counterparts.

'These islands are changing ...'

He said it almost despairingly, partly to himself but also for Elenola and Alex.

'There was an innocence here. But as Efate and our other islands grow, as non-islanders come here, we are losing it ...'

He stopped from going on any further.

'... but we have a job to do, and right now it's probably the biggest job we've ever faced here ... three murders, yes all three, we're not just looking at the deaths of Winston and Lena, we're also looking into Bob Rudd too ...'

He looked at Elenola and Alex, as if reading their eyes.

'I'll deal with our friends from Australia when they return. They need to start seeing sense and that it is better if we all work together.'

Greg's day had started well – and had kept on the same path

through the afternoon and early evening with two sessions, both lighter affairs. There would be enough hard hits in the actual games without causing themselves additional problems.

There was a good feeling in the England camp at Breakas. The new guys 'Brickie' Duncan and 'Rocking' Docking were two of eight club-mates from the title-winning Jagston Jaguars now in the squad, including Ash Tyson, Phil 'The Butcher' Parkin, Tyler Rodgers, Regan Phillips, Owen Fenchurch and Gary Walker.

They were vying with the Rockfield Ravens for the biggest group of club teammates in the squad. Their eight were Aaron Fielding, Jericho Pallagi, Sam Rivers, Mason Bell, Big Mick Green, Billy Ecktenstall, Jason Neve and Troy Whittingham

Neil 'Brickie' Duncan was the new joker in the pack adding to Gary Walker's presence. Neil was always ready with his Scots and Irish impressions and stories from his other career. There had been talk of him pinning his allegiance to the boys in blue over the border rather than the cross of St George. 'Brickie' had made his decision over a bottle of single malt. He'd spun the bottle once it was empty.

'Hi Dad!!!'

Kyle was overjoyed to hear from his dad when Greg rang. It was around 6 o'clock in the afternoon when Greg had tried. 8 in the morning back in Hopton. Greg had thought he might catch Kyle before Diane took him to school and for once his timing was spot on.

Kyle proceeded to give his dad the lowdown on his two tries. One had been a run on the wing, the other had been where he had taken the ball near the line *'and I span round in the tackle Dad, like you told me.'*

Greg was smiling so much listening to his son.

'I liked your song Dad … did you make it up?'

Greg laughed. Next up had been Col.

There was nothing new to report on Greg's dad. Col had sent a text earlier telling Greg there was no need to call but he had anyway.

'Amazing performance last night bud … I know you were only playing a little nation but it looked like being a disaster until you came on …'

Greg would have made another call, the one he had every day since leaving for Australia, every day since she had told him, in a way that he now took to have been final.

He decided not to ring Susie this time. Maybe it was all over after all. He hadn't been one for losing hope but this was, he corrected himself, this looked like it could be the end.

His phone sprang to life as he thought this way.

Susie? He knew, in that moment, when suddenly he'd still hoped it would be her, that he should have rung.

It wasn't Susie.

'You don't know me. But if you don't do as I say you will be dead in one minute. Run! … Run for your life! … Now!'

Greg was in his suite. Karla arrived out of breath. Her face told him what he'd just heard was true. She was crying, tears streaming down her face.

'Greg …?'

Her next words that followed his name meant he was in trouble, and it was hurtling headlong in his direction.

One minute later Greg's near-perfect last 24 hours was over.

CHAPTER 40

'*I'm so … so sorry …*'

Greg hadn't heard the last two words.

Fuck it! He was already under way.

Greg blasted out of his suite, through the doors that led to the beach. He was heading towards it as the door to his suite opened.

First thought. Why did he ever think being with Karla would work? He'd walked into this with his eyes wide open. Fucking idiot! No time for that now. Run! Create space between himself and whoever was on his tail – and quickly.

Greg hadn't had any option. Where he had been at the time of the call had given him only one route and now he was going hell for leather towards the ocean, diagonally away from the suite and heading away from Breakas.

As he ran Greg heard Karla's voice again in his head. She sounded upset, as though perhaps she hadn't intended this. But she had brought it about. She must have.

Greg knew. He'd known all along.

His shield had been up but somehow he'd let it down again. Same as ever. Pretty girl. The sweeties on offer. Surely it had meant more than that to her? It had to him.

In the past two days Greg had felt more than just a connection, something a lot more. But fuck it, fuck it, fuck it! Run!

That was all he could keep telling himself as he ran, barefoot across the stony beach. Normally he would feel every last pebble, but there wasn't the time for that. Adrenaline had taken place of pain. It was time to make distance.

Why him for fuck's sake? Why did these things always happen to him?

Still powering on, Greg reckoned he was well ahead of whoever was coming after him.

As he looked down at the stones, trying to avoid anything that would stub a toe or cause laceration of his barefoot existence, he thought briefly about how he was at least better dressed this time, albeit without footwear. He was still in his training gear. He'd made his phone calls when he'd come back.

'*Fuck!!*'

Forget the adrenaline, he'd cut the underside of his right foot on something sharp. Hurt like hell! Shit, keep moving, keep going.

It was approaching dusk. The light was on the wane.

What the hell was this all about? Receiving phone calls just prior to someone coming into his room? Twice now, in the matter of a few days.

Somewhere from within, Greg managed to summon up another gear, despite the cut to his foot and now feeling every rock, stone, pebble. He stepped up his momentum.

Greg had no idea where he was exactly just yet, apart from around maybe quarter of a mile from Breakas. He'd run on the road out of Breakas on his first morning there. The squad had run from Port Vila the night before the game against Vanuatu but that was the extent of his rudimentary geographic knowledge of Efate.

The direction he was running appeared to have been parallel with the morning run.

Up ahead, as he ran, he began to see what looked like individual beach bungalows. They were dotted around and individual. It wasn't a hotel resort like Breakas. This was more like a small community, village or hamlet. He kept running towards it.

He could hear what sounded like the pounding of feet behind him, but then how could it be? Surely it was just the waves against the shore or his heart beating.

Greg banked on his fitness. Anyone following him would have to match his endurance, and right now he felt confident that unless there was some kind of Mo Farah on his tail he might have made up a lead from whoever had been about to invade his room.

What did all of this have to do with him? Why was he being targeted? There had to be a reason. It kept coming back to him while he was running.

Greg tried to keep shaking it off. Really a waste of time thinking about any of this. He could be dead in seconds. Shit! Think! Think about how to get out of this situation first.

He had no idea who was behind him, whether there even was still someone behind. And if there was, whether they were armed.

He'd been running out of beach for the last 100 metres. The stony sand had now tapered off to earth, rock and clumps of grass, bushes and more bloody stones. He was still bleeding.

The settlement he'd seen and had pinned his hopes upon finding somewhere safe for a short while was getting closer but the new tougher terrain of bushes, weeds, sand and stone was slowing his progress.

In the end he couldn't help himself but look back.

There were two pursuers. Neither could have been anticipating a foot race on their entry to his suite, that much was clear. Why was he receiving warnings before people came? Who knew what was going on yet couldn't tell him until just before? It didn't make any sense.

Greg was dressed in shorts and a t-shirt; they were attired in trousers, shirts and what looked like normal shoes. One of them looked all in, finished, and was gasping for air. The other was still making a fist of it but not making serious headway.

Most importantly, Greg could not see either holding anything that looked like a lethal weapon. The caller had said if he hadn't run he'd be dead. How? Another thing that didn't make any sense.

It was now about finding a safe place, finding cover, somewhere these guys couldn't track him. Second base would be to work out what to do from there.

As he turned back to run Greg's world vanished!

CHAPTER 41

'Do you have any idea why my team is really here commissioner?'

Det Supt Erin Jackson's manner was borderline seething in her remonstration with Danford. She and Det Marlon Razni had returned from their abduction courtesy of a cattle truck that had been transporting beef animals to abattoir for export to Japan.

It had been the best transportation available at the time as the policeman who had made the trip to collect them from Kakula Island had only been able to deposit them in Paonangisu on account of having nothing more than a motorcycle, which was currently out of action.

Jackson and Razni had been treated to a ride that had been a million light years away from their existence in Sydney, and which had seemed to take forever. The driver was a Ni-Vanuatuan who spoke no English and showed them his paperwork time and again to back up what he was saying in his native language, that he had to collect more cattle from two other farms along the route and then unload the truck full of beasts before he could get them into Port Vila.

'Mi no save,' which he pronounced 'savvy' was how he answered every question. It meant he didn't understand, which is pretty much what they had both gathered. *'Talem mi long Bislama'* was something neither of them could work out but the driver had meant for them to talk to him using the local Vanuatu lingo.

The truck was part of Vanuatu Beef Inc., as it appeared fully liveried up in the island's colours of black, red and green. Exportation of beef was an established part of the country's economy with over 100,000 breeding cattle across the islands of Efate and Espiritu Santo.

Although the journey had been arduous, the truck itself was a brand-new Kenworth, a massive road train truck that was meant for thousands of miles in Australia. It looked incongruous on the small island of Efate.

Vanuatu Beef Inc. was part-owned by Brahman Australia Beef which in turn was part owned by Brazil Beef and money was being invested massively in the further building up of Vanuatu's beef herd due to its appropriate terrain.

The opulence of the cab, driven by Aleki, they'd managed to find out his name as it was badged up in the cab, had not gone unnoticed by them.

Aleki was proud of his vehicle, so proud that he was happy to drive far slower than either detective would have wished.

Overnight on Kakula Island Jackson and Razni had found themselves exploring their own potential. It had been a long time coming, a relationship that had never had the opportunity to seize the day as much as it had the previous night. Their time together had not been wasted so far as Razni was concerned. The abandoned hotel had come in useful.

All of that had now been put to bed, Jackson winced as she thought of it that way, at least for the time being.

The tipping point for Jackson's fury had been when Commissioner Napakauranga had just told her that he and his team were going to look into all three murders, rather than sharing them out with Jackson and her team.

Erin Jackson had been enraged. It was time to get real with this jumped-up island chief of police.

'Mr Rudd's suspected murder is only one small part of why we are here ...'

Jackson was eyeballing Napakauranga now.

She and Razni had been dancing around handbags since they had arrived.

'... but then you already know that don't you? ...'

She delivered the line with venom, watching the faces of Danford's allies, Elenola Taneo and Alex Lui, as she spoke.

She was going for Danford's jugular right now. This local yokel.

Danford Napakauranga was seasoned enough not to show any distress by what she had said. Let her win for now, or feel as though she had.

Deputy Commissioner Taneo was surprised by the verbal assault on the man who held the position above her. She had pledged allegiance to him a couple of days ago but in truth she still had reservations. Things that she hadn't been able to put her finger on.

His holier than thou attitude was something she disliked. She hadn't bought it years ago when she'd first met him and she didn't again now.

'... *that's why you wanted in on our investigation right from the start and why you've now decided to step in ...*'

Jackson moved closer to him, now in his face. She wasn't about to let this go.

'... *funny how a group of island thugs were able to get in here, just at the time we were here last night ... funny that ... funny that they knew the cameras to block ...*'

The volleys coming at Danford were nothing that Jackson could yet substantiate. She was trying him out for size. Getting her eye in.

Danford Napakauranga had other ideas.

'*Please leave this building. You have no business here.*'

He said it deadpan. He wasn't about to get hysterical.

He saw her open her mouth, possibly just agape as he had stunned her. He held his right hand up in front of him, fingers splayed.

'*I think you've said enough. Please leave. That includes all of your team ...*'

Danford left an appropriate pause.

Elenola Taneo could not help but stand in awe of what was now taking place. She didn't like Jackson either. Now, put to an immediate response of which she would pin her colours to, she would favour her boss.

Danford turned away from Jackson, then turned back.

'*Are you still here? ... Do you have any idea why my team is here Detective Superintendent?*'

Commissioner Danford Napakauranga looked Detective Superintendent Erin Jackson straight in the eye.

CHAPTER 42

'Mrs Reuben? I am Detective Ashton. I'd like to ask you a few questions. Could I come in?'

She had no intention of letting this man do so. And she also had no intention of asking him why. Instead, she sent a text immediately, to another contact.

Five minutes later three white Range Rover Evoques thundered along the road to where Mrs Reuben was staying and six men with firearms jumped out. One team of two taking up position alongside the detective's vehicle, while the other two pairs advanced on where the detective was standing.

By then the detective's initially polite speak had taken on a more sinister approach in order to make the woman let him in. She had been defiant. She hadn't responded.

'I don't think the lady wants to answer your questions Detective Ashton ...'

Ashton was suddenly the person feeling the heat.

The man with the voice and firearm was calm.

'I think it's time for you to go, don't you?'

Ashton turned, just in time to see his tyres being shot to pieces. He turned back towards the man with the voice, dressed all in black and with a black balaclava, as were the rest of his troop.

'Yeah, shame about that. Are you with the RAC?'

The leader of the gang then finally raised his shotgun at Ashton's head.

'Now, be a good lad and leave your phone on the floor.'

As Ashton was doing so one of the others of the group frisked him, nodding back to the leader that Ashton didn't have a firearm.

'I think that will do for tonight detective ...'

He hesitated slightly.

'But before you go on your way ... drop your trousers ...'

The others couldn't help but laugh within themselves as the detective did so.

'Ah, commando ... you've picked your night for that haven't you? ... Come on, jacket ... shirt ... right, off you go, get out of here ...'

Three minutes later, and with a naked detective now streaking away to wherever he could find some form of cover and hopefully speedy assistance in the form of clothing, Mrs Reuben appeared.

In the time she'd had Mrs Reuben had packed a case, put on her makeup, brushed her blonde hair, slipped on a sexy electric blue off-the-shoulder dress that accentuated everything she considered best about her body, put on her matching heels and stepped out and into the leader's Evoque.

CHAPTER 43

Everything was black. Silent. His head throbbed. Hurt like hell. First instinct, touch it, feel for blood. No chance of doing so.

His wrists were tied and ropes were also around his body holding his arms in place, restricting his movement. Blood? Could he taste it? Was it a trickle coming from the side of his head, or was that just sweat?

His mouth was taped up. The taste of the tape was rank. One of those tastes that produce nausea. It smelled like something from a farmyard and made him gip.

Greg had no idea what time of day it now was, how long he had been out cold or how it had happened. All he knew was that he couldn't see, couldn't shout for help and was immobile.

Why me? Why always bloody me? What was it about him that kept on finding himself in these situations? It was all that filled his brain for a few seconds on coming around. Then things began coming back to him.

He'd tripped. Or had he? Trip wire?

He felt his ribs. Jeez.

That's when it started coming back more. The ribs. Something had hit him hard. It had been as he had turned. The thud. A plank? An arm? The wind taken right out of his sails. He'd gone down hard. His head hitting stone.

That was all. He had no recollection of anything afterwards. No sense of time. Now all he had was darkness. Something being placed over his head. Hood.

Focus on the now, rather than try to work out what had happened. Think. How to get undone, get away from wherever he was. Where was he?

He couldn't easily flop his head forward and down, to give it respite, because of the way he was tied, but he could rest it back against whatever he was leaning on.

Outside or inside? Which was he? Had to be inside, didn't

it? But then the warmth could still have led him to believe he was outside. No, inside. Too still. No sounds of any type of wildlife. No breeze. Inside.

It still kept coming back. Why him? The women on the plane? Phone calls to warn him to run? He said he was good? The women had said that. What did it mean? Maria Cavaleros? That last frame they had shown on the Airbus? Even, now he thought about it, Shane Chislett's face when he was to go on for the game, looking at the clock. That note about when to come on?

Follow all the threads. Take it easy, nice and slow. After all, he had nothing much more he could do with his time than try to work things out and hope he would be found.

CHAPTER 44

'That's another great performance by this England team. They've built on the Vanuatu game and here, back at the Port Vila Municipal Stadium, they have simply blown Greece away!'

Brad Kearns was summing up the England performance with just a couple of minutes left in the match, for Channel 17. Ex-player Laurie Northey was alongside him once again.

'Aww mate, this team is really starting to play. All right, the Greece team doesn't have the same firepower and they're still an emerging nation in the sport, but they still have to be beaten and this England team is now looking mighty impressive.'

Brad Kearns took over once again.

'Too right mate! And when you consider they've rested Greg Duggan, the hero against Vanuatu and guys like Gary Walker and Big Mick Green, and with some of the earlier casualties to come back, they're starting to tick.'

When the final hooter sounded England had run out easy winners by 68-0. It had been an accomplished performance with the new boys to the squad Steve 'Rockin' Docking and Neil 'Brickie' Duncan scoring a brace of tries apiece and Vinny Venus crossing the whitewash for five, in a twelve-try demolition of Greece. Jericho Pallagi, Freddie South and Phil Parkin had bagged the others.

Pitchside reporter Karen Stonehouse interviewed Man of the Match Vincent Venus.

'Vinny, five tries in one game. How many times have you done that before?'

The six-foot-four winger gave a slight shrug of his shoulders and a gigantic smile. He said he'd maybe scored as many when he'd played at Under 11s.

'Terrific performance from the whole team. We were all a little surprised not to see your Eruption teammate Greg Duggan play after the last game especially. He's not here tonight either ...'

Karen was itching to ask exactly where he was. It didn't stack up that he wouldn't be at the game even if he was being rested. Had there been a bust-up?

'Just resting ...'

Vinny's good-natured response led Karen to move on with her questioning.

Nobody in the England camp at Breakas knew where Greg had gone. There had been speculation that he had been seen leaving, but that had turned out to be another hotel guest. He'd simply vanished.

Coach Shane Chislett and England team media relations expert Annie Laing had made the decision to keep Greg's disappearance hushed up. They hadn't wanted the publicity to detract from the team's objective, but they had the natural concern over his safety.

Fortunately, they had been able to come up with a story for the short-term, which wouldn't or shouldn't have unsettled the players, on the advice they had received from a new source for both of them who was desperately trying to find Greg.

They had chosen to rely upon the source based on two factors – one, the source gave them enough previous factual evidence of Greg and what he had gone through; and two, because neither had the first idea of how to deal with the situation.

Chislett was next up in the after-match interviews with Karen Stonehouse.

'Shane, explain what has happened to your team in the last two games, especially following on from your two warm-up games. You must be super excited about your prospects right now.'

Shane Chislett gave his answer straight from the coach's manual of how to sum up a win when you're over the moon but keeping a lid on it in front of the cameras. He did the usual thing of saying the scoreline hadn't reflected the effort the opposition had put in, praised his team's ability to go for the full 80 minutes and he talked about areas of the game that they still needed to work on.

'And the loose forward position? Is that one area where we will expect to see a change in the next game? Will Greg Duggan be back for that one?'

Chislett played stonewall defence over the question. His lips were tight together. His head rocked slightly from side to side.

'Well, Karen, we've a great squad of players, some coming back from injury. Everybody will play their part in our journey. One more game in the group.'

'So, no bust up in the camp? The reason why he's not here tonight?'

Chislett had been ready to answer immediately on the first question, but the second was trickier. He paused. Decided on a different approach. Raised his eyebrows. He stayed calm.

'No bust up.'

He smiled charmingly back at Karen.

CHAPTER 45

Greg still had no idea where he was. He hadn't seen anybody. Strike that. He hadn't heard anyone. He couldn't have seen them because of the hood, which made his head constantly warm, but had enough air coming in that he could breathe, albeit sometimes overheating.

He must have been here days by now. Why the hell couldn't he do something about it? He was certainly dehydrated. He remembered reading or hearing somewhere that the body can survive for three days without water. He didn't think he'd gone three days, but it gave him concentration. Why hadn't he had this motivation before now?

He had to do something. Try in some way to get free. Nobody was coming for him. Where would they start looking?

His mouth felt desert dry, his lips were starting to chap, he could feel them under the tape. Something had to be done. If it was three days the human body could go without water, he felt by now he must have been at least a day and a half, maybe two days, here. He'd probably missed the Greece game. Bloody idiot! Bloody stupid idiot!

He shook his head at himself. Karla? How could he have been so bloody stupid. Taken in again by a gorgeous woman.

He'd tried plenty of ways to get free, but nothing had worked. He was stuck. Bound, blindfolded by the hood, gagged. Dry. Overheating.

Why the hell had he let Karla seduce him? Why couldn't he resist temptation? What was happening to his dad? How was Kyle getting on? And Susie, for God's sake!

Right. Time to shove all of that to one side. Time to get out of here. He'd gone through all of this rigmarole on and off throughout his time here, wherever here was.

Why would anyone, whoever, want him like this? It didn't make any sense. He'd had no issue with anyone. He'd not done anything.

Stop it now. The thinking. Find a way to get out. It wasn't as though he hadn't already tried, but the dehydration thing was weighing heavy, playing on his mind.

He had simply no light. Daft enough to say when you're hooded, he thought, but indicative that he had to be somewhere inside and probably underground or in a cellar. Think. Clearly.

Tethered by the wrists and ankles, bound by ropes that held his arms firm to his sides and without any sight due to the hood and no opportunity to holler because of the tape it was proving useless.

Greg had tried finding anything he could to free himself for what seemed like over an hour solid, probably more like two, since he'd begun his latest mission in earnest when he heard a sound.

CHAPTER 46

'Breaking news from Vanuatu this morning is England's star player in their first game is missing. Loose forward Greg Duggan who turned around England's fortunes in their opening group match against the islanders has not been seen at the World Cup team's hotel on the island of Efate for what sources believe to be around two to three days.

'Last night the England team won their latest game on the island versus Greece when Vincent Venus ran in five tries. After the game he spoke with our pitchside reporter Karen Stonehouse and explained Duggan was 'resting'. This now appears not to be the case. Or if he is then it certainly isn't at the team's hotel. The England team leaves Efate for their final group game against Papua New Guinea in Port Moresby today. We'll have more on this story as it develops.'

Channel 17 Sport's editorial team had taken up residence at Breakas Resort following the Greece game and had ascertained that Greg hadn't been seen for days.

Chislett had not expected Duggan's absence could be hushed up for long and he knew that when it was out in the open the press would tell the world. He had absolutely no idea where Duggan was and since he could do nothing about it, saw it as just another possible loss of focus for his team.

Two victories out of two games meant England were assured of progressing to the quarter-finals regardless of the outcome against Papua New Guinea.

Tournament favourites Australia had put their trophy quest back on track by beating Fiji 26-16 in their latest game and now only had emerging nation Lebanon to face in their last group match. All of the four groups were progressing with the seeded teams for the quarters looking good.

Commissioner Danford Napakauranga's team was working hard on the murder inquiries. Detective Superintendent Erin Jackson and her charges, for all the might of their greater resources back on the Australian mainland, had been struggling.

A truce, of sorts, had been struck between the two respective leaders despite their earlier spat. They were now pooling what they had. There was little in the way of trust.

'Bob Rudd was here on business, allegedly.'

Alex Lui said it with a certain irony in his voice.

'He was staying as a guest of ex-prime minister and businessman Sela Natavanu at his Paradise Beach Estate. Made several visits to Port Vila Municipal Stadium and the National Bank of Vanuatu. Was seen around some of Port Vila's best-known restaurants including The Blue Marlin. Always seemed to have a different woman with him. We're trying to identify which were with him.

'He'd been coming to the island several times since before the decision was made to host World Cup games here. It's thought that's why he kept coming and that perhaps he was facilitating better deals for the Rugby League World Cup – and personally.

'Best we have in placing him before his murder was that he'd been eating at The Blue Marlin. Waiter there remembers Rudd was with an attractive woman, English accent. Hadn't seen her before. Hadn't noticed anything out of the ordinary'

Elenola Taneo took over from Alex.

'Lena Kalotiti had enjoyed the fame of her underwater post office role and it seems she may have had a relationship with Bob Rudd at some stage. The Hideaway Island beach bar manager saw them together several times.

'It seems Lena had a string of admirers. She was a beautiful woman and was never short of attention. Her mother, Oleta, who lives in Pango told me Lena had big dreams and had told her she had received an offer to appear on a TV show that would launch a career away from Vanuatu.'

Alex Lui saved the briefest description of the three that had been murdered until last. He felt that his boss already knew enough about Winston Sablan – and he wasn't too bothered about pandering to Jackson and Razni.

'Winston Sablan had many enemies and many allies on Efate and in Vanuatu. There is word out on the street that he was corrupt, but that's hardly news among any of the politicians on these islands.'

Lui was watching his boss's reaction. So too was Elenola, who had still been coming to terms with the revelation she'd heard from Jackson previously, casting aspersions on Danford.

She'd only just begun starting to trust him and now this had knocked it out of kilter. Since then she had been undertaking her own research into her boss, but that could wait until she had something more.

Alex continued.

'There are always rumours about politicians and our prime minister was no different. The only leads we have that may have any substance are that he was instrumental in the Rugby League World Cup coming here to Port Vila, hardly earth-shattering given his position – and that he was seen recently with Bob Rudd at Cove of Paradise Restaurant … and with Nene Natavanu.'

Alex had saved the last name as a bombshell. Sela Natavanu's daughter. Sela had been grooming her for becoming prime minister. Had the grooming taken on other proportions?

'We've not been able to locate Nena …'

Alex Lui had left this second bombshell until last.

'What is happening on this island?!'

Danford Napakauranga was beyond exasperated.

'Three murders, two disappearances …'

He shook his head.

'This tournament. It all keeps coming back to it.'

Detective Superintendent Erin Jackson had kept her counsel until now. She had been perched on the edge of a desk.

'Bob Rudd was twisted, so he could have been compromised in some way. We've still not been able to interview Zoe Miller. I am not sure how your other two murders fit in with your theory but her coming here certainly looks suspicious.'

Mentioning two World Cup officials in the same breath was as near to an acceptance of Danford Napakauranga's diagnosis that Jackson was going to give him. The two police leaders gave what amounted to the briefest of head movements to each other before heading their separate ways.

They still had nothing.

CHAPTER 47

Greg looked directly out into the sun. Unhooded, untied and unmuted. He sat. For someone who hadn't been able to move for days, he now found that uncannily, for the moment he didn't want to move. His eyes kept blinking, refocusing. He kept drawing them wide open, moving them around.

The tape had been removed gently from his lips using warm water. At one stage he'd had the urge to tell whoever was doing it to just rip it off.

When it came off and he drank water for the first time since being bound he felt like a child that didn't know how to drink. His lips were dry and numb. He was dehydrated and hungry.

He was also a mess from not being able to do the things that come naturally, although most of this had dried onto his body or had formed urine stains on his legs.

Whoever had arranged for this show of affection had not intended to come back for him, that much was clear.

It had only been when he had heard a light scratching that had turned into feverish scraping and urgings to get on quickly that Greg had finally realised where he must have been – and why nobody had come. He'd been in some form of underground cell, covered over by earth. He saw it now. God, his ribs hurt too.

He'd been buried alive.

Greg now saw the opening to his chamber. From his seated position he tried to work it all out. Bewildered, he sat looking at the opening. He had no words and at this stage was purely thankful that he had been rescued.

But who the hell knew where to look? And if someone knew where, then they must have known something of what was going on that led to him being there.

How long had he been down there?

Had he gone the distance? Managing the three days without

water?

He remembered Karla apologising. He recalled giving himself a hard time in being allowed to be taken in by her. His first instinct had been right. She'd been trouble.

'*I've got to get going ...*'

He made to get up from where he'd been sitting. There was someone with him. The one who had found him and untied him. And another who had been careful removing the tape from over his mouth. Their opinion was that Greg should stay right where he was, for the moment.

As Greg had very little by way of strength he chose to flop back down again and take stock, re-evaluate his position. Whoever these people were they had clearly helped him.

Just how much longer he would have been able to carry on breathing in his underground chamber Greg hadn't a clue. He sat back down, then allowed himself to rest to one side on a rock and fell asleep.

CHAPTER 48

'This is bliss!'

Zoe Miller was looking out from her host's Azimut 55 Mini K yacht off the coast of Efate. She and her host had taken the seaward route the day following Zoe's escape from Port Vila police headquarters.

'Ah, it is much more than bliss, darling. It is perfection.'

She put her arms around Zoe from behind her and held her close, their cheeks side by side looking out to the ocean. Dolphins playing below.

'It is perfection with you. I could stay out here forever.'

Zoe closed her eyes and let any other thoughts she had, and any other troubles simply melt away. She'd had enough of everything else, had been sick of life the way it had always been, always chasing. This was something else. But she also knew it couldn't last.

She turned to her host, opening her eyes to see her lips parting. Zoe bit softly on her lower lip before gliding her tongue lightly, wetting her own lips. The two gorgeous, beautiful women looked affectionately into each other's eyes with the promise of what was to come. Their breath was short, their longing for what was to come lending a smile to their lips as they were to meet.

It was then that Zoe lifted up her host and threw her into the ocean.

CHAPTER 49

Greg woke up laid in a hospital bed. No idea where. Was he still on Efate? Or back in Oz? Tubes all around him. He had a saline drip attached. What the hell? He'd just come round, didn't know how long he'd been asleep, how long he'd been there. How had he got there? His immediate reaction was to get out.

He made one move, one ever so slight movement and quickly realised that simply getting up and getting out was perhaps a bit previous.

He now looked around him. He'd had no sense of anyone being close by. He went back to his own amateur analysis of his condition. This started with his body feeling like it had just done ten rounds in a boxing ring. How could that be? He couldn't recall any fight.

The last time he'd been conscious he hadn't known where he was and hadn't known what had happened to him. Here he felt worse, even though he was now without restraints. No hood, at least he could see. Not bound, at least he could move.

Instinctively he tried moving every part of his body, every part. It felt like everything was intact. He was no doctor, but his first thought was that the aches were more muscular pain and bruising than anything serious.

The drip, he quickly figured out, must have been down to the time he had been held, wherever that had been and assuring that his salt levels were back right. He must have been drained of energy having had to cope after days without food and water.

Greg suddenly felt a hand on his arm.

Female. Or at least that's how it seemed. He closed his eyes rather than look at who was there. He was wishing. He so wanted it to be Susie when he opened them.

Part of him didn't want to open them again as he knew he'd be disappointed.

'*Mr Duggan …*'

Greg kept his eyes closed. It wasn't Susie. The female voice, he'd been right, mentioned his name again. He opened them.

'*Can you hear me? Do you understand what I am saying?*'

Greg nodded. He chose not to ask anything straight away. His whereabouts, what had happened to him. This pretty face might give him the answers or at least he'd be able to deduce what best to say based on her next questions.

This wasn't a nurse, he'd quickly ascertained. No uniform. Did Vanuatu nurses wear uniforms? Was he even on Vanuatu? But she wasn't a nurse, he knew that much because of her manner. She'd have been asking about whether he needed anything.

He didn't know who the hell she was, which made him keep his counsel, let her blow herself out before he had to get involved.

He had masses of questions that he would want to ask anyone who could fill him in with the detail, but they could wait.

Suddenly the pain he'd felt on waking was on the wane as his adrenaline kicked in. He could feel himself getting back in the game. Back under way.

Get back with the England team, talk with Kyle, with Col, try to talk with Susie.

And now Greg needed to know what was going on, why he was being targeted. Nothing still made any sense. Who were the people who had saved him? Where were they?

The visitor smiled again before continuing. Pretty smile. Nice face. Cracking figure. Probably about mid-20s? Greg could already feel his own carnal instinct normality.

'*I'm Grace … I'm a journalist. I hope that doesn't mean you won't talk to me.*'

Grace left the briefest of pauses to check on Greg's immediate response before quickly carrying on.

'*I'm with Australia Today.*'

She took a breath.

'*I'm a freelance. I came to Vanuatu for a very different story but there is something much bigger happening here …*'

She stopped briefly again, looking into Greg's eyes.

'I hoped you might be able to help?'

Greg had no idea what she meant. How could he help? All he wanted was to be out of the hospital bed, wherever he now was, and back with the England party. And also to start figuring out what had happened to him and why?

Grace was smiling at him, waiting for him. There were no nurses or hospital staff in sight.

Slowly, and checking every movement did not cause him to wince with pain or that he could feel something was not right, Greg raised himself upright.

Greg released the saline drip. He was fine. Aches, bruises, things healing but otherwise good enough to move. The drip must have been precautionary.

Greg was on the move. He could have waited, talked with nurses and other medical staff, but he needed to get moving.

He'd been apprehended while fleeing Breakas. He'd been tripped or beaten, or both. He'd been bound and locked up somewhere. Anyone who had gone to that trouble might just be looking for him if they knew he was back above ground.

'Grace. Get me out of here.'

Grace wavered momentarily. This hadn't been in her script.

She knew that Greg's directive hadn't meant for her to have a word with someone about getting him out. He just wanted to be out. Okay, she could do this.

Less than two minutes later they were making their way from Port Vila Central Hospital. Greg was wearing the shorts and t-shirt he had been wearing in bed and had left with his arm around Grace as though they were a couple.

'Just keep smiling …'

Grace had found herself in enough difficult situations in the past. It was her words now that had seen them past several hospital staff. She even managed more than simply a smile from Greg when she looked at him after saying the words,

'Well, do the best you can …'

She'd said it in such a sarcastic way, with her eyebrows raised and a slight shake of her head in exasperation that Greg hadn't been able to suppress a little laugh as well as a smile.

He still had no real idea about this girl, but he liked her spunkiness. She'd hardly batted an eyelid at what he'd asked her to do in helping him. And nobody had questioned them as they had made their move from the ward or down the corridor or through the reception.

'They are all too wrapped up in their own problems to be concerned with us ...'

Grace was ultra-confident. She had learned early in her journalistic career that blagging was one of the most fun, most adrenaline-fuelled activities. She was in the zone. Who knew where this would lead?

Greg was not so confident. As they made their way from the hospital building and into the grounds he began looking around furtively. He didn't know who he was looking for, it was more that his antenna was up. He said nothing about this to Grace. They had just met, she was getting him out of the hospital. That was enough for now.

But someone somewhere and for some reason was after him and Greg was about to find out why. Forget all the wonderings about why always him, forget feeling sorry for himself. Action time.

'He's out. Yeah, for sure. Leaving with a girl. Do I follow?'

The voice on the other end of the mobile phone conversation wavered. The person asking the question followed up quickly.

'Make it fast. They're not exactly loitering.'

Grace had a hire car. She hadn't parked in the hospital car park, preferring instead to use a nearby street. She knew she was on to something here. She'd made the right decision to visit Greg.

'Follow.'

This was the instruction from the other end of the mobile phone as Greg and Grace left the hospital grounds.

'I need my mobile.'

Greg's first words to Grace on their move out into the streets of Port Vila were not of thanks but of immediate necessity. He needed to be back in touch.

'*Sure. You want to enlighten me …?*'

Grace looked at him expectantly based upon her own efforts so far. Payment, in her language, was information. She wasn't sure Greg got this, so she made it simpler.

'*… about what's going on?*'

Grace and Greg were now in Grace's hire car, a white Suzuki Jimny. Grace had asked him her question before starting the car. It seemed the right time. She needed to know whether Greg was going to play ball. She looked at him. Greg felt her eyes on him even though his were closed, his head resting back against the headrest, composing himself.

He kept them shut. Exhaled deeply through his nose, his lips together. He was part-relaxing, as much as he could, and part-thinking.

'*I've no idea what's going on.*'

He shrugged, as he exhaled deeply once again, this time opening his eyes and turning to Grace. God, she was pretty. Lay that aside quickly, he told himself. He shook his head slightly, pressed his lips together firmly once again.

'*I came out to Australia to see my dad. He's dying. I got called up for England. I've only played one game. It's crazy.*'

Grace tapped the screen of her mobile and handed it to him. Greg's ordeal had just hit social media and the *Vanuatu Daily News* website only an hour previously.

England rugby league star found buried alive!

Greg Duggan, the World Cup star who became a friend of Vanuatu through his sporting behaviour at Port Vila Stadium, has been found in an underground cell after what appears to have been three days held captive.

Mr Duggan went missing from the England team's accommodation at Breakas Beach Resort and was found earlier today. The player is reported to have been taken to Port Vila Hospital for observation.

The news report helped at least clarify some of the detail Greg had not managed to calculate totally accurately. Three days and an underground cell. Not exactly buried alive as the headline had inferred. Bloody journalists!

'*Do you want to let me in?*'

Grace had gone for a soft, friendly approach second time around. Maybe Greg hadn't cottoned on previously.

She had already researched Greg. She'd been to Breakas. She knew about Karla, but she wanted Greg to tell her. She knew about Hopton Town's demise, about Greg's divorce from Diane, about his son Kyle, about his dad, about his girlfriend Susie, what had happened in Lanzarote, Greg's heroics on and off the pitch for Hopton and in Playa Blanca.

Grace knew there was much more. Now she wanted to get inside Greg's head. To her mind his abduction could be the key to all of what was happening on Efate.

Greg looked across at her. He dodged her question. Look at what had happened the last time he put his trust in a pretty woman.

'… *I need to contact people, let them know I'm ok. I need my mobile. It should be at Breakas. I didn't take it with me when I was chased out of my room. No time. If I had, I'd have been able to call to get myself out of trouble.*'

'*You think? …*'

It was another of Grace's sarcastic tones. She explained herself as Greg looked at her quizzically over her quick-fire riposte.

'*You were in an underground cell. Highly unlikely you'd have had any signal. And without a charger your battery would have died anyway.*'

'*Can you just take me to Breakas?*'

Greg was getting tired of this already, this questioning. He wasn't one for words and explanation, preferring action. Grace could hear and feel his mood. She decided that what she was chasing needed him more than he needed her just at the moment, maybe just maybe she could get him to start trusting her.

As Grace guided the Jimny out from Port Vila another car followed.

CHAPTER 50

'So, tell me …'

Grace was driving. It wasn't a long drive to Breakas. She knew that much and wanted to get what she could from Greg in the time she had before they arrived.

She had started the car and had weaved through stationary vehicles in Port Vila initially before reaching the wider streets. She had left a silence, to give Greg a little time to himself. He'd just left hospital after all, and without the approval of medics. Who knew where his head, his mind and his body were at? He had closed his eyes, had taken a deep breath. She didn't have much time.

'C'mon Greg, give me something here …'

Grace returned her eyes to the road after briefly looking across at Greg. They were now moving out of Port Vila and heading towards Pango on the Elluk Road. It was more of a country lane than a road.

'I'm sorry about your dad …'

Grace was trying a different tack. Try to be friends. Empathise. But she didn't want to waste time and this story had a long way to run, she was sure of that.

Still no reaction from Greg apart from a minimal shrug of acceptance and slight smile that Grace was trying to be nice.

Grace stopped the car. Greg looked. They weren't at Breakas. What was this?

'Look, I totally get that you don't know what's happening … that you're here to play for your country, but whatever is going on here involves you, whether you like it or not. I'm a journalist. I want the story. You're my lead …'

Grace had been looking Greg in the eye throughout. She wanted his reaction, some kind of confirmation back from him that what she was saying was at least making sense. She saw very little.

Greg, for all his recent experiences in difficult situations, was still not the most forthcoming when it came to allowing outsiders into his problems. His mouth opened marginally, he clicked his tongue against his lower lip, then made an indentation with his front teeth against it too. That was it. Sum total of his reaction.

Grace had left room for Greg to say something, but he hadn't. Her exasperation with him was plainly evident. She started the car again and tried once more. This time her eyes were fixed on the road.

'I know you're not as dumb as you're trying to appear ...'

She gave a quick sideways glance. Saw his face react marginally better to sarcasm.

'... I just don't know why you wouldn't try opening up to me ... why not tell me all of what has happened since you came from England and let me help in any way? ...'

Another sideways glance as she continued driving now on to Pango Road and only half a mile from Breakas Resort.

Grace had had enough of his stonewalling. She genuinely could not see why Greg was keeping schtum. She hung out the white flag. Spread her hands while maintaining control of the steering wheel.

'Okay, okay, I'm done ... I'll just drop you off at the hotel ...'

Greg was grateful for the lift back to Breakas. He had also been grateful for Grace's help in getting him out of Port Vila Hospital, but none of that warranted opening up to someone he didn't know. Grace appeared genuine, but Greg's confidence on who to trust had taken a massive knock.

Grace saved her last effort for when Greg was about to get out of the car as she stopped it in the resort car park.

'You know, I do know more about you than you think ...'

Greg looked at her, his expression fixed on blank. Grace couldn't just give up on him. This was her one and only lead. She'd worked hard on this case already, her research on Greg had told her one thing. Trouble seemed to find him.

'Saving lives, beating the bad guys, bedding beautiful women, a

dad, a hero, stop me if I'm not right won't you ...'

Greg gave an involuntary slight smile. Not much of one, but enough. To Grace it was the first sign of the dam wall bursting. It was what she wanted. Greg realised now how pretty Grace was when she screwed her eyes at him as he looked. Grace caught the look, the feel and a possible intent immediately. She gave her best affected affronted voice.

'This is not a come-on Mr Duggan!'

Grace then laughed.

'But I am pleased that we finally appear to be making headway. You know, you really make a girl work hard ...'

Grace left a pause. Raised her eyebrows and resumed the more humorous approach which now seemed to be getting the results she was looking for.

'Shall we attempt to retrieve your phone ... together?'

Greg didn't know quite how she had done it, but Grace had made him relax. She had broken his defences and there was something about her that he really liked. She had been great in the hospital. She hadn't had to help in getting him out, even though he recognised that she had done it in her own interests. Nonetheless she had still gone through with it.

He'd also enjoyed her company and her piss-taking of his manner when she had been trying to get him to smile. He'd tried all he could in the car not to give her any information, yet now they were walking into Breakas together almost as a couple of friends. How had that happened?

'Mr Duggan. Welcome back ...'

The hotel manager and owner was Reid Jefferson, an Australian who had moved out to Vanuatu 15 years ago, initially on a 12-month contract, and had fallen in love with the resort and the island of Efate. He was genial, as well as being ultra-proud of his hotel that he had purchased five years ago.

'We were all shocked to hear what had happened to you ...'

Greg hadn't known what to expect on his arrival. He had already calculated that the England players and officials would by now have landed in Papua New Guinea for the match which was scheduled for tomorrow in Port Moresby.

'I have several messages for you and also …'

Jefferson turned behind his desk for the messages and at the same time produced Greg's phone with an epic flourish.

Greg and Grace glanced at each other and both appeared to hold back a snigger at the way in which Jefferson had over-acted his role. It was only handing over a bloody phone for God's sake!

'Mr Duggan, we are all at your disposal. If you need anything just let me or any of my team know.'

Once again Greg and Grace looked at each other, now almost betraying their smiles as they made their way down the corridor to Greg's suite. When they were out of eyesight of Reid Jefferson they let their smiles out more broadly.

'At least he's a lot more friendly than the one you had in Playa Blanca …'

Grace raised her eyebrows and cocked her head somewhat cheekily in response to her own comment.

It was intended to show Greg that she knew a good deal about him and his heroics.

She was going to now keep up the momentum over what she had already found out about Greg. He'd dealt with a previous hotel manager extremely dramatically while under different pressures on Lanzarote.

Greg let it go. Grace had already cemented her position with him for the foreseeable future with her charm and well, grace. And yet he still hadn't told her anything more. It was Greg's turn to raise his eyebrows back in her direction on hearing her next line.

'We are all at your disposal, Mr Duggan …'

Grace now pined towards Greg. Once again mocking him.

She might not have been trying to come on to him, but it certainly appeared to Greg that she was.

In Grace's land this was her way of continually breaking him down. She had seen that dam burst ever so slightly previously, she now felt it had given way almost completely and she was determined it would not be rebuilt.

Jefferson had told Greg that the suite he'd occupied was still his. The England squad was due to return after the game in Port Moresby as two of the World Cup quarter-finals were scheduled to take place at Port Vila and regardless of whether England finished first or second in their group both games would be played on Efate.

All of the rooms had been paid for while the team was away and as such the hotel was now extremely quiet.

'Well, *this beats the dog's doings out of my little room in Port Vila.*'

Grace whistled low through her teeth as she took a look around the room while Greg set about opening his written or typed messages.

Greg couldn't help but feel a bit strange about being back in the suite he'd fled from several days ago. It seemed an age since he'd received the call to flee. But that strangeness could be put to one side as he took in all of these notes before embarking on the phone calls. His phone having needed charging first.

First up was a note from England Rugby League's press and media relations executive Annie Laing, who basically reiterated what Reid had already told him.

Everyone delighted that he was back, not to worry about anything, just to convalesce until the party returned and try to stay on site and safe. Fairly businesslike memo. Next was the note from head coach Shane Chislett who kept a similar line.

The third was from Karla.

'Greg. *I am so very sorry. I hope you are okay. Forgive me. Karla xx*'

What had she to be sorry about? What was it he had to forgive?

Greg had known right from the start that Karla having been there hadn't seemed right. He'd felt it but had given way to her, and he'd enjoyed being with her.

He lingered over the note.

There was more he needed to know about her now. She was

implicated in some way for her to have offered her apologies. She had turned up just before he had fled, again with an apology. She knew what was going on. Find her and maybe he'd have an idea what this was all about.

'*Anything?*'

Grace had completed her tour of the suite, including the bedroom which she had been pleased that she had conducted on her own. Greg was sitting on the sofa in the living area.

Greg shrugged, made a face that said he wasn't sure and handed Grace what he'd just read.

'*Girlfriend?*'

Greg wrinkled his nose, grimaced ever so slightly and made an iffy kind of gesture with both hands, fingers outstretched rotating them a little left and right.

'*Kinda.*'

Grace's fast becoming regular raised eyebrows steadied her from over-mocking her reluctant talker.

'*Kinda either was or wasn't?*'

Grace ventured, trying to get something more while returning her eyes to the note.

'*You'd had sex?*'

It was out of her mouth before she'd pressed her filter. Sometimes Grace berated herself for coming out with what her head was thinking before even she was ready for it. She wasn't about to take it back though. He avoided the direct answer.

'*She showed up here, might have even been here before we flew over. She was all over me ...*'

Greg watched for Grace's reaction, anticipating some form of Grace-type humour. Eyebrows, the mocking tone or look. He received nothing back. Grace was finally receiving information from him. She wasn't about to cajole or make fun right now. This was pay-dirt time for the past half hour. The dam finally giving way completely.

'*... I knew there was something not right, just instinct, beautiful girl, on her own, here, making a play for me that was just so obviously put on, me just being me, taken in by another beautiful girl ...*'

Grace hadn't had the opportunity until now to pick up on how self-deprecating Greg could be, mainly because he'd said sod all. She now saw this wasn't some kind of superstar in front of her, as projected by the rugby league media, but just a man.

She started to find him more endearing than she had previously thought. She'd had him originally in the mean and moody bracket but had now changed her mind. To her Greg was a man who appeared to have no airs and graces. A normal man who just happened to be in the spotlight because of how well he played.

It was her turn now to keep quiet and listen while Greg carried on recounting. Greg shook his head as he rose from the sofa to head toward the doors that led out onto a patio. He was agitated with himself. He carried on.

'But typically ...'

He shrugged again. Blew out an exhalation through puffed cheeks and lips. His voice lowered.

'You know my track record ...'

Grace let it pass. Greg seemed to be beating himself up about this, but now that she had finally got him talking Grace wasn't about to get in his way.

It was a knock at the door to his suite that brought about his conclusion.

Greg had a moment of panic. He'd not waited the last time there was someone at his door. He'd run. No phone call this time. No warning.

This time Grace was with him. Was that good or bad? Had he done the wrong thing coming back? Had he just walked into something he could have easily avoided?

CHAPTER 51

Grace moved towards the door. As she did so she held a small handheld gun. Glock 42 miniature.

Where she'd had it stowed was a mystery. Grace just seemed to have produced it from nowhere.

Some journalist thought Greg. Journalist with firearm. How many carried them? Maybe it was an Australian thing?

Grace looked across to Greg, put her finger to her lips for him to keep quiet. It was a look of askance. She raised her chin, eyes wide, head slightly cocked.

It was Grace who chose to speak.

'Who is it?'

Grace wasn't about to mention who she was and had made the decision that it might be better, to perhaps catch the person or persons at the door off-guard, if it was her voice rather than a male voice, Greg's, that was perhaps anticipated.

'Grace Elliott, put your gun down and just let me in. I'm here to see Greg.'

The voice was businesslike yet informal.

It was Grace who had been caught off-guard. Her eyes had widened, eyebrows couldn't have been more raised. Almost comical. She looked at Greg. Who the hell knew who she was? And who in hell's name knew she even had a gun?

Greg nodded at her, motioned for Grace to put her gun down. Grace was dubious about doing so but did as Greg had said. What if he'd got it wrong? She re-stowed the firearm but with her hand hovering over it.

'Greg!'

Grahame Pythagoras Kraft, otherwise known as GPK, entered with a beaming smile, open-armed and embraced Greg briefly before giving a cursory nod towards the attentive Grace.

Greg had known his voice immediately from the other side of the door, which is why he had responded in the way he had with Grace over the firearm. GPK's voice was unmistakable, like some kind of genial country pub landlord.

'*Dear God man, you sure do know how to get yourself involved in some serious shit and drag everyone else through it with you.*'

Greg had no idea what Grahame Pythagoras Kraft meant.

'*What are you doing here Grahame? I mean, it's good to see you …*'

The veteran newspaper editor and investigative journalist had led a team that had helped bring about the demise of Geoffrey Quinigan QC. The man who had been involved in the killings of his deputy editor Jeff Markham as well as Hopton Town owner and his newspaper owner Bob Irvine. Quinigan hadn't actually pulled the trigger but was implicated due to the heist he was pulling off at the time of Hopton's ground for development.

GPK had hunted down Quinigan on Lanzarote. Greg had been involved in his demise, working alongside GPK, performing heroics. Susie had become embroiled in the events too. Greg had saved her life, as she had talked affectionately about the last time they had been together.

Now GPK was here, out of nowhere and Greg knew there had to be good reason.

Grace didn't know quite where she stood and was frustrated that just as she had felt she had been getting somewhere with Greg this had happened, but it was all more information for her to take in. She let the two of them get on with it.

Greg clearly hadn't needed to introduce her. Kraft's mentioning of her by name from the other side of the door had seen to that. How had he known? The hotel owner perhaps?

GPK now turned his attention to Grace.

'*International Centre for Integrity in Sport. What do you know about it, Grace Elliott of Australia Today? That is the cover you're using isn't it?*'

Grace looked at GPK as formidably as she could. Who was this guy? She held her lips together tightly and shook her head almost apologetically.

'*Integrity in Sport?*'

It was Greg who had intervened.

Grace was grateful for the swerve it brought about in GPK's attention.

GPK swiftly shifted from Grace to Greg.

'*What do you know?*'

Kraft was surprised. He hadn't anticipated Greg being aware of the name.

So far as GPK was concerned Greg perhaps having some kind of inside track was a bit out of leftfield.

Greg relayed his experience on the plane, the two women on the Airbus and their plush apartment on board the flight. The pictures they'd shown him. Maria Cavaleros and the other woman at the end, in compromising positions with the male face blurred out.

GPK rubbed his chin. Rested back on the sofa with Greg now sat perched on a chair and Grace stood near the doors toward the beach.

'*Two years ago, after Quinigan, I retired …*'

Greg nodded. He'd not had any dealings with GPK since.

'*… then out of the blue, about three weeks ago I received some information that I just couldn't ignore … it came from a woman … that woman was Madeleine Jardine.*'

GPK paused. He wanted the elements to sink in.

'*I met her. She said she had contacted me because she'd read about the Quinigan case and that I hadn't had the whole story. She couldn't live with herself any longer if she didn't tell me what she knew.*'

Kraft turned more fully to Grace.

'*I was the editor of a newspaper. We had published the story and had syndicated it to the nationals.*'

He now turned back to Greg, while maintaining his tale to them both.

'*Madeleine Jardine said that her husband had been just as guilty and had been the one calling the shots …*'

GPK paused momentarily. Taking a glass of water that Greg

had provided.

'… *that night when Bob Irvine and you were shot – and when Jeff Markham was murdered days before. And that she was mentioning it now because she and her husband were finished.*

'*What matters to me is justice for the murders of my old boss Bob Irvine and my colleague Jeff Markham, as I've always wanted. That's why I'm here.*'

Kraft rested back a little, only for a second or two before turning again more fully towards Grace.

'*Which is where you come in my dear.*'

GPK took out the laptop from the slim bag he'd brought with him.

'*I work better with these than I do with tablets. At least my fingers know what they're doing with actual keys on an actual keyboard rather than catching the wrong key and having to alter text as I go along.*'

He opened up a download which contained two photographs. They were the ladies from the plane. It still made no sense to Greg.

'*So far as I can make out there is no official organisation that goes by the name International Centre for Integrity in Sport. And I'm not talking just about Google searches. We have looked everywhere. There are several regulatory bodies within sport that seek to eradicate cheating or drug misuse, and there is something known as the International Partnership Against Corruption in Sport, but this isn't known at all.*'

Greg was finding this hard to process.

'*I don't get it. Why would they say they are something when they are not? And how come you knew the name?*'

'*Where I come in?*'

Grace had added. Where did she suddenly come in? How did GPK know? About her cover? GPK carried on.

'*You see, Grace Elliott, my contacts at Australia Today tell me there is no journalist, on their staff or freelance, print or online by your name. Would you care to enlighten?*'

CHAPTER 52

'He's back at the hotel, but with a girl … Yeah … Couldn't follow him inside straight away but found a way in a few minutes later … An older guy is now with them … couldn't hear what he said clearly enough though … he went in … still there now …'

'Get a photograph of this older guy … and the girl … forward them both to me when you have them … and stay with Duggan.'

Grahame Pythagoras Kraft was waiting on a response from Grace.

This was all messing with Greg's mind. Why the hell had he been made a target? And why were people not who they said they were? It was becoming a theme.

'My father is Bob Rudd.'

Grace was composed. Straight-faced. She was showing no sign of breaking down as she mentioned her father by name.

'He was a liar, a cheat, he used people but, he was still my father. I came out here to find him. He was in trouble. I was too late.'

'But you stayed?'

GPK already knew what Grace had told him. But he wanted the rest.

'Come on Ms Elliott or Ms Rudd or whatever your real name is. You expect me to believe that someone carrying a Glock 42 miniature has it just in case her father or anyone needed a hand? Don't try my patience here.'

How the hell had he known what she was carrying?

'Elliott was my mother's name before she married. I've always felt more comfortable with it, especially given Father's …'

Grace hesitated.

'… history. You're right. I've not yet been published by anyone and if you've done your homework you already know I graduated recently with a first with honours in investigative journalism at Griffith. The gun now goes with my territory. I'm lead marksman at Gold Coast Gun Club. Licensed firearm. It's handy to have around.

Especially as I'm here to hunt down his killer and gun down the bastard. But then you already know this, I presume?'

Kraft relented, nodded his appreciation.

'So … where do I come in then, Mr Grahame Pythagoras Kraft?'

She had searched him on the net on her phone. GPK elaborated.

'First, I need to know what you know …'

He turned to Greg also.

'… what both of you know. Your father, Grace. And what has happened to you, Greg, since I last saw you. And then Grace and I, and my team will aim to make some sense of all this … and we might finally get justice, Greg for three years ago.'

Grace had listened intently and had a feeling that this was developing into something way less than the real story.

This old man Kraft was seeking vengeance and yes, she too wanted retribution for what had happened to her father no matter how wayward he had been.

But to Grace the story here was way bigger than that of justice for murders. This story was huge.

She was going to be no bit-part player for this old man turning his final trick.

'Mr Kraft, GPK, let me now enlighten you. This whole Rugby League World Cup is corrupt. My father was part of it. Zoe Miller, the chief executive, seems to be so too, but I have not been able to corroborate that just yet. This island has had its worst ever spate of high-profile murders. Did you ever reason why this little island in the middle of the ocean was made a host for not just one, but four games!? It just doesn't make any sense until you look around and under.

'Somebody or some people see Vanuatu as the next big thing. I'm not sure quite why and I certainly don't know who just yet, although based on my work I have names that could be involved, but someone, somewhere is behind all of this and there is a very good reason. It's greed.'

Grace stopped for a second, mimicking her elder journalistic counterpart. She took a drag from a glass of water. Eyes fixed on GPK.

'This isn't some 'let's get the son-of-a-bitch' wild west. We are dealing with sharp people with sharp brains who will stop at nothing, as they have already.

'We are talking billions worth of investment here on Efate, we are talking hitmen who will have more than my paltry Glock 42 miniature and we are talking individual people getting seriously wealthy out of it all. That's what I know so far. And for your information one of those men destined for this new hyper-wealth appears to be your man, Julian Jardine.'

Grace stopped again. Held her head back, lips tight together she looked GPK straight in the eye.

'Now do you want to see this through and run the risk of not enjoying your retirement? Or are you out? And I wouldn't blame you if you were.'

Fuck me, was Greg's reaction. Grace could see that much in Greg's eyes too. She turned to him next.

'And I wouldn't blame you if you wanted to get home to that son of yours, go and see your dad before you know what, see your girlfriend again. After what you've been through is there really any point you being out here? You can't play any further part in the games can you?'

It was as Grace moved around the living area that her own world disappeared.

CHAPTER 53

'*Do it!*'

In the split second following the command and the trigger being pulled Grace slumped to the floor.

'*Get down!*'

Greg bellowed to GPK who was already on the move.

Grace now lay still, lifeless. Blood spilled out across the rug on the floor.

Where the hell was Kraft going?

Greg's body was in no shape to run, or so he felt. He had hit the deck immediately, but GPK hadn't wasted time. He had run. Adrenaline pumping fast.

The gunshot had been silent, but Greg had quickly worked out where it had come from. The doors. Those bleeding doors again, leading to the beach.

But they also led around to the swimming pool and bar area. The perpetrator would have attempted to get away as fast as possible and Greg knew from personal experience that the beach wasn't the quickest means of escape unless there was a boat.

GPK had made his exit through the hotel room door. Greg was relieved for his friend.

Part of Greg wanted to check on Grace, that she was okay. But he made a snap decision that to chase the gunman would prove more productive.

Greg had expected a twinge or two from his earlier captivity and whatever the blow had been, but as he ran he was pleasantly surprised. He told himself, ironically, that any twinges might not matter in a second or two if the gunman turned and blasted him out of sight. He stopped for a second. Where the fuck was this gunman. Think. Look. Listen.

Greg heard a commotion coming from the bar and swimming pool area. Then an almighty splash. He attempted a sprint around a corner of the hotel where the bar and pool would come into sight.

An island dance and entertainment troupe of indigenous Ni-Vanuatuan men, several sporting rugby league style strong upper body physique, had been the gunman's downfall.

The gunman had rounded the corner with no expectation of them, had charged into one, who had reacted quickly in holding him, and two others had held on as the group's momentum had taken them all into the pool.

The hotel restaurant's diners laughed and applauded as they thought it was part of the show. GPK appeared from the hotel reception that ran through to the dining area.

Greg explained to the troupe what had just happened, that a woman lay dead and that the man was the murderer.

The man protested his innocence but the empty gun holster on his body gave the game away and one of the troupe, while maintaining his position as entertainer for the diners, politely and with a permanent smile on his face towards them, cupped the gunman's balls in his hand and tightened his grip on them like a carpenter's vice.

As the man howled another of the troupe pushed and then held him underwater while another slammed his head against the pool wall several times.

Two of Danford Napakauranga's police force appeared on the scene five minutes later, alerted by GPK having spoken with Reid. Another car arrived two minutes later and Alex Lui five minutes after them. The ambulance had sped into Breakas car park in between the first and second arrivals. Hotel manager Reid Jefferson had gone straight to Grace.

'Is she going to be alright?'

Greg's voice was more hopeful than it would have been when he had first seen Grace slump to the floor. Paramedics were around her.

'We need to get her to the hospital right now ...'

That was all Greg could get out of them as they left as speedily as possible.

Dazed, beaten and bedraggled the man responsible for Grace's shooting was hauled ignominiously out of the pool after being held under for longer than was good for his health and having been assured that any playful days he had ever had in store were no longer on the agenda. The common story was that his testicles must have caught something exceedingly sharp off their costumes.

Alex Lui and his men took statements from Greg, GPK and the entertainers while the gunman was escorted away to the hospital under armed guard.

Alex Lui first asked after Greg's welfare. He then voiced exactly the questions Greg was already asking himself. Why did he think Grace had been targeted?

Greg explained to Alex Lui that he had no idea, he'd only met Grace earlier in the day. GPK said that he had just arrived at Breakas that afternoon. When Alex asked the purpose of Kraft's visit he received the predictable reply of the Rugby League World Cup.

He seemed more concerned on getting off to the hospital to hopefully question a recovering Grace and the gunman.

CHAPTER 54

'Wow! Wow! Wow! That is another amazing piece of magic by the Kumuls! And it is Isaac Izamua again! The Papuan half-back has taken this game to England in this first half and this time he's scampered over the try line for a score of his own!'

Commentator Brad Kearns had made the trip on board the same flight as the England team.

'Laurie, this isn't the same England team we saw play against Greece or Vanuatu in their earlier games. I mean, it's more or less the same personnel but without that spark. Papua are on another level to their previous opponents but I'd have expected more.'

Laurie Northey agreed with his Australian compatriot as they relayed their thoughts on Channel 17 and Cloud TV.

'... and there's half-time ... it's Papua New Guinea 12 England 0 in what has to go down as a very disappointing first stanza for the England boys. The atmosphere, as always in Port Moresby, is highly charged and there's nothing the Kumuls like better than putting one over on the bigger nations than here in their own backyard.'

Greg was watching the game in the bar at Breakas. It had been nearly 24 hours since the attempt on Grace's life. She was in recovery. She had been very fortunate with no more than a flesh wound and shock. She had been sedated when Greg had visited, but he was assured she would be fine.

Following the shooting and subsequent mayhem Greg had finally made contact with Col and with Diane.

Dad was no change. Mum was struggling. Col said she'd been holding it all together for so long but that the strain was now beginning to show. Greg's own dilemma hadn't helped. News of his personal drama had been everywhere on all media.

Diane was relieved to hear her ex-husband's voice, more relieved than Greg had anticipated. He reckoned the relief was more about not having to give Kyle terrible news, but he was touched by Diane's voice which was breaking when she had spoken with him. Kyle wasn't around to talk to his dad.

He tried Susie. No reply, just an automated message saying to try later. Nothing.

GPK had been with Greg when they had visited Grace together. She was being kept in for observation overnight. Greg and GPK had split afterwards with Greg heading back to Breakas while Kraft explained he wanted to talk with a few people.

The game restarted. The Papuan crowd, renowned for providing visiting teams with a hostile welcome during matches, but perfectly charming and affable when the 80 minutes were up, was a seething mass as the England team fought to bring themselves back into the game.

Freddie South, Steve 'Rocking' Docking and Neil 'The Brickie' Duncan combined in a devastating charge down the left side that saw 'The Brickie's' legendary sidestep and swerve wrongfoot half of the Papuan side, only to be tackled close to the line by Popoli Baru who, along with earlier try scorer Isaac Izamua had played with Greg in Playa Blanca.

Big Mick Green had come on from the bench for his second spell and charged for the line from the next move, taking four tacklers with him he was also stopped just short.

The Papuan crowd was now set at high on volume as they cheered on their national heroes.

Once again the England team advanced. Once again the Papua New Guinea side repelled their flow. England were on full power after a circumspect first half.

Brad Kearns was impressed although had a word of caution.

'These England boys have come out with a whole different perspective in these early minutes of the second half, but they will need to turn pressure into points. Ohh! My word what a hit-up that was! Makali Gene take a bow!'

The Papuan second row forward had taken out Mason Bell with such force that he had propelled his England counterpart back from the line by seven metres. It was a massive hit that left Mason Bell wiped out and the ball spilling from his grasp.

With bewildering pace it was another of Greg's ex teammates

from Eruption, Manuwai Manuai, who gathered possession and set off on a run that saw him weave magic to the try line that even a supercharged Vinny Venus couldn't cover.

'Well that's g'day Manuai and maybe good night Vienna to England's hopes of getting back into this game after looking so good in these opening minutes … 16-0 to the Kumuls.'

Greg watched from the bar at Breakas as the Papuans took the game out to 18-0 with the kick at goal. It was starting to look beyond England already.

Greg watched on helpless. England repeatedly bombarded the Papua New Guinea defence but the one element they were missing was a bust of the defence or a kick through. The Papuan defence was so strong.

Five minutes from time Neil 'The Brickie' took the ball up, shimmied, stepped off his right foot, sidestepped once, then again, dummying to his teammate Steve 'Rocking' Docking on his way to the line and touching down in the corner to bring the score back to 18-4 but it was too late for a big finish.

'Hello stranger.'

At first, he couldn't believe what he was seeing.

She was there. Radiant. That perfect smile he'd fallen for years ago. Those eyes that sparkled. It still took him seconds to believe it, but here she was and looking more than fantastic. Greg was overwhelmed.

She was wearing a beautiful, alluring white thin strapped summer dress with grey polka dots and matching grey stilettos. Susie looked a million dollars.

All Greg could do at first was smile, the biggest smile he'd had in weeks as he drank in her look, her eyes, her smile. The game didn't matter anymore. It had gone for England and it had gone for Greg before the final hooter sounded.

Susie cocked her head to one side as she now stood in front of Greg, smiled again that smile he loved, put her index finger lightly to her lower lip with her tongue resting delicately against the finger and lip. She could see that Greg was happy.

'Have you missed me, darling?'

CHAPTER 55

'She's here … yes … watching her … nope, nothing … okay, will do …'

The call had come in as she had arrived. He was to stay, see what happened, report back on any movement as he had been, apart from the time when he hadn't! He wasn't about to mention that. The other end of the call was oblivious to what had occurred earlier.

Greg was the most contented he had been in weeks. The remainder of the evening had been quite simply very special. It hadn't been as though he and Susie had been energetic in their lovemaking. It had been a tender togetherness in which both had found sweet fulfilment.

He had known. Felt it. Just before touching Susie's body. 'Go carefully, be loving, hold me.' He had listened to the unspoken message and heeded its content.

'Yeah …'

Greg smiled. He had rested up on his elbow alongside Susie in bed. Susie smiled back, gave a little move of her head and the slightest of giggles from the back of her throat, narrowed her eyes a little without losing the smile.

'Yeah what?'

She rested up on her elbow too, mirroring him, her hand cupping her cheek and chin.

Greg rested his head back. Looked up at her smiling above him now.

'Yeah, I missed you …'

Susie rolled her eyes at him and gave him a little playful poke on his chest.

'Naughty Mister Greg. I asked you that question last night and you've only answered it this morning …'

Susie poked him playfully a second time as she looked into his eyes, hers now glistening in what seemed to Greg a lovely start to the day. Susie kept up the cheeky role.

'… *I hope Naughty Mister Greg is not so slow in other things …
oh! … It seems not!*'

Greg and Susie shared a morning of gentle and passionate lovemaking that was satisfying for both of them.

Greg still wanted to ask what Susie had meant with the last embrace they'd had in the UK. He wanted to get whatever it was out into the open. But in some ways he also didn't, because he didn't want to hear that they were over – which they couldn't be now, the way last night and this morning had gone so far, could they?

But if there was something Susie had been trying to tell him because of some dreadful illness or that there was somebody else he would rather have known. But would he?

Susie purposely hadn't told Greg what had happened back home before Greg had left and how later she had been whisked away in the Range Rover Evoque. She had made the decision that Greg had already faced up to enough dilemmas again. She knew of his latest abduction. They had talked about it the previous evening as he'd brought her up to speed.

Susie had reckoned that if she had told Greg about what had happened to her, he would have become over-protective. He'd already saved her life on Lanzarote and she knew he would go through brick walls to save her from anything. She had received every call, every text. There had been times when she had looked at her phone, seen it was Greg, but hadn't had the heart to answer him.

The one thing that Susie knew over anything else was that there was no way she could tell him what was going on.

She had come to Vanuatu. They were enjoying every moment of being together now, but Greg knew that these times had so often been short-lived previously. Stuff popped into his brain about other occasions.

He thought back to when Susie had appeared so gorgeously and dramatically in the Rooftop Bar of the Lanzarote Eruption stadium wearing that amazing white, figure-hugging dress that had stopped everyone in their tracks. She had been gone less than 48 hours later, back to the UK. There had never been an explanation.

Greg had never wanted Susie to have to explain herself. He'd always been more than happy with their times together however brief they had been, but increasingly he had felt a longing for those times they had to be far more.

'What is it …?'

He said the words gently. They had finally spilled over from what he had been thinking.

They had eventually moved from the bedroom after sharing each other for the morning in bed and in the shower. They were now having a light lunch in the bar area. They had missed breakfast by some considerable distance. They'd been talking about nothing consequential, just chat, and somehow the words had just come.

He'd asked them in such a way that Susie had to know what he was saying. That he was trying his best to open up the conversation and deal with the elephant in the room.

No sooner had he asked the question than he wished he hadn't.

He saw Susie's expression change immediately from happy girl to what he couldn't calculate. What was she hiding from him?

Greg could read plays in a rugby league game, he could see things before they happened, understood what was going on and was now known as a magician on the field because of it. He wished now that he could at least trade a modicum of that talent for the same here.

Was Susie ill? He didn't think so, judged by their recent endeavours that morning and the night before.

Was Susie in trouble? Maybe. But she hadn't given any impression of things being so.

Was Susie moving on? Had she moved on? Was this a last chance saloon? He couldn't see that, again judged on what had just been happening. He was at a loss.

Susie looked away at the ocean. She smiled, that smile. Held his hand across the table. There was something, Greg knew there was.

'*When's your next game?*'

It was as good a sidestep as Neil 'The Brickie' Duncan had used against Papua New Guinea for his try. But why?

Greg decided on the same as Susie. He let it go. They talked about other things, how he was. He told her he wouldn't rate his chances highly of playing in the quarter-final against France. Susie returned to her playfulness.

'*There's nothing wrong with your fitness, so far as I can see Mister Greg ...*'

Greg decided this was infinitely more preferable than asking the question again. Susie clearly didn't want to share whatever it was. Greg could cope with that.

His phone sparked to life.

'*Hi Dad ...!!*'

Kyle's voice, and Susie's, were the two that put a smile to Greg's face every time he heard them.

He now had Susie with him, which was fantastic, and suddenly his heart began pounding with the thought that perhaps soon, somehow, when he was back in the UK it would be the most amazing feeling to have his son with him too.

It was a recorded message. Kyle had left him a note to say he was playing in a Cup competition as his next game tomorrow, which would now be today since it would be the early hours of the morning back in the UK.

'*... just like you Dad! Hope I can get another try! See you Dad ... love you!*'

Greg couldn't help himself but smile. Susie knew how much Kyle meant to Greg.

'*You miss him.*'

It was said affectionately. Straightforwardly. Greg gave a tightlipped smile and the slightest of nods.

'*Kyle and you ... my everything ...*'

Christ! He'd done it again! Where was his filter? He never

usually let out this kind of emotion verbally. What was going on with him? It was like he'd taken some kind of truth pill that meant whatever he was thinking was just spilling out. He felt his eyes going moist.

This time Susie's reaction was to melt. She had been playing it all so coolly, but now he saw her eyes fill with tears, her face lose its composure.

'Oh, darling ...'

Susie's voice was cracking. She put her hand over his, she turned to face him, tears now running down her face.

'That is so ...'

But she couldn't finish her sentence as she chose instead to kiss. It was a kiss that he'd never experienced before. It was not just a kiss, but an emotional tidal wave. Greg felt the same kind of thing that he'd felt the previous evening when he had first touched her again, and when Susie had held him when they were in the UK.

Something told him that sometimes maybe saying what came into his head, without holding back, might actually be okay.

Susie dabbed her eyes with a napkin and made a visit to the bathroom in order to regain her composure, dry her eyes and fix her makeup. She too had also felt that she'd held so much in for far too long. Greg's beautiful words had been the release of it all.

CHAPTER 56

'Mr Duggan?'

Greg had made the move from where he and Susie had been around the bar area for lunch to around the pool. It had hardly been an excursion from one to the other, all of five or six metres at best. He was taking in the rays. He'd slipped off his t-shirt and was just in shorts and shades. Susie had headed back to the suite for a change into her bikini.

Two figures now blotted out his sun. Greg sat up from the lounger. Erin Jackson introduced herself and her partner Razni.

'You mentioned a Karla Karelia to one of our officers in your testimony when you were in hospital. Is there anything else you can tell us about her?'

Greg was relaxed. It was a fair enough question.

'Did she hit on you ...'

Greg swiftly had his filter back firmly in place. Something told him to do so.

'She came on a bit, that was all ...'

'And did you? Have sex?'

It was Razni who had asked. Greg hadn't wanted the question, especially as Susie could return at any minute. He nodded, tightlipped, no smile.

Susie appeared. She was around ten metres away and nearer the bar. Erin Jackson was on the case straight away.

Watching Greg's eyes, she turned to see the stunning blonde woman, clearly a good deal older than Greg but with a fantastic figure that looked great in her white two-piece bikini with a white tasteful drop shoulder open knit cover up.

Erin's first thought was that this woman may even have been old enough to be Duggan's mother, but that was tempered by this woman's beauty and the way in which Greg had looked over to her.

She was certain of something between them.

Susie had already made up her own mind. She wasn't going to go anywhere near what was going on. She drifted towards the bar. She'd perfected the art of moving away whenever had been necessary over the years and had already spotted whoever it was that Greg had with him before the woman had turned and spotted her.

Susie knew any more eye contact was too much. She had taken up conversation with the Vanuatuan barman, Lani. She settled in enjoying a long, cool beer.

'Hey! Greg, mate!'

'You're so Good, Good, Good, you're so wonderful!'

Freddie South was known in the rugby league playing world as someone who revelled in pranks.

It had been Freddie who had hollered out the greeting and then quickly joining with him around a dozen of the returning England party had not just sung a welcome back to their talisman, they had also paid no heed whatsoever to whoever was with him.

They picked Greg up from his sun lounger while singing and hurled him straight into the pool, which fortunately had nobody else around as they dumped the six-foot-three forward in with an almighty splash.

'You're so wet, wet, wet. You're not so wonderful!'

The players that hadn't been involved in the hurling now joined with those that had and added to the choir.

Freddie had had something in mind for Greg when the squad had been on their way from the airport having touched down from their flight.

Freddie had called Breakas and had spoken with the lady on the reception desk. He'd asked where Greg was.

He was concerned for his teammate, he'd said. Could she just check on him? She'd taken a quick look and had reported Greg seemed fine and where he was.

Freddie had then organised the troops like some ninja warrior style attack. He wanted the big lads and Big Mick Green, Phil Parkin, Neil 'The Brickie', Regan Phillips and Sam

Rivers had all jumped at the chance.

The song rang out around Breakas. The laughter was just what everyone needed even if it was at Greg's expense. Greg appeared rather like King Arthur's sword of Excalibur from the lake, gloriously glistening in the afternoon sun.

'*Are we done?*'

Greg's spluttered words were as much intended for the Detective Superintendent as they were in humour with his teammates.

But he was far from having been done!

During the time it had taken for Greg to resurface from his unceremonious splashdown into the pool, several other players had slipped in or dived in. This time he wasn't just pulled under by the new in-pool squad but also debagged. The protagonists making an appearance with their trophy – Greg's shorts!

The hi-jinx that had taken place in the past minutes had been enough for Jackson and Razni to decamp from where they had been questioning Greg to the bar area. Erin Jackson had chosen their destination because she wanted to find out more about this mystery woman.

There had been something about her that was a connection between Duggan and her. It could be simple and nothing to do with them. The two of them lovers, no more, but Erin just wanted to see. Ask a question.

'*You've known Greg a long time?*'

Susie was at the bar. Erin had sidled next to her. Susie had turned while the action in the pool had been taking place. She had smiled, but then had returned to chatting with the barman.

Susie wasn't taken aback by Erin. She had primed herself just in case the woman had come over.

'*Pardon me?*'

She turned to face Erin Jackson. Smiled her big winning smile. Erin took her time. She wanted to see movement, to see her confidence drain away by being laborious.

'*Greg … I saw the way you looked at him just now …*'

'*Is that his name? I had no idea. Would you like a drink?*'

Susie played it as though she was almost an alcoholic. She turned to the barman, quite pleased with her performance. Better than she had thought. She turned back to Erin. Susie raised her eyebrows. There was questioning in them. She chose not to voice anything, leave that to her.

'*I'm sorry ...*'

Erin chose to accept the woman at face value.

'*... I must have read too much into a glance ... I'm Detective Superintendent Erin Jackson and this is Detective Marlon Razni ... and you are?*'

Jackson was still trying. She felt she had something here.

'*There you are!*'

Susie felt relieved. Grahame Pythagoras Kraft had arrived right on cue.

'*Darling! Great to see you!*'

GPK was loving this, playing it for effect. Susie had first met him on Lanzarote. GPK took up the baton, removing the line of fire for Susie. He gave his most generous smile to Erin Jackson.

'*Introduce me darling ...*'

Susie introduced Erin and Marlon to GPK.

'*Ahh, Australia's finest! Tell me, how are you getting on with tracking down the culprits of those three murders on the island? Terrible thing. We came here for a relaxing holiday. It has been anything but so far ... excuse us ...*'

And with that the newly formed couple of GPK, with his best put-on gentleman's accent, and Susie headed off in the direction of wherever they could that was far out of the reach of the Aussie couplet.

Erin Jackson wasn't certain what kind of smokescreen she'd just had blown in her face, but she knew it was something. What she also knew was that she wasn't going to get very far here.

The earlier splashdown in the pool had by now turned to games. A rugby ball had appeared and was being hurled the length and width of the pool by the players in missile like style aimed at inflicting maximum damage either by direct hit without touching the pool or via the equivalent of skimming stones with a pumped-up Exocet.

It had to end badly. High spirits were in charge and the adrenaline was pumping.

And so it had. Owen Fenchurch had caught the end of the ball smack in the eye and it was closing up immediately.

Shane Chislett was enraged.

He'd just completed a press conference and had made his way to where he'd heard boisterous activity. He wasn't against team bonding and guys enjoying themselves. He'd been involved in enough himself, but he was incensed by what he saw.

'Are you all so bloody stupid!!'

His voice was several decibels louder than anything the hotel guests had ever heard around the pool. Owen Fenchurch went past him covering his eye apologising as he made his way to his room already knowing he could be out of the next game.

'We've just lost to Papua and in two days' time we play a quarter-final. We are only two games away from the World Cup Final. Do you really not see the sense in looking after each other?'

Shane had bellowed so all his squad could hear.

'Since you're so desperate for exercise, get yourselves changed into your training gear and be back here in fifteen minutes!'

Greg hadn't minded Freddie and the boys' antics at all. Whatever injuries he was carrying or fatigue he was experiencing from having been clobbered and held captive for days, this had been fun for him too.

As he'd been grabbed and thrown like a huge rag doll into the pool he'd thought about the damage it might inflict on his body, but when he'd splashed down it had been a great feeling and everything seemed okay as he checked it all out with little stretches and tweaks.

Greg had been known for his quick healing of knocks and pulls through his career and it appeared he had come through his latest trials and tribulations with flying colours. He was ready for whatever Shane Chislett was to demand of him. His first one was swift as Greg made his way out of the pool.

'And Duggan! Get some bloody clothes on!'

CHAPTER 57

'Boss! Paradise Beach Estate! Now!'

Alex Lui had taken the call. He was already moving from where he was in Port Vila as he called out to his boss.

'It's Sela Natavanu. He's dead!'

Laughter was coming from Greg's suite as he made his way down the corridor to change into his training kit after the pool antics. He hesitated before entering but then swiftly calculated who it was.

At first he'd wondered whether somebody else had taken over his suite, but when he opened the door it was as though he'd crashed some private party. Susie was enjoying herself. Her eyes sparkled and danced with that excitement and enthusiasm she always seemed to have when they had first met.

Susie was having a great time.

'Darling, you should have seen Grahame just now. He was great. He saved me from this policewoman. I'd tried to avoid her. This lovely man rescued me like I was a damsel in distress.'

Susie patted GPK's arm as she relayed the tale. GPK was enjoying the attention but splayed the palms of his hands in an 'I did nothing' gesture. He switched his concern to Greg. Susie sensed the shift in mood too. Again, she was first to make the move.

'Darling, are you okay?'

Greg was okay, particularly because Susie was safe. He gave the ball hurling data while changing, taking Susie in his arms for a reassuring embrace and asking her to stay with GPK until he was back and then talked briefly over what his friend had come up with during his day in Port Vila.

'Nothing definite yet, no sign of Jardine, no sign of your two women on the plane, no sighting of Zoe Miller since your game against Vanuatu. Think she's still here somewhere. Go and get to your session. We're good here.'

Sela Natavanu had been a prominent figure in Vanuatu. Not

just a previous prime minister but president of a number of Efate and the country's business organisations, a man who influenced what happened in this nation's archipelago of islands.

He'd been philanthropic, gifting towards new buildings, new developments in housing, Port Vila Hospital, Port Vila Municipal Stadium. He'd basically robbed from everyone – rich or poor – and he'd given back to everyone when he'd had enough of his own. In his terms, basic accounting.

But now he too was dead and within days the country's most well-known figures were gone. As well as a popular young woman who had had the world at her feet.

Danford Napakauranga thought again of all this as he took in the scene that presently faced him at Sela's home. He thought of the days when he, Winston and Sela had been in their youth. When the wine and kava flowed freely, when they had each sported six-packs and the world, or at least the world of the nation that was then called the New Hebrides was at their feet. They had all celebrated the Republic of Vanuatu being founded in 1980.

Those days they'd been happy in each other's company, could have taken on anything.

'He didn't stand a chance, boss.'

Alex Lui relayed what he had just been told from those who had witnessed Sela's execution.

'Shot at close range. Three shooters, maybe four. Our witnesses say that Natavanu's bodyguards disappeared just before the shooting. He was a sitting duck.'

'No way! Absolutely no way!'

Greg had come out of the shower after his hastily arranged England training session.

GPK and Susie were both still in the suite. While Greg had been training they had come up with something that had brought about Greg's strong reaction.

'You must be off your heads ... both of you ... you do remember what happened in Lanzarote?'

Greg could never get out of his mind just how Susie had been left in the Ghost Hotel, chained up and with explosives set to go off. That's when he had saved her. He'd left the Eruption game when she had come up on the big screen. It would stay with him forever. He had been so scared for her life.

'You've had too much to drink, let's just put it down to that shall we?'

The last thing Greg wanted was for the love of his life to put herself in any kind of danger

'I have enough of a hard time wanting to be with you. Now that you're here, why?'

Susie's heart was melting again at Greg's words. He'd never shown this side to him as much as he had recently. She had always thought that their relationship was something they had both picked up and put down, otherwise she wouldn't have … she stopped herself from where her thoughts were going. She softened her voice.

'Darling, please just think of this as me trying to give something back for you saving my life … all I'm going to be doing is hanging around … and you know how good I am at that …'

Susie smiled the smile that always won Greg over. She wasn't so sure he was up for giving way. GPK knew better than to get involved in this.

Susie moved over to Greg and whispered in his ear.

'Darling … we can seal the deal tonight if you like …'

Greg shook his head very slightly, softly and finally allowed himself a glimmer of a smile back to her. He couldn't help himself. It wasn't what she'd just said that had made the difference, it was just her. Everything about her.

Susie kissed him briefly, on the lips. Greg responded. The kiss now not so brief. GPK knew when to disappear. He didn't say a word.

Greg's towel around his waist fell to the floor, Susie's off-the-shoulder dress and panties followed suit. Greg lifted Susie, holding her soft bum as she wrapped her slim legs around his waist. They began moving in rhythm. The deal was eventually sealed sometime later.

CHAPTER 58

I think it's about time we talked, don't you?

Zoe looked at the text again. She had been looking at it on and off for the last hour. Hadn't replied. Wasn't sure whether to. Wasn't sure if it was the right time. If any time would ever be right.

She looked again and began her reply.

Detective Superintendent Erin Jackson was watching her iPhone screen aghast, turned to stone, but with her stomach churning as though it was a tumble dryer on a slow spin with a heavy load inside, her heart racing and her brain completely numb. She couldn't speak, whimpered inside, wanted to cry. There was nothing she could do about it. This would ruin her credibility if not her career.

This goes live in five, unless we have an understanding. Do we?

Erin hesitated. Five minutes. She had no idea who this had come from, but she was between a rock and a hard place. She didn't believe in succumbing to threats. This was exactly that. Blackmail.

She also knew that there was no use reasoning with whoever this was. Fuck! This godforsaken island was doing her head in. The commissioner particularly. Now this.

It was 10am. Greg and the rest of the England squad had only 34 hours before their quarter-final game against France.

Each nation had been playing a game every three or four days. It was crazy for everyone, hardly any time for recuperation.

The tournament had been planned that way through much consultation post-global pandemic which, although it was now fast becoming a distant but painful memory for many, had brought about a quick turnaround competition.

The fans didn't seem to care about the games being close together. They had been turning up in their droves in the various Australian venues, Papua New Guinea and Vanuatu.

England fans were in great spirits and had repopulated Port Vila in the past 24 hours since returning from Port Moresby.

The England players and Chislett already knew most of the French side as they all largely played in the Super League or the Championship.

Among the huge throng of fans landing in Efate were several big names – and one was the most powerful man in world rugby league, Sir Julian Jardine, newly knighted for services to the sport and chairman of the Rugby League International Authority.

CHAPTER 59

'Yeah, mum, I'm waiting, it's gone to message … Hi Dad! … Guess what? …'

Greg's heart melted again as he heard Kyle's voice the next morning. Greg hadn't been able to catch him directly to wish him well, although he had tried, but just hadn't spoken to him. He had left a text wishing his son a good game – and that none of it mattered anyway, win or lose, so long as he was enjoying it.

Greg didn't truly sign up to this last bit, but felt he had to say it, as his dad. It was the first time he'd thought that way, putting it like that. He found it quite cathartic.

'… We won!!!!'

Greg could feel his 7-year-old son's enthusiasm and his massive smile as he continued listening. Kyle sounded so happy.

'… it was amaaaaazing! … and Dad … I scored again, it was amaaaaaazing …'

Kyle laughed almost uncontrollably at this point having stressed the word so much. Greg could hear Diane trying to calm him down just a little in the background, although he also heard the fun and laughter in her voice too.

'Bye Dad! … Byeeeeeeeee!'

That was it. And it was again too late for Greg to respond, or at least not with a phone call. It was 10am and that meant it was midnight back in the UK. Greg sent another text.

It wasn't what he really wanted to do, and he vowed to try and watch the time better, so that he would be able to talk with Kyle at what would hopefully be the right time in future.

He called Col.

Latest update on Dad, hardly anything happening. Dad hadn't moved, said anything for days. There was a calmness in Col's voice that expressed the real situation without actually saying it. Dad was dying. They all knew it. Mum was wobbling a bit.

The brothers talked about the World Cup and sport in general. Just as they were about to finish Col mentioned something that meant little to him but struck an immediate chord with Greg.

'I meant to tell you ... I know you don't read it, but the media here and social media is turning against this World Cup. It's starting to read ugly. There's a lot of bad feeling being generated ...

'The games you're all having to play in such a short space of time – and the shootings where you are of the World Cup accountant, their prime minister, the local girl who everybody knew because of the underwater post office and now today some other local celebrity, another ex-prime minister whose name sounds something like Vanuatu; and then what happened to you ... there's also talk of all sorts, corruption, match fixing, sexism over 'The Pink' ... it's all making things look really dirty about the competition ... and rugby league isn't coming out of this very well at all ...'

This hadn't been the kind of comment Greg had steeled himself for, but it was also the first time he had really begun to take in what was going on around him.

These must have been what Grace had been talking about when she had been with him and GPK. Where was Grace now? She'd been in hospital the last Greg had known. Was she writing all this?

Greg hadn't even known about this latest murder.

Col fired a warning shot to his brother.

'Just play your games, Greg ... and try to stay out of trouble ... I know that bit's not easy for you ...'

Col had meant it in jest, as Greg had taken it, but then thought about his brother's mental and physical state. What he'd gone through.

'Are you even up to playing?'

Greg really didn't know the answer to that one until half an hour later when it was unequivocal. He was crashing into his fellow forwards who were holding tackle pads. He wasn't at breakneck pace, but he wasn't taking it easy either.

GPK was back in Port Vila. He'd spent the early morning

on the Paradise Beach Estate posing as a past business associate of Sela Natavanu. He was also doubling up as the same past associate of Winston Sablan.

All he wanted was names, links, something that would join the dots on the freehold murder spree that was fast becoming part of Vanuatuan life.

Just how that all related to Greg's woes of having been hounded out of two hotels and held captive for three days – and how that had an involvement with Jardine – GPK wasn't sure.

Jardine was part of the World Cup through his lofted position in the rugby league hierarchy and, as Grace had said, just how had this small nation of Vanuatu sealed the hosting of so many matches? Jardine had to be involved.

None of it still made any real sense to him yet, except that someone, somewhere was probably going to end up pretty rich or even more rich than they were already.

Jardine, plus whoever he was in cahoots with, came to mind first – at the expense of those casualties along the way who hadn't stood in line. He so wanted it to be all about Jardine to nail him for this.

It wasn't enough that Madeleine Jardine had shopped her estranged husband. He needed something to pin on him and send him down.

But then GPK's current undercover operations were to come crashing to a halt as a voice spoke delicately to him.

'I've just seen someone who I hoped I'd never see again ...'

Susie was whispering into GPK's right ear, not physically right alongside him but through an earpiece using a mobile phone. The earpiece had been an insurance policy GPK had sought to use so that, hopefully barring any loss of signal, they would be kept in constant touch.

He could feel Susie's confidence draining quickly away. This was Susie at her most insecure. He also knew that at this moment her instinct would be to run, to get out of where she was.

GPK was on red alert. He knew that remaining calm was his

best policy although his heart was pounding.

'Has he clocked you?'

GPK was straight on the case. No messing. He was instantly more concerned with Susie and ensuring she was safe and out of any firing line.

Having Susie with him had been a wrong decision. He knew that now.

They talked as he walked, got into his car and started driving towards the airport. Susie said that she couldn't be sure 'the someone' hadn't seen her.

Susie couldn't be certain that he hadn't shown any signs of having seen her, but GPK knew that his mere presence had been enough to knock her completely off centre. Everything would come back to haunt her.

Susie still had the sense to whisper, even though it was now a strangulated whisper. She was trying hard to keep herself steady, but she felt heady, woozy. She began swaying slightly, put her hand to the wall where she had moved to from having been seated in the arrivals area. She had tried to maintain her role as innocent bystander but seeing this man again had got to her. Again, she whispered in GPK's ear.

'What the hell is he doing here? I thought he was locked up.'

This young man she had just seen was the same man that two years ago in Lanzarote had been responsible for nearly ending her life. She couldn't hide her fears. She was trembling now. Her eyes filled with tears she was still trying desperately to hold back. She was starting to panic. Why had she done this? She couldn't do it.

GPK was now on the road as he heard the worry in Susie's voice.

'Just stay where you are. I'm on my way.'

GPK had been totally aware of the trauma Susie had suffered previously. She had travelled back to the UK with him after what had happened to her in Playa Blanca following her release from hospital.

Greg had wanted Susie to stay in Lanzarote, but she had told him there was no way she could remain on the island at that time. She knew that every day she remained it would just keep bringing back what this young man had done, what he had put her through, the words he had used while he had been feeding his fantasies and perverse nature as he had taunted Greg. All of these actions were now back in her head being replayed over and again.

GPK and Susie had kept up their friendship after landing back in the UK. It was purely platonic. They had made nothing of it with Greg. They simply enjoyed each other's company, found they liked some of the same things. Movies, music and food in the main. She had opened up to GPK much more than she had ever done with Greg. GPK knew things about her.

As GPK pulled out onto the main street, having left Marche de Port Vila where he had gone to prospect further leads he had picked up, about locals who could give him connections to the island's recent murders, another car began to follow.

CHAPTER 60

Julian Jardine hadn't landed on Efate with the masses. He had instead taken his flight to Luganville airport on Espiritu Santo nearly 200 miles north of Efate and just as popular with tourists.

Jardine had used it for quite another reason. It wasn't Efate. He wouldn't be seen by those looking for him until absolutely necessary and he could then arrive his own way. Nobody would know he was on the island until absolutely necessary.

Jardine had issues. Lately his plans had not worked out the way he would have liked, which had cost him a great deal of money. There was a fly in the ointment that had become more than any mild irritation. He was now there to make absolutely certain that everything he had staked was to bring about the greatest ever return on his investment – and dealing with the fly in the ointment was part of his plan.

There was one man whom he wanted to see crushed – and that man was Greg Duggan. Everybody else appeared to be dying on the island. Why not one more!

CHAPTER 61

Grace Elliott/Rudd had discharged herself from hospital.

The bullet had caused a loss of blood but nothing like as bad as she had first feared. It had brought about a flesh injury to her left arm and her initial reaction from being hit and with blood pumping from her wound had been one of shock, which had triggered a reaction to play dead.

She'd had no previous experience of this. She had gone with her own gut reactions. Better to play dead than be dead.

Grace had been the reason behind the stories of ill feeling against the World Cup.

From her hospital bed, in the previous 36 hours before discharging herself, she had generated as much copy as possible, across multimedia social platforms, blogs and podcasts. She had shared 'a victim's story' with every possible organisation and authority across Facebook, Twitter and Instagram.

And the muck she had flown had stuck.

Since sending each story also by email to the press she had also been busy consulting with the Australian national media, mainly over her payments. Her story had reached the *Sydney Morning Herald*, her Holy Grail, *The Australian* and all other regional titles across the country. National broadcast media had picked it up too. Channel 17 were said to be interested.

Grace hadn't been going to let a bullet stand in the way of officially starting her media career. Indeed, she had decided this was to be the real launch pad. She'd taken a bloody bullet for God's sake. Bloody well use it!

She told of her first-hand experience as a victim of the World Cup greed that pervaded on the sunshine island of Efate and of how those who ran the game were parasites intent on their own wealth at the expense of anyone who happened to get in their way.

BULLET FAILS TO SILENCE RUGBY LEAGUE

WORLD CUP SCANDAL!

The headline that appeared in the *Sydney Morning Herald* was above Grace's story that told of 'The Pink', the Women's World Cup, which had just started, and the Disabled World Cup, due to start shortly not being about an all-inclusive sport but a smokescreen for what was the game's biggest ever cover-up.

Through her media barrage Grace inferred corruption at the highest level in the sport and that leading officials were about to earn millions. The officials about to earn their fortunes had allegedly used the game's mantra of broadening the game's horizons through investment in the islands in the South Pacific and had taken backhanders from the island nation of Vanuatu, without ever mentioning by name Julian Jardine, Zoe Miller or Bob Rudd, who was not her father. She had made that bit up. She was a journalist after all.

Grace went on to label the island community's business leaders as 'small-time criminals using bribery and thugs to silence others while lining their own pockets'.

She listed Winston Sablan, Sela Natavanu and Lena Kalotiti as island victims of the sordid affair – and herself as having been caught in the crossfire in trying to bring justice.

'*This World Cup has never been about rugby league being the world's best sport, as some would like to believe,*' Grace had written.

'*It has been a vehicle that has been used to launch Vanuatu as a new destination to a world that had never known it before – and in return those who run the game will all live here, tax-free, happily ever after, so long as they survive the duration of the tournament.*'

And she had not given up. She had vowed on podcasts, blogs and social media not to let up in her determination to bring the whole story.

Grace's gunman had been Moses Pagoa, a Ni-Vanuatuan. He'd been held in a cell at Port Vila police headquarters since his arrest, his flee from the scene having been stymied by his fellow Ni-Vanuatuan traditional dancers at Breakas.

Moses's family had in the past earned their living from the land but had suffered as an indigenous people and had lately been regarded as 'displaced'. Ni-Vanuatuans like Moses were now working with the Vete Indigenous Organisation (VIO) in order to win their rights back to land that they had been forced off as a result of urbanisation.

Moses had been represented by a VIO solicitor and, despite having shot at someone and having hit his target, miraculously he had become free again, for the moment, being granted bail by a local judge sympathetic to the VIO.

Grace's career as a published journalist was about to become one of the shortest on record.

'*Twenty-five million Vatu ...*'

The figure was all Moses heard. It was the equivalent of over 300,000 Aussie dollars. It was more than Moses had ever earned in his life. It would buy him a house, some land too. It would give security to his wife and family. The only stipulation was that this time he must not fail.

He wasn't about to.

CHAPTER 62

'Good afternoon everyone …'

Julian Jardine was on the yacht that he had arrived on from Espiritu Santo. It was not any yacht but a Burgess Illusion Plus. £100 million pounds' worth of superyacht stretching out over 88.5 metres with six decks and one deck wholly devoted to himself and his partner, and rooms for 16 guests.

It was a magnificent engineering masterpiece that had benefitted from naval architects Azure and the world's leading interior design specialists Estima. It had won Superyacht of the Year at the Monaco Yacht Show.

Jardine was presently chartering it, with a view to buying when his latest masterpiece came to fruition. The Illusion Plus was moored in Mele Bay just off Paradise Beach. He'd felt it better to be here, less possibility of any kind of interruption – and he wanted to get a handle on where they now all stood.

He wanted to know that the last acts were going to play out as he intended.

On his 292-inch Samsung TV screen known as The Wall were four other faces. Three of them women and one man. It was time for a conversation, to check that all was in place.

'Ladies and gentleman … we are approaching the biggest pay-day any of us might ever see …'

Jardine looked at his screen, at all four separately. He would have preferred meeting face-to-face, but this had all been about keeping apart so that there could be no opportunity for anyone else to see them together.

'Susie?'

GPK was talking into the ether on his mobile phone having reached the airport. He'd parked up and was making his way to arrivals. He'd lost contact with her as he'd approached Bauerfield and was currently trying his best not to be in panic mode. She'd told him where she would be, but when he arrived she wasn't there.

What the hell had he been thinking of? Getting Susie involved with his snooping around. He should have engaged someone else, from somewhere. Somebody who was used to this.

But he hadn't had anyone else. The rest of his team were on their way, it had taken time bringing them back together. GPK had assumed their job had been done. Geoffrey Quinigan was no longer. End of. How wrong could he have been?

Kraft looked around the whole expanse of arrivals. Looking for Susie or for the man she had spotted.

What the hell was he doing here? He'd been locked up so far as Susie and he knew. This was now GPK's living nightmare as well as Susie's and it would soon be Greg's as there had to be only one natural conclusion to make. He was here to kill Greg.

His phone sprang to life.

'I'm outside … he's getting into a car … hurry …'

Relief coursed through GPK's veins. She was safe. Thank God. In the same instant he swivelled and broke into a run, or as near to one as his bulk could manage.

Susie had been tougher than he had given her credit. She had followed.

Jardine finished up the virtual meeting far from satisfied. His opinion was that although there were huge sums involved in what was about to transpire the other participants had all paid lip service to the meeting. He didn't trust them, but right now he had to.

It had been a chastening thought after all this time, but he also had other issues unrelated to the virtual colleagues he'd just been speaking with – and those other issues would be dealt with separately.

Jardine picked up his mobile and called his own version of an insurance policy. Starting tomorrow there were to be no more mistakes, nor amateur involvements. This time every action was to be decisive.

'Querido, ven conmigo …'

She said it in such a sultry way that Jardine just had to smile.

'*Quieres haser el amor?*'

Jardine turned and she was there. She kissed him, then took his hand in hers and led him to the exquisite, gorgeous bedroom. He knew what that meant.

Maria Cavaleros was dressed in nothing more than a gold thong and matching heels. Julian Jardine was soon to be wearing even less, welcome relaxation after the stress he was beginning to feel with his business partners.

Susie had spared no time waiting for GPK to get back to the car. Seeing the man getting into a taxi, she had done the same. She was still in contact with him.

'*I've just said that line they all say in films …*'

She was whispering as GPK, now out of breath, made it back to his hire car.

'*… follow that car! …*'

GPK heard the giggle in Susie's voice as he roared his car out of its parking space.

'*Just be careful. You of all people know what this man is capable of … I'm coming out of the airport car park now …*'

GPK was more than happy that Susie had regained her composure and also pretty amazed that she now appeared to be enjoying herself. He chose not to mention what could happen if the person she was following came to realise he was being tailed. He hoped Susie wouldn't think that way.

Grace was in Le Café de la Vue d'Ilfira which looked out on Iririki Island and further beyond it to Ilfiri Island. She was using the café Wi-Fi for research while also fanning the flames to an eager online audience now caught up in her story of shootings, charred corpses and corruption. She was loving it. And she was getting paid.

She had struck deals with five newspaper groups in the past 12 hours and two online media operators. Her blogs were now attracting over 1 million views and she was earning advertising revenue from them.

Fake News once again. When will people ever learn?

The response to her blogs, vlogs, podcasts and social media activity had not all been positive.

Another failed journalist trying to make herself famous. Sensationalist rubbish.

'Go fuck yourselves, you sons of Satan … and daughters too …'

Grace uttered the words not quite out loud, but probably enough for anyone close by to hear her. At that moment there was nobody close.

She was about to return to her research. She'd been looking more into Lena Kalotiti's life, or she'd been attempting to without much success. There had been the usual press blurb about her being postmistress of the world's only underwater post office, but there had been precious little else. A bit about her sporting past.

Grace's laptop pinged. A brief of the latest message to have landed appeared in the top right-hand corner of her screen. She clicked on it.

Two seconds later she dived for cover as the café window was pierced and exploded, glass shattering in shards all around her. This time there was to be no run for cover by the shooter. Wearing a motorcycle helmet and covered head to toe in black leathers, Moses Pagoa made his way forward toward the now windowless window frame to finish the job.

Grace's left arm had been in a sling. As she had hit the deck she had howled in pain, stitches from her wound bursting open, her arm flung from the sling. This was it. The point of no return. Fake news? Fuck you, you keyboard warrior. Come and take a look at this first-hand!

'Get down everybody! Descendre!'

England rugby league fans and French were in the street, but so too was Alex Lui with two officers.

'Now!!'

Alex gave the command as the gunman took aim again ready to finish what he'd started. The officers let rip with not just one shot each but two rounds of bullets that punctured every part of the motorcyclist's arms and torso.

Alex had followed Moses since he had been let loose. He hadn't believed that someone who had shot and maimed a member of the public could have been released on bail. There was no logic to it. He was already looking into the release. The judge who had allowed it. It stank. Alex had chosen not to inform Danford that he had gone out on a limb.

The café owner, Maurice, had been in shock when the window had smashed as the bullet had hit. He'd seen the girl who had been at the window on her laptop hit the deck. He now tentatively crawled his way towards her just in case there were to be more shots.

'*S'il vous plait viens rapidement!*'

Maurice screeched out the words as Alex Lui and his officers were first making sure that Moses had made his last movements, his last breath. Alex had immediately called for paramedics. There was a blaring in the distance as an ambulance began its run.

'*La fille est touchee!*'

Moses had done his job.

CHAPTER 63

'*Still following ...*'

Susie was concentrating on the car up ahead while keeping GPK informed. She had been entertained by saying 'follow that car' but had since discovered it was her pointing that had been what the cab driver had understood, not her words.

'*No comprendo, no hablo Ingles.*'

He had tried to explain as best he could.

Bislama wasn't a language Susie had ever heard before but the 'no comprendo' bit had been easy to translate and the 'no Ingles' bit certainly worked out as no English.

'*I'm two cars behind you ...*'

GPK didn't add anything more. He hadn't known quite what to say. Susie wasn't used to all of this. He didn't want to knock what appeared to be her new-found confidence by making her worry unnecessarily, but he wanted her to be aware of danger. She was in a cab. She was surely safe while she was in there? But she was tailing a loose cannon in the shape of this man.

'*The cab is pulling over ... what do I do?*'

'*Stay where you are. Get the cab driver to drive on.*'

GPK's response had been unequivocal. If Susie got out of the cab now and the man spotted her and something happened he'd never forgive himself for bringing her closer to danger.

'*Where are you?*'

'*Close ...*'

'*How close?*'

She could tell by his hesitation that he wasn't close enough.

'*I'm going ...*'

Susie was out of the cab. She was out in the street at Fatumanu Bay with colourful stalls selling shirts and sundresses, fruit and fish to one side and kava bars, coffee shops and the island's most impressive structure, the magnificent newly built, glass and steel building housing the South Pacific Offshore

Banking Corporation.

England and France supporters were everywhere adorned in their national colours and enjoying the warmth of another baking hot day on Efate. Susie glided along behind a group of them for cover.

'*Heading for the bank …*'

Susie could hear GPK's now laboured breath. He had ditched the car.

'*Just don't … put yourself … where he can …*'

'*… See me, yes I know … He's not turned around, doesn't know I'm here …*'

Don't be too sure was GPK's first thought. His second was that despite Susie's apparent confidence she was naïve if she felt in any way secure.

'*Why would he be going here?*'

'*Where's here?*'

'*Big glass place. How far behind are you?*'

Susie looked behind to check briefly. It was her first mistake since spotting him at the airport. She turned back.

'*Bugger!*'

'*What?*'

There was a pause.

'*What? … Susie? …*'

Nothing. He'd only reckoned on being 100 metres behind, but it had been difficult to see up ahead as islanders, holidaymakers and rugby league fans populated both sides of the road.

He was now close to the South Pacific Offshore Banking Corporation building. Where had she gone?

Deputy Commissioner Elenola Taneo had joined Alex Lui at Le Café de la Vue d'Ilfira where Grace was being attended to by paramedics who were now desperately trying to keep her alive in the back of the ambulance while trying to get her to hospital. She had lost consciousness, couldn't give them any verbal indication of her state, but she was hanging on.

One of the paramedics couldn't believe Grace's bad luck.

'Wasn't this the young lady we picked up a couple of days ago?'

Alex Lui motioned for Elenola to look at the notepad alongside Grace's laptop.

'What do you make of this?'

Julian Jardine was not taking any chances. He wasn't going to be seen anywhere near Port Vila until absolutely necessary and he was preferring life on the Illusion Plus to where they had intended to stay on the island.

There had been something he had picked up from the virtual conference call earlier that had unsettled him. He couldn't put his finger on it, but he knew there was possibly even more work to be done if his plans were to come together.

'Querido, regresa a la cama … Sea lo que sea, puede esperar hasta manana …'

Maria Cavaleros was as dissatisfied in bed as Jardine was in his mind. Leave it till tomorrow, whatever was to be done she implored. Jardine knew better than to not take care of her wishes.

'Right, that'll do for today everyone. Look after yourselves. Tomorrow's the biggest game of this tournament – and if you don't think so, then we've already lost. Now go!'

The quarters were a step up from the group games. All or nothing. England would be out inside 80 minutes or they would have reached what many pundits had considered their likely best case for this World Cup.

The semis were now considered to be their zenith. And there was no way any pundit was going to go for an England win the way they had been playing and the injuries they were now carrying.

'What's up?'

Greg was knackered. He'd been all set to jump into the hot tub when he'd returned, around the back to his suite, aiming to take off the kit, quick hop into the shower and straight into the tub. Bliss. But now clearly not bliss.

GPK stared at him vacantly, sadly. He put out his hand for Greg to sit down.

'Just tell me!'

GPK bit on his lip.

'*Col couldn't get you on your mobile …*'

Greg hadn't known what to feel, but now he knew. He immediately closed his eyes and saw his dad in vivid detail, laughing, joking, splashing about in the river. He saw his mum and Col too. But it was his dad's face now that suddenly meant everything. He'd never see it again apart from this way and in photographs. He leaned against the tub.

He put his thumb and forefinger of his left hand to the bridge of his nose pinching the fleshy skin just above and then using the forefinger and nail-to-knuckle of his thumb to try to hold back the tears.

GPK moved across and patted Greg on his left shoulder a couple of times before returning to where he had been seated.

After a short time Greg collected himself, put his hand back over his face, took several deep breaths, enough to regain his composure as much as he could, put his hands through his jet black hair and then down to his chin.

'*I'd best give Col a call …*'

Greg suddenly realised that there had to be something else. GPK was watching him. Greg tilted his head to one side. There was more?

Nothing was said. Greg just raised his eyebrow and made a swirling movement with his hand to tell GPK to give him the rest of the news.

The next realisation in Greg's mind was that GPK was here – in his suite – but that the one person he wanted to be there was missing. Where was …?

'*Darling, I'm so sorry … about your dad …*'

Greg's relief was palpable. He couldn't calculate wholly how he felt right then, but the kiss and embrace that he received from Susie wrapped in a towel that covered the essentials but little else meant the world right now.

'*See you both in the morning …*'

GPK disappeared.

'*Oh Gregory …*'

It was only his mum who called him by his full name. Tina

was in bits. She'd been holding everything back for weeks, maybe months so far as Greg knew. She couldn't speak, even though she had tried.

'I'm sorry you're having to shoulder all this mate.'

Col was always steady, a good firm hand on the tiller. His voice was a bit shakier than normal but he was okay.

'He went peacefully ...'

Greg could hear the catchiness in the back of Col's throat.

'A blessing really ... I'm good ... you do what you have to do and get here when you can ... Mum's good ... sends her love ...'

Greg could tell that she would have been attempting to mouth something while in tears. He didn't want to finish the call too soon, nor go on too long. Couldn't really do anything right in this position 2000 miles away in the ocean. At least he'd been in the right hemisphere when it had happened, not exactly comfort for his mum!

After speaking with his mum and with Col, Greg also called Diane. It was the right thing to do.

He told Diane about his dad. She would have wanted to know. She'd known his parents when they were first together. He'd told her that his dad was the reason why he had been heading out to Australia when he'd left.

He asked her about whether she wanted him to tell Kyle. He didn't want to get in the way of things in her life.

Diane was good about it. Said she'd talk with Kyle. Then she asked how Greg was. How he had been through *'your most recent'* abduction experience.

'You should be getting used to those by now.'

She had said it with a little fun to it, but also matter of fact. Greg liked that they could talk that way. He raised his eyebrows and hoped the minute pause he'd left at the time might somehow translate into Diane seeing it.

'You okay?'

He'd thrown it in just routinely, heartfelt, no expectation of anything coming back. It was the elongated pause and breath he heard before what she said that brought about something different to the norm from their conversations.

'Yeah,'

she said with the end of the word on a downbeat curve, still with that breath that gave Greg concern. But she followed up quickly.

'Bit stressed, tired … I'll be alright … you go. Do well tomorrow.'

She'd tried to finish on more of a high but hadn't really got there. It had been the first time Greg had heard her this way since losing their baby five years ago, the little girl that would have been their second child. He flashed back to it all. There was something wrong. He might not have been married to her anymore but he still cared, and not just because she was the mother of his son. They went back a long way.

The shower and hot tub beckoned. By the time he had finished in the shower there was a call on his mobile phone. Dear God what now? He picked it up without even looking at who was calling.

'Is this the hotline for the very handsome, exceedingly attractive and occasionally very naughty Mister Greg?'

Greg kept the mobile to his ear as he moved from shower to hot tub. He smiled at Susie as he slipped in alongside her.

'Let's just hold each other tonight, darling. Think of your dad.'

Susie stroked his hair, held his hand. Greg closed his eyes. His body had been through so much, he'd now been trying to train as though he was fit when he wasn't. He was nowhere near ready for tomorrow's game where he'd been asked to play in the half-backs due to Owen Fenchurch's eye injury.

Now he was nowhere near right mentally. Sure, he could deal with that, block things out but his dad dying, mum grieving, Col holding fort, guilt about not being there for his dad and them both, guilt for not being with Kyle and now something up with Diane? It all brought him back to Susie too. What was it that she hadn't told him, that she had held him so tightly for previously?

In the end it came out spontaneously.

'What is it you haven't been telling me?'

CHAPTER 64

'It's the Battle of the Old Colonials here at Port Vila Municipal Stadium tonight where France and England will lay claim to a place in the World Cup semi-finals.

'And it's the last game for us here on Efate on the islands of Vanuatu as the World Cup circus finally moves back to Sydney and Brisbane for the final games in the men's tournament.

'Join us tonight to see whether the England team can put behind them so many disappointments, injuries and lack of form to re-establish their credentials as possible World Cup winners and whether the undefeated, underrated and unfancied France team can maintain their 100 per cent record in the competition.

'We're all here with the big match build-up from 6.30pm tonight on Channel 17 with kick-off at 8pm. That's me – Brad Kearns, him George Northey and special guest Vanuatu team captain Ben Mara.'

Julian Jardine flicked from channel to channel, checking everything from the Rugby League World Cup to boat prices and share prices. Being on this magnificent yacht calmed him. He was still as uncertain about his colleagues as he had been yesterday, but the boat did something for him. He considered chucking everything in, but he couldn't.

This had all proved costly to set up, but greater outlays usually led to even higher returns and with the additional insurances he had spent time on putting in place he saw that his end goal was in sight and looking good. He'd buy this boat yet – and reach the real jet set. A jet! Great idea too!

The Super League and the Rugby League World Cup could go swivel after all this.

'Got it!'

Alex Lui had given the job of getting into Grace's laptop to one of the team that could reset and revive any such device.

It had taken a little longer than usual because Grace had put in several codes and walls to stop such activity.

Alex and Elenola had to know what Grace had been making a note of in her notebook when she had been hunted down for the second time.

'This goes nowhere but between us ...'

Alex turned to face Elenola.

'If we need to involve anyone else we do it when we are ready.'

Det Supt Erin Jackson arrived. She was brighter than she had been in recent times.

'Anything for the group to share?'

She checked out both faces, knew something was up.

'Whose is this?'

Alex was caught between two choices. One, he fancied bringing Erin Jackson in on the case because he felt it was now the right thing to do, given some of the ways in which their investigations had turned; two, he didn't truly know what would happen with the case if they began involving her.

'It's mine ...'

He made a move of his head to suggest there might be more to follow, but not there. Erin nodded briefly without offering any other facial mannerism and walked on.

At last she felt part of something with the Vanuatu police, strangely it now meant something to her for it to be that way.

'Okaaay,'

she drawled.

'... and I may just have something for you too ...'

Erin took up a pen and wrote two words.

'You don't have to run at this pace all the time you know!'

Freddie was keeping pace with Greg but only just. Neil 'The Brickie' Duncan was tucked in behind with Tyler Rogers. Up way ahead were the backs Sam Rivers, Jericho Pallagi, Troy Whittingham and Vinny Venus. They were the two leading groups, out early on Pango Road at 7am.

'No pain, no gain ...' Greg managed in time-honoured and clichéd fashion. And in truth he was in pain, but right then more mentally than physically after last night's news. The two groups had set off first as the other intended groups of four were

waiting for their third or third and fourth members.

Shane Chislett had decided, on Annie Laing's advice, that it would be better security-wise if they were in groups of four.

South, Duncan, Rogers and Greg were going at a steady lick. They had settled to a healthy 6 minutes a mile pace that just about suited Greg. They'd emerged out of Breakas Beach Resort Hotel and had turned left on Pango Road going past Sano's Kava Bar and Pango Football Ground.

They made their way around a long bend to Pandanus Bay where they marvelled at the amazing beach apartments littered around the harbour area with white and golden sands.

Greg reflected on the poverty or at very least seeming poverty he had seen in Port Vila Fish Market and Fruit and Vegetable Market, where those who were trading looked like they needed to eat more of what they were selling and looked homeless, and the contrast in wealth out here just a handful of miles or so from the island capital.

'I built that one ... and that one ...'

Neil 'The Brickie' Duncan pointed out as they passed. He really had been a builder until his swerve and sidestep had become more lucrative than sand and cement.

'Really did ...'

he protested, as he felt they didn't believe him. He was blowing a bit now. They all were. The warmth of the day was starting to kick in. It was already 23 degrees and only 7.15am.

They rounded Pandanus Bay clinging to the coast for a while before the road branched to the right which was to bring them to the coast again at Pakoa Marina.

'Wow!'

Tyler Rodgers whistled in almost disbelief at the size of some of the boats in front of them, a mixture of glistening bright white, blue-and-white and black-and-white superyachts.

'Some money in them ...'

Tyler quipped as they passed what must have been at least thirty to forty of them.

'... not exactly a poor island then ...'

'*Millionaire's playground …*'

Freddie chipped in.

'*Dear God, have you seen that?*'

Up just beyond Pakoa was the most dazzling, glass edifice all four had ever seen. It literally sparkled everywhere, the sun shining on it and creating a vision that was almost blinding.

Greg had intended to keep up the pace he'd set but Rivers, Pallagi, Whittingham and Vinny were transfixed. It had become as good a time as any to take a breather.

'*Man, that's some sight …*'

Vinny was entranced.

'*I could live there …*'

He put on his big sunny smile, then set off once more with his group as Greg's four followed suit.

'*Owned by the same guy that owns the Marina and just about everything on this side of Port Vila.*'

'*Bloody 'ell, have you seen this one?*' This was now becoming more a sightseeing exercise of properties none of them would ever own. This time it was Freddie marvelling once more, at the ultra-modern white building with the unimpressive name Sindiso Beach Hut.

'*Beach hut, my arse! It's another fucking palace! They're all bloody palaces! Where do they get their money from around here?*'

'*Means bliss,*'

Tyler offered up.

'*In Zulu.*'

There was a look of incredulity between the other three. Tyler Rodgers was not known for his grasp of all things cultural. Grasp of a yard of ale maybe, but not culture.

'*Get you, Mr University Challenge …*'

Brickie Duncan offered in between breaths.

'*Fuck you Dunc,*'

Tyler retorted, but in good humour.

'*I was watching it on the telly in my room, interesting stuff, owned by a Jap …*'

Next up was Paradise Beach Resort. The local news had been

all over it in the past few days since Sela Natavanu's murder.

If the boys had been taken with Sindiso it was to be nothing compared to Sela's as it had become known to its residents. Six glorious individual gleaming white and gold villas strung out around a beautiful golden sandy beach.

'*Billionaire's Row … so this is where the action has been …*'

Brickie shook his head as they continued running.

'*Come on Greg, get us back to our humble 5-star beach hotel, I'm feeling kinda insufficient now. How do people afford all this?*'

'*Some clever people out there …*'

Tyler put in.

'*Clever … and fucking devious, criminal bastards …*'

Freddie added.

Port Vila Police Headquarters was on Rue de Paris near to the harbour and the main fish, fruit and vegetable market.

Just beyond the busy market was Iririki Island Ferry Wharf.

'*Why here?*'

Alex and Elenola had both slipped away separately.

Today was another massive day for policing on the island. Efate and specifically Port Vila was once again awash with tourists and more specifically French and English people there to support their teams in what was once again the biggest sporting event ever staged throughout Vanuatu.

Additional police had been drafted in, utilising the whole of Vanuatu's reserve force of volunteer, part-time police from all of the islands and Australian police.

Erin had written Iririki Ferry on the note she had passed to Alex. She, Alex and Elenola were now together at the terminal.

'*Out there.*'

Erin pointed to the ocean.

'*Somewhere is a man called Julian Jardine. Sir Julian Jardine. He's a megalomaniac. My sources tell me he's on a yacht. He's the chief executive of the Rugby League Authority in England … and he is responsible for the World Cup … in fact he is currently solely responsible … as Zoe Miller has disappeared … and Bob Rudd is dead …*'

'And you're telling us this … only us?'

Elenola Taneo sought confirmation that this was purely knowledge for herself and Alex, at which Erin duly nodded. Elenola continued:

'... because he's responsible for what has happened here? Rudd? Sablan? Natavanu? Kalotiti? Duggan? Elliott?'

'... because you two, and only you two, are the ones I trust right now ... you'll see I have someone missing ... and so do you ... Listen. I have no proof of anything yet. I have a lead. That's all. But it is more than I've had so far ... and certain things start falling into place when you put his name firmly in the pot ...'

She stopped. Erin Jackson knew she was good at her job. She had only needed the first spark to ignite the flames, but she wasn't going to get anywhere unless she had Alex and Elenola onside.

She made a face to inquire of them if they were sufficiently onboard to go further. Her wide eyes, outstretched fingers from open palms, were enough to engender the reaction she wanted.

'And there's another thing ...'

For the first time, since Erin Jackson had landed on Efate, the two younger Vanuatu detectives began to realise that this woman made sense.

GPK and Susie had reconvened by the time Greg had returned from the run, showered and had gone for breakfast with the squad, which was also to merge into Chislett's briefing and analysis of the opposition for the rest of the morning.

'Any excitement planned for me today?'

Susie was in an easy-going frame of mind. She had no intention of being lured further into a role of snooping and loitering around airports. That was yesterday's news.

She raised her eyebrows and gave GPK a smile and slight movement of her head. Kraft simply shook his head similarly slightly.

'You, young lady ...'

He knew how much she loved that. He wagged his finger in her direction.

'You, are incorrigible ... I'm not letting you loose on your own *again ...'*

Susie felt absolutely the same. She'd had her fill of being a private eye.

'I'll drink to that ... believe me I've had enough ... I'm happy just to lie here in the sun.'

They clinked orange juices before Susie asked about the next steps he intended to take.

'So, what are you intending to do about our friend?'

Susie enquired, with ironic emphasis on the description of Oliver Quinigan, son of Geoffrey Quinigan QC who she had been tailing. The young man who could only be on the island for one reason, to avenge his father's death. And that would be at the expense of Greg Duggan.

Grahame was disparaging about Quinigan.

'Already in hand. My team arrives today. You are officially retired from active service.'

He looked across the breakfast table at Susie's moderately inquisitive expression.

'Don't worry, he won't get to you ... so long as you don't put yourself in danger, that is ...'

He looked at her this time with a smile, wagged his finger, but just as swiftly changed back to his main task.

'It's Jardine who is the one we need to get ... caught in the act.'

He leaned towards Susie, in conspiratorial fashion, across where they were eating in the breakfast area of Breakas.

'He's here somewhere, we know that much. We know he could just be putting being here down to the World Cup, his involvement with it and Super League, but that's not it ... he's got an agenda ... this guy's worse than Geoffrey Quinigan. At least with him, he made no disguise of the way he felt ... this guy ... he's a right two-faced bastard ... so his wife tells me!'

Jardine had no intention of being seen anywhere in public anytime soon, except the game that evening.

Maria, on the other hand, was up for retail therapy and couldn't care less whether Julian was with her or not. She had one of her girlfriends from the crew who would gladly go with her.

'El no es el hombre que quiero,'

Maria related to Penelope as they made their way from Vila Bay and around to Port Vila Marina in the Spectre Illusion 35 Powerboat specifically designed to be stored in the Illusion Plus for when it was required.

'Are we good to go?'

Final preparations were in place. Each player had been contacted individually. Targets had been set. The time was approaching. Jardine was ready.

Grace was still under observation, but that observation was now not only from the doctor.

She was still on the critical list. No way she could have been anything but, the bullets having this time ripped through her body, through her chest and abdomen. She was lucky to still be breathing, and there was no guarantee she would see through the day. It had been a miracle she'd lasted the night.

But she had recovered consciousness and although her voice was very weak, she could talk.

Alex Lui's face was the first she saw. He had cradled her in his arms the previous day before the paramedics had arrived, praying that she wouldn't be the latest victim on the island but acknowledging she probably would be.

'We have found messages on your laptop ...'

Alex added after first explaining who he was.

'Can you tell me anything about them?'

Grace was fighting for her life, trying to keep living. Alex felt mercenary. This wasn't important. It was more important she continued her battle. He saw her struggling and was prepared to leave. Her monitor was bleeping, her blood supply was still pumping. He shouldn't be there.

'No,'

Grace managed.

'Don't go ... I'll try ... to help ... if I can ...'

Grace tried to breathe steadily. Then she tried again. Alex managed a smile, couldn't believe how brave she was. She was going to die, but she was going to help.

The rest of the England squad's day had been geared to rest, relaxation and watching their opposition. Chislett's backroom team had been busy compiling video dossiers on the French team, including their three group games and more in-depth analysis of the main playmakers Laurent Galia, Jean-Paul Alainne and Michel Marseilles.

Greg had already rested up a little more than the others, having not played in either of the previous games. He'd only played in one game so far. His afternoon's relaxation had included making another call to Col, checking on mum and something a little more energetic than Shane Chislett may have wished, with Susie.

'Welcome to Channel 17's Rugby League World Cup coverage for the greatest prize in rugby league!'

Brad Kearns was on the build-up phase of the last big night of the tournament in Vanuatu.

'We are now at the business end of the competition where it's knockout footy. Lose and you're goin' home. We're here on the beautiful island of Efate part of the nation republic of Vanuatu, which is made up of hundreds of islands here in the South Pacific.'

Brad Kearns turned to Camera 2.

'But these islands were once home to both of tonight's quarter-final opponents England and France when it was an Anglo-French condominium called the New Hebrides.

'We have Ben Mara here with us tonight, the Vanuatu national team captain, who skippered his side to a victory over Greece and very nearly turned over England in the first group match.

'Ben this could nearly have been you leading your team out tonight if you had pulled off the shock of the tournament …'

Ben Mara was loving being in the studio which was doubling as the commentary box at Port Vila Municipal Stadium where the crowd was already streaming in two hours prior to kick-off.

Greg and the England team were already there. They'd been out on the paddock in their tailored suits, waving to the fans, enjoying the moment.

'It don't seem real, man.'

Vinny Venus had a beaming, generous smile and was lapping up the attention from the fans.

'Like, it's more like when we played at Hopton Town than a World Cup quarter ...'

Greg understood what he meant. For all the colour and spectacle the Vanuatu organisers had put on, it didn't somehow feel grand enough. As though they should have been in a stadium with a 40,000 capacity for this stage of the competition.

'I think it's spot on.'

Gary Walker was in for Stu Wainwright, whose thigh injury hadn't had enough time to heal.

'Great little ground.'

Det Supt Erin Jackson was watching, as were Dep Commissioner Elenola Taneo and Detective Alex Lui. They were watching activity inside and outside of the ground from a mobile studio that was home to 24 TV screens all showing a variety of action from cameras set up and recording.

It had been a logistical nightmare organising it in such a short space of time but Erin had pulled strings in Australia and the mobile studio, equipment, engineers and technicians had all been flown out in the past 12 hours. Equipment had been rigged up, there were editors, monitors, soundmen and women, runners, it was almost another Channel 17 coverage, but this time unconcerned with what was going on amongst those with the odd-shaped balls.

'I want these people ...'

Erin was totally on her own game now. She brought up pictures of each person she wanted the cameras training on.

'If we haven't got them bang on, you need to get out there and shift the camera to where it's needed.'

'Erin, they're all being held by cameramen and women, every single one. You just speak and they will hear. Everyone is wired up to here. You want them to move, tell them where ...'

Erin Jackson was more than impressed. She had no idea whether any of this was going to work, but World Cup quarter-final on Efate, four murders all seemingly related to it, possibly five, and people attending who could have been responsible for them. It was worth a shot.

'Julian Jardine – I have no idea whether he'll be here, here he is for all of you … including you cameramen and women … He's our prime suspect for all that has been going on here on Efate, in the past few weeks. His name links everything and everyone, but he's not our killer.

'Zoe Miller – chief executive of the World Cup Organising Committee and former Olympian if any of you go back that far … disappeared while here on the island … disappeared while in Australia … she could be involved … last time she was here at the ground was the first game, when she was a guest of Sela Natavanu, one of our murdered list.

'Karla Karelia. Mystery woman. Eastern European. Had a fling with England player Greg Duggan. The guy who was abducted and found after nearly three days. Worth keeping a camera on him too. Seems to have a habit of being caught up in anything dangerous or illegal, but nothing ever down to him. Attracts trouble.

'Nene Natavanu. Not seen since the first game here also. Daughter of Sela Natavanu. Supposedly shoe-in for new prime minister if anyone can find her!

'And these two … very much hush-hush … I don't want anyone in here other than you guys and myself and Det Insp Lui or Deputy Commissioner Taneo … but if someone else gets in then get any cameras off screen that show these two immediately … Det Marlon Razni …. And Commissioner Danford Napakauranga.

'Report to me of anything you see that appears as though these people or any others, but predominantly these, are up to something other than watching and being involved in the game … I know this may seem like we're trying to find an unknown needle that may or may not be in a haystack, but just concentrate … and report … that's all I ask … thank you!'

The door to the studio, situated just outside of the ground opened.

CHAPTER 65

'Sabia que querrias venir, querido.'

Maria Cavaleros was happy to be at the game and from what she had said, felt that her partner was happy to be there too in his positions with the game and the competition.

Julian Jardine just smiled at his sultry companion. He'd enjoyed destroying Greg's Eruption career through his relationship with her, but that was as far as that went. It was the boat that was keeping them together, but soon he would have more riches than ever and would throw her overboard – figuratively of course, not for him that kind of dirty work.

He spied cameras like a bird of prey spots its food. There were far more here than would be needed on a normal camera crew for a top rugby league game. And they were trained on the crowd. Noted. Best expression then. Give them something. He turned to Maria.

'Tenias razon carino, y me, siento bien.'

He really was feeling good and kissed her passionately, almost to the point of violently on the lips. Maria was pleasantly taken aback. Maybe things were looking up.

'Not exactly subtle, is he …?'

The director/producer in the van wasn't taken with him.

'Keep on him …'

Brad Kearns was in front of the broadcast TV cameras.

'And I'm delighted, if not also pretty amazed, to introduce you to Zoe Miller, chief executive of the World Cup Organising Committee and of course our former Australian Olympic hero on the track … Zoe, it's great to see you …'

This had been a coup for Channel 17. Zoe had literally walked in off the street, out of nowhere, no great fanfare for her arrival, and was here. The whole of Australia had been looking for her and Brad Kearns had her, his very own pre-match scoop!

Zoe hoped she knew what she was doing. It was a calculated

risk. By being right in the TV spotlight she had hoped that perhaps it would also be the safest place. She beamed at Brad.

'*Aww thanks Brad. It's great to be here with you. It's such an exciting competition isn't it? Who would have thought that Australia would lose their opening game, that Vanuatu would take England such a long way, that France would top their group having beaten New Zealand, and that Wales wouldn't even qualify for the quarters after beating Australia, losing that amazing match to The Lebanon three days ago?*'

Brad wasn't some former player who had been shoehorned into TV, he'd come up through the journalistic ranks in newspapers and radio before making it on screen. He'd retained his reporter's nose for a story and having dispensed with his soft opening to his surprise guest he couldn't resist a brief stab at uncovering a story, even though the game ahead was his main priority.

'*But Zoe …*'

Brad paused, deliberately. He knew how to turn dramatic.

'*You're the chief executive of this competition and you haven't been at any of the games, so far as I'm aware, and you weren't at the official opening? … where have you been, have you been ill?*'

Zoe kept her cool. She had anticipated this, expected it. She knew Brad. She smiled demurely at him, no flicker of concern.

'*All confidential right now Brad. Nobody really wants to see the organisers they just want to see the footy and I've been watching all the games even if I've not attended. As you can see, I'm fine, and I'm here now and looking forward to tonight's game …*'

Zoe was also clever enough to realise that Brad Kearns would only have a finite time to devote to her. She knew there were VTs to play, the match buildup, but she was also aware he may try one last little go, which is why she extended her reply just to make sure he couldn't come back with another attempt.

'*… and one thing I must say is massive congratulations to those who have contributed to putting on all of the games here on Efate. It is such a beautiful island with wonderful people. Every game here has been a very real celebration of rugby league and, if you'll allow* *me the time during the half-time break …'*

Zoe made her own pause for effect.

'… I may have some really sensational news to share …'

She beamed once again, before turning it into a coy smile.

Brad hadn't been expecting another gem to land in the palm of his hand, but he was excited that he had more breaking news.

'That was great, Zoe.'

He applauded her as they went off-air, as the show went to a VT.

'Look forward to half-time!'

Greg had returned to the dressing room with his teammates in readiness for the game. He was getting there, the feeling inside him turning from thinking too much about lack of match fitness to motivation. Seeing the crowd had triggered it.

He'd only played a handful of games for Eruption at the back end of the Super League season often having being spelled for 20 minutes at a time during the games. That's why his selection for England had been deemed too much of a liability for the initial squad.

Since joining the lads in Australia he'd only played his part in one game. He'd subsequently been bashed up, locked up and had suffered from dehydration for three days in captivity! Not exactly the best preparation for the quarter-final of any competition let alone the World Cup.

Greg checked his phone for the last time before making his final preparations. Text messages were there wishing him well from Kyle, via Diane; from Col, and his mum; from Susie. He felt their warmth. Their love. Thought for a moment or two about his dad. Decided that this one was for him.

And as Greg was about to put his phone back into his pocket it pinged.

CHAPTER 66

'And this is it ...'

Brad Kearns was now in full-on match commentary mode.

'The Old Colonials – England, who laid claim to these islands in 1774 through Captain Cook; and France, who arrived here six years previously in 1768 when French navigator Louis Antoine de Bouganville landed on these shores ... well, actually that was on Espiritu Santo, but it's still what was the New Hebrides until 1980 when the Republic of Vanuatu was born.

'Tonight's prize is no longer these beautiful sun-kissed islands but a place in the World Cup semi-finals. I have Ben Mara, Vanuatu's captain alongside me, and our regular summariser Laurie Northey.'

While talk of injuries, team changes and strengths and weaknesses of the teams took place and music boomed out around the ground from reggae artist Stan Antas who had joined Port Vila's finest Vanessa Quai and her band, singing their duet anthem 'Spread The Love (All Over The World)', there was one man spreading his own words to what seemed an appreciative audience alongside him in the stand.

'Can we get anything closer to see what he's sending?' The producer/director in the van outside the ground had one camera trained on his every movement.

'Camera 10, can you get anything?'

Jardine knew they'd be watching him, not because he was psychic but because he had contacts. He moved his face forward towards Camera 10, smiling.

The national anthems were played for both France and England. The players and whole crowd were then silent for a minute in respect of Sela Natavanu before a cacophony of noise erupted around the ground as the ball was placed in the centre of the field.

'Here we go ...'

Brad Kearns was looking forward to his scoop at half-time,

let alone what was to come on the field of play.

'*Eighty minutes. One winner. A place in the last four. And it's France to kick to England ...*'

Both teams looked well and truly pumped for the game. Greg's adrenaline would by now normally have kicked in, but what he had just seen before coming out on to the pitch had changed everything. His mind wasn't at the game.

The ball sailed high into the early evening night sky.

'*Look at this for a charge from the French! Jullien, Maison-de-Boeuf and Jordain are hammering towards the England full-back Charlie Cole. He's come towards it, he's up ... ohh! ... that's an amazing leap by Robert Jullien, he's flipped it back ... it's in Maxime Maison-de-Boeuf's hands, he's shovelled it quickly out to Laurent Galia ...*'

Brad Kearns was supercharged along with a now super-enthused crowd. Brad's voice reached a new level of intensity.

'*... and England can't get to them quickly enough ... Galia's jinked inside! ... He's gone through this desperate England defence ... we've not even had a tackle yet! This is sensational stuff from France ... Galia's still looking to get the ball away, he's basketballed it over ... and there it is!! ... It's the opening try!!! ... It's Gilles Baltieri, in at the corner! Well ... Ben, Laurie, I need a lie down after all that and we've only been going for 13 seconds, just thirteen!*'

'*Aww mate, that was terrific play. We spotted Galia earlier, said he'd have an impact but that was just top drawer ...*'

Ben Mara followed up Laurie Northey's comment, similarly enthused.

'*Such a great leap by Robert Jullien. The England full-back did everything right technically, he just couldn't get high enough.*'

The Tongan referee Maketi Obeng looked towards his touch judges. He handed the decision over to the video referee, in so doing also signalling that subject to confirmation of no infringement he was awarding a try.

The next minute the crowd saw the try being replayed in slow-mo at the pinch-points where Mr Obeng wanted to be sure.

Had Jullien tipped the ball back? Or had his momentum made it look that way when it was really tipped forwards? Had

Baltieri grounded it correctly?

It didn't take long for the video referee to make his call. Try! It hadn't been in question by the crowd. There hadn't been a doubt in their minds.

And worse was to come for England. Right out from the touchline goal-kicker Anton Jeuneville deftly slotted the conversion through the uprights.

Brad Kearns stated the obvious.

'It's France 6 England 0. This is not the start Shane Chislett would have wanted that's for sure. And your boys did the same against England, Ben. Must be slow starters.'

Many had still thought England's patched-up side strong enough to see them past the post against France, but with all of their key playmaking roles at full-back, stand-off, scrum-half, hooker and loose forward now taken up by non-regulars in the side or non-regular in that position and now immediately shipping 6 points the England fans were just as immediately on edge.

Fielding, Fenchurch, Wainwright, Tyson and Duggan had occupied those roles in the first group game but now all except Greg were out injured, and he was playing out of his regular position even though he had occasionally played in the halves previously with Hopton and Eruption.

To some it looked a mess, an accident or in this case a defeat waiting to happen. It hadn't been an impressive tournament for England.

Things needed to change. And they did. Steely determination became the hallmark of both teams. Brad summed it up.

'… the clock's now at 25 minutes and since that opening try this game has become a real arm wrestle …'

Greg hadn't been able to make any significant impact.

His mind was elsewhere. Here he was again at the centre of something that he had no idea of why. He suddenly had plenty of time to think.

'… and it's the first interchange of the game. Greg Duggan, a hero in this stadium little over a week ago comes off with Ricki Brown taking his place.'

'*Disappointing first stanza for Greg …*'

Ben Mara was amplifying what many England fans on the terraces and in the seats were thinking.

'*You know, he doesn't look right. This is not the Greg Duggan we faced. He was amazing that night. I really don't think he's fit, which isn't surprising given what we know about his recent misfortunes.*'

'*I'm surprised he's even managed to get on the park so soon,*'

Laurie Northey added.

'*Rugby league is physically demanding and psychologically draining, especially when you are the kind of impact player Greg is … but he's out there, good on him …*'

'*Well, he's not right now …*'

Kearns corrected.

'*He's back on the sidelines.*'

As Greg walked off the park he looked up to the main stand and the directors' box where the privileged few, those with money or fame, were seated, including the Vanuatu-based sponsors Copra International, Kaman Kava, South Pacific Offshore Investment Bank, Bank of Vanuatu and Vanuatu Beef Inc.

Greg couldn't make anyone out for definite. He thought he saw at least two familiar figures.

'*Duggan's looked up to the grandstand … could be nothing …*'

Jericho Pallagi made way for Rich Dee as the next interchange.

The control room, which hadn't had a sniff of anything was suddenly on alert. The producer/director was on it.

'*Try any of your cameras to give us people in the grandstand.*

'*Editors, can we get a close-up of Duggan's eyes on playback? Which direction we think he was looking? Any expression as a result of seeing whatever he may have seen?*'

'*Jardine's in his eyeline …*'

came back the initial reply.

'*Get any cameras on him now …*'

'*It seems France are the real beneficiaries of Super League in England, based on what we've seen so far …*'

Brad Kearns offered.

'They now have two teams in the competition and with a third due to be added next season it's looking good for them as a rugby league nation ...'

The third club, based in Pau, was being financed by Anglo-American businessman Dennis 'Monty' Montgomery and his English artist wife Janet, an ex-table tennis world champion. They were the couple who were sitting alongside Jardine and to whom he had been talking with so animatedly before the game.

The Pyrenees Royals, so named because Pau had been the only city in Europe where two royal dynasties had been born – Henry IV of France, of the House of Bourbon; and Charles XIV of John, Sweden of the House of Bernadotte born in 1818 – were looking forward to joining their French companions in Super League.

Talk was that Monty and Janet Montgomery were checking on the Greg Duggan 'situation' with regard to his contract termination at Eruption, as well as other possible signings.

But they also had other reasons for sitting alongside Maria Cavaleros and Julian Jardine.

They were rumoured to have family connections with an underworld gangster operation with the initials HHM and recently they had developed financial interests in Vanuatu. Monty had various dealings with banking throughout his career and presently involvement with the South Pacific Offshore Investment Bank.

Their 73-metre Dragonfly superyacht *Charlie Skipper* was currently moored in Undine Bay to the north of Efate.

'Any idea who they are?'

The producer/director focused in on Monty, Janet, Maria and Jardine.

'Let's get closer guys, watch for any lip movement ... we got a lip reader here?'

France made their first interchange, bringing on Fabrice Joulliet and Georges Dacourt to replace Bastien Albert and Charles de Vries. Shane Chislett made his third change with Mason Bell on for Billy Ecktenstall.

Brad Kearns was famed in his commentaries for watching and commenting on what he saw off the ball, the plays that were developing, the instructions that were being given.

'*Gary Walker is trying to get his team organised out on the park. There has been nothing to choose between these two sides after that opening few seconds, but Walker, who has come in for injured Stu Wainwright has been working everything he can without too much support as yet. George, what's going to be the game-breaker here. Which side is going to crack first?*'

Brad handed over to Laurie Northey who gave a mock look of 'I haven't a clue' before summarising as best he could.

'*You've just got to look at the way both sides are set up, Brad. France are in the front seat. They got the early points. But neither side has really played the kind of expansive game, throwing the ball around the park. It's like neither is prepared to chance their arm in case they give the ball away.*'

'*That's right, Laurie, it's good possession of the football,*' Ben Mara added. '*They've both respected it. They've completed their six tackles, but that has made it all a bit mechanical apart from that first move of the game. We've yet to see any real flair apart from that …*'

Greg was sitting on the bench mystified.

He'd felt heavy legged on the park and his head was whirring with thoughts of what he'd seen just before kick-off.

His mind wasn't at the game. His concentration on what was playing out in front of him was blown.

The hooter sounded for half-time.

The capacity had been scaled up to 15,000 since the last match with the addition of new larger temporary stands, but the crowd was subdued. Apart from the opening seconds there hadn't been that spark to ignite them.

Vanessa Quai was back with her 'Life Is So Good' song.

It had become an overnight online sensation since she had played it at the Vanuatu v England game. The YouTube video was now at over 16 million hits and it had been a chart No 1 in 17 countries including the UK, France and Australian charts.

'Now!'

CHAPTER 67

It had been just one word, uttered silently via text.

The whole ground was suddenly plunged into darkness.

Beyond, Port Vila went black. Shrieks were heard instantly. What in heaven's name was this? Vanuatu was used to natural disasters.

Fifteen seconds later all power was restored. It had been sudden – and it had been intended.

Julian Jardine was all smiles. He shook his head and shrugged looking rather bewildered over what had just occurred.

It was the happiest Maria Cavaleros had seen him for weeks. Jardine had transformed into an agreeable mine-host to their party.

'Shall we all adjourn for refreshments?'

Julian Jardine was quite possibly the least fazed person in the stadium over what had just occurred.

Up in the commentary box and out in their unit in the car park Channel 17 studio officials were carrying out all necessary checks before the temporary off-air status caused by the momentary blackout was restored on-air. Their Australia-based headquarters had taken over briefly, filling with additional airtime for advertisers.

The blackout had brought about no casualties. No fatalities.

Monty was curious.

'How does that kind of thing happen? I mean, in this day and age of back-up power?'

'I haven't the faintest idea,'

Jardine bounced back, now trying hard to wipe the Cheshire cat smile from his face. They both smiled as they clinked glasses together.

Shane Chislett had deliberated over his half-time team talk. If he didn't act in his natural manner, was he being true to himself? He wanted to rave, to shout. Why shouldn't he? This might be his one chance to lead a team to World Cup success. But he was under pressure. If only they knew. If only they all knew what it had been like for him.

'He's gonna blow ...'

Regan Phillips, playing at hooker in place of Ash Tyson, had experienced Chislett as his club coach previously.

He had said the words under his breath to Neil 'The Brickie' Duncan as they reached the dressing room.

GPK knew without doubt that the brief blackout was not a surprise to some. His questions to himself were why and what was to be gained by it?

He felt he knew who the who was already.

He had been in the mobile studio. GPK had been the one who opened the mobile studio's door just as Erin was talking with Alex and Elenola. It was GPK who had set Det Supt Jackson on this course by bringing her to speed on Jardine's past. He'd contacted her after their earlier meeting at Breakas.

It was currently mayhem as the studio sought to ensure everything they had shot in the first half was backed up, while also maintaining a presence on the ground with cameras running while the break took place.

GPK had been in the mobile studio alerting them to who should be filmed. He had left them to it for a short while and was currently entering the hospitality lounge in the stand where he could see Jardine, Maria and the Montgomerys, plus Danford Napakauranga who was seemingly enjoying their company along with a Japanese gentleman.

'Excuse me young lady.'

GPK nodded in the general direction of the throng.

'I'm sure I have seen the Japanese gentleman before, but I just can't remember his name. I don't want to have to ask him, as I feel I should know ... do you know?'

The girl, who had been circulating the room with complimentary glasses of wine and kava, shook her head apologetically.

'Sakamoto ... Maratoto Sakamoto ... lives at The Hut ... not

much of a hut, more a palace …'

GPK would have known her voice anywhere.

He'd not expected her to be there, as was evident by his expression.

His colleague of many years, Janet Hague filled him in briefly, privately and quickly.

'Got your message. Ann's here.'

She nodded in the direction of Ann Cummings holding up her glass, another of GPK's investigative reporting team back in England.

'Plane landed at 7. Came straight here.'

She then shifted her head in the group's direction.

'Sakamoto. Took over Vanuatu Beef Inc. three years ago. Linked with drugs, gambling, nothing proven but all very definitely part of his empire.'

She let the news settle before adding.

'The Montgomerys? A bit more mysterious, not sure what their game is yet but banking, you can't get more criminal than that can you?'

Janet smiled at her ex-boss.

'Getting on well, aren't they?'

They clinked glasses.

'You're good, but then I don't need to tell you that do I?'

GPK was overjoyed to have his team back in place.

Janet gave the hint of a smile while turning to face the 'rat pack', as she'd just decided to call them. She continued looking at them as she delivered her final heartfelt line.

'We want this as much as you Grahame – for Jeff. That's why we're all here, James and Ken, me and Ann …'

She looked at him now.

'We got Geoff Quinigan, we'll nail this guy. Whichever way we have to.'

CHAPTER 68

'*Welcome back to Port Vila Municipal Stadium!*'

Brad Kearns was composed and ready to go as the first half action was replayed on screen.

'*The action started with a bang when France hit the straps with the fastest ever try scored at the start of a World Cup knockout game. It was recorded at 12.4 seconds. Since then, it has been all a bit nip and tuck with a lot of bluster from both sides, until the lights literally went out!*'

The camera showed the blackness just after the end of the first half before coming back on to Brad.

'*We're just minutes away from the second half of this game that will see one of these sides go into the semi-finals … or will they?*

'*Have the World Cup organisers had something up their sleeves? … Before the game tonight the chief executive of the Rugby League World Cup Organising Committee, Zoe Miller, taunted us with a special announcement she said she would make at half-time … come back to us after this commercial break and find out our very own Channel 17 exclusive breaking news!*'

The cameras had panned to a smiling Zoe in the commentary box/studio when Brad had mentioned her by name.

While the brief ad break took over Brad had leaned towards the chief executive.

'*This had better be good Zoe …*'

She winked at him. She looked great. This was her gaining back control.

Since her boat expedition she had purposely laid low, readying herself. Dressed in a thin cotton material Ravish Me HQ red midi dress with matching heels she looked composed, radiant and back to the woman she saw herself as – sassy, classy and on top form.

A burst of information came through on a mobile phone, just prior to Zoe's announcement.

'*All good here!*'

'*Same.*'

'*Ditto.*'

Julian Jardine looked down at his phone as it reverberated in his hand. All three texts were sent on the same app share he'd set up.

Jardine was doing backflips inwardly while maintaining a straight face outwardly, then slipped the phone back in his pocket to turn back to his friends. Only then did he smile, but it was enough for eager eyes.

'*Yep, saw that,*'

Ann Cummings replied to Janet.

'*If we could get that phone …*'

England and France were coming out of their respective dressing rooms when Channel 17 returned to air.

'*You've 20 seconds, 25 tops,*'

Brad Kearns told Zoe.

'*No link. No time. Camera straight on you. You're on screen now.*'

Zoe Miller was as cool as they come.

'*Thank you Brad and Channel 17, for allowing me to bring you a fabulous piece of news. I hope you are all enjoying the Rugby League World Cup. This truly is a wonderful game for all men, women, those in wheelchairs, the PDRL and LGBT.*

'*The people of Vanuatu and particularly here on Efate have been amazing – and that's why the Rugby League World Cup Organising Committee has decided that the first semi-final will also be held here in 3 days' time. Thank you!*'

Brad gave Zoe a thumbs-up just before he came back on screen. He was always great with feigning shocked expressions, but this time no feign was necessary. He acknowledged the breaking news with gusto.

'*Wow! That's us booked in for three more nights! Terrific news for these islands!*'

Brad left aside the howls of derision and pandemonium this news was probably now causing across either Brisbane or Sydney, with one of them losing out as the original semi-final venue; with travel plans that would have to be altered and tickets that may already have been purchased.

He knew that part of it could turn horrendous and litigious, and so did Zoe, as she strode out of the commentary/studio area.

She held her head high, clicked her heels and gave herself the biggest almighty smile.

'Does anyone know what just happened here?'

Brad Kearns spoke to his producers as pitch commentator Karen Stonehouse gave her feedback on what both coaches had said to their players during half-time.

'Has she gone crazy? She's just creamed the whole of one ground's plans! How can she do that?'

Karen Stonehouse handed back to the studio. Brad recomposed in an instant.

'Right, here we go everybody! For the right to play here again in the semi-finals in three days' time ... you heard it here first ... it's England kicking to France to get us underway!'

Greg was still on the sidelines and had now been joined by Neil 'The Brickie' Duncan and Freddie South. Phil Parkin and Mason Bell had taken their places.

'That's a really odd line-up from Shane Chislett ... does he want to win this game?'

Laurie Northey was scratching his head in the commentary area.

'By odd do you mean rugby league coaching suicide?'

Brad Kearns found himself now constantly shaking his head. What was happening to the world? Pitch black one minute. A crazy 'last minute' announcement about gifting this island another game. Now a coach playing roulette with his players in a quarter-final game. Ah well, he thought. Adds to the fun of commentary.

The crowd had loved Vanessa Quai's 'Spread The Love (All Over The World)' which she had just performed again with reggae star Stan Antas.

And now the word was spreading around the ground that the World Cup party was set to carry on, just when the people of Vanuatu thought this was going to be their last night.

The noise began swelling from the Vanuatu people who were delighted that it was all going to roll on for another few days.

Neil 'The Brickie' Duncan nudged Greg and the others to get up and encourage the England following to add even more. At least they could do this much from the sidelines.

Freddie and Billy joined in and Gary Walker, Vinny, Tyler Rodgers and others on the field built it further. Stu Wainwright and the other injured members of the squad moved from their positions to join them.

The French team caught the mood too.

'This game never ceases to amaze me.'

Brad Kearns was now chuckling away to himself.

'Somehow just a handful of guys have turned the atmosphere in here from subdued to a cauldron of noise!

'And it's getting everyone going!

'It's Tyler Rodgers kicking to France, oh! ... Here we go ... he's gone for a short high one ... and there's a stampede here ...'

The crowd loved it! There was a roar all around the ground with the Vanuatu locals and each nation's fans fist pumping and hollering their players on to what was destined to be shattering impact.

Phil Parkin, Rich Dee and Big Mick Green were the hit-up boys. Their mission was to destroy anyone from the French side, to hit hard if one of their players got to the ball first.

Sam Rivers was their other weapon, to run fast and hard – leap and reach.

'Ohhh!!!'

It was a collective, highly audible sound from the whole crowd as French hero Laurent Galia leaped above everyone to take the ball, only to be taken out in the air by Phil 'The Butcher' Parkin.

'That's one big hit! And it's a big moment coming up here from Mr Obeng as that could be trouble for Parkin. He's taken Galia out. And he looks completely gone to me. Mr Obeng has stopped

the clock while Galia receives treatment ... and now he's moved his hand towards his pocket ...'

The French fans were shouting 'Rouge, Rouge'.

'They're wanting Mr Obeng to show a red card here ... but it's yellow ... ten minutes in the bin for Parkin, and that's nearly as bad as when they started the first half, Ben.'

As Ben Mara took his lead from Brad Kearns, and Laurent Galia was led away from the park to be assessed for a head injury, the French fired the ball downfield from the penalty and set themselves up for a charge at the England line from thirty yards out.

'Romain Robin takes the tap of the ball and passes to Fabrice Joulliet who runs towards the oncoming England tacklers. Joulliet spins in the tackle and offloads to onrushing Maxime Maison-le-Boeuf who charges into a welcoming committee of Green and Rodgers before going down.

'He plays it back to Renaud Jordain who spins it out to the little general Michel Marseilles who comes off his left foot to wrongfoot half the England team, which opens up a gap and throws a pearler of a pass to Anton Jeuneville who comes racing on to the ball and it's a try!!! Another well worked try from France as he goes over unchallenged.

'Now that was how to score a try, Laurie ...'

France 10 England 0 was expanded to 12-0 with Jeuneville converting his own try adding a further two points with the conversion attempt.

Ten minutes later, following Phil Parkin's return from his sin-binning, the French side had crossed twice more with tries for a returning Laurent Galia and half-back Jean-Paul Alainne, both converted by Jeuneville.

'Twenty-five minutes are left on the clock and England need twenty-five to win, with arguably their most inspiring player in this tournament having spent only around twenty minutes out of fifty on the paddock ...'

Brad Kearns turned to Laurie Northey and Ben Mara.

'... England really have to score next boys, if they're going to *have any chance, but what is going on out there?'*

While Brad's summarisers gave their thoughts, there was one man in the crowd who looked smugly satisfied.

'Jardine's smile. He's trying to hold it back, but it's there ... check this out ... check out who he's looking across at ... see that? The mannerism ...'

The cameramen and the producer/director in Det Supt Erin Jackson's operations room were on-point.

'And check this out ... oh ... uh-oh ... get the whole of this ... and keep on all our main characters so far ...'

The cameras had also found another look, another mannerism, another face. The look was not from the grandstand. It was a look of astonishment, then fierce words, anger and then it boiled over.

Channel 17's cameras caught the action shortly after Erin Jackson's team.

What their audience saw was a flick over to what looked purely like just a heated moment on the bench.

Brad Kearns picked it up immediately.

'Woah, steady on boys! There's trouble around the England bench. It's England coach Shane Chislett. Oh, there's punches being thrown! It's all getting mighty messy! ... and the referee Mr Obeng has stopped the game.

'Oh, man, now everybody seems to be wading in ... this is not a good advertisement for rugby league right now ...

'Let's go down to pitchside reporter Karen Stonehouse. Karen, it looks like Gangs of New York! What's happening down there?'

'Brad, it is pandemonium down here. It's calming down now, but I have more sensational news for you! ... Shane Chislett has just been sacked! Mid-game! ... I have never seen anything like it in my life. No-one gets sacked during a game, do they?

'Well now they do!'

Brad Kearns was shaking his head once again, and if viewers could have seen him he now had his head in his hands. Karen Stonehouse continued. This was her moment. Normally she only had about fifteen seconds to relay information, but this was big news, bigger even maybe than Zoe Miller's announcement.

'*And from what I've just seen and heard it is Greg Duggan who has been given the task of steering the ship for the rest of this campaign!*

'*Which may well be over already if this game doesn't get restarted … and there is some talk of that at the moment too … Mr Obeng is not a happy man!*'

In the Erin Jackson studio the situation was developing further.

'*Get that! Look, he is absolutely livid! And he's leaving his seat! …*'

The producer/director was privately loving this. He had three cameras trained on Jardine now. They were watching him move, giving his apologies to his guests, but he was most definitely on the move and had completely lost it.

'*Get someone following him wherever he goes. Two cameras. Camera 6, Camera 3 – go!*'

It was all true. Shane Chislett had been relieved of his position as England coach with immediate effect. Wow!

Greg had been given the job temporarily. One of the England officials had been handed the task of going across to the bench to deliver the news. He had shown Chislett a confirmation from the chairman of the England Rugby League International Team, former scrum-half Walter Armitage.

Chislett had been enraged. He had grabbed and thrown down the official's phone and had taken him by the throat before players and his off-field team tried to calm him.

Greg hadn't known what the hell was going on, and knew nothing of his impending role, but was one of those who was aiming to quieten down the rumpus.

Chislett flew out a hook as hands tried to restrain him and floored the official.

Greg and Neil 'The Brickie' Duncan put up their hands, aimed at diluting his hostility.

Chislett knew about Greg's new job before he did and aimed an angry swipe at him. Greg ducked just in time, but Chislett wasn't done. He aimed a kick at Greg, catching him on his left leg, but next second Chislett was decked by Big Mick Green, the six-foot-seven powerhouse then towered over him.

Deputy Commissioner Elenola Taneo had three Vanuatu policemen at the game arrest Chislett for breach of the peace, threatening behaviour and bodily harm. He was led from the ground in disgrace.

GPK had been in among the police presence and used the brief opportunity he had to deliver a message to Greg.

Brad Kearns loved the drama. It made his commentary.

'I keep saying this game never ceases to amaze me but tonight … well, it has stepped into the surreal … a last-minute decision to host a semi-final here in three days' time, an international coach sacked while the game is in play … pinch me somebody, when I wake up this will all surely have been a dream …'

Brad Kearns was pedalling his own brand of hysteria.

Greg's brain was suddenly clear, his adrenaline pumping like fury. He'd been in a stupor on the park and on the bench.

The message he'd received before the game had done that, but now this last two minutes of absolute madness had given him clarity.

For the next twenty-four minutes he had one purpose.

Referee Obeng was ready to start the game again, to set the clock back rolling.

Greg got to work. Four changes.

'Tyler – to full-back, Charlie – you're off mate; Neil – to centre, Troy you're off too; Freddie – you're on for Phil; Rich, you make way for Billy.'

Greg took to the park.

The cheers all around the ground from England and Vanuatu fans was immense. And the atmosphere kept building as the France fans became louder too.

Mr Obeng restarted the game. Brad Kearns restarted his commentary.

'Rugby league's newest international coach Greg Duggan has instantly made four changes, but is it already too late? George?'

'Well Brad, Greg Duggan has immediately put everyone back in their right places. That's at least a wise first move, but France only need to get down the park and slot over a drop goal for them to be out of sight.'

'And that looks exactly what they have on their mind ...'

Ben Mara added.

'Hey! Think we may have something ...'

Camera 5 from Det Supt Erin Jackson's operation was talking back to the production crew. All eyes went straight to their screen.

'What's he doing?'

The producer/director was questioning himself or indeed anyone who was watching.

'And who the hell is he?'

CHAPTER 69

Julian Jardine was beyond furious.

'*Get me Walter sodding Armitage right now!*'

'*I'm sorry Mr Jardine, I'm afraid Mr Armitage is temporarily unavailable at this time. Would you like me to take a message?*'

Jardine had already finished the call by the time Walter Armitage's secretary had finished delivering her reply. He'd quit at 'I'm sorry ...'

The chairman of the England Rugby League International Team had been feeling under the weather prior to the World Cup and had stayed at home, but he had been watching the games and he had been fed important information.

He was alongside his secretary when she had been answering the call and now patted her gently on the shoulder and gave a smile of satisfaction.

'*Thank you, Denise. Now, would you be so good as to call this number ...*'

'*And France are running the ball exactly as Laurie and Ben predicted.*'

Brad Kearns was readying himself for the contest to be as good as over before Greg could even launch into it.

'*France have three more attempts in this six-tackle set, currently just on the halfway line. Jeuneville is setting himself for a drop-goal attempt when they've gained about 15 metres more, but they also have Galia and Alainne who can kick too.*

'*Robert Jullien runs the ball up to the England tacklers, spins and offloads to Maison-le-Boeuf, who is wrapped up by South and Green. Two tackles to go in this set. Maison-le-Boeuf plays it back to Romain Robin, who makes ground and darts through a gap, before being hauled down by opposite number Regan Phillips. They're 35 yards out. This is it. It's in range.*'

'*Might be a bit too much for Jeuneville, not the distance but the time to get the accuracy,*'

Laurie Northey submitted.

It was panic stations on the park. Greg hadn't had time enough to get words out to any of his team. No instructions, just actions. The one thing he knew was that if the French were about to go for goal someone had to get in the ball's way, or pray that it was a poor, unsuccessful kick.

'Romain Robin plays it to Michel Marseilles. Oh, he's taken a step to the left and come back on his right. Now he's flicked it back to Fabrice Joulliet. The French are looking here, trying to make space, but they just can't find a way. Ohhh, that's a great little flicked pass out of the back of his hand to Gilles Baltieri. And he's bounced off one would-be tackler. They're still looking to get it to Jeuneville.'

England players were firing in hard. Desperate defence was the order of the day. Greg wanted possession, but these first few seconds of his new international coaching career were all about France.

'Baltieri somehow, don't ask me how but somehow, has shovelled the ball out to Jeuneville but has no time to set himself for the kick. He offloads to Galia, who dinks the ball over despairing England hands to Jean-Paul Alainne who has no space to work, or does he?

'Oh, he's going through! He's found a gap, he's motoring here. He's within the England 30-metre line, he's nearly at the twenty, but the England team are bearing down on him. Tyler Rodgers is covering. He's kicked!!!! …'

It had been a grubber kick, bounding along towards the England try line. From out of nowhere French full-back Philippe Longchamps sprinted through and dived on to the ball and went over the line!

'It's a fantastic try from the 'Machine Bleue' as they French fans now call them! And that's it for Greg Duggan and his England team. Laurie, this could just be the shortest coaching career ever! …'

Maketi Obeng looked to his on-field touch judges.

'… oh, now, hold on! … Mr Obeng and his team may have something to say about that … it looks like he's giving the try, yes, but he's going to the video referee for confirmation … he's looking for something in back play leading to the try and he wants the grounding

*of the ball checking ... these are nervous times indeed for the England
fans, but if you're a France fan this could be the game right here ...'*

Greg lost no time at all in gathering his team. The video
referee was looking at the action, the crowd was watching it
too, there was doubt all around the ground.

*'Don't look at that bloody screen! Listen! ... Now I don't fucking
care whether that comes up TRY or NO TRY. We have just over
twenty minutes to bring this game back and we are all good enough
to do it. Get your minds set, get your arses into gear and let's play
like we all can! ...'*

There were roars going up around the ground both for France
to be awarded the try and for it to be chalked off. The England
players maintained their concentration on Greg, who was still
on with his team-talk while the action was being replayed and
replayed on the big screen.

*'It is only us who have got ourselves in this mess, and it is only us
who can get us out. Discipline! Nothing stupid, don't lose it with the
ref or them! Think about those moves. Belief ...'*

Greg hammered his clenched fist on his chest.

*'We can't win this game with words. It's about belief and playing
our fucking hearts out that will get us through ...'*

Just then a roar went up all around the England fans.

'NO TRY!!!'

*'The video referee has seen something in the move. I'm still not
quite certain what, but it looks like it was an off-the-ball infringement,
obstruction, by Renaud Jordain. And it is a penalty to England back
at the halfway line.'*

As Brad Kearns prepared to take a sip from his drink Greg
took hold of the ball to kick for touch.

He looked up in front of him. He was going to kick it into
touch, gain yardage, but instead quickly changed to sidefooting
the ball forward. The France players had been anticipating a
kick for touch, they'd moved further back than they would if
he'd just been tapping the ball.

*'Oh! Duggan has caught the France players with their pants
down here! He's played an audacious little grubber, he's collected*

and he's on the France 30-metre line! And this France team are all at sea here. Neil 'The Brickie' Duncan comes up on his inside, Duggan passes ... no he doesn't! Oh that was magic ... he's in open space! ... Just Longchamps to beat ... the crowd is going wild! ... Duggan feigns to pass ... Longchamps takes the dummy ... and he is over!!!! From absolutely nothing Greg Duggan has carved out a masterpiece! They'll call him The Sculptor next! TRY to England!! They're on the board!'

While Brad Kearns bigged up Greg's try even further Greg took it upon himself to kick the conversion.

He didn't know quite why, but he did not want to trust it to Jericho Pallagi who had been taking them previously while he'd been out. Something about Jericho's eyes when he'd been talking.

Jericho had not been happy when Greg had taken over. Another decision from Greg.

A last interchange. He prayed that no injuries befell them in the run-in to the end of the game. Before he kicked what was an easy conversion, he called for Troy Whittingham to come back on.

'Jericho, off. Troy on.'

Greg hollered out to the bench, back to his brief words again. He then turned and coolly slotted over the conversion. France 24 England 6.

'Wow! What a one-man show that was! ... But it can't all be one man if they want to get back into this game ... and France are still in the driving seat ...'

The crowd was already getting excited 'Greg Is So Good, Good, Good' began being sung again in the stands.

'That's not what they think,'

laughed Ben Mara.

France didn't appear rocked by Greg's wonder try. Laurent Galia was a seasoned campaigner. He knew that all they had to do was hold the ball, run it up, get good field position and restrict England. And that's what they succeeded in doing for the next ten minutes. They tried a drop kick from 40 metres, that sailed close but landed wide and out of play.

'*Eleven minutes to go. England have upped their game, there's no question about that, but they need points again soon. France have played resolutely since that Duggan try. They need three tries and all to be converted just to get level. Ben, George, can they do it?*'

Greg couldn't come up with such a cheeky play as he'd made for a second time and get away with it. He took out his gumshield and had words with Billy, Freddie and Big Mick.

'*Get me down this park, boys. Come on!*'

Greg tapped the ball on the 20-metre line and passed to a rampaging Big Mick Green who hammered the ball hard up to England's 30-metre line. He spun out of the arms of the first French tackler Georges Dacouret but only into Maison-le-Boeuf. His legs pumping hard took him a further three metres but he couldn't break free.

Green sent the ball back to Regan Phillips who fed the next man mountain Billy Ecktenstall who made a further five metres before his reception committee of Jullien, Joulliet and Garcia, but he was still moving forward, another two metres with Baltieri joining the tackle to bring him down.

Freddie South and Greg looked each other straight in the eye, the briefest of nods. Ecktenstall played the ball quickly while the French players were still reorganising. Freddie hit full throttle as Gary Walker fed the ball. His face full of intent he took the ball straight up to the halfway line before Maison-le-Boeuf, Jordain and Joulliet loomed up close. Just prior to impact he flicked the ball out from his right hand and like an express train Neil 'The Brickie' Duncan came through.

'*Oh, that's an amazing swerve and sidestep from Neil Duncan and he's in acres of space ... just Jeuneville and Longchamps ahead ... oh, he's done Jeuneville with another ludicrous sidestep! ... and now he releases ... it's Venuuuusss!!*

'*Try, England!! This game is alive!! France 24 England 10 with a kick to come.*'

Vinny had made the kick as easy as you like for Greg who slotted it over. 24-12. Eight minutes left. Brad Kearns had seen the effect the latest try had had on the France team.

'This France side is suddenly looking ragged for the first time in this tournament. And listen to that crowd! This place is becoming England's second home.'

The England and Vanuatu fans were embracing each other. Ever since Greg's act of sportsmanship during their game there had been a real bond between both sets of fans. It was now cemented.

France's kick to England was high, it was deep, it was out!

'Anton Jeuneville has gifted England an opportunity. He's kicked the ball straight out and England have a penalty kick on the halfway line … it is the first real mistake France have made all evening. The cracks are beginning to show. Captain Galia needs to get them back to where they were before, but Ben, it is proving difficult with the noise now in this stadium. The French must feel like everyone and everything is going the way of England.'

Ben Mara was quick to respond, as well as brief.

'It is, Brad and the Vanuatu people, my people are really, really helping England here. We are so good, good, good …'

Ben was enjoying himself.

Greg had his head switched on to just one thing. Not the scoreline, nor the crowd or time remaining in the game, not his dad, nor Kyle nor Susie. The ball.

He stared at it as though looking for inspiration. He stepped back from the ball, six paces, then two to the left, his customary run-up to striking the ball high up into the night sky or to sail through the posts.

He ran. But as his ball-kicking leg came down to connect he skipped over the ball. Scrum-half Gary Walker who had been one of the line of players to follow up the ball went on an opposite diagonal to Greg's feigned kick.

The France team was momentarily bewitched and bothered as well as bewildered. They had loaded one side more than the other in expectation of Greg's kick, it had gone the other way. Worse still Gary Walker had kicked it along the floor. Nonetheless Jean-Paul Allaine looked favourite to collect, but the ball was travelling at pace and was bouncing wickedly. At its last bounce before he had intended on collecting it took a sudden jag. Allaine switched his body as best he could but only succeeded in staggering and tipping the ball forward.

Referee Maketi Obeng allowing the game to flow chose not to blow immediately for a knock-on infringement and Sam Rivers kicked the ball on beyond the now despairing front line of the France defence, it was still turning over and over and full-back Longchamps was trying to make up ground as Vinny Venus bore down on the ball.

Five metres out Vinny took the ball in one clean swoop and threw himself at the line. Try!!!

'England have just cut this French side to ribbons and that's an outstanding second try from Vincent Venus who is now looking every inch a world-class winger. Laurie, this game is going to the wire!'

Laurie Northey put what they had just seen into rugby league perspective rather than using Brad Kearns' hyperbole.

'That was a play that you cannot help but admire Brad. There are not many moves where you should be applauding a man who didn't even touch the ball during it, but Greg Duggan has prised open this France team doing exactly that. The rest played their parts superbly, but the architect was this man taking the kick.'

Brad Kearns joined Laurie Northey

'Hold on to your hats everybody. Three minutes left on the clock. England, yes Duggan has just slotted over another conversion, are just six points adrift. France 24 England 18.'

As Greg raced back into position following his latest kick he fist-pumped to his whole team. No words now, just action.

France kicked back to England once more. Galia ordering Jeuneville to *'gardez le ballon en jeu'*. Keep the ball in play.

Twenty minutes ago they had been 24 points in front. Now just six. But with only minutes to go. *'Un point,'* he instructed. *'Tenir le ballon'*.

But before they could hold the ball the France team had to get it back. Three minutes if both sides held the ball through their tackle counts might mean around two more chances for each team. Maybe they wouldn't even need a drop goal for that extra point.

Greg was focused. Nothing was going to get into his brain in the final three minutes other than the ball.

Jeuneville had sent it almost into orbit, high and hanging, to give his teammates as much time as possible to get under it, to pressure the England team and win the ball.

Maison-de-Boeuf, Jullien and Dacouret thundered towards where the ball's trajectory was bringing it down under Troy Whittingham who rose to meet the ball off the ground. Jullien flew into the air to tip the ball back. Whittingham had his arms cupped in front to take the ball cleanly into his chest.

At the last nanosecond Troy decided to instead raise his left hand even higher and tip the ball back to Tyler Rodgers who ran a weaving line across the onrushing tacklers, searching for an opening, but was gathered up by Baltieri and Jordain and bundled back five metres.

Ricki Brown took the ball, and with an exquisite reverse pass found Mason Bell who was immediately stunted by the France surge of Maison-de-Boeuf and Albert who had interchanged with Dacouret.

'*Follow him!*'

Det Supt Erin Jackson's camera team was fast dispersing. Two more cameras were now en route to catch what they could of what had been their mystery man in the crowd.

'*Alex, are you on this?*'

Alex Lui responded positively to Jackson.

Elenola was already following Jardine.

'*England are under immense pressure here. Whatever happens this has been a remarkable comeback, Ben …*'

But before Ben Mara could answer …

'*… oh, that's a monster kick from Duggan … he's kicked from the England 10-metre line and it has sailed into France's half of the field. It's all they could do. They'd made no ground at all in their last set … Longchamps has the ball … he's at the France 40-metre line, now he's at the halfway where he is met by South and Ecktenstall.*'

'*Ninety seconds left on the clock. It's ticking down. All the France side have to do is hold it.*'

Brad Kearns felt the atmosphere building once again.

'*Tenir le ballon!!*'

Galia hollered at his charges. He took the ball and held it himself to lead by example. He took the tackle, twisted and would have released but wanted to show his team what he wanted from them.

Three successive charges followed by a returning Charles de Vries, fresh legs in Rene Lammonet and Pierre Pietemonet. Galia's teammates had done as instructed. Two tackles left.

Drop goal to put the game out of sight? But only 55 seconds now left. Was it necessary?

'*Tenir le ballon!!*' had become Galia's watchword. He ran the ball again into the tackle. One tackle remained. 45 seconds.

'*Full credit to Laurent Galia who looks as though he has saved this game for France. He's played the ball back for France's last possession maybe, to win the game, and it's Baltieri who takes the ball up to England's 10-metre line, he's flipped it inside to Michel Marseilles and he's taken the tackle … oh, he's spun out of it, he's trying to keep the ball as long as he can … but … he's had it wrenched from his grasp in a one-on-one tackle with Duggan! Who else could it have been! …*'

Brad looked up at the clock. 30 seconds! His commentary was rendered worthless.

The crowd made its own, the action plain to see.

Greg wrong-footed the France side with a sidestep of his own. He'd have a word with The Brickie about it later, and galloped through the flailing arms of an out-on-his-feet Maison-de-Boeuf. Greg's momentum seemed to accelerate in time with the crowd's reaction. He was over the halfway line with France's fastest men in pursuit – Jeuneville, Pierre Le Blanc and Alainne – he knew they had speed in their locker. He arced his run to make them alter their opportunity to tackle. Over the France 40-metre line, into their 30 metres.

20 seconds were left on the clock. He dared not look at

anything other than the line. He reached the 20-metre line and was within sight of the 10-metre line when Jeuneville launched himself with every fibre of his body extended – and clipped Greg's right heel, sending it against his left heel and, unbalanced, Greg felt himself going down.

No time for a pass. Greg knew that any regrouping would eat up precious seconds. He knew that one man would be there, somewhere, as he had for the past three years for him. As he fell he flipped up the ball and there he was.

'Vincent Venuuuussss!!!! It's Try-Time England!!!! This IS the most amazing game!! And it's another easy kick for Duggan as Venus goes in close to the posts. France 24 England 22 and the kick to come. Keep it right here boys and girls. This is going to Golden Point.'

Greg slotted over another without even thinking that had he missed, it would still be game over.

There were 15 seconds remaining on the clock when France once again kicked back to England. The hooter sounded. 24-24.

It was party time all around the ground with the England and Vanuatu fans in ebullient mood. The England fans blowing a collective sigh of relief.

Their team had earned an amazing reprieve. But now it was down to a lottery, so far as many were concerned. The golden point was the rugby league equivalent of a football penalty shoot-out that goes to immediate sudden death rather than five attempts each.

'I'm on him!'

Alex Lui was following his prey. Erin Jackson's recording team had sent him a photo of the man on his mobile. The man they hadn't yet been able to put a name to. In Sydney her team were also working non-stop. Alex now looked and instantly recognised him.

'I've seen this man before, boss.'

Alex hadn't intended to call her boss. It just tripped out when he was talking to a superior. He hadn't done it with her before.

Erin smiled at the other end of the phone. She had worked hard for this. She didn't have the time for wallowing in the pride she felt at having turned around her relationship with the Vanuatu Police department, but she could allow herself a second or two to smile.

'Just what in hell's name is going on here?'

Danford Napakauranga was on screen. The cameras captured his movement. No histrionics, no face like thunder as Jardine's had appeared.

Erin transferred her attention back to her producer/director who had made the comment.

'Can we get a closer look at his face from those shots, maybe we're missing something here.'

She had been suspicious of Danford right from the start. Always the good guy, always genial, never a foot put wrong. She didn't get that. She wanted to know his demons, what made him put up his wall of what she saw as bland policing.

The remaining members of what had been Jardine's happy band at half-time were still there and still, it appeared, happy.

The Montgomerys and Maria Cavaleros appeared in light-hearted conversation, but there was now someone else who had just joined them.

Greg had gathered his team together just off the pitch.

Port Vila Municipal Stadium had a running track around the playing surface, just a four-lane track but sufficient to keep a distance between the crowd and the players.

'My team' he thought to himself for a second. I'm the England head coach. I only came over to see my dad. He thought again briefly of his dad as he crouched on his haunches taking on water. He'd just led an epic 25-minute fightback as England coach, he said it again to himself.

It sounded ridiculous. It was ridiculous. But it was real. His only other coaching role had been with Hopton Town three years ago and that had ended in disaster for the club and for Bob Irvine who had lost his life. Enough.

He shook himself out of any further backtrack. He glugged water down, rehydrating then took up with his team.

'Fantastic effort boys! All of you! Two outcomes here from kick-off. If France kick to us I want that ball, come hell or high water, inside their 40-metre line to drop the goal. One chance. If we kick to them we do not let them get beyond their 40-metre line. Got it?'

Seventeen firm fists met in the middle of their circle.

'Stand by everybody. These two sides have given us a real game of two halves. It's now down to this. In the next few minutes, maybe even seconds, we will know who is to reach the World Cup semi-finals ... to be played here among these wonderful people of Vanuatu!'

Brad Kearns was loving every minute of it.

Maketi Obeng brought Greg and Laurent Galia together in the middle of the park. He flipped the coin. Laurent Galia called. It came down his way. England were to kick to France.

Greg placed the ball, moved back. He sent a spiralling ball towards the France posts. It hung in the air. The England line moved forward as one. There was no way they could reach the player who would collect it before he had.

Greg had had one focus with the kick, something he'd never ever tried previously in a game. He'd purposely aimed at the posts rather than the more regular kick from kick-off to one side or the other.

The ball was heading for Anton Jeuneville. He was setting himself to collect. The England line was nowhere near him, but as the ball descended he began recorrecting.

Horror came across the Frenchman's face as he took in what was about to happen.

The ball hit the crossbar! The France team could not believe what was happening. The onrushing England team had time to see, to calculate, the ball was coming their way!

Greg was leading the charge from his kick.

He'd played 'crossbar challenge' as a kid with a football and then a rugby ball. His success rate had been negligible.

But here! Oh man! His heart was racing.

The crowd raised its volume to fever pitch again, roaring England on. For a moment everything went into slow motion in Greg's world, even though he had been at top speed. The ball was coming down. The France team were trying to cover.

Baltieri had recognised the danger. He attempted to dive on the now bouncing ball. He succeeded in knocking it backwards. It cannoned off Romain Robin's legs as he had been coming to meet it.

Greg readjusted, he had little time to think.

'The ball is ricocheting between the French team! It's still bobbling around and ...'

Brad Kearns was astounded at what he saw happening in front of him once again.

Greg, at pace, flicked the ball up with his left foot, into the palm of his right hand which was still facing downwards as he was running, and somehow, with the ball seemingly defying gravity, made it five of the remaining seven metres towards the whitewash before launching himself, fingers now spread on the ball but still holding it downwards.

The crowd went wild! To say nothing of Brad Kearns!

'... that is the try of the season!!!! In fact, scratch that, it is the try of all time!!! Forget golden point! Greg Duggan has scored four of them! He's not just rescued this game for England, he has now won it for his charges with the most astonishingly brilliant piece of off-the-cuff football I have ever, ever, ever seen!!!'

As Brad Kearns went into superlative land the England team raced as one to embrace Greg and each other. And then to the fans.

Several seconds later they were also gracious with their France counterparts whose disappointment was nearly as great as their utter disbelief over what had just taken place.

The England team then joined in as one with the England, Vanuatu and, it had to be said in all fairness to them, the French fans as everyone applauded the greatness and majestic of all rugby league many would ever witness.

'Greg is so good, good, good. Greg is so wonderful!!'

The supporters rang it out now, throughout the stadium. It was party time again on Efate and the England fans knew they had three more days of sun, sea and whatever else they chose before the World Cup semi-final.

'*Look at their faces!!*'

Erin Jackson's filming team were trained on the Montgomerys, Maria Cavaleros and the new member of their group.

'*That's not about the game. Look at them. They are ecstatic. There's something else here. Pause that!*'

Erin was looking hard. The pause showed a phone being held. There was a finger pointing at the screen and Maria Cavaleros gave the biggest smile she had possibly ever given in her life.

'*We need to know what that says!*'

CHAPTER 70

'You're so good, good, good, you are so wonderful …'

Greg woke with Susie, head propped up by her hand with her elbow on the bed, singing lightly while smiling and stroking the hair on his chest.

Greg raised his eyes to the top of his head in mock dismay.

He just wanted to stay here in their bed and relax. Proper relax, not any other extra activity. His body wasn't up to it.

Then again, he quickly thought, well maybe, smiling to himself. Susie saw it.

'What?'

She smiled. She knew what Greg's smile meant.

'You knowww …?'

she said temptingly.

'They do say it is a powerful aphrodisiac …'

Susie raised her eyebrows. Greg played along.

'Oh yeah? What is?'

'Success. Especially among sportsmen …'

Susie ran her fingers a little lower than where they had been previously.

'My my! … and especially among growing rugby league players … called naughty Mister Greg …'

Greg hadn't realised he'd have the energy, but sleep had obviously proved a wonderful recharger.

Susie had stayed at Breakas and had watched the game with Lani and Makele, the barman and keyboard player who played each week and was particularly fond of The Eagles classics.

The remaining hotel guests, even those not sportified had become even more engrossed as England had come back into the game. When Makele told them over the microphone that Susie was Greg's partner the party had started in earnest.

The Australian sporting media had gone into a frenzy.

Greg's heroics had been well documented. England's

comeback was recognised as one of the Rugby League World Cup's and indeed any sport's most outstanding achievements.

Such had been the manner of their determination in the last stanza of the second half that they had been reinstalled as second favourites.

The quarters had all been played and the semi-finals were to be England vs Samoa plus the absolutely massive Australia vs New Zealand.

Zoe had known just how much she would be setting herself up for a dynamite reaction when she had announced that Vanuatu was to host a semi-final, but she also knew she had powerful backing and while the media ranted and raved about the decision, she also knew it would all blow over.

Money talked.

Brisbane's owners of the Sunshine Stadium had already been recompensed; and for the Samoan fans it was half the distance from Samoa to Efate than it was to Australia; there was a sense in it.

It all made absolute sense to Zoe.

Efate would benefit, she would have more time, and she could go back to Australia head held high for the men's and women's final – and The Pink, if she really wanted to.

Right now, she was more than happy on the island.

Shane Chislett had been detained by Vanuatu Police where he had been questioned but had been released the next morning.

Walter Armitage had given strict instructions that Chislett should not return to Breakas and that his belongings be transferred to him at Bauerfield International Airport where he was to be flown back immediately to the UK.

What had Chislett done wrong? the Australian and England rugby league press had conjectured.

He certainly hadn't pulled up any trees in his World Cup campaign and the only times England had looked impressive had been when Duggan had come on to the park. But that was it as far as some were concerned. Why hadn't he used him more?

Others expressed that maybe Duggan was an impact player first and foremost, staying on Chislett's side.

There was talk of curious decisions, no more so than when he had sidelined all of arguably his most influential players at half-time in the France game, but other pundits said that those same players had been largely on the park when England had shipped 24 points.

'Shane! … Mr Chislett! …'

Janet Hague had followed Chislett after GPK had seen the former England coach's bags being deposited into a taxi that had arrived at Breakas. Annie Laing had been doing the honours, making sure they were taken. GPK had alerted Janet thinking that Chislett might react better to a female than a male asking questions.

'Do one!'

Chislett was angry and emotional.

'Shane, I'm not after a story, I'm not a journalist …'

Just hope I've not come across him in my stories before, she thought quickly.

'… and I'm not the police either … I know you've been a victim here …'

She saw his look, knew she had him. He stopped.

On the boat that had been moored in Undine Bay a rather different exchange was taking place.

'C'est combien nous avons gagne la nuit derniere cherie!'

The phone was shown with a figure that exceeded £20m. It would do for now. The couple clinked their favourite French wine from Madiran as they set off into the ocean.

'No se porque eres tan infeliz querido.'

Maria Cavaleros had returned with Julian on her boat in Mele Bay, it wasn't his. He'd talked as though it was, telling people he'd chartered it and was going to buy it. That annoyed her. She could not understand why he was so unhappy.

To her, it looked as though everything was going well.

Watching Greg play last night had reminded her of his prowess, in all departments. She had been as delighted as the

England fans when he'd gone over for the winning try. Greg was truly 'un gran especimen de hombre'. She couldn't help but smile to herself thinking back to the times they had spent together. Maybe she had been hasty in sacking him?

She thought back to when Julian had gone crazy. Why would what happened to the England coach matter? She was curious.

GPK had set up operations at Breakas. Ken was with him, back to his data gathering.

Det Supt Erin Jackson, Dep Commissoner Elenola Taneo and Det Alex Lui were having coffee at a local bar. The general consensus had been it would be better that way than at the station. There was still no Det Marlon Razni.

'So, it looks like we had a corrupt rugby league coach. That we also may have a couple of corrupt rugby league officials. That they have associates or friends with lots of money. And we have murders that have been committed that relate to all of this. Plus what happened to Greg Duggan in the lead-up to the games, and what has happened to Grace Elliott. And a possibly corrupt police commissioner …'

'Plus a possibly corrupt detective?'

Elenola added to Erin's list.

'Complete transparency on both sides? Isn't that what we said?'

'Yeah, possibly corrupt Australian police detective.'

Who I slept with just a few nights ago, Erin added to herself, my God woman what were you thinking!

CHAPTER 71

'Hiya Dad!!!'

Kyle was back on the phone, Diane next to him. Greg could hear her breathing, ready to help her son.

'You did GREAAAATTTTT!!!'

Kyle let himself go on this one and laughed out loud, as Greg couldn't help but do also.

'That try you scored. It was AMAAAAZZZINGG!!!'

'Dad! Dad! ... Mum was crying when you scored ...'

Kyle hadn't meant to give anything away, but Greg heard Diane go 'ssshh' as silently as she could in the background.

'... and Paul's gone ...'

What? Suddenly, Greg's mind began to whirl. Diane had appeared unhappy last time they had spoken. There had been something. His performance last night couldn't have been responsible. Maybe Kyle had just meant Paul had gone out.

Greg decided to take control. To find out.

'Hey, Kyle, put your mum on a sec ...'

'Okay Dad! Love you ... Mum! ... Dad wants you ...'

Greg had purposely rung when he had. It was now 7pm Vanuatu time. Making it 9am in England. If Paul went to work, and if he didn't work from home, he would have probably left by now. Maybe that's what Kyle had meant, he now thought, Paul had gone ... to work. Idiot! He was reading too much into things. They talked. Things seemed okay. Greg didn't ask.

The day had been, at last for Greg, one of uneventfulness, peace. He'd been able to laze around with Susie. GPK had dropped by, but only with updates on things that Greg couldn't be bothered with.

Greg had been able to relax, let his body recover from the previous night's game. It was a big ask to go again in just two days' time, but it was the same for everyone. They'd have just two sessions the next day. A run and a gameplays session. The day of the game they'd look at Samoa on video in the morning after a light run. Nothing more.

'We've got the date through for Dad's funeral.'

Col had sent it in a text. Greg rang to check in on his mum. He knew it still seemed wrong that he wasn't there and apologised yet again to his brother and to his mum when she had come on the phone.

'Don't be daft, Greg. Oh, and what a try that was! Your dad would have been so proud!'

Greg felt his mum waver, but quickly bring herself around. He knew his dad had been proud of both he and Col. He also knew his mum wasn't some old woman with nothing else going on in her life. She was in good shape, fit and she and his dad had by all accounts led a full and active social life, whatever that meant. He hadn't asked for any greater detail on the active side, hoping it was just about sport. This had been his mum and dad after all.

'Anyway, son. Got to go. Col and me are gonna hit some waves!'

'Way to go, Mum!'

Greg was pleased his mum was already sounding okay. Col confirmed that it wasn't some front either.

'She's really good, bud. Getting in the ocean every day, hitting the bars for food and drinks. Still a few little moments, but otherwise all good. Think Dad going was a blessing in the end. Like she said, great game! Just Samoa now, eh?'

It was GPK who broke the news two minutes after Greg had come off the phone with Greg. GPK was flustered. He had rattled on Greg's suite door before entering, just in case he was breaking something up between he and Susie.

'Greg, the Vanuatu police are on their way to arrest you!'

CHAPTER 72

'What? ... I mean, why?'

Greg shook his head. He was confused. He hadn't done anything. There was nothing for him to be worried about. But GPK was.

He knew how things would be skewed, how reputations could be built up and knocked down. He'd been a part of a sector that did exactly that.

'This ...'

GPK had been clutching his phone as he had come in, as though he'd just been on it. He had, not on a call but to check news, developments.

Ken had alerted him half an hour ago to what was just breaking, since then it had snowballed.

'Check your bank account.'

Greg was dumbfounded. The last time anyone had asked him to do that had been his mum before she and dad had left for Australia. They had left both him and Col £5,000 each to help them get started in whatever they were going to do with their lives.

He had hardly ever looked at his bank account in the past two full seasons at Eruption. He'd earned the biggest amount of money he had ever earned and he wasn't one for flash cars and property.

'Check it now, before they get here ...'

GPK played the news feed from his phone. It was from Radio V, but it could have been any channel because it had gone viral.

'Last night Oceania was hit by its biggest ever bank robbery. And it was all conducted online. It is believed to have occurred at around 7.46pm and to have affected The Bank of Vanuatu and The Efate & Espiritu Santo Banking Corporation. Unconfirmed estimates have been predicted at a robbery value of over £500m. More news as the story unfolds. The Vanuatu Police Department is following various leads.'

Greg was perplexed.

'What's any of that to do with me?'

'Your account,'

GPK laboured.

'Look at it for God's sake! Because you won't believe me if I tell you.'

At that moment several Vanuatu police officers, including Det Alex Lui, arrived in Greg's suite.

Susie appeared from the shower. They had been readying themselves for a relaxing evening meal in the Breakas restaurant.

'What's going on, Greg?'

'Greg Duggan. We are arresting you for conspiracy leading to robbery and for the receipt of stolen money. You do not have to say anything, but I must caution you that it may harm your defence if you do not mention, when questioned, something which you may later rely on in court. Anything you do say may be given in evidence. Do you understand?'

Greg just laughed. He couldn't believe what was happening. Alex Lui led him away.

Julian Jardine laughed too. But he was on his, correction Maria's, as he'd been reminded by her, yacht. It didn't matter where he was now, he would soon be buying it, or another like it.

Nobody would find his bank account.

Duggan had been easy meat.

Jardine's angry persona as he left Port Vila Municipal Stadium had been a suitable diversionary tactic. An act. It had outfoxed those idiots with their cameras, that he'd been warned about through a close contact. His girls had done the trick and the old man had played his part in ensuring the lights went out. Sakomoto would love it. The Montgomerys too.

'Would you say you were a rich man, Mr Duggan?'

Greg looked at Alex Lui, now at the Vanuatu Police headquarters in Port Vila. He spread his hands. Shrugged his shoulders.

'Not so far as I'm aware.'

Alex Lui followed up with another question.

'Could you tell us how much you would normally have in your bank account or bank accounts?'

'Look, Alex, Mr Lui ... you're probably about to tell me that I suddenly have a lot more than I ever have had. Okay? ... I know that I shouldn't. My account shouldn't be showing a sudden massive figure ... and you can't for one minute believe I'm guilty of anything, which I'm not.'

Alex Lui said nothing in response. He slid a copy of Greg's closing balance as it stood from the time they had arrested him. Greg didn't even look at it. Alex moved on.

'Your mobile phone, Mr Duggan. You sent a text at 7.46pm yesterday, we have the call log here. Alex slid another sheet across the desk. You sent one word 'Now' to three mobile phone numbers on a group text, whose numbers are all scrambled.'

Again, Greg shrugged.

'Your phone Mr Duggan. Nobody else's. Sent at the exact same time as the fifteen second blackout that created the opportunity for the internet bank robberies to take place.'

Greg wasn't having any of it.

'I'm a bloody car mechanic! Not some kind of keyboard warrior! My phone was in the dressing room. The game stopped for half-time at 7.45 or a bit after. How could I get in there and send it?'

'Do you recognise this woman?'

It was Karla. Greg stopped. What was this? Had Karla been involved in the robberies? He didn't answer immediately.

'Simple question, Mr Duggan. Do you recognise this woman?'

'Yes.'

'When did you last see her?'

'Why?'

'A woman's body was found earlier this evening.'

'Well, I didn't do it!'

Greg's patience with the proceedings had not been brilliant, now they were non-existent.

'If you're gonna lock me up, just get on with it. But it won't make any difference. You'll only look stupid when it all comes out who did all this. Otherwise just let me go. I've done nothing.'

Lui locked Greg up.

CHAPTER 73

Greg had never been in an actual cell before, a real jail. He was calm, reflective, strangely subdued. No need for any histrionics, just let it take its course. They had got the wrong guy. They would realise. He settled in for the night. Poor Karla.

He'd been taken in by her, but her apologies and now this. Whatever had been going on in her life must have been some bad shit.

Grahame Pythagoras Kraft and his team were on the island for one main reason. They were going to bring down Julian Jardine.

GPK had his team around him. They were working through the night, trying to find anything that would give them an angle on Jardine, but Grahame was also growing more concerned about Greg.

He'd visited Annie Laing, the England team's media and relations executive, who had assured him that Greg would have representation at Vanuatu police headquarters in the morning. Briefs were flying out overnight from Australia.

'It all leads back to Jardine.'

Ken Knott had finally rested back in his chair. He had been analysing, searching and researching Jardine since he had arrived, with James and Ann alongside him.

'Three and a half years ago it was Jardine who made the decision that the side that finished at the foot of the Rugby League Division One, two leagues lower than Super League but still deemed to be professional, would be thrown out of the league.

'Jardine wanted newer clubs – like Lanzarote Eruption and the soon to be installed, Pyrenees Royals – to replace the older dead wood as he sees it. A brighter future for the game. Then he stumbled on Bryan Caill, whose family brewing company Caill's Ales were struggling.

'Caill let it slip to Jardine that there was some old clause in the *contract over his family's tenure of the ground, that meant it reverted back to the family's ownership if professional sport was no longer played there. They'd finished bottom several times previously. It would be no surprise if they finished there again.*

'The ground was worth millions for development. Caill needed the money. Agreed to sell the land. Jardine did his level best to make sure problems were stacked against Hopton Town.*

'When Bob Irvine, business magnate, unexpectedly took over the club and when Greg became player/coach it was the worst news Jardine had had. Irvine was investing, Greg was enthusiastic, popular and inspirational and Hopton started to win again.*

'Jardine had to step up his catastrophe machine. Greg was beaten up, his wife lost their second child, the club physio was injured in a driving accident, Greg was abducted, the Hopton Town ground was wired with incendiary devices that exploded.*

'Jardine had brought Quinigan in to sail through any legal procedures that might come up relating to the overturning of the restrictive covenant issue being challenged if Hopton finished bottom, and another man by the name of Brent Dugarry, a developer who had the balls of the planning authority in his hands, to facilitate the development – and Jardine continued to ensure in every way that Hopton Town couldn't survive.'*

'And now?'

GPK knew Ken was building up to a crescendo. They had been concentrating on Quinigan in the past not Jardine.

They probably couldn't nail Jardine for what he'd done in the past as it would take too long to go through the courts, but here, if they had enough to go on, they could instead destroy him.

GPK and his team would do it gladly in the name of Jeff Markham, their fellow journalist colleague, who it now appeared, had lost his life to a bullet fired at the behest of Julian Jardine as the media began uncovering his dirty work. One way or another Jardine was a criminal who needed to be brought to book.

Ken now explained what he had found out about Jardine's latest nefarious activities.

'He's doing the same thing again here. He has used his position.*

First, he chances upon Vanuatu through being involved with the World Cup Organising Committee. He loves it because it's a tax haven. He loves it because it is a beautiful, idyllic, warm, sunshine island. He loves the sun. That's why he supported Lanzarote too, only that was more about having somewhere close to home for freebie holidays based around business expenses.

'When he becomes involved with the World Cup Organising Committee he can't believe his luck. Efate, in particular, is an island waiting to explode on the tourism market. He can roll over his dirty money gained from the Hopton and Eruption deals he has done, not get taxed and contribute to further income.

'Vanuatu had earned a place in the World Cup through the qualifying stages and he suggests it is a great location for games and for rugby league to show it embracing emerging nations. Zoe Miller likes the idea. Backs it.

'But he gets greedy. So does Bob Rudd. Bob starts coming here for meetings. He makes friends in high places here. He starts cutting out Jardine.

'Big mistake. Zoe Miller catches wind of what they are both up to. She tackles Jardine.

'Jardine arranges for Bob Rudd to meet his end, keeping himself clean in the process being over 10,000 miles away. He tries something similar with Zoe Miller too, but she's astute and works out there's some bad smell. That's why she has been so difficult to get hold of. She's laying low most of the time.'

Ken hadn't finished.

There was an odour. Greg smelled it. And sunlight. It felt so strong, one of those times when it feels as though you can see the sun through closed eyelids. He didn't open them. It felt warm. Airy. He felt a tension in the back of his head, to the left near his ear.

Greg moved his head gradually from side to side. It felt like ball bearings clicking around in his neck. He continued to breathe deeply, slumber rather than sleep. This cell felt air-conditioned. The sunshine coming through he hadn't expected last night when he'd been banged up. Sleep. That was all he needed. Sleep. He slept.

Susie took the call. She couldn't believe it. Didn't know what to say. The timing couldn't have been any worse. She should have known her past would catch up with her sometime.

She flung her phone across the bed. Greg in jail. Now this. She began packing her bags as she fought to hold back the tears.

She was out of the suite, into a taxi and heading towards Bauerfield before the staff had arrived to serve breakfast at Breakas.

Zoe was feeling good. All of her plans had been coming together nicely. The PDRL World Cup quarter-finals had just taken place the previous evening in Sydney to worldwide acclaim. A crowd of over 25,000 had watched all four games take place in one day with England, Australia, Japan and the USA prevailing.

The Women's World Cup had also reached the semi-finals stage with great crowds at both games in Brisbane seeing England, Australia, New Zealand and France through; the Wheelchair World Cup Final was to be played between England and France; and 'The Pink', Zoe's personal triumph in getting accepted, was a real box-office hit with a Gay Pride Festival due to take place at an already sell-out 40,000 Sydney West Stadium with artists such as Lil Nas X from the USA and Anne-Marie from the UK along with legendary Jimmy Somerville of Bronski Beat and The Communards.

'Zoe Miller? … We need to talk … can you meet me?'

She had seen a call come in, but no number had come up. She'd thought it was a spam call or sales call. The woman had left a message.

'G'day mate!'

It was the brightest wake-up voice Greg had heard. He'd just stretched, yawned and had opened his eyes. He couldn't see its owner. The sun was beating down.

Hold on. Sun beating down? Where was he? This was no cell.

The voice went into a fit of laughter, so loud. Too loud. Greg's head hurt.

'*Aww mate, you should see your face! You look like …*'

The laughter was bordering on hysterical.

'*Ha! I don't know what you look like …*'

Greg tried to shake himself awake more fully, put his right hand to his head rubbing his temples with his thumb and his middle finger. Just couldn't seem to focus.

'*Where …?*'

It was all Greg could manage before he collapsed again.

'*CCTV? Footage? You must have that? … Right. I'll be there.*'

Det Supt Erin Jackson had contacted GPK.

She had wanted to get to Greg at the police headquarters before Commissioner Danford Napakauranga. Alex Lui had reported to her. He had felt wrong in interviewing Duggan but Danford had insisted. Nothing stacked up about what he was asking of the rugby league star and Danford hadn't even been around.

He'd locked Greg up. Now Greg had gone.

When Greg next opened his eyes the laughter he'd initially received had been replaced with concern. He was more compos mentis this time. The sun's rays not quite so strong, but it still felt warm.

'*Now mate, you back? … Here …*'

Greg was finally able to focus, while moving his head from side to side and then his shoulders and extending his arms. The young man in front of him looked familiar but not the voice. He took a swig from the bottle of water he'd been passed.

The young man clicked his fingers as he walked in front and around Greg who was on the ground. Greg looked around at where they were and shrugged by way of a question.

'*Yeah, not a prison cell huh? … I stole you …*'

He saw Greg's quizzical reaction. He became wide-eyed and started laughing again, not uncontrollably this time.

'*It was easy really …*'

He'd dropped the Aussie accent. Clarity came Greg's way.

'*You're Oliver Quinigan.*'

CHAPTER 74

'He doesn't know what he's got himself into …'

Det Supt Erin Jackson was talking with GPK and his team. They were watching the footage from the CCTV of a man who had posed as a cop, who had delivered food and drink to Greg in his cell.

Half an hour on in the recording he had come back, bringing a wheelchair, and had lifted Greg in, wheeled him out to a police van and had left.

'Audacious …'

Ken Knott shook his head in despair.

'How come nobody else was around?'

Janet Hague asked.

'Drugged them too. Just two of them on duty, the Vanuatu guys would have known their own, but I'm guessing he said he was from my team, made them a drink like the nice guy he is …'

Erin's sarcasm was to the fore. She was passed more information from one of the desk officers.

'Headed out north, that's all we have … both teams, here and mine, are covering every social media channel and we have every officer briefed …'

She followed up her initial comment.

'This man is either related to what has been going on here or has issues with Mr Duggan. You shed any light? …'

Greg was still coming round, his head clearing. He flexed limbs, swivelled ankles, tested joints and tendons, rocked his head from side to side. Everything appeared in working order, but also felt so heavy.

He wasn't bound in any way but couldn't move. Couldn't work it out.

'Rohypnol.'

Greg looked up. Oliver Quinigan was staring at him.

'Date rape drug. You're my date. Renders you incapacitated for

hours. Gave you another in the drink you've just had.'

Quinigan said it nonchalantly. Greg didn't give him the satisfaction of a reply.

'This isn't about my father.'

Greg didn't answer. He simply raised his eyebrows slightly in a couldn't care less style.

'If it was, do you think I would still be here talking with you?'

Again, Greg stayed quiet. Let him talk.

'You killed him …'

Oliver was now walking as he was talking, back and forth in front of Greg, before squatting to face him. To get close.

'… or at least you were the one to blame …'

Oliver stared right into Greg's face. Greg kept dead straight. There was no point in antagonising. And he could feel his head going again. That second shot contained in the bottled water.

'… but …'

Oliver stood up abruptly. He smiled a grimacing smile.

'… that's not why I'm here, as I said … who knows, maybe another time …'

Oliver Quinigan walked away. Two minutes later Greg heard a roar, a crunching of tyres on stones, he turned to see, but his eyesight was fading, his eyelids closing. Sleep, need more sleep. The sun warmed him, helped him relax into a deep slumber.

'Det Supt Jackson … In my office … now, if you would be so kind …'

Commissioner Danford Napakauranga had just walked in.

Erin left her operations centre where she was working with her team.

'Close the door.'

Danford rubbed his chin with the thumb, forefinger and middle finger of his left hand. He breathed in deeply before exhaling. And before talking.

'What are you doing?'

She looked at him inquiringly. She would not be spoken to in the manner he had begun, especially by someone she had no respect for whatsoever. She waited for his next line as she flicked her chin up in disdain.

'You have constantly undermined my authority since you arrived. I don't know what you think about me, and I don't care either ...'

Danford raised his hand as he saw her about to comment. He carried on. He passed her a sheet of A4 across his desk.

'... which is why I have contacted your superiors in Australia, explaining my disappointment in you ... and your somewhat ... shall we say ... lack of professionalism while you've been here, using this more as a fantasy island?'

Danford kept his face like stone. Erin looked at the correspondence. She looked up at him. She was being relieved of her position in charge of the case on Efate. She looked over at Danford's laptop screen. He'd purposely slanted it so that she could see the pic of Marlon and her making love on the island.

'You bastard!'

CHAPTER 75

'Just make sure he's there. Everyone's in now. They're loving it. This should be the biggest yet.'

The conversation had been another video link.

Oliver Quinigan had performed a useful purpose, the Commissioner too.

It was now nightfall. In less than 24 hours the semi-final of the World Cup between England and Samoa would take place at Port Vila. Bauerfield International Airport was already busy with more incoming flights from Faleolo International Airport near Apia, the capital of Samoa; and Brisbane and Sydney airports with England fans having first landed there from England before making another three-hour flight.

'Do you know a David Pic-wah?'

Ken Knott had rung GPK from Breakas where he'd now become a permanent fixture, coordinating activities and carrying on with his analysis of all they had to go on, checking on who was around in different locations and who was moving to and fro. Something would give somebody away eventually.

GPK, Janet, Ann and James were all out in the field covering as much as they could of the various areas of the island to find Greg, with Alex Lui, Elenola Taneo and the support of the rest of Danford Napakauranga's force and the Australia contingent, minus Det Supt Erin Jackson.

GPK had found it enlightening that the commissioner had seemingly sidelined his murder investigations for the sake of finding Greg. He responded quickly to Ken's text.

'Name's really Pickup, just pronounces it that other way, why?'

'Because I think we have a glimmer of hope.'

Greg was back awake. The sun was no longer bearing down on him, but there was still warmth. It was getting near dusk. He felt something move close by. He flinched. Then moved quickly, realising that he could now move again. It had been about a metre long, emerald green with black rings, but it had possibly been as frightened of Greg as he had been initially.

He found he was now able to stand. Went through the motions of checking everything was in full working order once again. Then looked out around him. Where the hell was he this time?

He was on top of a bloody mountain!

Although he didn't know it by name at the time he was at the peak of Mount Taputoara in the north of the island. He could see another larger peak nearby and in the far distance the ocean.

'For fuck's sake!'

he uttered aloud. How the hell did this keep happening to him?

'Why me!!?'

As he started making his descent a sudden thud sent him sprawling to the ground.

CHAPTER 76

The 11.15pm touchdown at Bauerfield brought another 300 to the island, most of them wearing the iconic blue rugby league jersey of Samoa; the 11.30pm touchdown brought a further 400 wearing mostly the white shirts with a red cross of England. Excitement was building and Port Vila was absolutely bursting at the seams in World Cup fervour.

Two of those now waiting to collect their bags from the carousel, amongst the 700, were being watched more closely than anybody else at the airport.

'*Alex?*'

Grace Elliott had been in intensive surgery. She was now recovering. The shots she had received had been through a lung and another where the bullet had lodged in her kidney. She'd lost copious amounts of blood, had internal injuries that would cause her problems for however long she lived. But she was still alive.

Her voice was weak, but the corners of her mouth moved upwards as she made out who was with her. Alex had visited whenever he'd been able since the shooting. He'd prayed she would recover. He put out his hand to rest in hers. She closed her eyes. There was no hope of discharging herself this time.

'*Did you find the information?*'

Alex gave a little shake of his head, told her it wasn't important. That's not why he was there. She had only been able to give him limited words previously. She wasn't feeling in any way that much better now, but she knew.

'*There's a list.*'

CHAPTER 77

'Maria says to meet her tonight. She'll be at the game. Half-time. That's all I can tell you.'

GPK had met David Pic-Wah at a chandlery at Port Vila harbourside. The two were talking as though customers who had come to buy supplies. In Pic-Wah's case it included all manner of minor purchases for the upkeep of the Illusion Plus, the superyacht he and Penny (Penelope) crewed on behalf of Maria Cavaleros.

'Someone has to stop all of this, before any more are murdered. I didn't sign up for this. I'm just a faded pop star, one-hit wonder, who enjoys cruising around with my girl on a boat. But just not with this guy.'

He looked nervous as he left. Probably for his own life, thought GPK. They were making progress on Julian Jardine, but there was still no sign of Greg.

Greg was miles away on a mountain, now trying to work it out.

Millions now in his own bank account. The accusation of the murder of Karla. Implications that he'd been involved in an internet bank heist? Who the fuck did these people think they were?

Why had he now been drugged and dragged out of jail by Oliver Quinigan of all people? How had Quinigan become involved? Had to be Jardine surely? And why wasn't he, Greg, now dead?

None of it made any sense apart from one thing.

Money. That's all Greg could put it down to. Money. If he had millions in his account there must be multi-millions involved.

That money in his account had been put there to frame, for some reason. Again, he couldn't think why. Why would they, whoever they were, have then sprung him if they wanted him there in the first place?

Why weren't they out hunting him down?

Jardine, fucking Jardine!

His memory flicked back to the two women on the plane in The Residence. What they'd said. They'd said, 'He said you were good'. Jardine's women? No way they were working for that spurious sounding International Centre for Integrity in Sport! What a joke!

But why would they show him pictures of Maria, with Jardine? To make him jealous? And the last picture? What was that all about?

And why was he being targeted all the time? In Brisbane at the hotel? At Breakas on Efate?

If Jardine was doing all this to get at him, then why, if what he was about was the money?

The murders. Bob Rudd. The two politicians on Efate. The woman who ran the underwater post office? Now Karla. They couldn't all have been Jardine, could they? Something clicked.

'Hey, Carlos! You get me to Hideaway Island first?'

It was time for Greg to get involved.

The thud he'd felt and heard the previous evening had been from an arrow. It hadn't hit him, nor had it been aimed at him. The archer had been extremely apologetic. It had been the first time he and his team of Ni-Vanuatu traditional tribesmen had known anyone be on the mountain at night.

They had been conducting an island tour from the Melanesian heritage village of Ekasup, just north of Port Vila and were camping overnight on the mountain before the hike back to their minibus in the morning.

The bows and arrows were simply giving experience of days gone by. Greg had felt that it could well have been his days that could have gone by if he'd been struck.

Greg had been made welcome into their party. One or two of them had recognised him as the 'He's so good, good, good' guy that they had seen in action on the park at Port Vila Stadium. Greg had given a softer version to them of why he'd happened to be on the mountain. That he'd always been a walker, into climbing mountains.

Carlos was the driver and leader.

'*Sure thing Greg! You scuba diving? Sending a postcard? There's a job going as postman down there since Lena ... you know ...*'

'*You knew Lena?*'

'*Everybody knew Lena, man. And I don't just mean because she was famous.*'

Carlos gave the biggest laugh Greg had ever heard.

Two hours later, having visited Hideaway Island, Greg returned unheralded to Breakas. He thanked Carlos for his hospitality and for his taxi service and made his way to his suite.

CHAPTER 78

'Dad!'

Kyle jumped for joy at his dad, running straight to him and leaping into his arms.

Diane simply said: *'Hi.'*

Greg's immediate disbelief turned fast to smiles for his son and ruffling his hair, then to mouthing *'What?'* to Diane.

Everything had changed in the course of the past day. Where was Susie? Nobody seemed to know. Why had Diane come?

She'd said it had been spontaneous, that Greg could win the World Cup, but to win it with his son there, wow!

She had wanted to come for the funeral too. She'd left Lily with her mum and dad. She'd didn't want to talk about Paul.

There'd been no time other than to ask GPK about Susie, whether he knew about what had happened to her.

She'd left a note with him for Greg.

All charges against him had been dropped. The lawyers had arrived and done their stuff as GPK had put it, or to put it more accurately he'd said they'd shoved it all up their arse.

It was now 3pm. Semi-final Day. Greg had freshened up from his outdoor look and had been reunited with his team. Hardly the best preparation.

Get arrested, get date-rape drugged, get impaled by an arrow (fortunately that hadn't happened), spend a night on a mountain. Was he turning into The Grinch? But he was back, he knew more than he ever had about what was going on, and he was not just playing for a place in the World Cup Final, he was also coach and captain.

By 4pm he'd arrived at the ground – with his son!

Samoa had performed above their world ranking of 7 in reaching the semis. They had overachieved – and they fully intended to carry on doing so.

Freddie South and Big Mick Green, not knowing what had

happened to Greg had selected the same side that had finished on the park in the game against France, apart from Owen Fenchurch returning from injury to replace Ricki Brown who was suffering from a knock.

Greg was relieved to see that he'd been selected!

'And right there just might be a future England player!'

Brad Kearns was giving his customary pre-match build-up and the cameras showed father and son Greg and Kyle passing a rugby ball between each other up and down the Port Vila ground.

'Kyle Duggan with his dad Greg, who has set this World Cup alight. He's had his moments off the park too, not least being wrongly accused of crimes after the quarter-finals, but he looks in good form there, George. Every bit the family man.'

Laurie Northey was alongside Brad once again.

'Looks a great kid, doesn't he?'

As kick-off approached the crowd grew to what seemed even greater unprecedented numbers. This was to be Vanuatu's last game as hosts and the whole country had adopted Greg Duggan as their favourite player.

There were banners made of 'We Love You Greg' and 'Greg Is So Wonderful'.

Vanessa Quai and her band were now in residency at Port Vila Municipal Stadium.

Greg and Kyle were introduced to the Vanuatu pop sensation who was now celebrating her third week at the top of the UK and Australian charts. Vanessa was sound-checking for the half-time concert and she took Kyle on stage with her.

When it came to the chorus he joined her singing with his own version of her song, 'Dad is so good, good, good' and danced in such a cute way that anyone in the stadium at the time also joined in with him. Everyone instantly fell in love with Kyle. Laurie Northey had been watching and listening.

'And he's already got his second career … I think Vanessa might be taking him on tour with her at this rate! Listen to that applause!'

Kyle was enjoying himself so much. He ran back to his mum

afterwards and Vanessa went over to talk with Diane and sit with her in the grandstand.

Jardine was in the sponsors hospitality area with Maria. The Montgomerys had just arrived, and Maratoto Sakamoto. Danford was to join them.

GPK and his team were stationed all around the ground. There was no additional camera presence this time. They would all have to rely on eyesight. Elenola Taneo and Alex Lui had joined the GPK throng.

'This has been one of the greatest pleasures of my commentary career.'

Brad Kearns eulogised over his experience in the past couple of weeks.

'We've seen some tremendous games, sensational tries. We've experienced the colour, the warmth and the sheer happiness of the people on this wonderful island of Efate, part of the extraordinarily friendly nation of Vanuatu.

'Ben, I'm sure all of us at Channel 17 and viewers around the world would join with me in thanking you and your countrymen and women for welcoming us all.'

Ben Mara was humble and gracious. He spoke of the World Cup as having been one of the greatest moments of his life and something his nation would remember for many years to come.

When the two teams walked out onto Port Vila Municipal Stadium's turf it was to the most earsplitting, deafening cheers.

It was time to forget everything else. Greg could deal with what had happened with Susie later. He would get to his dad's funeral. He had his son watching him.

And he knew there was something going on with Diane that he needed to get to the bottom of. He also had Jardine to sort – and he would.

But first.

There was a World Cup Final place at stake.

CHAPTER 79

Samoa had seen off Fiji in their quarter-final after having finished second in their group behind Tonga. Their earlier victories against Ireland and the USA had been routine without being stunning, but their two Oceania 'derbies' had been epic struggles of warriors versus warriors.

It had been a war of attrition three days ago and it had been even more remarkable that their 31-30 victory over Fiji, which had been just as nail-biting as England's against France, had left them with a team to put on the park.

'This World Cup has to be the most gruelling of any world sport …'

Brad Kearns was keen to emphasise.

'… rugby league is such a demanding game, but the decision to play the whole tournament in such a short time frame, decided because of the epidemic a year ago when restrictions were at their height, has shown just how fit these players are …'

'That's so right, Brad. Every single player out on the park here tonight and at the other semi-final in Sydney deserves special credit for just getting out there. For some of them this is their fifth game in fifteen days!'

Laurie Northey admitted he had never played that many in such a period and that injuries were bound to occur.

Greg's team talk had consisted of just one line before they had emerged.

'Do not think this is done until it is.'

He gave his words upbeat. His fist clenched. There was to be nothing more.

As he lined up to kick to Samoa after the national anthems and toss had taken place he looked to the stands, one brief moment, to catch Kyle. He caught Jardine! It triggered a memory of being in the police station that he'd not remembered before. 'Now!' That's what the detective had said that he had sent in that message on his mobile. It clicked.

Jardine! Jardine had somehow got hold of his mobile phone to give an instruction that had led to the internet bank robberies. Now he understood the look he'd seen in those eyes, the look that he'd been suspicious of and had led to him sidelining Jericho later.

Someone who had the time, before half-time.

Think! Do not think this is done until it is!

'Greg Duggan sends the ball up, up and away. Samoa, right now the pride of Oceania and the underdogs here, against the might of the second-favourites to lift the trophy, England.'

Brad Kearns wasn't expecting anything like the drama of the game just three days prior.

'It's Vila Va'a underneath this high hanging ball with a combined mass of around 50-stone about to impact.'

The seasoned Aussie NRL player collected superbly and fed his full-back Joseph Talipeau who made ground before being brought down by Greg and Billy Ecktenstall.

Hard drives characterised the opening 20 minutes with penalties not being awarded and field position being gained by both sides as French referee Alexandre Dumas showed the cavalier spirit of his namesake. It had been a similar start to the France game just without the explosive first play that had brought France a try.

'Both sides look good when they are running with the ball, but just a bit slower in getting back onside when they are without it, Ben ...'

'That's right, Brad. We've yet to see that spark that will lift this game ...'

Greg was more than happy with the start. He was battered, bruised, aching and quite content to let the game ebb and flow in the first half. He'd not played a whole game for months. He'd only played the equivalent of just over 80 minutes in the two games he'd played in the World Cup. Let it give, just a little. Conserve.

He had the hard-working Troy Whittingham on the bench,

plus Stu Wainwright and strong running John Cloudsdale back from injury, and the ever-reliable Phil 'the Butcher' Parkin.

'You and me off in five minutes Gary ... give 'em five minutes of hell before we go!'

Gary Walker had played out of his skin since stepping in for Stu. Greg knew he had three fantastic half-backs he could interchange, including Owen Fenchurch already on.

'Love it!'

Gary was always smiling. A great character in the dressing room where he was known as Farmer Gary with his chickens and sheep back home with his wife Tracy.

England had just been awarded a penalty by Mr Dumas for an offside infringement. Greg kicked the ball downfield giving them a starting position near Samoa's 20-metre line.

'Jorge Ropati has sent the message out here. They're getting ready for an England surge. It's mercurial scrum-half Gary Walker tapping the ball and he sends Billy Ecktenstall on a hammering run towards the Samoan defence. He's all wrapped up by Efie Elia, Devon Varama and Mataria Embua ... forget that, he's not! ...'

Billy had managed to flip out the ball to Mason Bell who had also charged into a wall of tackles from Fa'amanu Vagana, Thomas Elia and Eliot Tavagana. He'd been going down with the three of them when he'd shovelled out a pass to nobody in particular, because by now he couldn't see, but in training it had been Sam Rivers who had always been on his side.

'Sam Rivers has picked up that speculative pass from Bell and he's rounded the flailing arms of this sliding defence ...'

The crowd was raising the volume as England had made it to the Samoa 10-metre line.

'Rivers has nowhere to go now, he's jinking around, but there's nowhere ... he's running across the play, searching ... ohh, he's slotted an inside pass to Gary Walker, who has kicked through ... the ball is going through to the try line ...'

'And it's Neil 'The Brickie' Duncan!!! He flies over the line ... does he ground it? Is there downward pressure? Was he onside?

'Mr Dumas has given it as a try on the field, but he's taken it

upstairs to the video ref! The crowd has gone crazy here. That's what the game needed.'

'Yes, Brad. And it's got to be a try, surely?'

A second later and with the big screen on playback Ben Mara changed his mind.

'Oh, I don't know, you know ...'

As the crowd took in what the video referee was watching, with the screen going back and forth in slow motion over the various areas of concern there was delight, ecstasy and then doubt.

'Often the giveaway in these situations is the man who has scored ... or not ... but you really can't tell with 'The Brickie' ...'

Ben Mara was laughing as he said it.

'If you've ever talked with him you'll know what I mean. And he's not Scottish, even though he does a mean Scottish accent ... very confusing man ...'

'Well, confusing or not, our video referee, Cam Delay, please tell me he's changed his name by deed poll, has obviously made his decision – and the way it looks, as he's gone to the grounding and not even played that part back more than once, it looks like it's ... a TRY!! ... England hit the front!'

Greg popped over the conversion kick to take the score to England 6 Samoa 0 – and promptly dispatched himself and Gary to the bench for a breather, putting on Stu and The Butcher.

It had proved the right decision. Stu Wainwright, sidelined for the France game after having received a knock against Papua New Guinea, was on fire. He ripped the Samoan team to shreds with a mazy run. They couldn't put a hand on him, just before half-time, going in under the posts and then he took over Greg's role as kicker.

Half-time. England 12 Samoa 0. Walk in the park.

'This England team has certainly grown into this tournament. It's not so long ago they were being beaten at Alice by part-timers. Laurie, can Samoa get back into this game? It seems to be going away from them.'

Greg held his fist high to Kyle and Diane in the stand as he strode off the ground and into the dressing room with his team, telling himself *'Do not think this is done until it is!'*

Vanessa Quai and her band struck up with 'Light It Up'. The crowd loved it. It was now another national anthem of sorts, particularly the line 'Never Lose Heart, Never Lose Faith' in which the whole of the Vanuatu people joined in and many England fans too, who had heard the song several times since being on the island.

'Rise Up Warriors' took the Vanuatu people into new realms of volume. The England and Samoan fans both understood the passion and shared the emotion. 'No More' was Vanessa's personal anthem to end violence towards women in Oceania and received rapturous applause, but it was when the Vanuatu singer came down from the stage to her little friend Kyle that every heart, if it wasn't won over already, melted.

They sang the duet of 'Life Is Good' with Kyle reprising his earlier performance which had been to a much smaller audience. Diane had never been so proud of her son.

Maria had been waiting her moment. She had chosen it when Julian had been suitably engrossed in conversation.

'Senor Kraft, how good to see you …'

She then whispered softly,

'No time. Just take. Enjoy.'

The handshake transference was brief and successful. GPK just nodded. Game on.

GPK transferred it to Janet so that he could stay where he was. Janet transferred again to Ann while remaining in her position in the grandstand. Ann passed it directly to James, who took it straight to Ken. The whole process seeing the flash drive installed at Ken's Den in Breakas. And all within nothing more than the time it had taken for half-time.

CHAPTER 80

Jardine ushered his guests back to their seats with uncharacteristic bonhomie. Maria saw it as though he'd had a goodwill transplant. Something had happened at half-time. What had he done while she had been away?

Brad Kearns brought the commentary back to life, but not before he'd taken time out for a special crowd member.

'If it's not Greg Duggan who's stealing the show, it's his son Kyle! We were all in bits up here as he sang with Vanessa Quai, but now it's time for dad to take centre stage again as both teams take to the park for the biggest 40 minutes of their playing careers …

'It's England 12 Samoa 0. In these next 40 we will know which of these two sides will be playing in the World Cup Final against either Australia or New Zealand, who are currently locked at 6-6.'

Samoa kicked to England and bore down on Vinny Venus who was under the ball. Jorge Ropati, Reni Leilua and Vila Va'a were at the head of the charge as the rest came up in a line. The Samoan team looked suitably recharged and reinvigorated from their half-time break.

Greg had kept himself and Gary Walker on the bench and had interchanged Troy Whittingham and John Cloudsdale, another returning from injury, with Neil Duncan and Billy Ecktenstall.

If the guys on the park could maintain the lead, or even add to it, he was confident that he could come on later, Neil and Gary too, to make a difference. And if he didn't have to come on at all, so much the better. He knew his body needed the rest.

The game had reached fifteen minutes into the second-half with no further score when Mr Dumas was called into action.

'Ohh! That's a swinging arm from Phil 'The Butcher' Parkin on half-back Joseph Lisana … ohh, the Samoans are wading in here, England players too … it's getting a bit tasty …'

Laurie Northey put Brad Kearns right.

'It's all handbags, Brad. Nothing much in the rest of it. Bit of testosterone being applied, but Parkin defo copped him … oh, but there's a cheeky little punch gone in there … and now it's kicking off again …'

One player went down, clutching another. The brawl turned into a heap.

Mr Dumas and his officials tried to bring back some order.

Brad Kearns assessed.

'This has been brewing since the half got under way. The Samoans have come out like men possessed. They know this 12-point gap needs bridging, but they also know they cannot really afford to go further behind. The hit on Lisana has lit the blue touchpaper.'

On the field Mr Dumas parted the teams. The big screen was showing the melee and the Samoan fans roared their disapproval of the head-high tackle by 'The Butcher' and the bunny punch that had connected with Thomas Elia. The England fans knew Phil Parkin was up for a warning of some kind. Mr Dumas reached for his pocket.

'It's a red!'

Brad Kearns was stunned. The Samoan fans roared approval.

'I think that's because of the way he reacted after the infringement, odd from Phil he's normally such a mild-mannered bloke. He'll be disappointed in himself when he sees that back.'

Laurie Northey had played with Phil 'The Butcher' Parkin when he'd spent two seasons in England a decade ago.

'And Mr Dumas still has his red card out, this could be disastrous, it's only going one way – and it's exactly that! He's shown it to Tyler Rodgers! England are down to 11 for the rest of this game.'

The England team lost any cool they had.

Verbals were being thrown at the referee. Angry crimson faces of bitter vitriol. Laurie Northey had seen Mr Dumas many times before.

'England have obviously not played many matches where Mr Dumas has been in charge otherwise they would have known his penchant for discipline.

'Oh no!'

There was the slightest of chuckles in Brad Kearns' voice that he was trying best to strangle into a cough so that it didn't sound as though he was having fun at the referee's expense as the drama shifted.

'... Wait a sec. Mr Dumas has been pushed! He's staggering backwards, and he's fallen ... on his backside!'

Brad Kearns very nearly laughed out loud at the comedic way in which Mr Dumas, not exactly the tallest of gentlemen, had gone down. In the commentary box he was trying his best to restrain himself. He resumed his commentary.

'This does not look good. I don't think I have ever seen three red cards to the same side at the same time, but I think we're going to see it now ... you just cannot do that to an official ... and here it comes! ... It's red for Regan Phillips ... he's also taking the long walk! Ohh, boys, tell me what's going on?'

Greg could not believe it. Ten men against thirteen for the final twenty-five minutes of this game.

The Samoan fans, who had been subdued having not seen their team get over the whitewash once in 55 minutes, were suddenly urging on their warriors.

Team captain and half-back Frank Brown was a tactician and he had been presented with a real gift. There was no way England could plug all the holes in their line if Samoa kept moving the ball.

Greg had watched it all from the sidelines.

'Don't panic. Tackle well and when we've got the ball use it.'

This was his new mantra. He still hadn't put himself, Billy, Gary or Neil back on.

Freddie South reorganised the big players as best he could, Stu Wainwright jinked and danced, using up valuable time when they had the ball and his kicking game, along with Owen Fenchurch's, unbelievably kept Samoa at bay for around ten minutes.

'This is outstanding defence from the ten men of England ...'

Brad Kearns was impressed, but Laurie Northey was the harbinger of doom.

'... but it's just a matter of time, Brad ... they cannot stop this blue tide of Samoan forwards forever ...'

And with 13 minutes left on the clock Eliot Tavagana burst through a tiring defensive line heading for Charlie Cole and Sam Rivers. Tavagana launched an outrageous dummy which saw off Charlie and then dinked out a short pass to the formidable Vila Va'a who went over under the posts.

The extra points were added with an easy conversion kick by Joseph Lisana and it was game on.

'Samoa 6 England 12. This England team is tiring quickly. They've been overloaded with work and have performed brilliantly but it's catching up with them now and listen to those Samoan fans. They know they could be going to the World Cup Final!'

Greg resisted the temptation to change anything. He'd decided that if he could get to within 10 minutes to go with no further scores he would then make changes.

Brad Kearns had been fed the latest game stats by his production team.

'That's another penalty to Samoa! The penalty count in this second half, along with the dismissals has been all one way. Samoa have had 19 penalties awarded, including this one, to England's none!'

Laurie Northey had an explanation.

'I said he was a stickler for discipline ... and I understand he's a big fan of Tom Jones, so I guess ... It's Not Unusual ... I'll get my coat ...'

Laurie laughed as Ben Mara briefly took on the commentary baton. Brad couldn't speak. He was too busy shaking his head at Laurie.

'Make that penalty count 20-nil ... England are just not getting back in to their defensive line quickly enough and Mr Dumas has penalised them again.'

Brad Kearns resumed.

'England are powerless here. They're out on their feet. Samoa have taken the penalty and put the ball out at the England 10-metre line. They're moving it so fast here, this is great hands and they've

spun the ball quickly wide and there just aren't enough covering tacklers! It's Fa'amanu Vagana who is in at the corner! He's raced around to get it near to the sticks again making another easy conversion attempt for Lisana.'

Lisana duly added the extras. The game was locked at 12-12 with 11 minutes on the clock.

It was time for action.

Charlie Cole, Sam Rivers and Owen Fenchurch were all replaced by Neil 'The Brickie' Duncan, Billy Ecktenstall and Gary Walker.

Greg held himself back. Was it right or wrong? He had no idea. Gut instinct.

'Here are the fresher legs, but England now need to score to win … and so do Samoa. Maybe Greg Duggan is carrying an injury, which is perhaps why he is still on the bench.'

Possession was England's friend for the next six minutes.

Stu Wainwright darted around, Neil Duncan was sidestepping everywhere to use up time in possession.

Gary Walker sent a perfectly executed grubber kick through towards the Samoa try line, which had the England fans pumping fists and hollering Vinny Venus on. He couldn't get there, but Freddie South and Stu Wainwright following up managed to bundle the full-back Joseph Talipeau back over his line.

'It's a dropkick out from under the Samoa posts back to England. This is their first time in the Samoa half in the past fifteen minutes. This could be their moment.'

Laurie Northey responded to Brad.

'Under three minutes! It's getting to drop goal time.'

Brad Kearns couldn't see beyond a Samoa win.

'In the last game both these sides left it late, both coming back from half-time deficits, this time it's been a backs-to-the-wall effort from England with only 10 men, since 55 minutes. Samoa must be favourites for a first ever World Cup Final appearance. Their fans must be daring to dream.

'And here he comes!!!'

Greg had seen the play. He'd watched the move. This was his time. He interchanged with Troy Whittingham.

Brad suddenly changed his tune.

'And the decibel level in this crowd has just gone up ten-fold!

'Greg Duggan, who wasn't even in this England squad that came out to Australia four weeks ago, is the story of this World Cup. He is now captain, coach, outstanding player of the tournament, darling of the Vanuatu fans …'

'And currently without a club …'

Laurie Northey added gleefully.

'That will definitely change after this …'

Lisana kicked out from under the posts to the England team and only one man was destined to be under it.

'It just had to be didn't it!'

Brad Kearns was excited. He now knew that when this man took the ball something unexpected was usually about to happen. The atmosphere was suddenly at fever pitch again.

Greg had only one mission in mind. Run. Hard. Gain as much ground as he could and then see what it brought. He'd collected the kick on the Samoa 40-metre line. He reached just over the 30-metre line before being met by Mataria Embua and Jazz Perigini, who had just come on. He felt a crunch.

He knew instantly it didn't sound good and went down in the tackle.

'And if Duggan wasn't crook before, he certainly is now. He looks in pain there …'

Brad Kearns had seen it just as instantly as Greg had felt it.

Greg played the ball back gingerly to John Cloudsdale who had performed heroically on tackling throughout the second half. John turned and placed an inside pass to Mason Bell, who charged a few more metres before going down. Mason played it back to Big Mick Green, who passed it out to Stu Wainwright who scampered under the challenges of the Samoan forwards before being wrenched back.

'England have managed to get themselves a great field position. They are giving this everything and look as though they are setting *themselves for a one-pointer.'*

Greg was shaking his limbs out. He wasn't sure what had crunched but everything seemed okay. He'd set himself back for the play. Stu played it back to Freddie South, who looked briefly at Greg as he took the ball, then stepped off his right foot and charged across on a run that saw him straighten up and hammer into the Samoan defence.

It was a shattering tackle and Freddie, usually so dependable, saw the ball spill agonisingly from his grasp. Greg's heart slumped.

Jazz Perigini kicked the ball ahead for Samoa. England had committed all 10 players to attack.

Brad Kearns lived for this kind of moment.

'Ohhh, the ball's loose! Perigini's kicked onnn! ... Here's the match right here! ... It's a race for the ball, he's kicked on again ... it's going just over the try line! ... Perigini's getting there ... but there's Vincent Venuuuuus!

'This play has gone from the Samoa 20-metre line to the England try line ... the crowd is going crazy, but it is Vincent Venus who has picked up the ball in his own try area, he's come out from under his own sticks, he sprints back for England, bounces off one tackler, changes direction, this is Rugby League folks, hold on to everything ... he's at the halfway already ... he links up with the stepper Neil Duncan ... Duncan's away ... kicks it through! ... and look who's there, landing on the ball over the line ... it's Duggannnn!! ... That is from another universe!!! ... England are in the World Cup Final!'

The beaming smiles on the faces of all ten England players on the park were joined by the onrushing rest of the squad and every member of the coaching staff and England party. The final hooter sounded. The crowd went absolutely bananas.

Julian Jardine was taking the congratulations of his colleagues in the stand as though he had masterminded the England win.

'Greg Duggan. England coach, captain and World Cup finalist! How good does that sound?'

Pitchside Channel 17 reporter Karen Stonehouse was

carrying out the post-match interviews. Greg blew out his cheeks before projecting the widest smile possible.

'*The boys gave me everything and more …*'

He wiped away the sweat from his brow.

'*When we lost Phil, Tyler and Regan we knew that 12-point lead wasn't likely to last for long, but full credit … amazing team performance, and we're in The Final!*'

Greg raised his voice. For once he was letting himself go on a post-match interview and why not?

'*You must have thought it was game over when Jazz Perigini kicked that ball on …?*'

Greg raised his eyebrows. Smiled again. Rubbed the sweat away from his eyes.

'*You just never know with rugby league Karen, that's why this game is so great. And this place! …*'

Greg spread out his arms. The interview was also being shown on the big screen and the whole Vanuatu could hear.

'*… these people. This is an amazing place to be!*'

The crowd erupted!

CHAPTER 81

'Have you seen Kyle?'

Diane had been talking with Vanessa Quai at the post-match celebrations that had seen Vanessa and her band give another impromptu performance. The Samoan fans and players, despite their disappointment, had joined in the party with the England fans and the people of Vanuatu.

Greg was still in his England kit, as were most of the players. They'd not been given chance to get changed. And they weren't at all bothered. They were going to Stadium Australia!

Diane's question shifted Greg's world from euphoria to catastrophe.

Where the hell was Kyle?

Greg wouldn't have wanted to worry Diane any more than she probably already was, but his immediate reaction was a giveaway.

After all that had happened to him – and what he'd found out just before this game, this was the worst. His stomach was churning. He could hardly speak.

His son, for God's sake! Keep calm. Maybe he had just walked off somewhere having fun too, but Greg wasn't convincing himself. Instinct took control.

This was no time for pleasantries. This was time to show this jumped-up little piece of shit they were on to him. He'd never even spoken to Jardine before. This was going to be one hell of an introduction.

GPK intercepted Greg. He'd seen where he was heading.

'Greg, we've got this.'

'I don't bloody care what you've got, this prick's going down, he's got my kid ...'

Greg brushed Kraft aside as he made his way to where Jardine was standing with the Montgomerys and Maratoto Sakamoto in the hospitality area.

Greg was on the warpath, not to be denied.

He ran straight up to Jardine, who was dressed in casual but smart attire of designer jeans and buttoned shirt. He grabbed him by the throat with one hand and lifted him from the floor, hammered him to the wall and spat out his words. His right fist cocked to hit.

'Where the fuck is he, you little shit!!'

Julian Jardine had no way of getting away from this man mountain, but he had about 50 witnesses in front of him, from which he would claim an assault charge. His voice came out somewhat strangulated.

'I have absolutely no idea what you are driving at ...'

He was firm.

'And I would strongly advise that you put me down.'

Greg was having none of it. If anything, Greg now held him a little firmer and higher. He seethed at Jardine.

'You want to tell all these people about your relationship with Lena Kalotiti? And with Bob Rudd? And your extremely close relationship with the police commissioner? ...'

Greg knew better than turn away from his prey in order to make sure others heard. He merely raised his voice so that the now hushed room could take it all in.

He then shoved his knee sharply into Jardine's groin.

'... now tell me shithead, where is my son?!'

He spat the words at Jardine who despite discomfort managed to remain not only unflustered, he also smiled.

'You are an extremely talented rugby league player Mr Duggan, but as a man ...?'

He laughed in Greg's face. He then delivered a line that floored Greg completely. He seethed at Greg and spat venom back in return.

'Did you never wonder why your girlfriend is never around when things start going wrong for you?'

What the hell was this? Susie? What did he mean? This wasn't getting him anywhere. He was about to launch his fist into Jardine's face when Maria stepped in.

'Greg ...'

Maria's tone was affectionate towards the man she had booted out of the club just a few weeks ago.

'This will not solve anything. Let him go.'

Greg wasn't in any mood to do so.

GPK dashed over and broke the deadlock.

'Greg! There's been a sighting of Kyle ...'

Greg took one glance at GPK. Jardine took what he saw as an opportunity to wrestle free. Greg felt Jardine try. He turned back and launched his fist at Jardine's face. The result was not pretty as claret burst from his splattered nose. He collapsed in a heap on the floor.

It wasn't the answer. Greg knew that. He turned to Kraft.

'Where?'

'All we have is that he was seen with a woman. About five minutes ago ...'

While Greg and GPK made their way out of the hospitality area Jardine regained his footing, watching them go. The party resumed. He made his way towards an exit and took out his handkerchief, dabbed away the blood from his nose, tapped into his mobile phone and gave an instruction.

'He's fucking guilty as hell ...'

Greg was still seething.

'I know.'

'You know? Yet you just got us to leave him?'

GPK was driving. He had already told Greg that Kyle was okay. He was back with his mother. No damage done. He'd wandered off, still in the ground enjoying the party. A Vanuatu lady had realised who he was from earlier and had brought him back to Diane.

Greg and Kyle had spoken on the phone. Diane was relieved and was heading back to Breakas with Annie Laing who had taken charge of their welfare.

'We've still some work to do, Greg. First, we're taking you to be cut open ...'

CHAPTER 82

'Zoe! How good to see you! It's been a long time. Well, what an excellent World Cup we've put on. You must be incredibly proud.'

Zoe Miller had appeared in the hospitality area having been a guest on the Cloud TV UK commentary. She introduced her partner Nene Natavanu, Sela's daughter, and looked straight into Jardine's eyes. She knew he had not been in favour of The Pink.

'Mr Jardine.'

Zoe cocked her head in thanks.

'I heard you had been involved in an altercation with the England player Greg Duggan?'

Jardine shrugged.

'High spirits.'

Zoe smiled.

'We all have our ups and downs. Some of us make a splash when we go, don't we Nene?'

The couple laughed over their fun and games throwing each other into the ocean from Nene's father's boat, and then hauling each other back in, laughing.

Then Zoe delivered something much more acutely.

'... but there are also those who deserve everything they get, and eventually go with a bang rather than a splash, don't you find Mr Jardine ...?'

Jardine knew the atmosphere to the conversation had changed but was more interested in what had just pinged on his phone. He smiled and made his apologies, leaving them.

As he looked he saw it hadn't been a bad night at all. He certainly hadn't banked on the punch he'd received nor the knee in his balls, but on balance his night had been very good.

Money wasn't everything of course, but it would buy everything ... and everyone.

He'd done his homework. Found weaknesses, exploited them. And tonight, he'd made a fortune.

CHAPTER 83

'Karla?'

Greg was at Vanuatu police headquarters. He looked across at Karla, alive and well. And then at Det Alex Lui, quizzically.

'I never said Miss Karelia was dead Mr Duggan. I said a woman's body had been found. You assumed. I am sorry for the confusion ...'

Deputy Commissioner Elenola Taneo took over.

'We have, tonight, arrested Mr Napakauranga for his responsibility in the murders of Bob Rudd, Sela Natavanu and Winston Sablan.

'Mr Napakauranga had met with Mr Rudd when Mr Rudd first came to Efate. He had introduced Mr Rudd to Natavanu and Sablan. They all cooked up a plan to make a lot of money based around the Rugby League World Cup requiring a sum from Vanuatu if games were to be hosted here.

'They attracted millions' worth of investment from offshore accounts and businesses. The money was to go into the Rugby League World Cup Finance Department account held by Mr Rudd.

'Mr Rudd spent a good deal of time here building up business contacts. He set up an offshore account under the name Rugby League World Cup in Vanuatu. The account is still there.

'Natavanu and Sablan never put anything in. They attracted the investment. The total funding was never published, but the account shows it was nearly £50m.

'There was a fallout. Napakauranga was cut out. He was enraged and from then he was on a mission. Rudd had shared it out between them, £10m apiece for himself, Natavanu, Sablan and a sweetener for Julian Jardine. Napakauranga says they cut him out because he hadn't contributed any of the investors.

'They accounted for their contributions as management fees. Only £10m went towards the Rugby League World Cup.

'When Detective Superintendent Erin Jackson was sent over from the Australian Federal Police and took over the murder inquiry

of Bob Rudd, Napakauranga panicked.'

Alex took over once again.

'*Napakauranga had people he could use, who he had something over, to carry out the murders. He had a list, in his handwriting, which he had inadvertently left on his desk one day when journalist Grace Elliott came to the station asking for information about Bob Rudd.*

'*Miss Elliott photographed the list not knowing exactly what it was but having seen names and intended targets. Rudd, Natavanu and Sablan. Miss Elliott was unable to show us the note until she regained consciousness from having been shot at Le Café de La Vue D'Ilfira where Moses Pagoa, one of Napakauranga's men attempted to murder her.'*

Elenola took over once again.

'*That leaves us with the murder of Lena Kalotiti. The underwater post office lady. We don't have anything conclusive there. It's not Napakauranga. We know that much.'*

'*So why is Karla here?'*

Greg asked.

Greg had heard so many names, people he had no call to know about. GPK, Ken, James, Janet and Ann were present too. It was their turn now. Elenola nodded towards Grahame.

'*Because, Greg, Julian Jardine is at the heart of all of this. You were right. He is guilty as hell.*

'*Jardine is a puppeteer criminal. He works everybody, never gets his hands dirty. It was he who we believe coordinated the bank heist of Vanuatu's banks while you were playing your quarter-final. Napakauranga arranged for lights out and all power off in Port Vila, which triggered something cleverer than all of us here to enable his people to rob.*

'*The banks won't give away how much was taken from the online accounts of both banks targeted for fear of a run on their enterprises but early estimates, based upon those with funds missing already, are in the region of £500m. Could be far more.*

'*But it is the next part that is where you come in.'*

GPK held up the miniscule object that had just been

extracted from Greg earlier.

'It's a tracer. Amazingly these can be injected into your skin these days rather than stapled or being cut into you. Someone can know exactly where you are.

'Jardine really doesn't like you Greg. Never has, from the Hopton days when he was only amassing a small fortune. You have always been the fly in the ointment. The person who always seems to be in the way.

'So, when Jardine started rubbing shoulders with some of the investors for the World Cup he found similar people to himself but much wealthier. People who had built up vast amounts of money they would never ever have a hope of spending. People who liked gambling, but not just any kind of gambling.'

Ken Knott took over from GPK explaining the next part of Jardine's activities.

'Jardine runs an Extreme Gambling Ring on the Dark Web. It's all conducted behind hidden servers with intricate passwords and firewalls. Players log on from over 1000 spurious websites, all scrambled from the normal day-to-day Internet of social media twaddle.

'All rings are pretty much impenetrable. Governments lay off them because the people involved are multi-millionaires, billionaires. Their legal teams would cost the taxpayer billions fighting the cases.

'Jardine's Extreme Gambling Ring is rumoured to be one of the bigger ones. They are all very high risk. That's why these people are attracted. The minimum stake is £1m per bet. They are known as 'whale' punters, big punters to you and me. So long as Jardine gets his odds right the punters win occasionally – and he wins every time. Usually pulling in £100m per event.'

Ken stopped. He looked straight at Greg.

'You have been his plaything – his source of merriment. The women on the plane? Integrity for Sport? Two ladies he paid handsomely to put on a show. When he heard you were coming to Australia he paid off the people who had booked the flight in the Apartment in the Sky. Thought he'd have some fun.'

GPK intervened.

'He's been fixated on you since Playa Blanca. Maybe before.

Something about Susie? or Maria Cavaleros?'

Ken paused. He sniffed. Rubbed his chin

'Anyway, that's when he first used you in his Extreme Gambling Ring. You were at odds of 2-1 that you would bed the younger of the two women, 3-1 for the other, 4-1 both, and evens that you would walk without any of that. The TV screen in the room acted as a camera. Gamblers were able to see you, your reactions and had to gamble by a certain time.'

Greg was open-mouthed. His jaw couldn't drop any lower.

'He won a packet on that one.'

Ken shrugged nonchalantly.

'These punters don't live in the real world. They thrive off adrenaline rushes and Extreme Gambling gives them that. They all thought you would do them ...'

Ken quickly corrected his terminology to *'... go with them both'* as Janet gave him a kick on the shins and Ann sighed.

GPK took back over. Ken appeared to have been enjoying his role too much.

'Jardine manufactured your hotel runaways. He hired guys to track you down. Hired a guy to call you with an urgent message to get out. In Brisbane the bet was how far you could get in 30 seconds. He had cameras on the balconies and a drone flying nearby. He won another packet, but then like all maniacs he wanted to do something more. He enjoyed being the puppet master, like I said, making things happen.

'He didn't always win. You went on in your first game five seconds before he would have won another packet. Shane Chislett was supposed to have managed that one better. He also lost big on your comeback against France.

'He had Napakauranga in his pocket because he had looked after him financially when Sablan, Rudd and Natavanu hadn't. He had Karla come on to you. Karla is one of Napakauranga's girls, she would do everything he said since she was 12 years old, if you catch where I am going here.'

Karla hung her head. She was 22 now but the hurt would never leave. Greg looked over at her, now apologetically.

'Odds were fixed at how long before you were in bed together, not

whether. He knew that part was pretty much a sure thing ... it was one of your biggest audiences ... wherever you were he had people fix mini cameras ... you were a millionaires' TV show sensation ...'

GPK raised his hands. Shrugged.

'... based on your track record. It proved another winner. You were now a bit like The Truman Show *film?'*

Greg shrugged, he had never seen it.

'Your second hotel run was because he now wanted you caught to plant the chip on you. Punters saw you run. He'd hired people to take care of you. While you were unconscious, he had someone chip you. This time, it wasn't how far you could run but multiple bets on things you did. Times things took. The perverted punters loved it. Wasn't as huge an audience as the Karla Show, nor the balcony running, but he still made millions again.

'You became the man to watch and have a flutter on. So much so that he raised the ante to those taking part. It was now £2m per bet in the exclusive Duggan's Dilemmas Club, and he allowed accumulator bets on you over six separate happenings.

'Oliver Quinigan's exploits with you on the mountain were one of those. He was an easy buy-in for Jardine. Had every reason to hate you.'

Greg was shaking his head in incredulity.

'How the hell was that a gamble?'

'The time it took you to get off the mountain. That was a spread-bet. The TV punters loved the arrow. That hadn't been ordered,'

Ken had added, raising his eyebrows. GPK took it back on again.

'This is the thing, Greg ... this is all weird, depraved, ridiculous, but it doesn't bring about what we all really want.'

GPK settled himself ready to get to his point. Why he had come out to Vanuatu.

He was at the end of his career. This would be his team's final mission together. This had been about bringing retribution for a fallen comrade who they now knew fervently believed had been murdered at the behest of Jardine, but they would probably never have the proof.

'We need you to bring about justice for Jeff Markham ...'

CHAPTER 84

Greg was looking forward to making this call.

'Hello.'

'Paul? How are you mate? Listen, I just thought I'd let you know that there are some people coming to see you, in about thirty seconds?'

Google Earth Live was proving a useful tool on Ken Knott's laptop at Breakas. Greg and the rest of the GPK team were watching the action about to unfold as Greg spoke clearly to Diane's husband from 13,000 miles away.

Diane's husband Paul, father of her daughter Lily, had been part of Jardine's long-term plotting against Greg. Ken had found the evidence.

Jardine had rewarded him for insider information on Greg acquired from Diane.

Diane hadn't known or suspected a thing for the first two years of their relationship, but then little things had started taking place.

During the past week Ken had traced payments to an account, not in Paul's name but a spurious company name, that amounted to £100,000 a year, for the past three years, amounts deposited in the account monthly as though a salary.

Diane said that she had sometimes wondered why Paul had asked about Greg a little more as time had gone on but had thought that Paul was maybe a little jealous of Greg.

Greg had been right when he had picked up vibes from her that something was wrong. Diane was suffering from depression, taking medication.

She said that she could never have believed someone could have taken her in so much that she had had a baby with him. She was embarrassed, bitter and had been suffering from anxiety.

GPK's team had suggested the call be made to ensure Paul

was where they had thought. Greg, after hearing Paul's story, had said he would make the call. Paul was in his second house, one that Diane had never seen, with his other wife!

'Who is this?'

Greg heard a sound in the background on the line, as though Paul was now moving hurriedly. Google Earth Live showed three police vehicles arriving.

'Never you mind. Oh look, here they are now. Bye, Paul ... I hope you rot in hell.'

Greg turned to his former wife who had been sitting close by, watching on the big screen Ken had set up. Diane had been astounded to see this other house.

She had been unaware of his work for Jardine, hadn't questioned him when he said he would be away on business, often at weekends due to his management work in the leisure sector, and that much of her last three years had been a lie.

Ken had uncovered the lie, by working back from the payments. It had all been on the flash drive that Maria had passed to GPK at half-time in the semi-final, along with most of the other payments being made and banked.

Jardine had gone up several leagues from screwing a poor northern rugby league club out of its ground.

Diane had been apologetic to Greg and broken in spirit. Greg had consoled her as best he could. She had wanted to be present for Greg's call to her husband. She may have been suffering from depression brought about by him but she was also resilient.

Greg had always admired Diane for the way she handled things. She had suffered enough when she had lost their baby still in the womb as a result of the hit-and-run attempt when he was playing for Hopton. It only dawned on Greg now, but what if that car driver had been Paul too?

After Paul's arrest Greg took Kyle to the pool. Diane watched on, not feeling like playing happy families.

CHAPTER 85

It was now the morning after the semi-final. The England party was preparing to leave Breakas amid much good cheer from the players and the resort team. Neil Duncan was telling them in his best Scottish brogue how they should come to see his castle in Scotland, ever the joker.

Gary Walker was touting for business at his Cheeky Chicken Cottage back home, unlike Neil's a real residence that he and his wife Tracy ran along with a menagerie of animals including a dog called Panda.

There were only two days to the final against hosts Australia, who had come through in another tight squeeze in their game against New Zealand.

The flight from Bauerfield to Sydney was scheduled at 2pm.

England fans were flying out on the same plane as the team, along with those from Vanuatu who could afford it and now wanted to be there to support Greg's England.

Greg, Diane and Kyle were flying to Brisbane a little later in the day and from there driving south to Byron Bay, as Greg had done what seemed like months ago, but in reality was only around two and a half weeks.

His dad's funeral was tomorrow. The day before the World Cup Final versus Australia. Greg had left Freddie South and Big Mick Green in charge of the guys once more. Annie Laing would look after everything else.

Hideaway Island was only a 25-minute drive from Breakas. Greg had taken a trip there on his way back from the mountain, because he'd fancied seeing it. Carlos the minibus man with the Ni-Vanuatu tribesmen had taken him there. It was beautiful.

It had been the only sightseeing Greg had experienced and he'd had it in mind that it would be somewhere to take Kyle, to go snorkelling with his son, see the coral. Diane thought it a good idea. Their flight wasn't until 5pm. A family day out.

Kyle thought it was a great idea. He was so enthusiastic about everything, everything an adventure.

When Greg asked Breakas owner Reid Jefferson for a taxi, Reid generously offered to take them and then take them on to the airport later. He was desperate to show Greg how much his island had to offer.

It was as beautiful a day as it always seemed to be on Efate and Greg wished now that he had explored the island a little more, without the assistance of date rape drugging at any rate.

They all took the waterbus over to Hideaway Island with Reid acting as tour guide. Kyle was eager to try scuba diving with a new outfit that Reid had purchased for him.

It was as near as Greg and Diane would probably get to being a family unit. They both took in some rays for a short time as Reid played with Kyle.

'You going to be okay?'

Greg asked softly.

He knew how much the Paul revelation was hurting her. She still had Kyle and Lily to bring up. She had already said how much she was missing her daughter. She took a minute. Smiled the kind of smile that wasn't. She brushed her hair from her face.

'Yeah. I'll be okay ... thanks.'

'You know, I can always be there ... I mean not there, but ... well, you know, for Kyle ... help you with Lily, anytime ...'

She looked at him. She didn't hold out a hand to touch his cheek or hand, he didn't either. Too much old territory.

'Yeah, I know ... I know you're hurting too ... about Susie ...'

They had never talked about her, hadn't seemed right to Greg. He didn't speak now, gave a gentle shrug, didn't want to go there for Diane's sake. Old wounds and all that.

'Thanks ...'

He felt he had to respond in some way. It was the best he could do.

'Dad! Dad! Come on! Come and look at these! They're amaaazing balls!'

Diane and Greg laughed together. Their son. He was picking up phrases. Greg went towards him, but with a little parting shot turned to Diane as he spoke.

'You know there's nothing wrong in going somewhere with our son ... every now and again ... and Lily ...'

Greg splashed into the sparklingly clear waters with Kyle. He went underwater and saw what Kyle had been marvelling at, wonderfully multi-coloured fishes of all kinds, and wondered why he hadn't done this kind of thing more.

It was like being in one massive aquarium.

But it wasn't just the fish. Why wasn't he doing something more with his life when he wasn't playing rugby league? And it wasn't just about spending time with Kyle either. Why wasn't he doing something more with his life?

Kyle was swimming like a fish, darting here, there and everywhere. He then started motioning to his dad, pointing where he wanted him to go. Greg followed. They found Hideaway Island's claim to world fame – the world's first and only underwater post office.

Greg hadn't bothered with snorkelling when he'd visited for a few minutes with Carlos. They'd had a kava and then Greg had returned to Breakas.

This was Lena Kalotiti's workplace, where she would collect the postcards sent by divers and snorkellers to loved-ones back home.

What a great idea! Kyle swam through the frame of the fibreglass converted water tank mailbox as hundreds of thousands had done before and Greg did the same.

'Mum!! That was so cooool!! Can we send a postcard to Grandma and Granddad? Can we please? And Dad and I can go back down again and put it in the postbox. It's great!'

Kyle was literally bursting with excitement. Greg saw so much fun in him. Coming here had been a great idea.

It was Reid who had to be the bearer of bad tidings though.

'I'm afraid it has not been open for sending postcards since ...'

Reid stopped himself from saying anything further in front

of Kyle whose smile had dropped.

'… *since they haven't got a postman or woman at the moment …*'

Diane was typically quick at covering for moments like this. Greg was quick too. Team effort.

'*Never mind son … hey, why don't we go back down and pretend to be the postmen? … Tell you what, we'll get a postcard now, come on … and come on, Mum …*'

Greg wasn't attempting to play something he and Diane weren't, but he wanted her to know that him being around Kyle, when he was, wasn't to exclude her. They both held hands with Kyle as they made their way to the hut that sold snorkels, goggles, swimwear, tourist stuff, drinks, sweets and the waterproof postcards.

'*Not been too much of a call for these lately.*'

The hut attendant gave a sad grimace as she scanned the barcodes of a couple they had chosen. Greg gave a reciprocal nod with similar feeling.

'*What was she like? Lena?*'

Diane asked the question. The attendant's face lit up. She put her head to one side, closed her eyes for a second as she saw Lena's face again in her mind.

'*Aww honey, she was like our country, she was sunshine! Everybody loved her! She was so friendly … and you know, she had the world at her feet … she was so excited about a TV show she was going to be in … but …*'

Alani, Diane had asked her name, stopped herself momentarily.

'*You are from England, yes?*'

Greg and Diane both nodded.

'*Then I will be careful what I say…*'

This had been small-talk up until now. Greg and Diane looked at each other.

CHAPTER 86

'Diane! ... and Kyle! ... Ohhh!'

Greg's heart went out to his mum as she melted at seeing her daughter-in-law, as she still saw her, and her grandson. Tina wasn't one to get over emotional, just like her sons, but she couldn't help herself.

Nobody was dressed in black. The funeral was to be a celebration on the beach at Byron Bay, not a wake. Tina and Trevor had always loved their music, their wine and their surfing.

Their great friend, fellow surfer and wine purveyor Russ Berry had provided the best wines of Australia from his Luna Wine Store and Russ's fiancée Alexandra Laviolette had planned the whole day.

Tina, Trevor, Russ and Alex had also become friends with American-born, Byron Bay BluesFest regular Jack Johnson who brought his guitar to play 'Better Together' especially for Tina.

Greg was amazed at how popular his mum and dad had been in Byron. His mum was a star in her own right. He hadn't known, because she hadn't said, but she was known amongst her surfing friends as The Twister on account of her skills on the board, and that she had been Byron Masters ladies champion twice.

Tina was so touched by everyone being there, and once again Greg's thoughts went back to his dad, but now to his mum and dad together with him and Col. And then his mind went back to his thoughts at Hideaway Island and making more of his own life, as they had so obviously done with theirs.

Grandma Tina and her friend Russ teaching Kyle how to surf, would be an abiding memory later in the afternoon as The Twister took to the gentler waves with her grandson.

'It's like going back in time ...'

Col put his arm around his brother's shoulder.

'Go get that trophy Greg! I've got things here … you might not be welcomed back though …'

Greg looked across to where a couple of Aussie fans were wearing the green and gold as they walked the beach with the sun still belting down on the gold-kissed sand.

'You know what, Col … at this moment, I couldn't care less …'

He looked at his brother, with tears in his eyes.

'Wish I'd come here sooner …'

CHAPTER 87

'Hey, Greg!'

Coen had driven to pick him up from Newcastle Airport where he'd flown in from Ballina Byron Gateway Airport in the New South Wales Northern Rivers region, part of Australia's Fly Pelican internal flight network. Greg, Diane and Kyle were stopping over in Broke.

Zoe Miller had arranged for her folks to be an appropriate stopping off point for the night before the World Cup Final. She'd spoken with Greg at Breakas before the England party had set off for Sydney.

'If you're worried about anything just ask my dad about Grady Sorenson and the Broke People's Front. You'll know you are in safe hands.'

Newly appointed Vanuatu Police Commissioner Erin Jackson had wished Zoe well for the World Cup Final and had said she looked forward to them both having a much-improved relationship in the future. She then returned to her Deputy Commissioner Elenola Taneo and newly appointed Det Insp Alex Lui.

Zoe and Nene Natavanu had also flown in to Sydney to attend the inaugural game of 'The Pink' at the West Sydney Stadium, which had been an outstanding success.

The Southern Hemisphere had triumphed over the Northern Hemisphere in a really tremendous game of rugby league. It hadn't been turned into some kind of *Priscilla of the Desert* fancy dress game as the sport's purists had feared. It had been exactly what Zoe had intended – a game played properly, but just with those who had different sexualities – inclusive.

Greg, Diane and Kyle had watched it with Coen and Marli. They had loved the concert, particularly Jimmy Somerville singing his classic hits such as 'Smalltown Boy' and 'Don't Leave Me This Way'. And they had all been astounded by the skills and sheer brutality of the Wheelchair World Cup Final that saw England beat France for a second consecutive final.

'*Dad! Can we get wheelchairs and have a go! That looks sick!*'

Greg's eyes went to the back of his head and he smiled a tight-lipped smile, not at his son's idea but at his son using a word that he hadn't heard from the 6-year-old before. Diane shook her head in mock despair. Everyone laughed. Greg then explained a little more to Kyle about why the wheelchair game existed.

'*I don't care! I just think it's great! They are all amazing!!!*'

CHAPTER 88

Greg arrived in Sydney at 7am the next morning, alone. He'd taken the early morning flight from Newcastle at 6.20am thanks to another drive from Coen Miller, who had told him he must come back and see the site of Baiame, The Sky Father, enjoy the wines of the Hunter Valley and bring back your gorgeous wife and lovable son.

Greg didn't have the heart to put him right over any happy families Coen might have presumed. But, he thought how it would be great to take in more of Broke, the Hunter Valley, Byron Bay, Efate and Lanzarote come to that, sightseeing – just for fun, not for any other reason.

'But right now, I've work to do.'

Greg had told himself this as he touched down at Sydney Kingsford Smith International Airport where he was met by Annie Laing.

Twenty-five minutes later they were at Stadium Australia. He had wanted to be there early, take in the stadium, the atmosphere without the fans, without the rest of the squad.

Kyle and Diane were booked on a later flight with Coen and Marli. They were all to be guests of their daughter and her fiancée as of last night Nene Natavanu.

Greg was met at the ground by someone he knew only too well.

CHAPTER 89

The tousled hair was a little greyer than it used to be, but the famous, trademark gap-toothed grin was exactly the same.

The former teammates and imminent World Cup finalists clasped hands, then man-hugged each other.

'You do know that we are both completely bananas, don't you mate? But let's do this!'

Kenny said with his usual beaming expression.

They stripped off in their respective changing rooms and emerged in minutes, both wearing their international shirts, running shorts and running shoes. Greg Duggan and Kenny Lomax, back in harness.

'I've never seen Sydney Harbour Bridge or Sydney Opera House. How long do you think it'll take?'

The challenge was a morning run. The two great mates having a great time before the game.

'Aww, it's only about 12 miles mate. If we stick to the main route. You ready? Let's do this thaing!'

They fist-pumped and set off. Greg had reckoned they'd knock out a steady pace of around 7 minutes 30 seconds per mile for the first ten miles, then see what they both had in the tank. About an hour and a half. That would be sufficient. Then breakfast.

Kenny had been up for it straight away. They were both determined that being in their thirties, Kenny a few years on from Greg, wasn't going to stop them playing the sport they loved; and running was their second love.

Five miles in and they were both sticking close together, as Greg had hoped. He hadn't a clue which roads to use, but Kenny was holding true. Eight miles and the pair were still running alongside each other as the sun made its first real appearance of the day.

'You good?'

Kenny smiled at his buddy of the past three seasons at Hopton and Eruption.

'*Any time Greg … we all know you're so good, good, good!*'

The pair laughed, taking the pace up a little more as they reached ten miles.

'*I can see it!*'

Greg hollered in a childlike way, as though he could see the sea.

'*The bridge … Go there first, then the Opera House?*'

A mile out from the bridge Greg stepped up the pace again. Kenny went with him. It was still comfortable for them both.

'*First across?*'

Kenny went ahead with the start of the bridge in sight.

'*Let's see what you've got then!*'

Greg's competitive spirit was just as strong as Kenny's.

'*It's over 1000 metres mate, don't let the arch fool you.*'

A helicopter appeared overhead.

'*Just Sydney's 'Eye in the Sky' traffic 'copter, mate!*'

Kenny shouted as they reached halfway across.

'*And breaking news is that two of tonight's World Cup Final opponents have been spotted this morning running from Stadium Australia, tonight's venue, to the capital. Our 'Eye in the Sky' traffic team are following them now on Sydney Harbour Bridge. You can follow England's and Australia's players of the tournament Greg Duggan and Kenny Lomax right now on our social media platforms 'live'!*'

Channel 17 had picked up the buddies earlier and Kenny and Greg were now trending so much on social media that everybody they now saw were training their mobile phones on them for pics and cheering them both on.

'*Go Kenny!*'

Greg was hearing that more than his name, but he wasn't at all concerned as he stepped up the momentum across the bridge with the end only 100 metres away. This had been well worth their effort. Kenny was just out ahead with 50 metres left. Greg was putting it in, but so was the old master. They charged across what both fortunately took to be the finish with Kenny probably just about edging it.

'It's a sign!'

the gap-toothed wonder-kid said, as he'd first been called some 17 years ago when he'd made his debut. The pair were both now blowing hard, their hands on their thighs as they took water on board.

It was a steady trot for both to the Opera House that followed with a few stops on the way for snaps with fans and tourists. It had turned into an impromptu publicity campaign for the World Cup Final.

'What do you think? Will that do?'

Greg winked at his mate as the two returned to their respective teams.

'See you tonight ... don't be late!'

CHAPTER 90

'Good Evening Sports Fans! And welcome along to the Rugby League World Cup Final!'

Bethany Best was at pitchside with a packed stadium behind her as she introduced Channel 17's coverage, which had been ongoing since 2pm when the inaugural PDRL World Cup Final had been played with England eventually emerging victorious over Australia 14-12 in a spectacle that had touched at the heart of every fan of the sport and had not been without its share of controversy with a try having been ruled out for Australia in the dying seconds.

'We have already witnessed some amazing Rugby League in the PDRL World Cup Final and the Women's World Cup Final. England were victors in the PDRL and now Australia have done the trick over England with a fantastic display by both teams.

'That's four amazing games in the last two days with the Wheelchair World Cup Final and that amazing new competition 'The Pink'.

'We're now all getting set for the final game of this terrific all-inclusive Rugby League World Cup between England and Australia here at Stadium Australia. Stay right where you are, we'll all be back, all 83,500 of us, in just ninety seconds – count them!'

Bethany Best had proved just how all-inclusive she could be in her opener and now England and Australia were just fifteen minutes away from kick-off.

'Right boys, this game isn't about words, it's about what we do on the park. I'm not gonna give you many. Just these. Hold the ball when we have it, get the ball from them when we don't ...'

Greg's brain flashed up a picture of his dad smiling and laughing with him. Whatever he had been going to say transformed into what he now actually said, as he put on the broadest of grins.

'... and we are going to enjoy it! ...'

It was then that Greg opened up to his team, probably the first time he had ever been so open, so full of passion. He hadn't planned this.

'We buried my dad yesterday. I had never realised how much I would miss him until now …'

Greg could feel the tears inside, stirring him further as he fought them back from flowing.

'… you may have lost someone close to you, I know some of you have. I would have loved to share the World Cup Final trophy with my dad 80 minutes from now. But I also know from yesterday he is in here with me … and in my son Kyle out there …'

Greg beat his chest with his fist three times.

'Let all of them, the people who you love, whether they are here or not, urge you on inside when the times get tough tonight …'

Another bout of spontaneity hit home.

'… Fists High Guys!'

Seventeen fists met in the centre of the circle in the changing room. Every single player responding and in total commitment, with several adding 'Come ON!' until everyone joined in a continuous chant that rang out through the room.

Greg would have brought about some levity, by putting himself down over the number of words he had actually ended up using, but chose not to, he didn't want what he'd said diluting into a good-natured banter piece. He wanted his team out there giving everything they had.

'… and with me tonight, back in the hot seat is Wayne Ferryman, former World Cup winner. Wayne, what will these boys be going through right now?'

Channel 17's first string commentary and pundit team of Bruce Anderson and Ferryman had been given the nod over Brad Kearns and Laurie Northey, who had followed England's progress on Vanuatu and Papua New Guinea.

Bruce Anderson had threatened to quit Channel 17 if he hadn't been given the game.

'Come on Dad!!'

Kyle had shouted as loudly as he could from the grandstand

having come out of the hospitality area with his mum a few minutes prior. They were now in their seats with Zoe, Nene, Coen, Marli and the England officials, including international team chairman Walter Armitage who had made it over and was sitting one side of Kyle with his mum the other.

'That's a fine pair of lungs young man! And I hear you're going to take over from your dad one day!'

Walter, who had appeared in a World Cup Final against Australia four decades ago smiled across to Diane. Kyle looked at Walter very straight, his face turning extremely serious.

'I'm in a big game next week. It's not like this though …'

Kyle spread his arms wide and made his eyes really big and smiled so nicely. But then made Walter smile:

'You can come if you like …'

'I just might Kyle, I just might …'

Walter laughed.

'And here they come …'

Bruce Anderson had been turning up the gas slowly on the game until now, but he was ready to press the accelerator pedal.

The Australia and England teams strode out onto the Stadium Australia turf amidst a cacophony of noise from the fans, fireworks and Midnight Oil performing one of their biggest hits 'Beds Are Burning'.

Greg was at the head of his team and Australia coach Jaime Pagano similarly, but wearing a suit compared to Greg's training jacket over his kit.

Two minutes later it was time for the national anthem of both teams, a meeting of the captains in the middle, Greg and Australia's skipper Ricky Graham, and a toss of the coin from referee Glenn Stewarty that resulted in Australia kicking to England.

'It's the most tremendous noise I have ever heard before a game …'

Bruce Anderson was turning up his own heat even further.

'And it is Greg Duggan, the England team captain and coach who will get this game underway. It's the final final of this wonderful

Rugby League World Cup tournament … and we're under way!'

Greg had played in big games before, in Super League back home, but never in anything like this. It was only his sixth international game and he had never played against the big two, Australia and New Zealand.

He'd never played in a stadium like this. How the hell had he found himself as England coach and playing in the World Cup Final?

Then it came to him. His dad. If it hadn't been for his dad dying he wouldn't have even been there.

These had been Greg's thoughts in the final moments between the anthems and placing the ball on the kicking tee.

By the time he put boot to ball projecting it high into the Stadium Australia lights his focus was on one thing only. The game.

Aaron Fielding was back at full-back, Gary Walker stayed in the half-backs with Stu Wainwright in at hooker.

Australia had their mercurial full-back Don Jarrett also back from injury, Kenny Lomax was of course in at hooker and another of Greg's old teammates at Eruption, Ellard Vellidale (EV) was in at prop.

'It's a high kick from Duggan to the Australia try line … and it's taken by Don Jarrett. He passes to winger Wes Tessyman who takes it up to the England tacklers. Solid line from the men in white shirts and cross of St George.'

Greg led by example and was up with the England line as they sought to hold the Roos. The opening exchanges from both sides were hard, physical encounters as the two finalists gave no quarter.

'Neither Australia nor England have looked particularly impressive throughout this tournament …'

Bruce Anderson reflected, as the old rivals continued to lock horns.

'… but they've both found ways of winning games and although some may think it was always going to be these two, try telling that to New Zealand and Samoa in the semi-finals, France in the quarters

and Wales against Australia in the opening game …'

'*Aww, but mate, these boys are making up for any previous frailties tonight … these early hit-ups are really fierce …'*

Wayne Ferryman was commenting after a first twenty minutes that had offered a stalemate in terms of possession. Australia were just about edging it on the amount of yardage gained but even that was a close call.

Kenny Lomax and Greg had been on the park together many times before but never on opposite sides. There was no sign of friendship when they went in for their first clash as Greg carried the ball up into a tackle from Kenny and Frank Dailly.

'*He's here.'*

It had been sent in a text. He'd just arrived.

'*They're here too …'*

'*… and look who else!'*

Messages flew around the stadium.

Julian Jardine was sitting in the same section as Walter Armitage, Diane and Kyle. He was on good form. His latest Extreme Gambling event had ended rather well, especially considering how off-the-cuff it had been. He'd had to work pretty quickly on it and had impressed himself.

Maria was sitting with him. She had enjoyed their time in and around Vanuatu but she was overjoyed when they had arrived in Sydney Harbour.

'*Querido, es hermoso.'*

Maria had said how beautiful it was as they sailed through into the harbour. This man might have his faults and many of them, she thought. But he knows about money and having a good time.

Bruce Anderson exploded back into life.

'*It's Trent Scott with the first bust of the day! He's gone through Mason Bell and Owen Fenchurch, breaching the England defence which has been rock solid up to this point, but Freddie South tidies up the play bringing down Scott.*

'*It's the first line bust we've seen, Wayne. Indicative of the England boys tiring already?'*

'*Aww I don't think so Bruce. It's maybe more like interchange time for some of the big guys. It's a warm one down there.*'

'*And here you go … Both sides interchanging at the same time. It's Rich Dee and John Cloudsdale on for Mason Bell and Billy Ecktenstall; and Nick Valentine and Andrew Casey-Lewis for EV and Cam Sperrow …*'

Erin Jackson had been busy since her new appointment. She had been approached by Ben Santo the Deputy Prime Minister of the Republic of Vanuatu and had jumped at the chance to carry on working with Elenola and Alex and escape from the internal politics she had grown tired of in the Australian Federal Police.

She had come back to Sydney to settle some outstanding business before taking up her new role permanently.

Erin responded to her latest text. She was there.

'*It's a tough old game is this rugby league …*'

Bruce said, in a lead-up to his next point.

'*… and it's pretty tough out there now. These boys have been running into each other like monster trucks for nearly half an hour. Something's gotta give.*'

Greg hadn't played a full 80 minutes in the past year and he knew that he was ready for a break. Troy Whittingham had just come on for Sam Rivers, which left Ricki Brown to interchange.

'*Australia have the England team on the England 30-metre line after four tackles. Strategically the Roos are in a good place here. One more good tackle down in this area and England will have to come up with something special to get the ball down the park.*'

Bruce Anderson had called it exactly as it was and exactly how Greg felt.

'*… and they're not leaving it 'til then. They're looking for that play right now …*'

Wayne Ferryman had seen Greg set himself back for a 40-20 kick that would see England retain possession if he was accurate.

'*Get me that ball,*'

Greg had ordered from Gary Walker and Stu Wainwright, the livewires who would feed him the right pass. He replaced his gumshield.

'You're right again, Wayne. They're looking to get out of a heap of trouble here.'

Greg knew he needed to be up the park by a good ten metres to give himself a chance of executing it properly. It was a gamble.

It was Big Mick Green who had just been tackled. He played the ball back for Stu Wainwright who threw out a perfect pass to Gary Walker, who in turn matched it with just what Greg had wanted, but the kick Greg had planned would never be booted.

Bruce Anderson was in full voice.

'Ouch!! That's such a hit by Lomax! He's come through from nowhere and has wiped out Duggan.'

Greg was in agony as the result of his former teammate's tackle was turned into disaster.

'... and Duggan's day just got a whole lot worse! ... and Australia's day a whole lot better! ... Try time Kenny Lomax! And it's the first score on the board after 35 minutes.

'Lomax knew just what was going on there, he put the heat on Duggan big style and the impact forced the spill. Lightning quick reactions from the little master and he's dived over for the opening score.'

The conversion kick was an easy 2-pointer for Eliot Schoular and Australia were ahead 6-nil.

Even worse news was that Greg was still flat out. The medics were on.

'And this doesn't look good for England's skipper! Duggan has sometimes almost single-handedly dragged his team through this competition, but maybe no longer, he looks in real pain ...'

The Channel 17 and Cloud TV cameras were trying all they could to get an even more agonising picture of Greg's face.

'Just pop it back in and get me off, do it now!'

Greg's left shoulder was dislocated. He'd done it before

and it had been popped back in. He'd been out for a long time afterwards. He knew it would be the same again. It had happened as he'd gone down, the reason for spilling the ball.

He grimaced and tears were brought to his eyes as the physio managed to pop it back more easily than he had anticipated.

'It looks to me like the England captain has done his shoulder. That's a sad way to end his World Cup after all he's given to this tournament.'

Referee Stewarty had stopped the clock with four and a half minutes left of the first half. Ricki Brown came on.

'Get me a brace, Jim.'

Greg was not done. He was for now, but he was determined to give himself a chance for maybe later in the game. He couldn't just let this go. The World Cup Final.

James Darbury, England physio, was shaking his head. James said,

'I don't think we have …'

Greg was on him immediately.

'Just get one, I don't care who from or where from, just get me one …'

Jardine knew this was the time. He'd been waiting for a moment when he could launch it. Fill his boots with another absolute surefire winner. This would bring it all to a close. He left his seat to set it all up in the hospitality area.

Beautiful. Another plan was coming together. Within minutes he had most of his 'whales' on board. As he came back the half-time hooter sounded.

Kyle was almost inconsolable. Diane was working hard with her son. Walter Armitage was trying to help.

'Hey, Kyle, why don't you and I go and see your dad …'

Diane wasn't certain. Walter could see it in her face, but quickly countered to make sure she felt comfortable.

'If they will allow us in of course, so long as your mum's okay with that …'

Walter whispered.

'I might just be able to find a way.'

Julian Jardine was abundantly happy with life. The money was rolling in once again and there was no way he was going to walk out of the stadium later on without again having earned substantial millions, even given the amount he would need to pay out for those who gambled what turned out to be successfully.

Another 40 minutes, he told himself. And another fortune.

Bruce Anderson had a special half-time guest.

'And with us tonight is the woman who has ensured this whole tournament will last long in the memory, organising committee chief executive Zoe Miller …'

While Zoe took the bouquets that came from Bruce she thought back to just prior to the opening ceremony and what could have happened if she hadn't run? If she had attended that meeting at Manly? Would she have gone the same way as Rudd?

Greg put on a brave face in the England dressing room. His shoulder hurt like hell.

'You're all good enough to win this game. This Australia team is nothing special. 6-nil at half-time and the spill was my fault, not yours! …

'Neil! Sidestep them all you like mate! Step 'til you go dizzy! Aaron, run at 'em! Gary, keep smiling in their faces as you tear them apart! Freddie, Billy, Mason, Mick, John, Rich hit 'em like they've never been hit before. John, Owen, Sam, Troy – run fast, you'll be all over them! Ricki, Charlie – amazing from you two tonight. You don't get your share of praise for getting us here, now get us over the line!'

Greg left his two young guys who he'd brought on at Hopton 'til last.

'You two …?'

He clicked his fingers and held his face in mock loss of memory.

'… give me your names again? …'

Greg laughed as he said it. Looking across at Stu and Vinny. Then spoke to the rest.

'*These two guys were there at the start of this amazing journey I've had in the past three years. They're part of my DNA … whatever the fuck that means!*'

The rest of the team saw the humour.

'*… and they are winners! Just like you! … so for God's sake don't fuck this up guys! Win this trophy, for you!*'

'*Dad!*'

Greg hadn't known his son was there. But he did now.

Thankfully, Kyle hadn't heard the rude word. He just came straight up to his dad, and Greg picked him up instantly with his good arm. And holding him up, as he'd done with the fist salute earlier.

'*And do it for Kyle!!*'

Kyle was already their mascot after his singing exploits at Port Vila. They joined as one with a chant, started by Stu of 'For Kyle!'

'*That sounded like we were swearing about a Scottish island!*'

Neil Duncan had said seconds later as they left the dressing room.

'*Australia 6 England 0. There's nothing in it, Wayne!*'

Bruce Anderson was setting up the second half as the teams emerged.

'*Let's go down pitchside to Bethany Best for her update on what has been said at half-time.*'

'*Well as you might expect Bruce, it was difficult getting hold of Greg Duggan. What I can tell you is that his news is that he looks extremely unlikely to play any further part in the game and he could be out for several months including the start of the new Super League season … but he feels his team can overcome the Australia team. He's been happy with their defence, but feels they need to express themselves more.*

'*Jaime Pagano wants his green and golds to stick with the game plan, which he says has worked so far and to stay strong all around the park. He's happy with his team's defensive effort too.*'

Privately, Bruce Anderson's thoughts had been that this was the most boring game he had so far witnessed in the tournament. Why couldn't he have had the Vanuatu games? Brad Kearns' popularity had soared on the back of it.

'*Thank you, Bethany! ...*'

Greg now had his shoulder in a brace that physio Jim had found, as he made his way to the England bench.

Jardine was smiling, looking forward to the second half as he took his place back in the stand once again. He rested back in his seat feeling very pleased with himself.

'*And we are all set for the second half here at Stadium Australia ...*'

Bruce Anderson trailed.

'*Mr Glenn Stewarty has restarted the clock ... well, hang that out to dry ... he hasn't restarted ... there's movement on the England bench ... and ... really? ...*'

Julian Jardine's expression was one of incredulity.

He looked down on the park from his elevated position in the stands and then put his head in his hands. No, no, no! This couldn't be happening. He needed to act fast.

'*... and incredibly ... I think Greg Duggan is coming back on the park ...*'

Bruce Anderson was genuinely astounded.

'*... he is! Greg Duggan is coming back on ... He can't have recovered that quickly, can he Wayne?*'

Wayne Ferryman had played top level NRL rugby league for nearly 20 years. He gave his kneejerk reaction.

'*Aww mate, this game never ceases to amaze me with what players can do. They've probably assessed him in the hutch at half-time, he'll have had a massage, maybe as many painkilling sprays as they are legally allowed to, and he's obviously decided it's worth the risk, but he's a brave man.*

'*It definitely looked to be a real dislocation there just before half-time. If nothing else it's going to be incredibly sore and he could do far more damage that could keep him out of the game for longer and might even threaten his career ...*'

'*Look Mum! It's Dad! He's back!*'

Kyle was overjoyed. Walter was smiling, Diane too.

Jardine made no effort to offer apologies to Maria and their guests this time around as he made his way from his seat once again. This needed sorting. He had to do something and quickly.

'And now we really are under way! 40 minutes to decide the Champions of the World ... err, maybe not just yet ...'

Anderson was still shaking his head at what he'd just witnessed. Kenny Lomax was shaking his head too, but with a smile on his face. Referee Stewarty couldn't believe he was waiting again.

Greg gathered his team together.

'Right boys, let's get this deficit out of the way first ...'

Referee Stewarty didn't like these delays. He walked over to Greg.

'Are you done with all this drama? Can we get on with the game now?'

Australia's full-back Don Jarrett took the kick that towered high into the night sky before coming down to be bathed in the floodlights. It wasn't the easiest of takes and with a long hang-time, but Jarrett's opposite number Aaron Fielding was under it and took it safely.

The first ten minutes of the second half developed along similar lines to the first. Both sides were working extremely hard at not losing the game.

Greg was moving gingerly. He was avoiding the heavy traffic as best he could and going in slightly one-sided into the tackle, often assisting with someone else making the heavy hit. He then decided he'd done enough.

'And Duggan is bringing himself back off again. He's been a passenger for these first ten to twelve minutes. It's a sad sight to see, but surely, that's the last of him in this World Cup Final, Wayne.'

Bruce Anderson passed the baton to his summariser.

'You're right Bruce. I can't really see what he hoped to do. Even his own team looked amazed when he came on for this second half.'

Jardine had only just returned to his seat when he saw Greg coming off. The past ten minutes had been his own personal Armageddon.

'Querido, estas bien?'

Maria had asked. All colour had drained from Jardine's face. He was as white as a sheet. Seeing Greg leave the park again suddenly brought an idea, some colour back to his cheeks. Without a word, he was out of his seat again. He turned to Maria this time, put up his hand.

'Business ... five minutes ...'

England hadn't been able to function as they wanted with Greg on the park earlier, but now Gary Walker began calling the plays. Freddie South and John Cloudsdale made great yardage, taking the ball up ten metres at a time. Neil 'The Brickie' Duncan went on a mazy run that saw him swerve and swivel around his Australia counterparts Luke Veron and Andrew Durrant.

The game was nearly at the hour mark and for the rugby league purists it had been a formidable tackling display particularly from the Australian forwards Cam Sperrow, Andrew Casey-Lewis, Johnnie Johnson and Trent Scott and England's top hitters Freddie South, Big Mick Green, Billy Ecktenstall and John Cloudsdale – but great half-back and back play of an inspirational and imaginative kind had been stifled and in short supply, until Neil Duncan decided to put his legendary sidestep on show.

'He's a stepper this lad Duncan!'

Bruce Anderson was getting excited.

'... and here we go! Duncan has slipped the ball out one-handed to Venus, who has come inside from his wing for some action. Ohhh-Who-Woh! And he takes an almighty clattering from Frank Dailly, and he's hit the deck.'

Vinny played the ball back to Gary Walker, who went on a run and was also clattered.

The only problem for the Australian defensive line was that Gary didn't have the ball!

Gary Walker had let the ball run through the gap between his hands and feet, but had made as though he had the ball. Instead it had gone straight through him to Stu.

'Aww, it's not *Walker* with the ball, it's *Wainwright*! The defence has all gone towards Walker, who has done a dummy run! Wainwright's gone through a gap and he's away! He's got Arko Turame and Luke Veron on his tail and Don Jarrett trying to cover half the park to get to him! He's arced his run! He's nearly there! Aww, sensational ankle tap by Jarrett, but it's still a TRY!! Wainwright let go of the ball just before hitting the ground and there on the end of it was Charlie Cole!

'Now that's the kind of move this game has needed, Wayne.'

Australia 6 England 4.

'It was a great move by the England boys that's for sure. When you're under the pump, as they were just probably starting to feel, to come up with a simple but effective play like that was really clever.'

Jardine returned to his seat again, but he still looked ashen. He nodded to his guests, the Montgomerys and Maratoto Sakamoto and smiled a simpering smile that radiated nothing but his concern and unhappiness.

'That's a bad miss by Aaron Fielding. That conversion attempt for the two extra points really wasn't that difficult, but it's a two-point ballgame with 15 minutes left on the clock.'

Bruce Anderson was giving all he could on the commentary. He still felt the game hadn't yet exploded.

On the bench Greg had been caught up in his own version of Jardine's 'Duggan's Dilemmas'.

Part of him wanted his team to get ahead in the game without him, but another part, the larger part was desperate to be on the park where he could influence the game. Another part told him not to be so stupid. He had an injury. He'd be no more use than a chocolate fireguard.

But that wasn't the point. This was the World Cup. This was possibly his first and last chance to win it. He wanted to be on the park to do all he could to ensure it happened.

If he didn't go on, he might forever wish he had. He wasn't certain about anything – whether by taking someone off and putting himself on he would weaken his team, probably would; whether he would break down in the first tackle he encountered, and the Aussies would be bound to go for him, he would in their position; whether he could tackle anybody; too many bloody whethers! Like too many maybes a few weeks ago!

Don't make a decision yet. Wait.

Make a decision, do it, do it. Get yourself on. Jardine was willing him to come back.

The game rolled on with a continual brilliant defensive effort from both teams. Five minutes were left on the clock when …

'*And it's another brilliant dart of a run by Gary Walker! This lad's even faster than his cheeky chickens he keeps back home! He's gone under a lunging tackle from Kenny Lomax, who has again turned back the years today, and Walker now plays the ball back to prop forward Freddie South who barges his way past Cam Sperrow and Eliot Schoular and offloads to Owen Fenchurch.*

'*Fenchurch finds the irrepressible Neil Duncan, who sidesteps as only he can to go past Luke Veron as if he wasn't there, and he's stopped at the Australia 20-metre line with one more tackle in this set to go.*

'*Duncan plays the ball back to Wainwright who launches a … no he doesn't! … The kick rebounds off Australia's Eliot Schoular and goes forward from him, but beyond the England attack and it's play onnn! … and would you believe … it's the old master again! Kenny Lomax zips on to the ball … and he's away! He's over the Australia 30, now the 40, now he's at halfway …*'

Wayne Ferryman joined in the Bruce Anderson commentary. They couldn't help their excitement.

'*Lomax has got to get this ball away, Bruce … he's not got the legs these days to keep up this against the pace of the England backs … Venus is nearly there, Cole too …*'

But what Kenny still had, even if his pace wasn't quite as it had been, was a rugby league brain. He changed the course of his run toward the corner, making Vinny change his angle on him but Vinny was still tracking him down. If he went down, he would still have made significant yardage. He was now at the England 20-metre line.

'He's going for the corner! This could be lights out for England ... but Venus is all over him, he's nearly there ... and Lomax kicks the ball ahead as Venus throws himself at Lomax ...'

The crowd was as loud as it had been all game. The Australian supporters urging Kenny on, almost sucking him towards the try line.

Kenny had known he had to take Vinny out of the game. The split-second Vinny reached to grab him, Kenny had released the ball and kicked. The ball had then scampered on, bouncing the way only a rugby ball can.

'It's a foot race here between Cole and Jarrett ... they're neck and neck ... and it's a ... ohhh! ... I don't know what it is! ... and neither does Referee Glenn Stewarty! ... he's looking across at his touch judges ... it's the grounding ... who got there first, who touched it down, did anyone have downward pressure on the ball? Cole looked as though he just about had the edge, but the ball jagged at the last moment and it looks like it could have been Jarrett's ...'

'Mt Stewarty has taken the decision upstairs. It's all now in the hands of the fourth official. And on the field he's given it as 'NO TRY'. That might be all important in this decision Wayne.'

The big screen was played backwards and forwards from several angles. Every single player on the field was looking. If the try was given and the goal was scored it could have made the game out of sight for England. The clock had been stopped with four minutes 20 seconds left.

Maria looked across at her partner. She had been sitting at one end of their guests with Jardine in the middle. She'd wanted it that way. He did not look good, biting his lip, fiddling with his fingers.

'Querido?'

Jardine looked back across at her. He knew it. Something about her eyes, instantly. She knew.

'You fucking bitch!'

Everything crystalised. He had to get out of there. He began making his move. But the crowd roared as they saw the slow motion replay on the big screen.

'*Where are you going Mr Jardine?*'

Dennis Montgomery asked politely, yet with a firmness that said he was going nowhere.

'*There's really nowhere to run, nowhere to hide ...*'

Mr Sakamoto now stood also.

'*Mr Jardine ... I believe you have a saying in England ... you reap what you sow ...*'

He blocked Jardine's other route.

Bruce Anderson was enjoying the controversy of the call by the fourth official.

'*The video referee has looked at this so many times. It looks like Don Jarrett might just have had downward pressure, a moment before Charlie Cole. I think this is going to be awarded!*'

The screen went from the replayed action to the graphics and then to the sponsors with a countdown to the TRY or NO TRY graphic. The Australia supporters, knowing how the replayed action normally then related to which way the try was to be awarded, was expectant, confident, but still everyone held their collective breath.

TRY!!!

Australia 10 England 4.

Greg put his head in his hands. He'd been standing alongside the bench, his arm over the Perspex canopy that offered cover. He ran his fingers through his hair. He moved his shoulder, felt it. It wasn't right, but this wasn't the time for deliberating.

'*And it's Schoular from the touchline with the kick. This should do it for Australia. Referee Stewarty has put the clock back on. It's ticking. Schoular takes his time. Sets himself. It's up, it's looking good! And it's clipped the post! Six points in it and now less than four minutes to go ...*'

Bruce Anderson loved the final minutes of any game when it came down to this.

'*Aww now this is ... well I'm not sure what it is, Wayne ... is this pure crazy? Greg Duggan, who has led this England team all the way in this competition and is carrying what we understand to be a dislocated shoulder that was popped back in at half-time is back on*' *the park!'*

'Aww mate, full marks for effort ... and for courage beyond the call, but really?'

Greg gathered his team again. Referee Glenn Stewarty watched on with a degree of disdain but also as a rugby league fan a degree of respect for a man who would put his career at risk to try for the ultimate prize in the sport.

'Yes! Yes! Yes! Ohhhh, come on! ... come on!!'

Jardine had retaken his seat as he'd been instructed, but now he was back on his feet and in ebullient form, transformed from his state of just a few minutes prior. Maybe he'd just saved himself. Or Greg Duggan coming back had saved him.

'Ok, no words about why I'm on. I'm on. I want this – and so do you! I don't give a shit about anything that happens in the next three minutes apart from one thing! Gary! Get us down the park! Freddie, Mick blast 'em like you just did! Neil, they cannot cope with you! Charlie, what a try! Do it again! Everyone!'

Greg took up the kicking duties. He could only put one hand behind his back to give the call. Vinny saw it.

'And Greg Duggan has put up a high one. He's got right under the ball and it's launched into the night sky. He's gone for a short but high kick. Oh, this could be trouble for anyone underneath! It's Morani Mai-Mai who's there for Australia, he's only been on five minutes. He's gone up for the ball and he's met by the fastest man on the park who leaps high and palms the ball back to his England teammates.'

Bruce Anderson was starting to get a sweat on in the commentary box.

Vincent Venus had practised the same move many times before for Eruption. It worked around four times out of ten and this time he had extended everything possible to reach the ball. So much so that he came down in a heap afterwards. Greg had been flat out after his kick too. In his determination to get under the ball and create a ball spinning backwards he'd keeled over on to his dodgy shoulder. Fuck! It hurt worse than any hurt he'd felt before – even the bloody bullet he'd taken at

Hopton on THAT night three years ago.

'And the ball has gone back to Wainwright who jinks and moves, but there's no way through. He goes down in the tackle. The medics are on in backplay for Venus and Duggan. But the action goes on. Wainwright plays it back to Walker who spins it out to Freddie South who charges into a welcoming committee of Dailly, Vellidale and Casey-Lewis.

'South gets the ball out! Fenchurch takes it up, snakes around Ricky Graham, he's making his way across the park on the Australia 30-metre line, looking for an opening. He goes down under a tackle from Turame. He plays the ball back to Bell who sneaks a pass away to Sam Rivers who goes direct from the play and is stopped by Schoular, Sperrow and Lomax. England are still just inside the Australia 30.'

Sam Rivers was hurt in the tackle. He took time, steadied himself. He played the ball back to Wainwright. Stu slid the ball out to Gary Walker who had signalled for The Brickie to come on his inside. Neil Duncan stepped as though he had the ball. It was another deception move they'd been working on.

Gary Walker had dummied to Neil Duncan and had pirouetted, taking Durrant and Veron out of the game and had scuttled through to the Australia 20-metre line, then 10 metres out he spiralled the ball over the hands of full-back Jarrett to reach, in amazement to almost everyone, the charging, bullocking run of Freddie South who stormed over right in the corner.

'And the referee Mr Stewarty doesn't need to go upstairs for that one! That is a sensational try by England! And what a prop forward! Freddie South, we salute you! The big man goes over like a winger!'

Bruce Anderson might not have been on Cloud 9 so far as his home nation was concerned, but the finish to this game would go down in rugby league history and his voice would remain with it forever.

'It's Australia 10 England 8. This kick is as difficult as they come. It's from bang out on the touchline and it's the wrong side for a right-footed kicker like Duggan, who is back on his feet again.'

Jardine was as happy as he'd been all game. This was his rise like a phoenix from where he'd been after Duggan had come back at the start of the second half. Everything wasn't alright, but it would be once he'd got away from this stadium and these people.

Greg hadn't planned on kicking being his main contribution. He crouched as best he could to plant the ball on the tee with the manufacturer's name facing him. Stupid, he knew, but another sporting superstition he'd become accustomed to following. He raised himself upright from having set it just right.

Bruce Anderson had been given Greg's kicking figures.

'Duggan is one of the best kickers in the game and his conversion rate in Super League is 87 per cent. Out wide on the touchline it's still a fantastic 78 per cent, but like most right-footed kickers kicking from the right-hand touchline it goes down. His is 68 per cent. Something like two out of every three. Add the pressure of a World Cup Final in the dying minutes of the game, plus an injury to your shoulder that is bound to have an effect … but he's on his way …'

Every ounce of Greg's body, movement and leg trajectory was focused on one thing only. His eyes, having focused on the posts, were now wholly committed to his boot's connection to the ball. He'd taken his metronomic five big steps back and two steps to the left. He took one final look at the posts and then his head stayed completely on the ball. He bent his back to stretch it and set off towards the kick.

'It's looking good, it's looking very good … and it's sailed between the sticks! … We are all tied here with just two minutes on the clock, Australia 10 England 10.'

Greg was on his haunches. The kick had required more than just focus. He took just a second and then trotted back for Australia's kick to England.

Jardine was fist pumping in his seat, to himself. He felt this could all be turning to his advantage, the way he'd planned.

'Just give me one chance, one more run, one more go.'

Greg had given his words to Stu, Freddie and Gary. He would have passed them to the rest but there was no time.

Don Jarrett had his own agenda from the kick-off. So too, Kenny Lomax and Ricky Graham, all nearing the end of stellar careers in the sport, they all wanted to go out on a high.

'I know you went to Vanuatu ...'

Jardine was looking down at his phone that had just pinged.

'I know you had a 'thing' for Lena Kalotiti,'

the messenger added. Another was being typed. His world was turning.

'I know you killed her.'

The number was unknown. Jardine's rollercoaster evening was fast going downhill once again. He felt a heat coming over him.

'Aleki told me.'

His eyes closed. He tried to appear calm once more.

Bruce Anderson was supercharged.

'It's a high spiralling kick back to England from Don Jarrett. Neil Duncan's underneath this one. He sends the ball straight to Aaron Fielding who is all wrapped up by Dailly and Vellidale.'

Jardine's phone pinged again. Another number unknown. Another message he would have preferred not to have received.

'Your last instruction. The one about Duggan coming back on at the end? It never computed. It's a tough world Mr Jardine.'

Ken Knott loved being the bearer of bad tidings to criminals.

Within seconds Jardine's phone filled with what seemed like over 100 texts, his phone constantly pinging. Demands for money.

'England are still in their own half of the park. Walker and Wainwright are calling the plays in the middle. Ohhh! And that's a big hit by Morani Mai-Mai on Sam Rivers! The England boys didn't like that, but referee Stewarty called it fair.'

Bruce Anderson was quickening his own pace of speech, matching the efforts by the players.

'The clock stands at 78 minutes 45 seconds. This could go to the golden point, Wayne! But these two teams are trying to finish it here. Freddie South takes the ball up again, as he has done all game. He makes hard yards with four Australia players all over him. Scott,

Johnson, Mai-Mai again, he's put in some stint since he came on, and Dailly who must be close to topping the tackle count.

'*South plays it back to Wainwright, who dummies and goes from acting half-back! He's scooted away! And he makes tremendous yards before being hauled down by Durrant and Tessyman. The clock's at 78 minutes 59 seconds. One minute of normal time to go …*'

Greg was a passenger. He'd contributed with his boot but nothing more. Could he even hold the ball if he was passed it?

Bruce Anderson's voice was becoming more strained as he put in his own maximum effort. The Australia and England supporters were now all on their feet.

'*… and Gary Walker now takes over from Wainwright! … he's inside the Australia 40 … Wayne, this has got to be drop-goal time hasn't it?*'

'*Aww, sure has to be Bruce, they've two chances here England, two tackles left in their set, but I can't see they can give it to Duggan. He's not Superman.*'

There were forty-five seconds on the clock when Jardine made his move. The crowd now on its feet, he jumped onto the next row in front, leaving his party behind before they knew what had happened.

Greg had sweat pouring from his brow as his body attempted to keep rectifying itself while being put through yet more stress. '*This one's for you Dad, fuck my career, just this, just one touch …*' The thought was all over in a flash.

'*… Walker has played out of his skin tonight … he's marshalled this England team all over the park, and he's found man-mountain John Cloudsdale on the charge. Cloudsdale takes the ball into the tackle of Sperrow, Dailly and Vellidale, he spins in the tackle, he's got an arm out, there's an Australia arm in there and the ball comes loose … it's Kenny Lomax … but has he knocked it on in his effort to try for it? …*'

Jardine had to move quickly.

Greg couldn't reach down to collect, that was way beyond him. But he could kick!

'... and it's gone to Duggan who has hacked the ball forward football style ... and the ball has gone beyond the Australia defensive line that is still struggling to regroup ... and Duggan is following it up! ... he might be short of movement in his left shoulder but he's moving like his life depends on it ...'

The crowd's noise was immense. The England support bouncing up and down, fists clenched and pounding the air.

'Jarrett was out of position but he's trying to collect as Duggan bears down on the ball, it's at the Australia 20-metre line ... you said he wasn't Superman, Wayne ... I think he just might be ...'

Greg had no thought for anything else but his boot reaching the ball first, before Jarrett.

'The clock is down to 35 seconds of this game remaining ... it's Jarrett versus Duggan ...'

Jardine was also kicking on. He was within sight of the end of the row when a figure loomed in front of him.

'... and Duggan and Jarrett have collided ... is that a penalty? ...'

Jardine stood transfixed.

'Why did you do it? Why did you kill my daughter?'

Aleki Kalotiti had always been able to speak English, he'd put on his best Bislama creole when he'd had Erin Jackson in his road-train cab that she and Marlon Razni had travelled in. Erin had recalled that he hadn't just had his name there, but under it had been a faded photograph of his daughter.

When Greg had visited Hideaway Island two days ago with Diane and Kyle, Alani, the lady in the beach shop had told them that a man called Julian had come some weeks ago, and that Lena and the man had snorkelled together, eaten together several times and they'd had fun.

'I believe he is a very wealthy man. He said he could get Lena into a TV show. Lena loved that idea and that they would be together, she saw him as her ticket to fame and she loved him, but then ...'

Commissioner Erin Jackson appeared from behind Aleki. She had brought him over from what was now her newly adopted island country.

Dennis Montgomery was coming up behind Jardine. He smiled at him.

'It's over Mr Jardine.'

Twenty seconds were left on the clock. Bruce Anderson was all over it.

'… and Greg Duggan is down … and he's staying down …'

The crowd was going berserk!

'… but astonishingly, as Duggan has gone down he has somehow managed to put a boot on the ball and has hacked it on! … the ball is bounding along towards the Australia posts …'

Alani had continued her story to Greg and Diane.

'… but then Lena found out it was all lies, he was already married, there was no TV show … Lena was angry … she had a photograph of the two of them that she had had printed as a waterproof postcard for herself only, like those that are sent from here … she was so mad, she decided to send it to his wife, but she had no address … he had mentioned some village, so she looked up the nearest post office and sent it there, marked to Mrs Jardine … I know because she asked me to send it …

'I sent it to Barwick Village Post Office & Stores with a note for a very nice man called Chris Bolton. We found his name on a Facebook page for the store. I found out later he is a very good swimmer …'

Kyle hadn't been able to see the action with everybody up, so his new best friend Walter Armitage had gathered him up in his arms and shoved him on his shoulders.

There were ten seconds left.

'Get up Dad! Get uuuppppp!'

Walter hadn't realised quite how much young Kyle was going to pound his feet against his chest and wobble so much on his shoulders being so excited. Diane asked whether Walter was alright, but Walter just laughed. This was the most electrifying end to a game he could ever remember.

The ball was still skipping on, now just yards away from the Australia line. There was a surfeit of bodies stampeding towards a possible victory or defeat.

'*Venus is galloping towards the ball, Walker is scampering through and Wainwright is there just behind them, Turame and Veron are in the race too with Kenny Lomax ... Venus has thrown himself at the ball, and so too has Turame! ... the ball goes on ... did Venus get a touch? If he did, it's a knock-on ... did Turame? ... it's going over the try line ...*'

Alani's tale had not been over.

'*Nice Mr Bolton sent me a letter back saying that he knew Mrs Jardine, and that he would ask another of his team, 'Whistling Bob' he wrote, or maybe 'Marvelous Marie' to hand it to her when she came in.*

'*When Mr Jardine, Julian, came back two weeks ago, I wasn't here. All I know is that he was here, someone said he had a gun and poor Lena ended up shot. There could have been nobody else involved. Everyone loved her.*'

Greg had passed all of Alani's information on to Erin, who having then interviewed Alani herself then made the connection with Aleki, Lena's father.

Five seconds were left in the game.

'*Daaaadd!! Get uuuppp!!*'

There was no way that Greg could possibly hear Kyle, in all of the commotion that was going on both on the park and in the stands, but as he had gone down with Jarrett, his dad's face appeared in his head. Just the way his father had always been, smiling with him all the time.

Greg and Kenny's run this morning hadn't just been an old pals together run, nor had it been about some kind of publicity stunt for the final. It had been the first of two elements that Greg had known Jardine couldn't resist.

Jardine hadn't just gone for single bets in his Extreme Gambling Millionaire's Club, he'd also arranged a 'Duggan's Dilemmas Accumulator'.

Ken Knott and James Vickers had uncovered it as they had unscrambled his site. Jardine had needed two more events. There had been four already, he'd promised six. The Sydney Harbour Bridge Run had become number five and had proved another success for Jardine who had been alerted to it through Ken Knott having made connections with an organisation called the HHM.

Greg's return from injury in this game had been the final gamble of the Accumulator and while Jardine had won handsomely overall, this had been his downfall.

Greg was always going to go down injured near the end of the first half. That had been the plan.

GPK, Ken and Greg had known Jardine needed a final accumulator bet and GPK had known that Jardine would not be able to resist a 'Duggan Dilemma' of whether he would come back on or not, or when.

GPK and Erin knew they already had Jardine on a murder charge, but this would completely destroy him.

They had met with the Montgomerys and Mr Sakamoto and had promised them there would be no looking into any of their affairs, so long as they went along with the plan.

When Jardine had flung himself into the setting up of the last gamble at half-time there had been significant sums and an unhealthy amount of gambles put on Greg returning immediately in the second half, Jardine's longest odds. Ken had found a way to ensure Jardine did not see these.

Three of the gambles had been from the three whose accumulators were still on fire. Their combined stakes running into the final gamble had been at a figure of £50m, easily coverable, giving Jardine a massive profit by the other gambling taking place but not if everyone jumped on at 40-1 as Jardine had delivered to entice what he felt was never going to happen. Greg coming straight back on at the start of the second half. The three accumulators alone would cost him £2 billion and they had!

Jardine had been bankrupted!

Three seconds were left on the clock!

'… *we have sprawling bodies, limbs stretching every sinew and fingertips outstretched in the Australia red zone … Venus thought he might have had it … then Turame … Ricky Graham thinks he's*

grounded it in the in-goal area! ... Freddie South is claiming it ...
Gary Walker too ... Kenny Lomax is under all this somewhere ...
and Neil Duncan ...

'*The ball's still loose! ... It's come back into the field of play ... I*
can't tell you why ... a hand from an Australia player? An England
player? ... it's another charge ... nobody's picking it up ... it's a kick
from Johnnie Johnson now for Australia ... they're coming clear ...
but it's bounced up ...'

Jardine had to get away, but there really was no way.

'*Come with us Mr Jardine, it's time for you to go ...*'

Erin was firm. Aleki made way for Det Insp Alex Lui and
two other Australian Federal Police to take him away. He was
cuffed. As he reached the exit from the seats another figure
loomed in front of him.

One second left!

All of Bruce Anderson's commentary Christmases had come
at once. The hooter had sounded for the end of the game. This
still wasn't over. Both sides were still in the game. It was a rugby
league battlefield with players everywhere, either running,
getting up to run, still down but attempting to get back to their
feet.

'*... and the ball has bounced up into Duggan's hand ... not even*
his arm ... he's running ... he's only two metres short but still going
... it's Duggannnn!'

Greg had seen his life flash before him. Kyle, Susie, Diane,
his dad, his mum. This might be his last ever moment in rugby
league. This shoulder. His body. He could feel it popping out
again as he stretched. He'd not intended an actual injury at the
end of the first half, he'd imagined feigning it to screw Jardine.

Bruce Anderson was as excited as everyone else in the
stadium.

'*... and there's Lomaaax!!! ... they go over the line together ... is*
it downward pressure from Duggan? Is it a try? Is Duggan held up?
Has Lomax saved the day for Australia?'

Wayne Ferryman allowed Anderson to catch his breath.

'*Aww now ... there's such a lot here mate ... first you've got the*

*kick from Duggan ... was it an infringement by him or by Jarrett?
... then you've got what happened over the line the first time, did
anyone ground it? The referee didn't think so ... then was it a knock-
on? ... then you've the second phase ... does Greg ground it? or
Kenny?'*

Bruce Anderson gave the news.

*'Well, understandably, Mr Stewarty has had to send this one
upstairs ... he's really not sure what to give as an on-field decision to
the video referee, you can see that ... but he's awarded it as a TRY
on the field ...'*

The England fans roared, ready to celebrate, but not quite.

Playbacks continued to bring cheers and gasps among the
crowd in almost equal measure between the Australia and
England fans and Greg and Kenny shook hands over whatever
would be the outcome.

Greg was still in agony. He might be out of the game for
months after this, but maybe, just maybe he could get his life
back together.

And there was another ending in sight.

Jardine was astonished to see her. He was even more
astonished to see her wielding a Glock.

'Goodbye, Julian!'

Enjoyed *Tough World?*

Read on for an exclusive extract
from the fourth Greg Duggan crime thriller
by Chris Berry

TOUGH SEASON
The French Connection

CHAPTER 1

Fast Car

The sleek, black Bugatti Divo, one of only forty ever made, with a top speed of 236mph was presently cruising at a mere 145mph on the E80 from Toulouse as its driver's face enjoyed the moment, the day and burst into what would be a last smile before unintended oblivion.

The smile had been one of great joy, of achievement, of impending destruction, but not, the final part, of the driver's own doom.

As the on-board computer flickered to an ever-increasing speed digit, there was satisfaction over the plan having appeared to have been constructed perfectly. Everything was now in place. It was a beautiful, hot summer's day. There would be many more.

As the supercar costing £5m exploded, its driver simultaneously evaporated in the heat. It was not a long, slow painful death but one that shocked everyone travelling on the motorway, not least the driver of the white Bugatti Chiron, costing a mere £3m that had been travelling at a marginally lesser speed in the Divo's wake.

Fast Finish

'*Baise moi!*'

As vocal expressions go this could easily have come from the Chiron's owner, but its English translation was better suited to the couple in a heightened state of passion at just that precise moment in the Chateau de Crouseilles.

'*Monsieur! Mmmm! Tu es un homme tres mechant!*'

The wagged finger and cheeky giggle that accompanied her words as the shapely raven-haired young woman wriggled over the straddled man, whose wrists and ankles were tethered with soft bed restraints and fluffy cuffs. Her playfulness was just enough encouragement to send her companion closer to the edge, given their present status of near naked copulation.

'*Ohhh … aah … oui, oui, oui …*'

Breathing from both parties had become increasingly intense and had led to a somewhat energetic and immensely satisfying afternoon, culminating in the most tumultuous climax at least one of them had ever experienced.

It was as she poured herself back into her pink sheath-style mini spandex dress, covering very little modesty, and with a scoop neck, as though any further accentuation was necessary, that she took out the machete-style small blade from her slim clutch bag and very quickly and accurately slit his jugular vein and trachea.

'*Monsieur, tu etait un tres mauvais homme. Au revoir!*'

She turned, took a look in the mirror to check that no specks of blood had sputtered on to her face, body or dress, put on her heels and left the room without rushing as his claret, not of the wine variety, swamped the bedsheets and her victim's eyes stared wide.

Fast Beast

'*This has to be the most stupid thing I have ever done.*'

He muttered, not quite under his breath as some 25 metres away athletic young men dressed in uniform of white ran for cover while a steaming, enraged and soon to be rampaging beast of around 400 hyped-up kilos was set up to charge remorselessly and mercilessly towards him.

Matthieu stood immediately behind him and began waving a white handkerchief and shouting to attract the attention of the animal and a second later, with his job done and the said animal's eyes aglow and sawdust spraying upwards in its wake, beat a hasty retreat to the sidelines.

He who remained could feel the slightest of laughter in his teammate's voice as he disappeared. He now looked at the onrushing, pound-for-pound disaster missile of hurtling flesh, bone and muscle marauding in his immediate direction at around 50mph. This could get seriously messy.

'Baise Moi!'

He stayed, as he'd been instructed, on the spot and having remonstrated audibly with himself seconds previously, now uttered the words much more loudly and much to the amusement of a packed arena and some of his teammates at Aire Sur L'Adour. He wasn't French, but he knew this phrase well. It usually summed up most of what he found himself entangled in.

This was hardly what he would have called the theatre of dreams, but to some this was clearly just that. Right now, he wondered briefly why he was wearing white trousers.

Steadfast

'How did you get my number?'

She felt her voice quivering. She had stopped walking. It had been a pleasant day until now. The voice at the other end had mentioned her name. It had been sufficient to send her on the defensive and to renew an old acquaintance she would rather not have done.

She looked all around her in the street. There was usually something more. The voice carried on. She couldn't believe what she was hearing while still furtively looking for anyone close by. Was it courage or foolhardiness that brought about her next words?

'Not again. I said the last time it was the last time ...'

Before she could add anything further the caller stepped in. She had been as brave as she could be. Perhaps foolhardy after all. She hung up.

The voice sent a text message for her to watch. She had no idea what the caller meant until she opened it and watched the video that the voice had attached on her iPhone. That's when she shut her eyes. Trembled.

She'd thought it was all over. It wasn't.